EDENS ZERO

6 WORDS WILL GIVE YOU STRENGTH

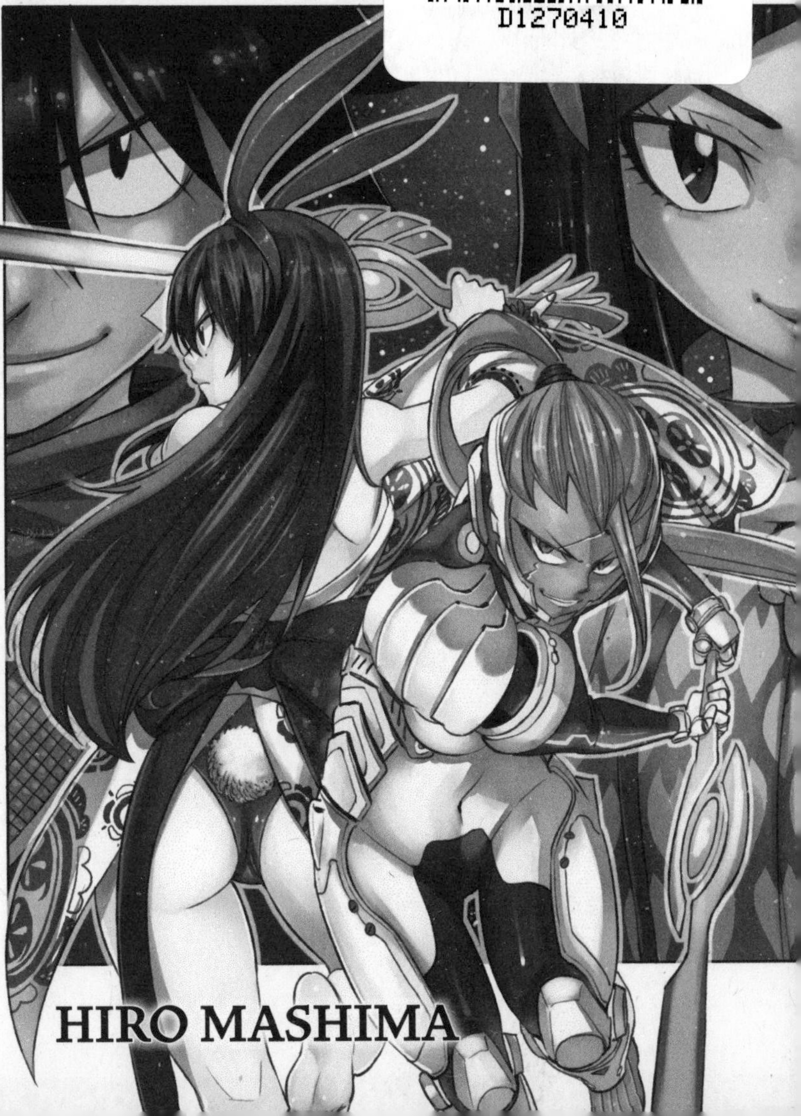

HIRO MASHIMA

EDENS ZERO 6 contents

EDENS ZERO

WE'RE GONNA MAKE ANOTHER AWESOME VIDEO TODAY!!
AYE, SIR!
FWEET
HOLD IT RIGHT THERE!!
FWIT
FILMING IS STRICTLY PROHIBITED IN PARTS OF THIS SHIP.
FWIT
FWIT
WHAT?! NOOO!
WHAT DID YOU EXPECT?! SOCIETY CAN'T KNOW SOME OF THIS SHIP'S SECRETS.
SCARY!!
SO INSTEAD, I'LL GIVE YOU A TOUR OF THE FACILITIES.

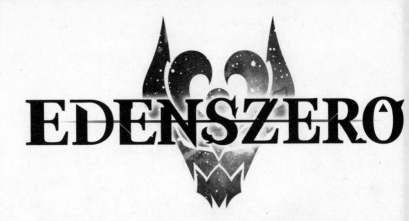

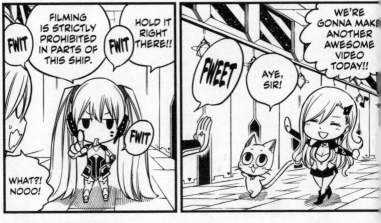

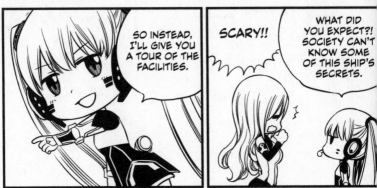

CHAPTER 42: PINO'S DREAM

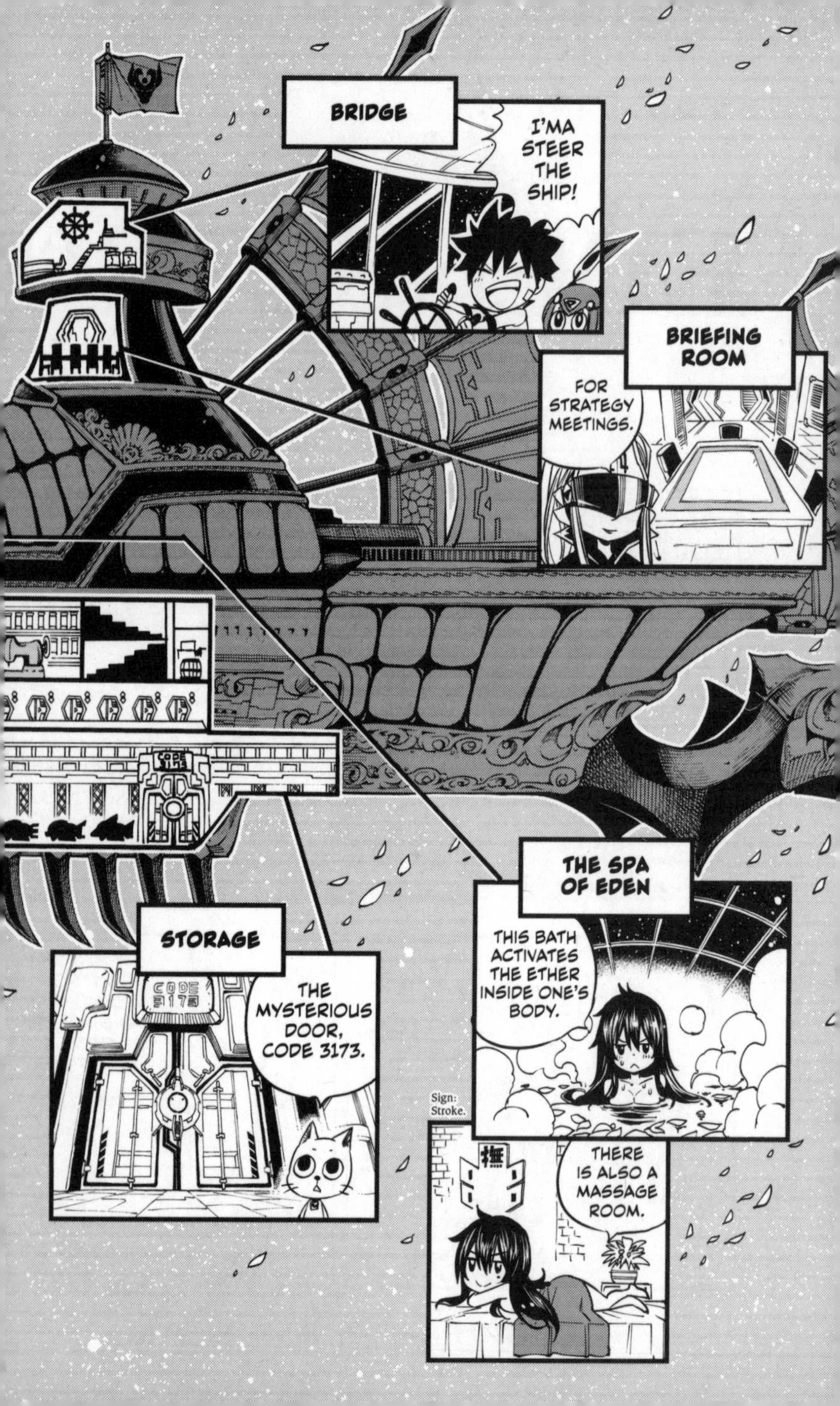
BRIDGE
I'MA STEER THE SHIP!
BRIEFING ROOM
FOR STRATEGY MEETINGS.
THE SPA OF EDEN
THIS BATH ACTIVATES THE ETHER INSIDE ONE'S BODY.
Sign: Stroke.
THERE IS ALSO A MASSAGE ROOM.
STORAGE
CODE 3173
THE MYSTERIOUS DOOR, CODE 3173.

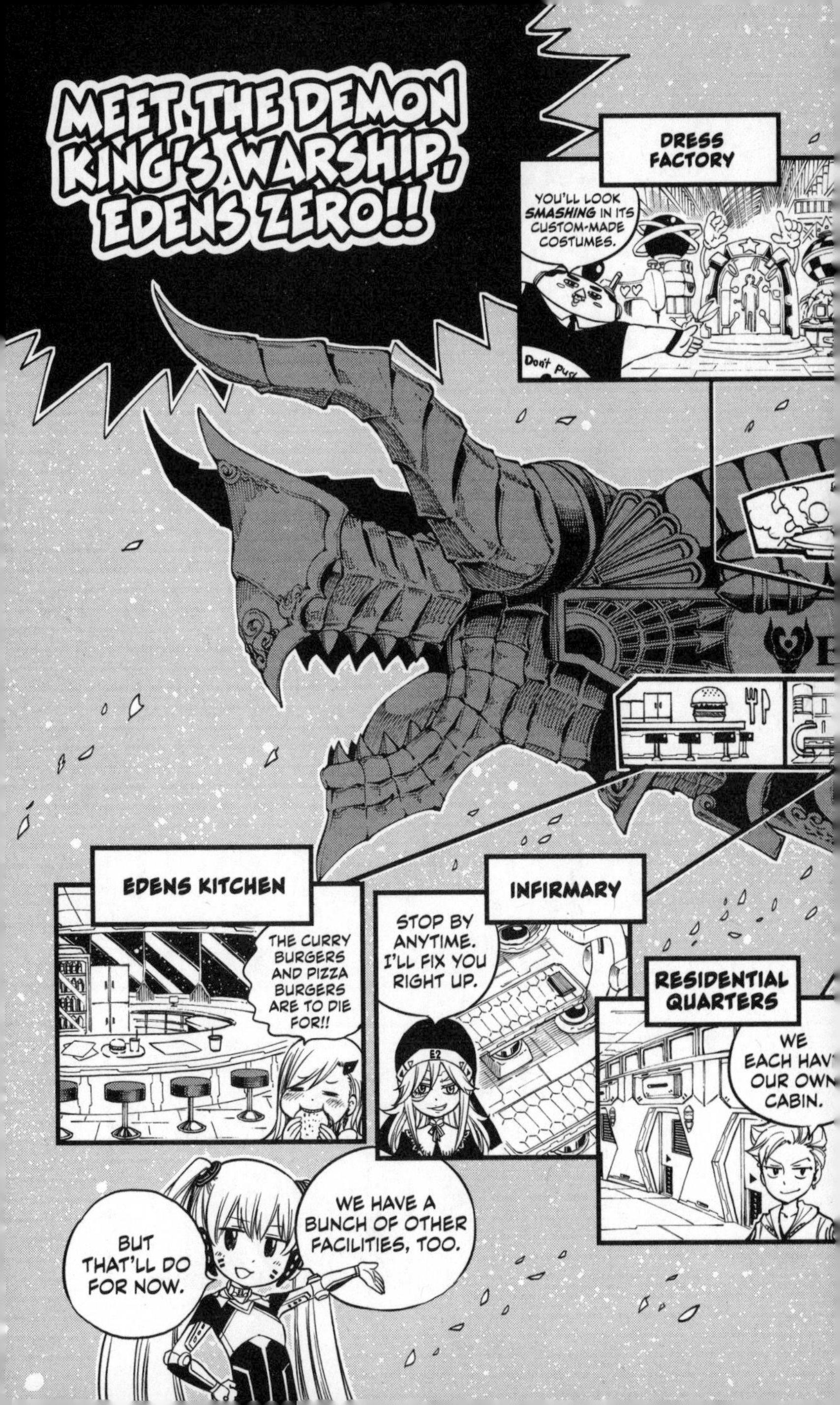

DRESS FACTORY
YOU'LL LOOK SMASHING IN ITS CUSTOM-MADE COSTUMES.
MEET THE DEMON KING'S WARSHIP, EDENS ZERO!!
RESIDENTIAL QUARTERS
WE EACH HAVE OUR OWN CABIN.
INFIRMARY
STOP BY ANYTIME. I'LL FIX YOU RIGHT UP.
EDENS KITCHEN
THE CURRY BURGERS AND PIZZA BURGERS ARE TO DIE FOR!!
WE HAVE A BUNCH OF OTHER FACILITIES, TOO.
BUT THAT'LL DO FOR NOW.

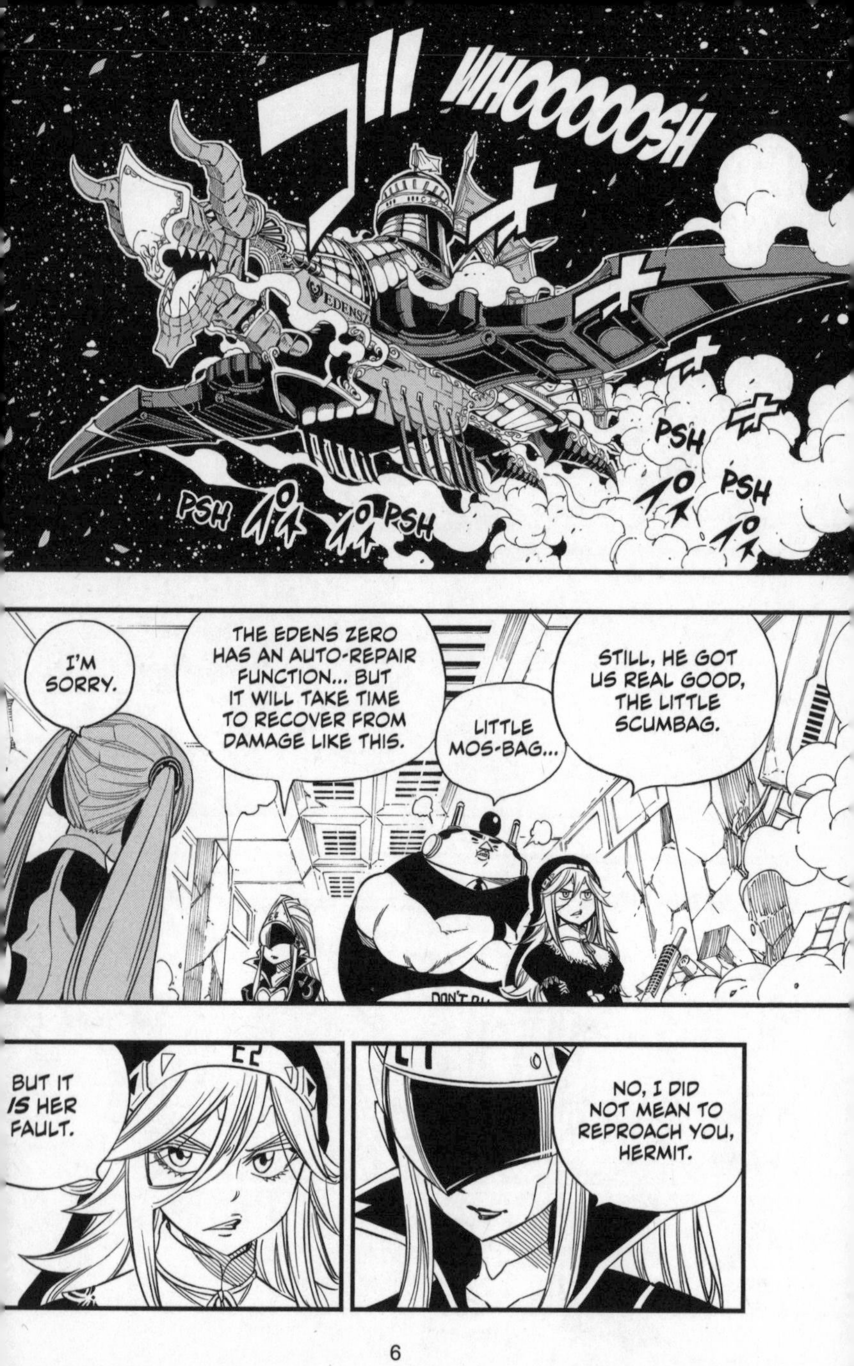
WHOOOOOOSH
PSH
PSH
PSH
PSH
STILL, HE GOT US REAL GOOD, THE LITTLE SCUMBAG.
LITTLE MOS-BAG...
THE EDENS ZERO HAS AN AUTO-REPAIR FUNCTION... BUT IT WILL TAKE TIME TO RECOVER FROM DAMAGE LIKE THIS.
I'M SORRY.
NO, I DID NOT MEAN TO REPROACH YOU, HERMIT.
BUT IT *IS* HER FAULT.

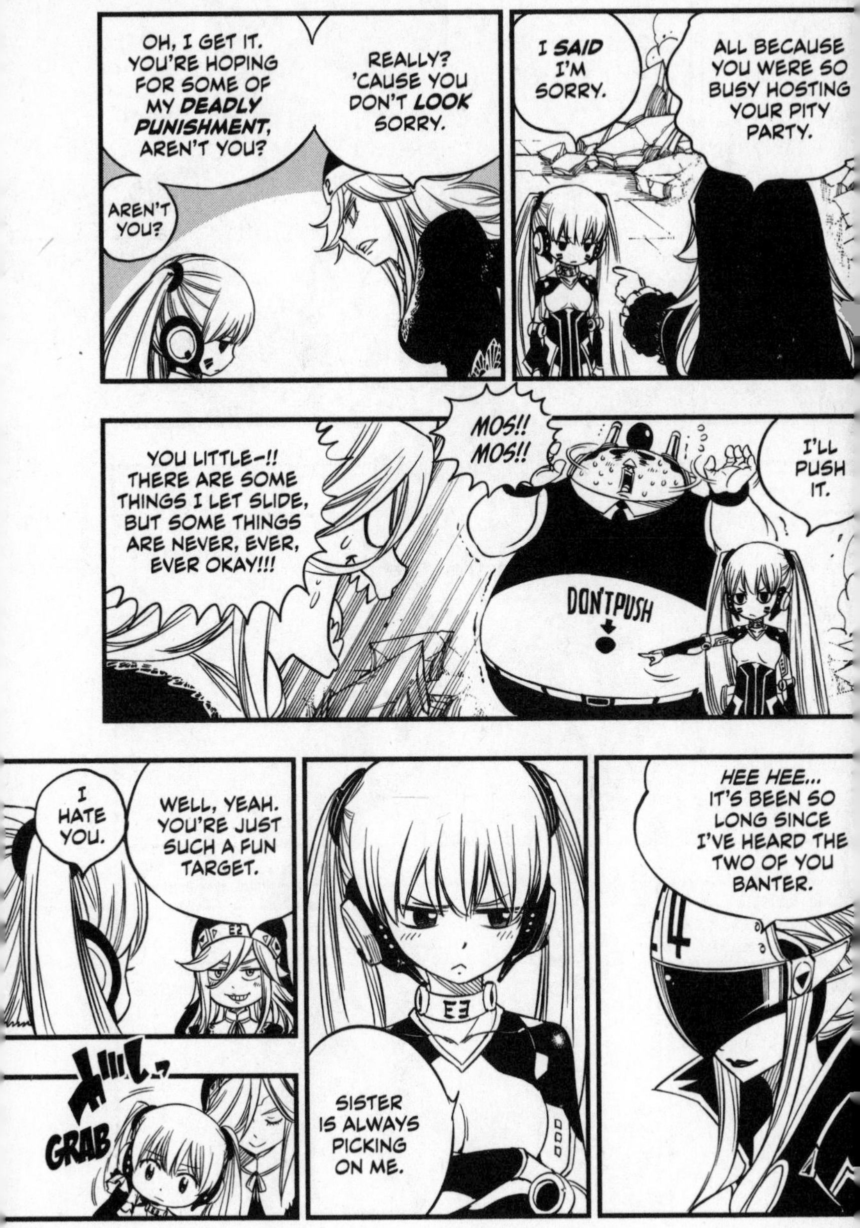
ALL BECAUSE YOU WERE SO BUSY HOSTING YOUR PITY PARTY.
I *SAID* I'M SORRY.
REALLY? 'CAUSE YOU DON'T *LOOK* SORRY.
OH, I GET IT. YOU'RE HOPING FOR SOME OF MY ***DEADLY PUNISHMENT***, AREN'T YOU?
AREN'T YOU?
I'LL PUSH IT.
MOS!! MOS!!
YOU LITTLE--!! THERE ARE SOME THINGS I LET SLIDE, BUT SOME THINGS ARE NEVER, EVER, EVER OKAY!!!
DON'T PUSH
HEE HEE... IT'S BEEN SO LONG SINCE I'VE HEARD THE TWO OF YOU BANTER.
SISTER IS ALWAYS PICKING ON ME.
WELL, YEAH. YOU'RE JUST SUCH A FUN TARGET.
I HATE YOU.
GRAB

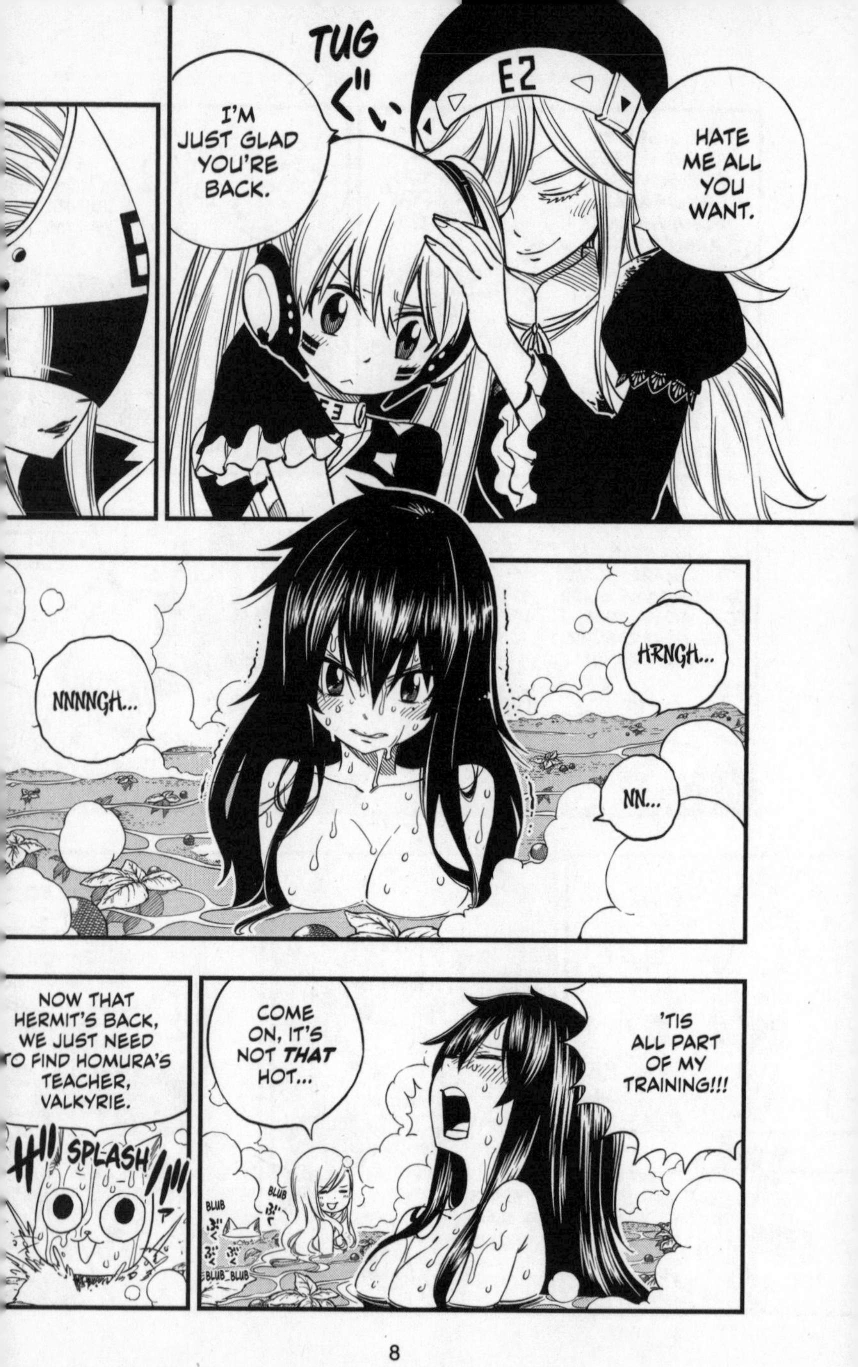

TUG
ぐい
HATE ME ALL YOU WANT.
I'M JUST GLAD YOU'RE BACK.
HRNGH...
NN...
NNNNGH...
'TIS ALL PART OF MY TRAINING!!!
COME ON, IT'S NOT *THAT* HOT...
BLUB
BLUB
BLUB BLUB
NOW THAT HERMIT'S BACK, WE JUST NEED TO FIND HOMURA'S TEACHER, VALKYRIE.
SPLASH

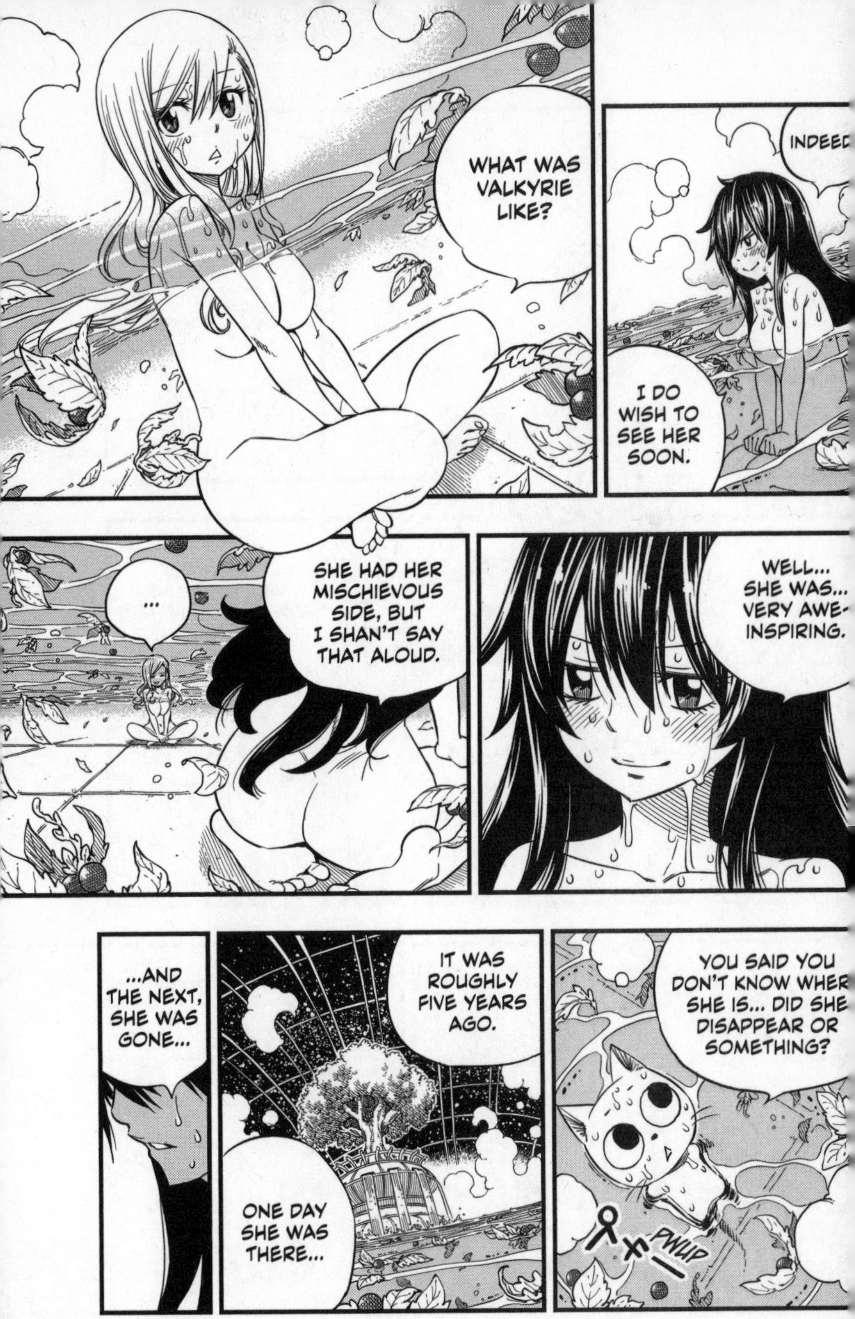
INDEED
I DO WISH TO SEE HER SOON.
WHAT WAS VALKYRIE LIKE?
WELL... SHE WAS... VERY AWE-INSPIRING.
SHE HAD HER MISCHIEVOUS SIDE, BUT I SHAN'T SAY THAT ALOUD.
...
YOU SAID YOU DON'T KNOW WHER SHE IS... DID SHE DISAPPEAR OR SOMETHING?
PWUP
IT WAS ROUGHLY FIVE YEARS AGO.
ONE DAY SHE WAS THERE...
...AND THE NEXT, SHE WAS GONE...

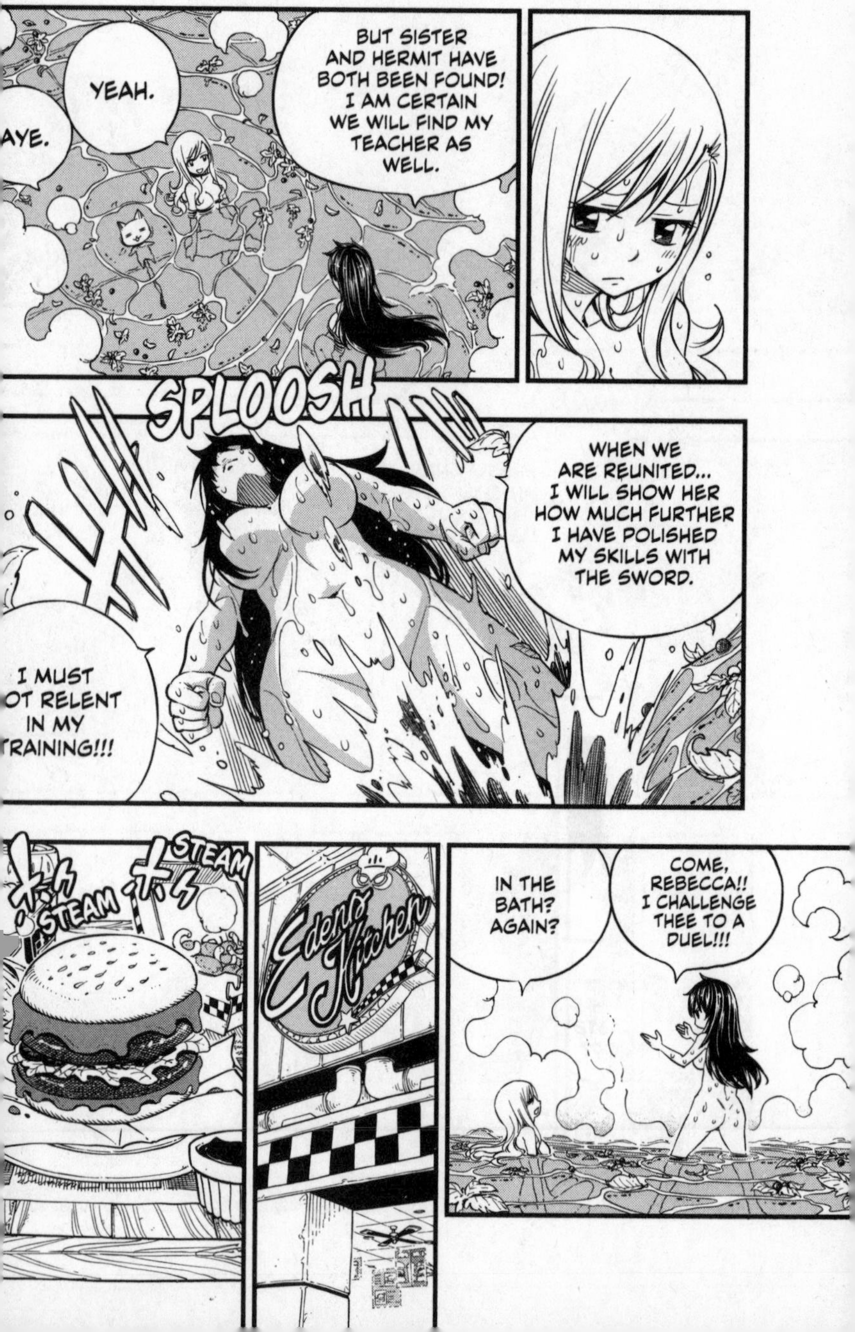
BUT SISTER AND HERMIT HAVE BOTH BEEN FOUND! I AM CERTAIN WE WILL FIND MY TEACHER AS WELL.
YEAH.
AYE.
SPLOOSH
WHEN WE ARE REUNITED... I WILL SHOW HER HOW MUCH FURTHER I HAVE POLISHED MY SKILLS WITH THE SWORD.
I MUST OT RELENT IN MY RAINING!!!
COME, REBECCA!! I CHALLENGE THEE TO A DUEL!!!
IN THE BATH? AGAIN?
Eden's Kitchen
STEAM
STEAM

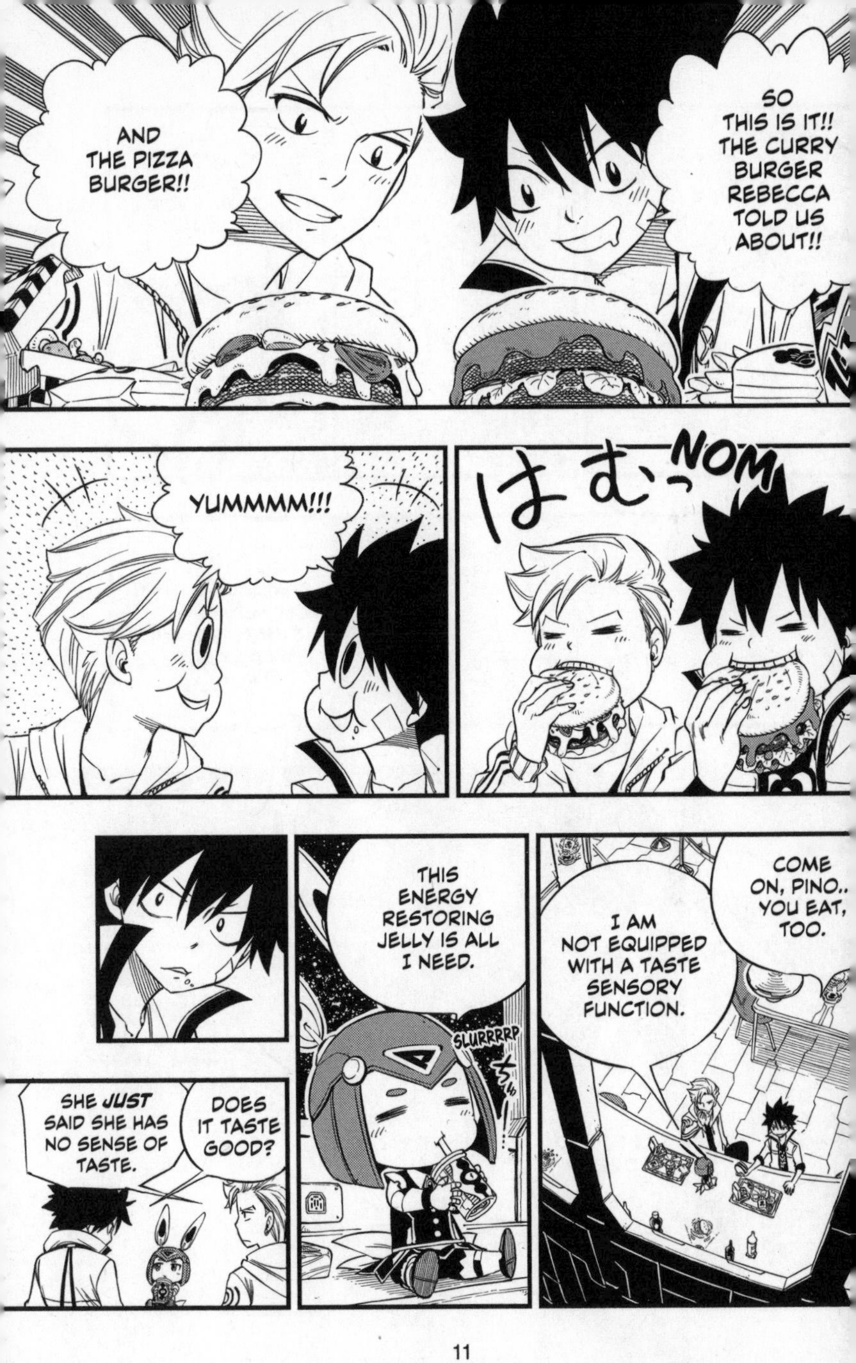
SO THIS IS IT!! THE CURRY BURGER REBECCA TOLD US ABOUT!!
AND THE PIZZA BURGER!!
はむっ
NOM
YUMMMM!!!
COME ON, PINO.. YOU EAT, TOO.
I AM NOT EQUIPPED WITH A TASTE SENSORY FUNCTION.
THIS ENERGY RESTORING JELLY IS ALL I NEED.
SLURRRRP
DOES IT TASTE GOOD?
SHE *JUST* SAID SHE HAS NO SENSE OF TASTE.

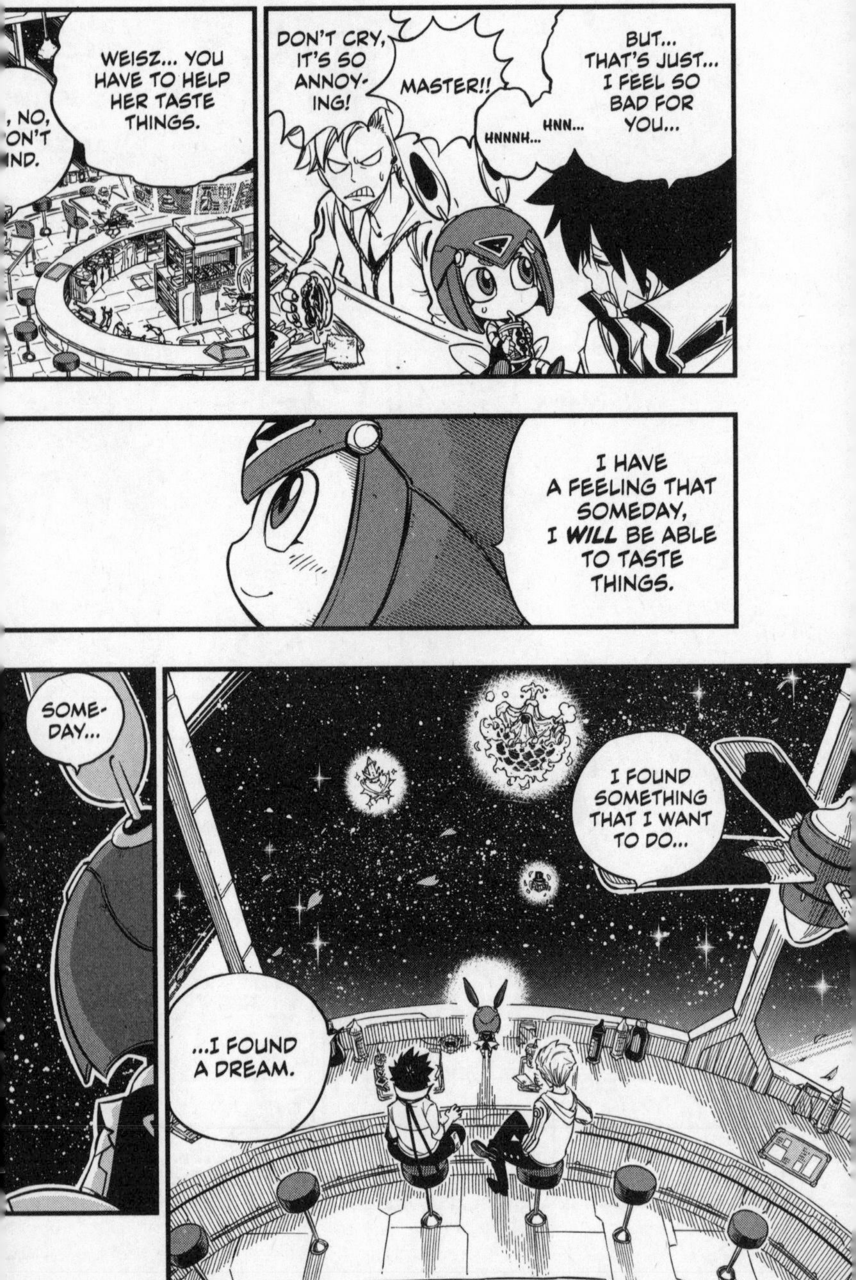
BUT... THAT'S JUST... I FEEL SO BAD FOR YOU...
HNN...
HNNNH...
MASTER!!
DON'T CRY, IT'S SO ANNOY-ING!
WEISZ... YOU HAVE TO HELP HER TASTE THINGS.
, NO, ON'T ND.
I HAVE A FEELING THAT SOMEDAY, I ***WILL*** BE ABLE TO TASTE THINGS.
I FOUND SOMETHING THAT I WANT TO DO...
...I FOUND A DREAM.
SOME-DAY...

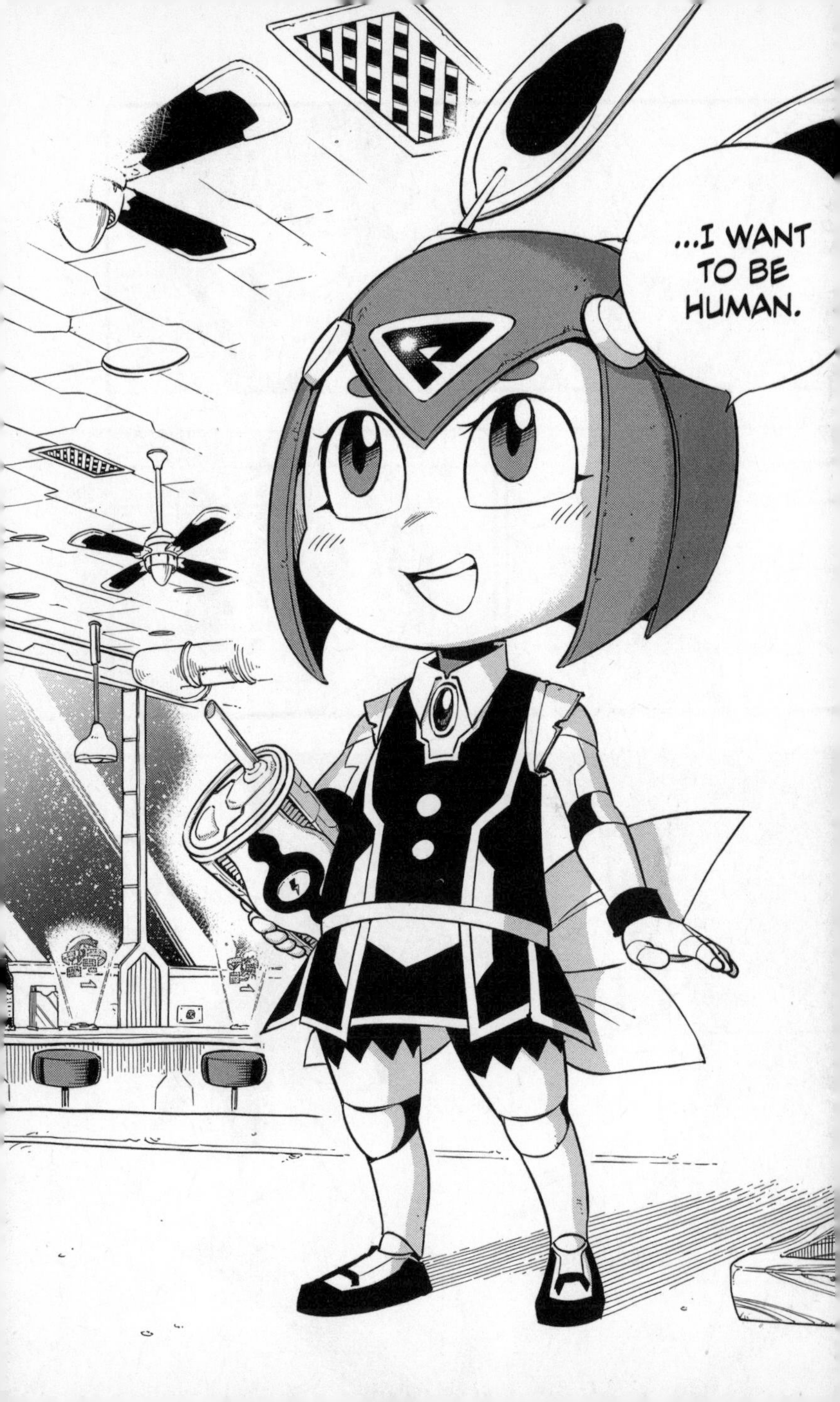
...I WANT TO BE HUMAN.

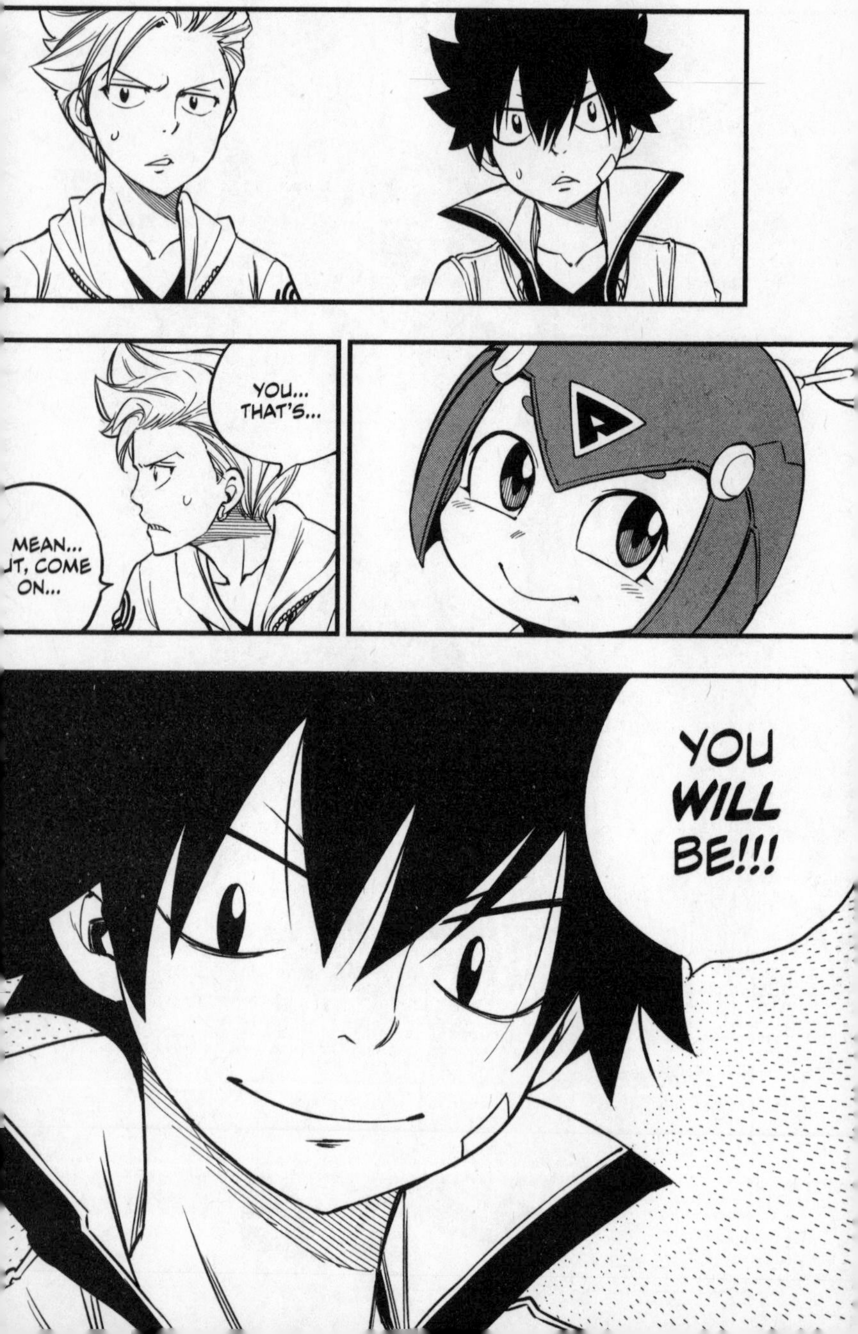
YOU... THAT'S...
MEAN... UT, COME ON...
YOU **WILL** BE!!!

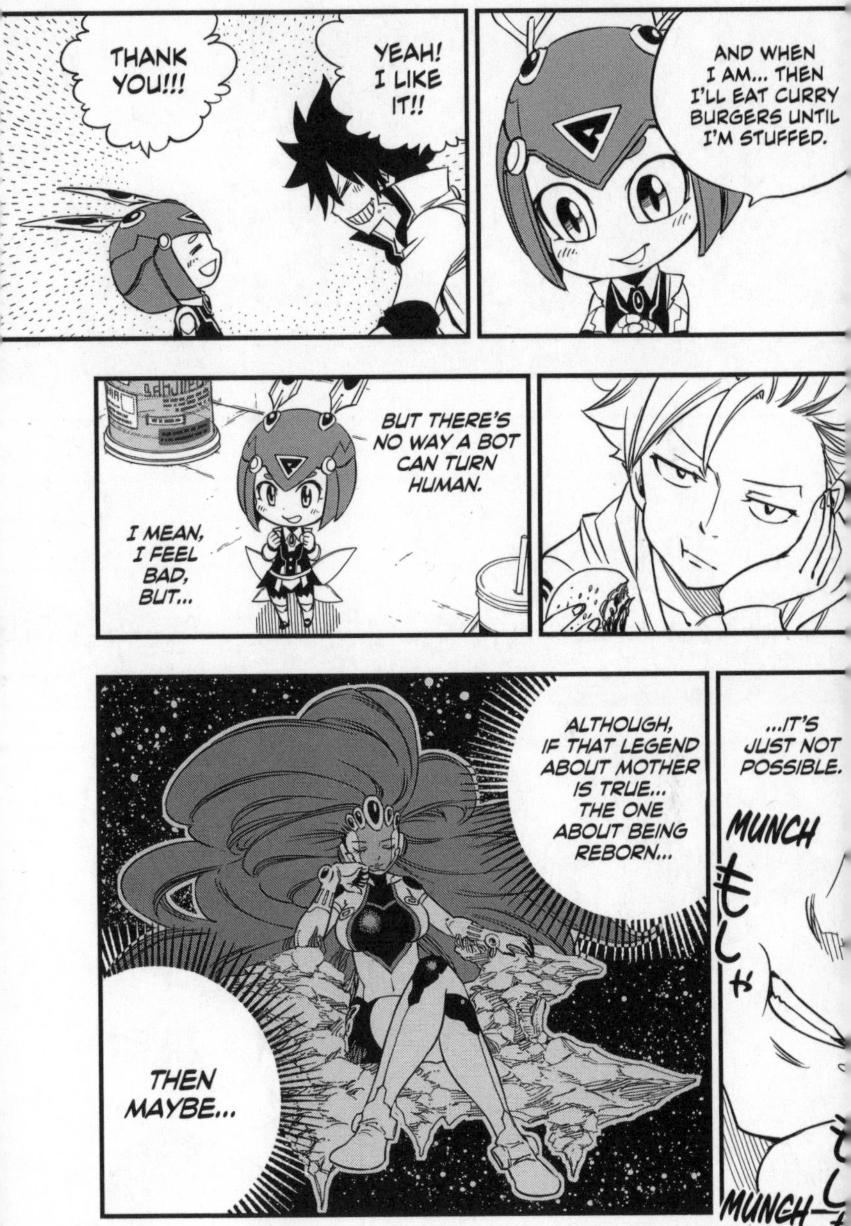
AND WHEN I AM... THEN I'LL EAT CURRY BURGERS UNTIL I'M STUFFED.
YEAH! I LIKE IT!!
THANK YOU!!!
BUT THERE'S NO WAY A BOT CAN TURN HUMAN.
I MEAN, I FEEL BAD, BUT...
...IT'S JUST NOT POSSIBLE.
MUNCH
MUNCH—
ALTHOUGH, IF THAT LEGEND ABOUT MOTHER IS TRUE... THE ONE ABOUT BEING REBORN...
THEN MAYBE...

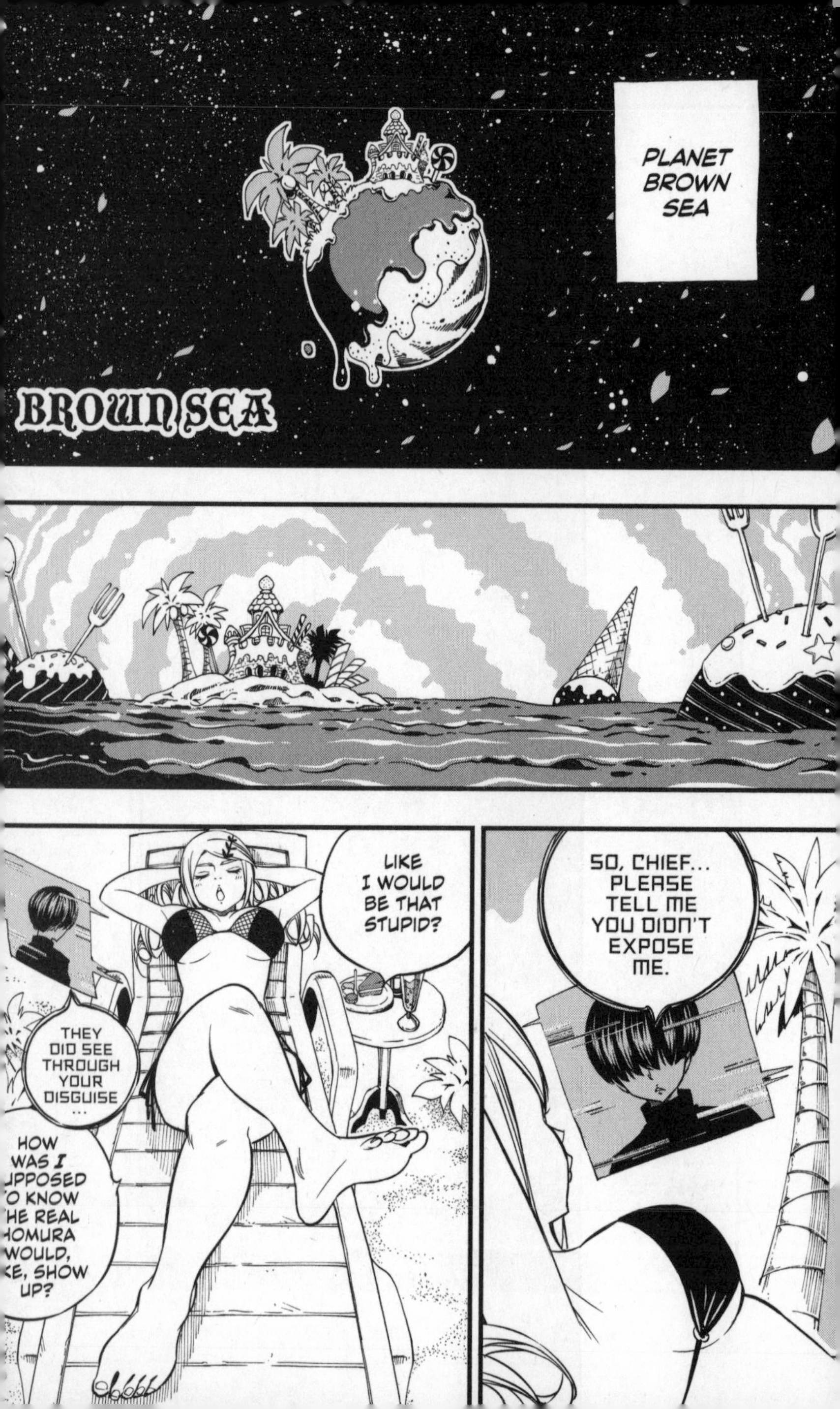

PLANET BROWN SEA
BROWN SEA
SO, CHIEF... PLEASE TELL ME YOU DIDN'T EXPOSE ME.
LIKE I WOULD BE THAT STUPID?
THEY DID SEE THROUGH YOUR DISGUISE ...
HOW WAS *I* UPPOSED O KNOW HE REAL OMURA WOULD, KE, SHOW UP?

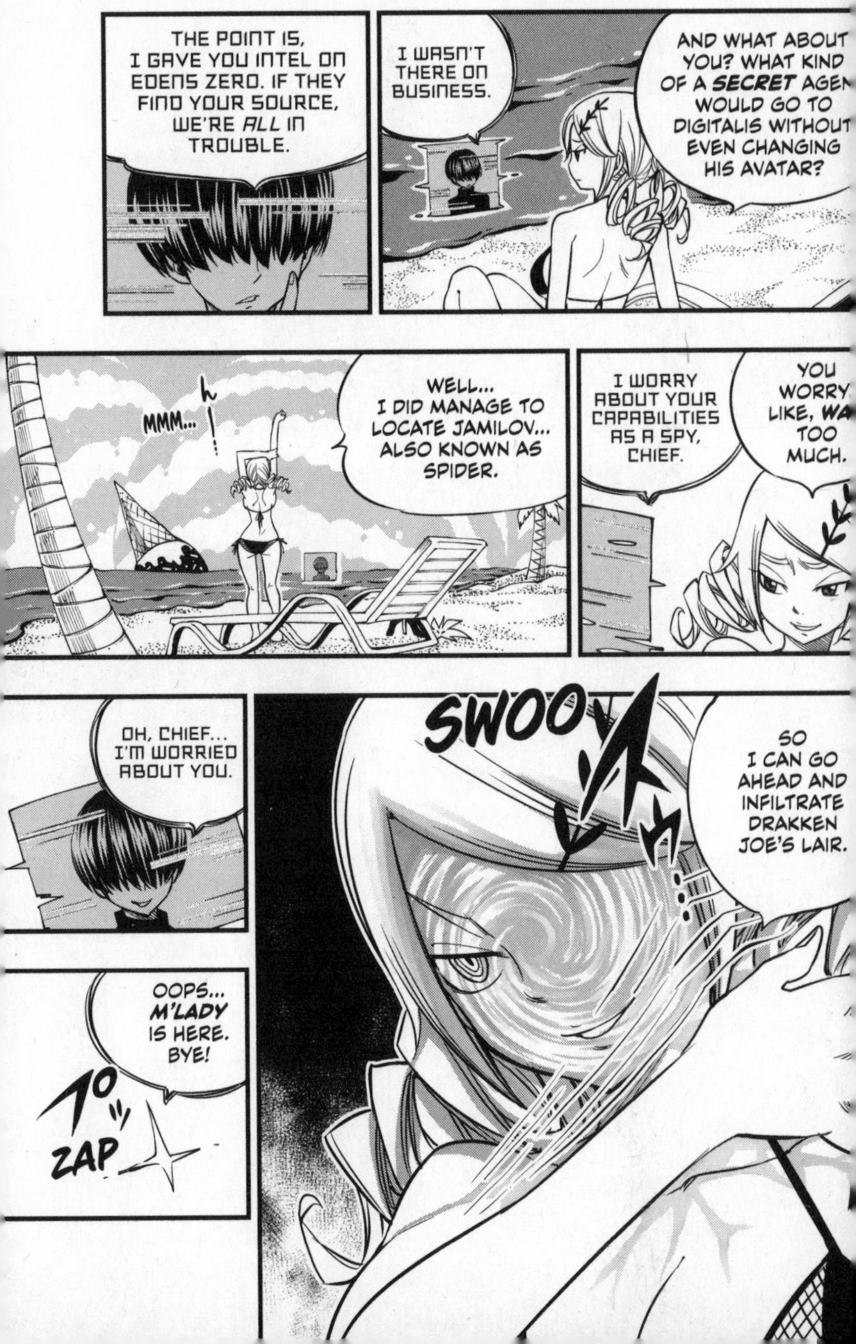
AND WHAT ABOUT YOU? WHAT KIND OF A *SECRET* AGEN
WOULD GO TO DIGITALIS WITHOUT EVEN CHANGING HIS AVATAR?
I WASN'T THERE ON BUSINESS.
THE POINT IS, I GAVE YOU INTEL ON EDENS ZERO. IF THEY FIND YOUR SOURCE, WE'RE *ALL* IN TROUBLE.
YOU WORRY LIKE, *WA* TOO MUCH.
I WORRY ABOUT YOUR CAPABILITIES AS A SPY, CHIEF.
WELL... I DID MANAGE TO LOCATE JAMILOV... ALSO KNOWN AS SPIDER.
MMM...
SWOO
SO I CAN GO AHEAD AND INFILTRATE DRAKKEN JOE'S LAIR.
OH, CHIEF... I'M WORRIED ABOUT YOU.
OOPS... *M'LADY* IS HERE. BYE!
ZAP

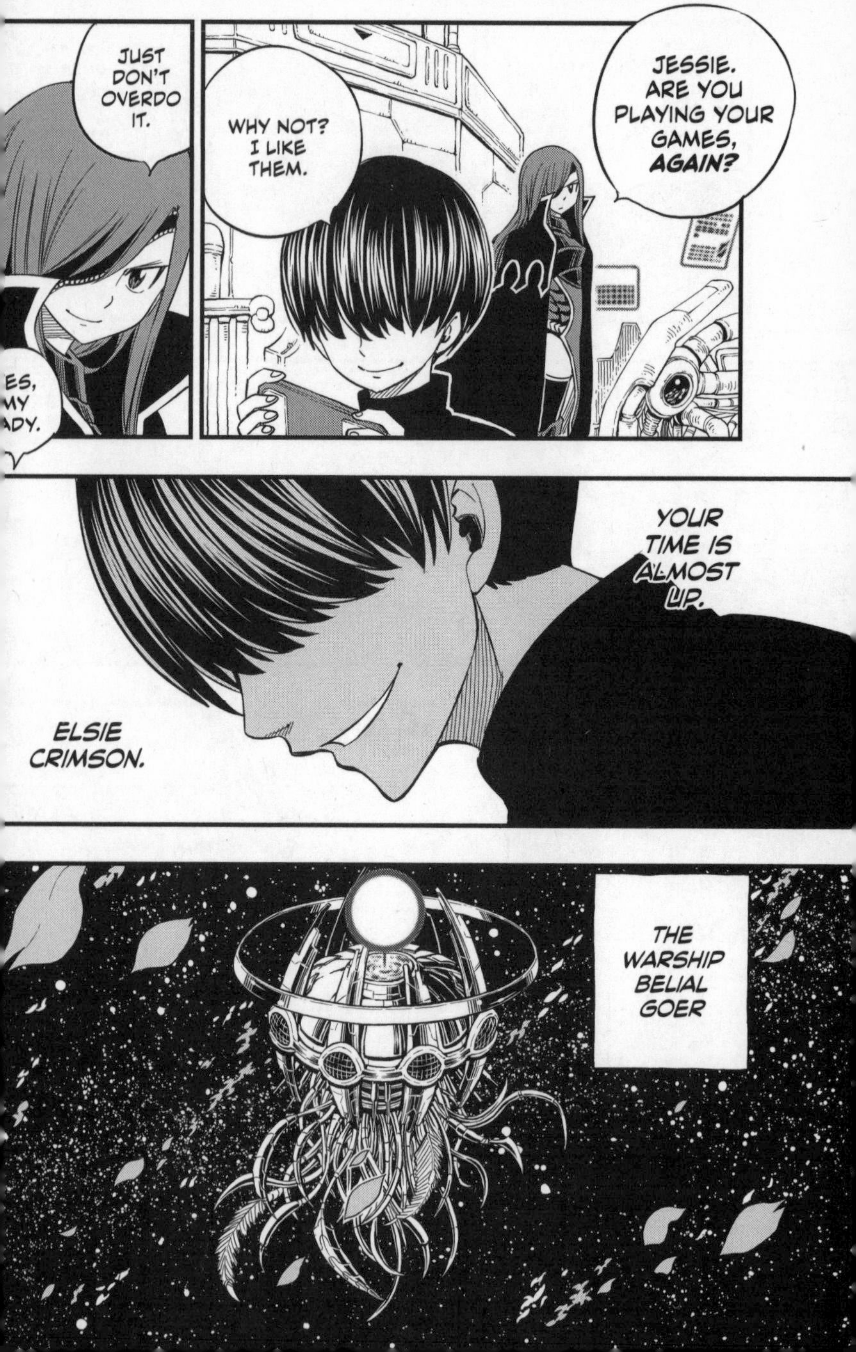
JESSIE. ARE YOU PLAYING YOUR GAMES, AGAIN?
WHY NOT? I LIKE THEM.
JUST DON'T OVERDO IT.
ES, MY ADY.
YOUR TIME IS ALMOST UP.
ELSIE CRIMSON.
THE WARSHIP BELIAL GOER

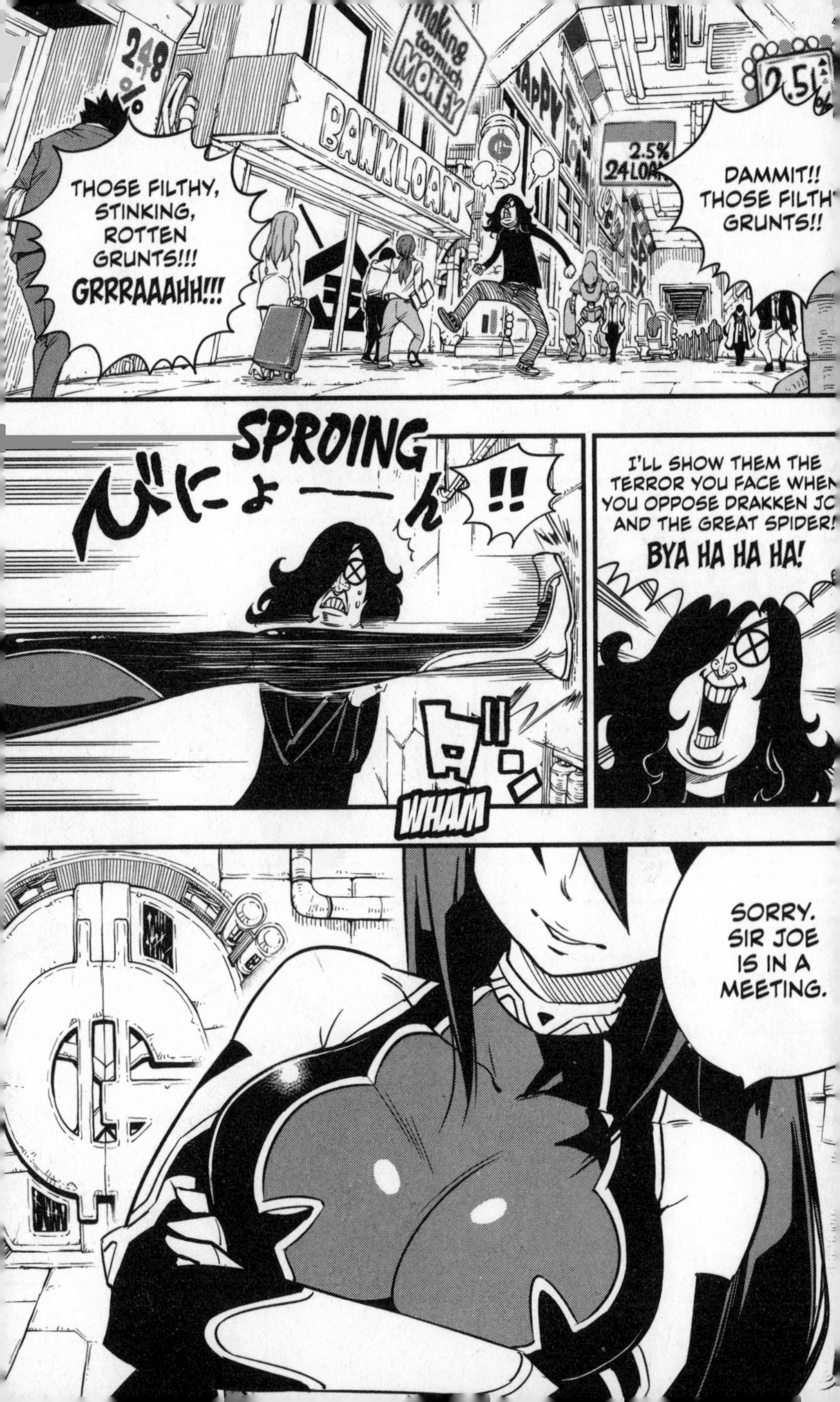
DAMMIT!! THOSE FILTH' GRUNTS!!
2.5% 24LOAN
making too much MONEY
BANKLOAN
2.48%
THOSE FILTHY, STINKING, ROTTEN GRUNTS!!! GRRRAAAHH!!!
I'LL SHOW THEM THE TERROR YOU FACE WHEN YOU OPPOSE DRAKKEN JO AND THE GREAT SPIDER!
BYA HA HA HA!
SPROING
びにょーーーん!!
WHAM
SORRY. SIR JOE IS IN A MEETING.

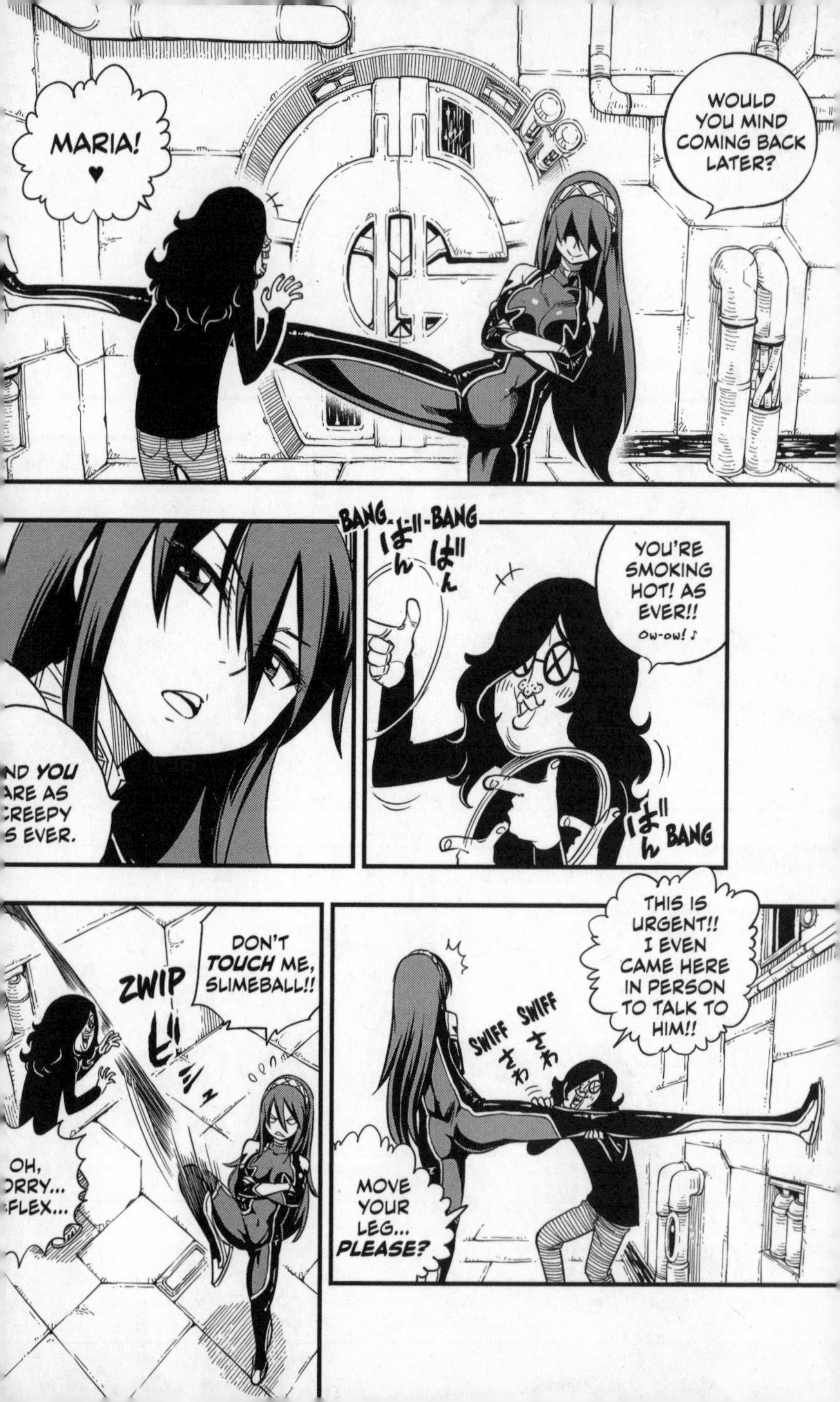
WOULD YOU MIND COMING BACK LATER?
MARIA! ♥
BANG-BANG
ばん ばん
YOU'RE SMOKING HOT! AS EVER!!
Ow-ow! ♪
ばん BANG
ND YOU ARE AS CREEPY S EVER.
THIS IS URGENT!! I EVEN CAME HERE IN PERSON TO TALK TO HIM!!
SWIFF SWIFF
さわ さわ
MOVE YOUR LEG... PLEASE?
DON'T TOUCH ME, SLIMEBALL!!
ZWIP
OH, ORRY... FLEX...

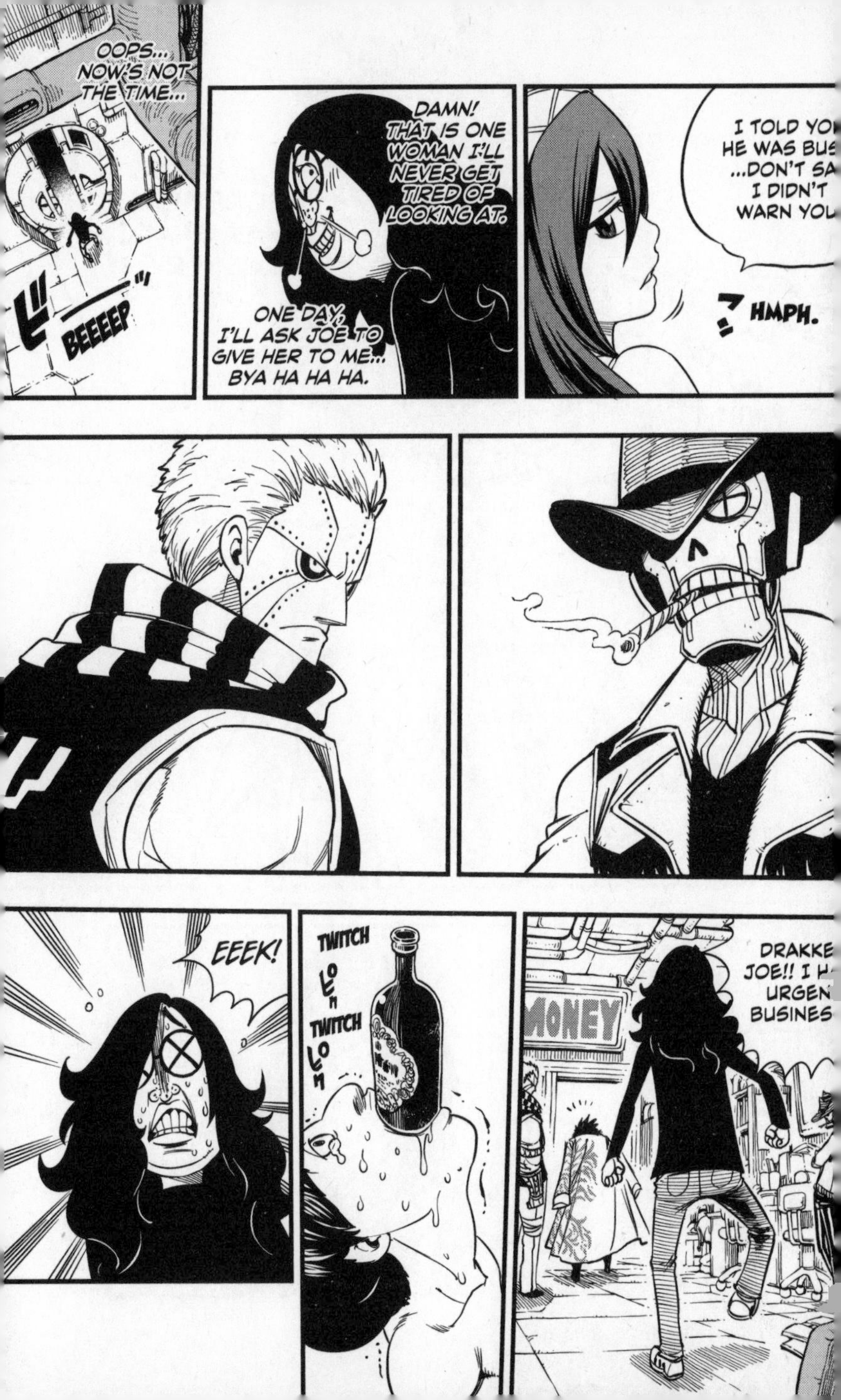
I TOLD YO
HE WAS BUS
...DON'T SA
I DIDN'T
WARN YOU
HMPH.
DAMN! THAT IS ONE WOMAN I'LL NEVER GET TIRED OF LOOKING AT.
ONE DAY, I'LL ASK JOE TO GIVE HER TO ME... BYA HA HA HA.
OOPS... NOW'S NOT THE TIME...
BEEEEEP
DRAKKE
JOE!! I H
URGEN
BUSINES
MONEY
TWITCH
TWITCH
EEEK!

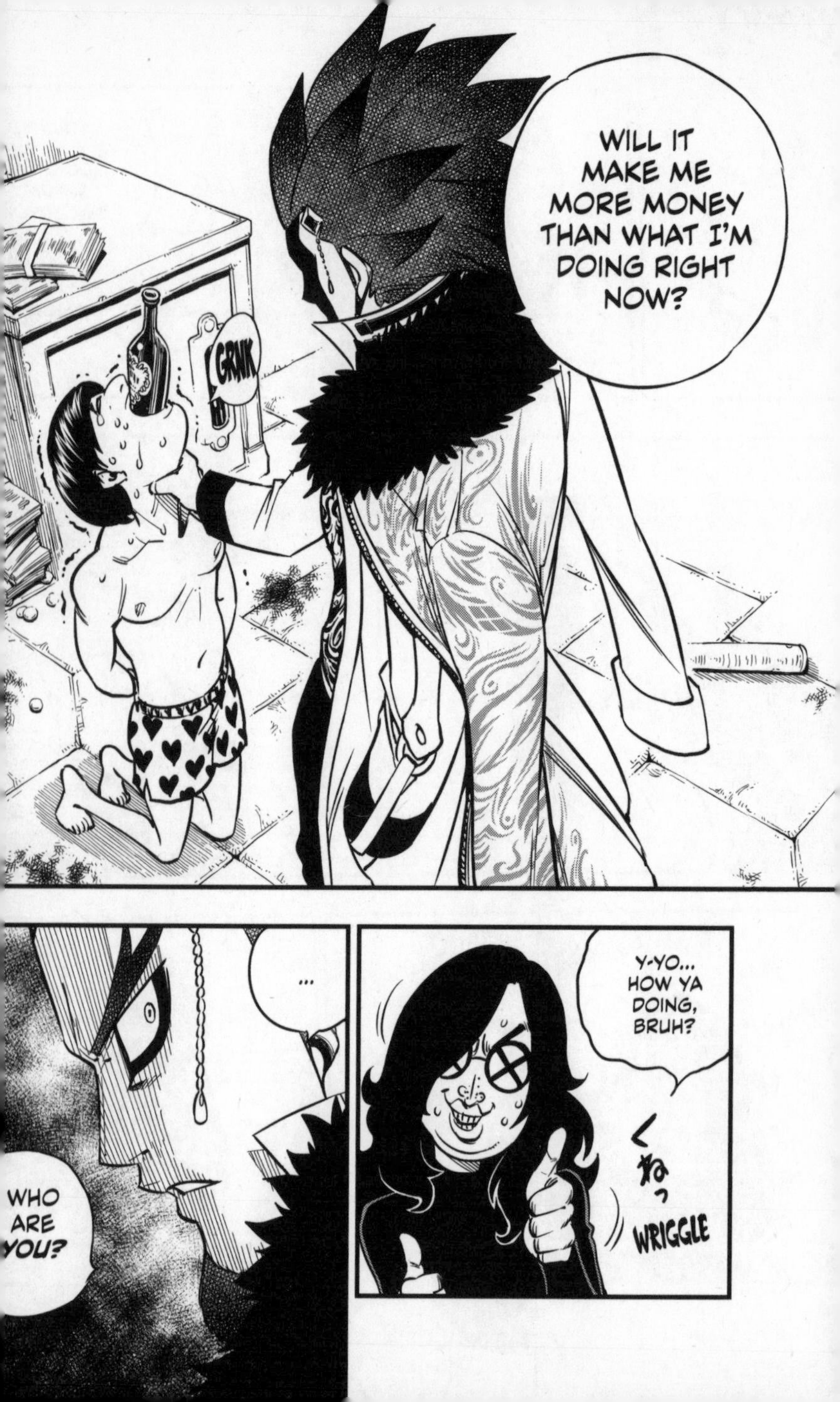
WILL IT MAKE ME MORE MONEY THAN WHAT I'M DOING RIGHT NOW?
GRNK
Y-YO... HOW YA DOING, BRUH?
くねっ
WRIGGLE
...
WHO ARE YOU?

EDENS ZERO

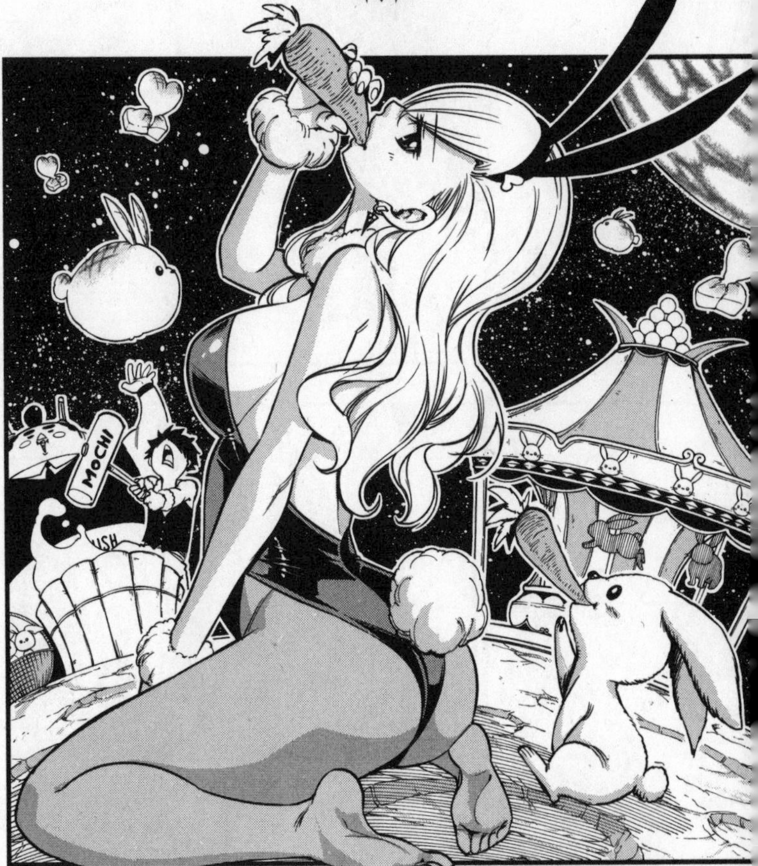
MOCHI

CHAPTER 43: SMELLS LIKE MONEY

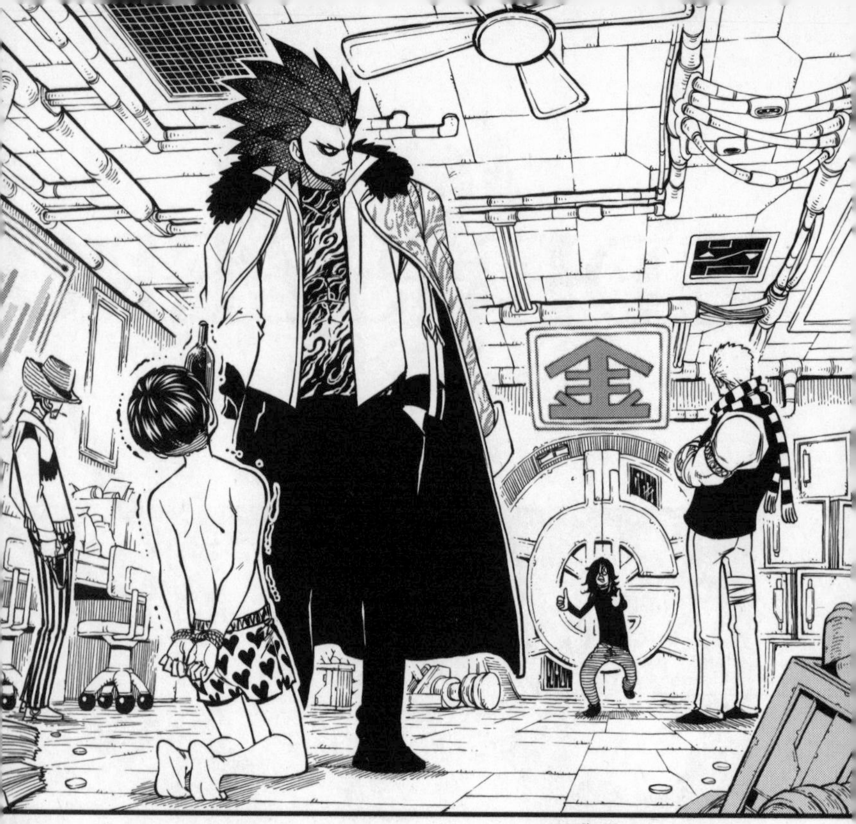

Sign: Money

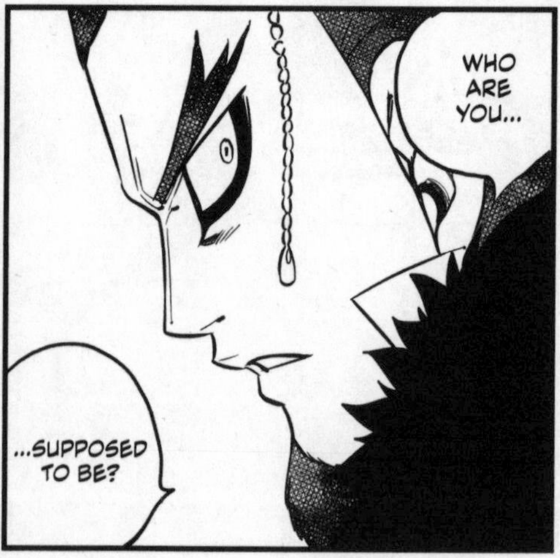
WHO ARE YOU...
...SUPPOSED TO BE?

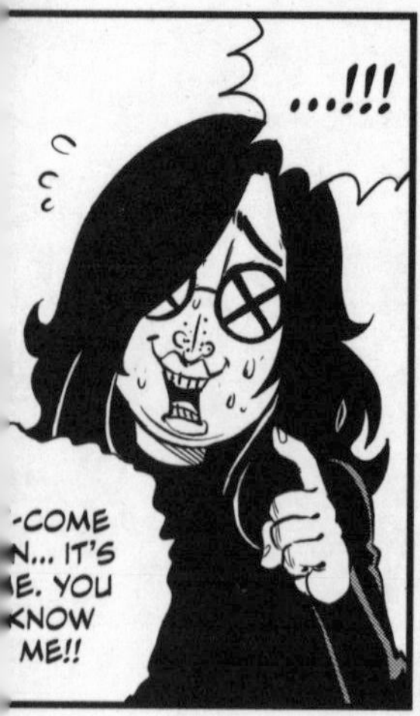
...!!!
-COME N... IT'S E. YOU KNOW ME!!

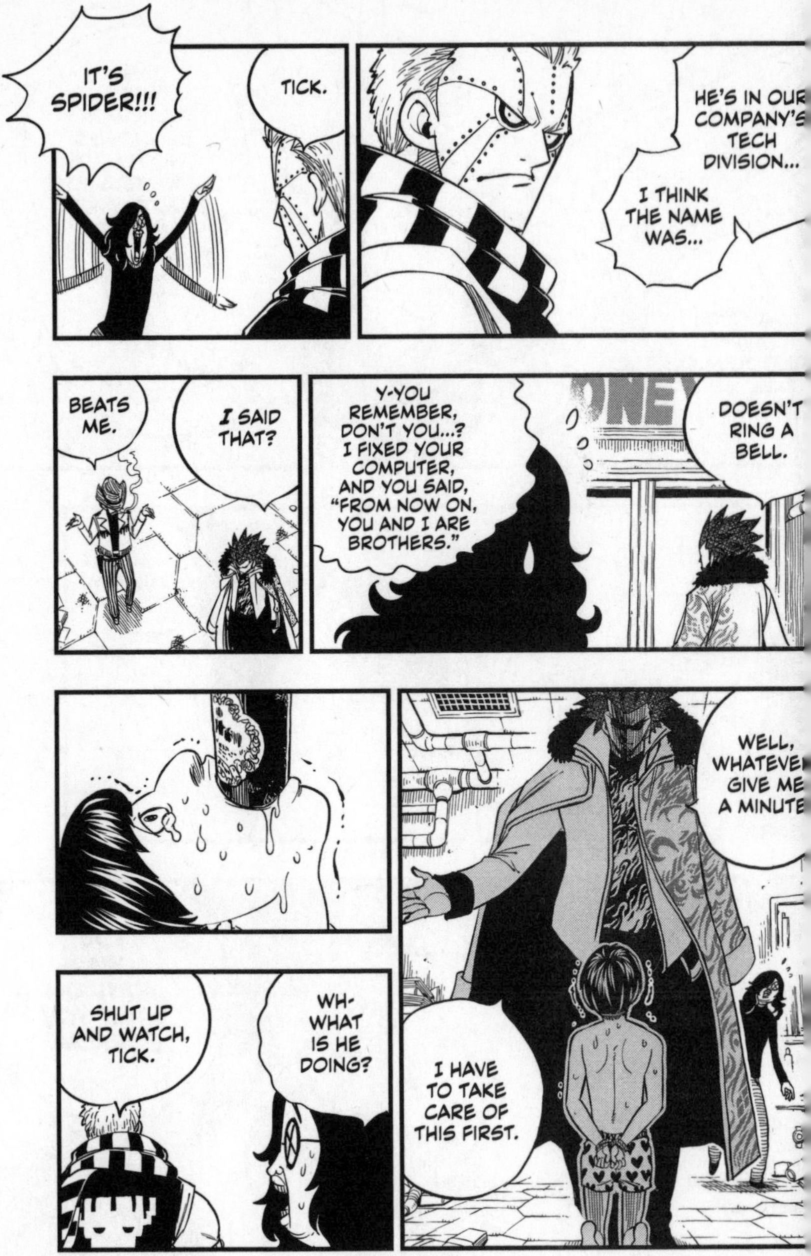
HE'S IN OUR COMPANY'S TECH DIVISION...
I THINK THE NAME WAS...
TICK.
IT'S SPIDER!!!
DOESN'T RING A BELL.
Y-YOU REMEMBER, DON'T YOU...? I FIXED YOUR COMPUTER, AND YOU SAID, "FROM NOW ON, YOU AND I ARE BROTHERS."
I SAID THAT?
BEATS ME.
WELL, WHATEVE GIVE ME A MINUTE
I HAVE TO TAKE CARE OF THIS FIRST.
WH- WHAT IS HE DOING?
SHUT UP AND WATCH, TICK.

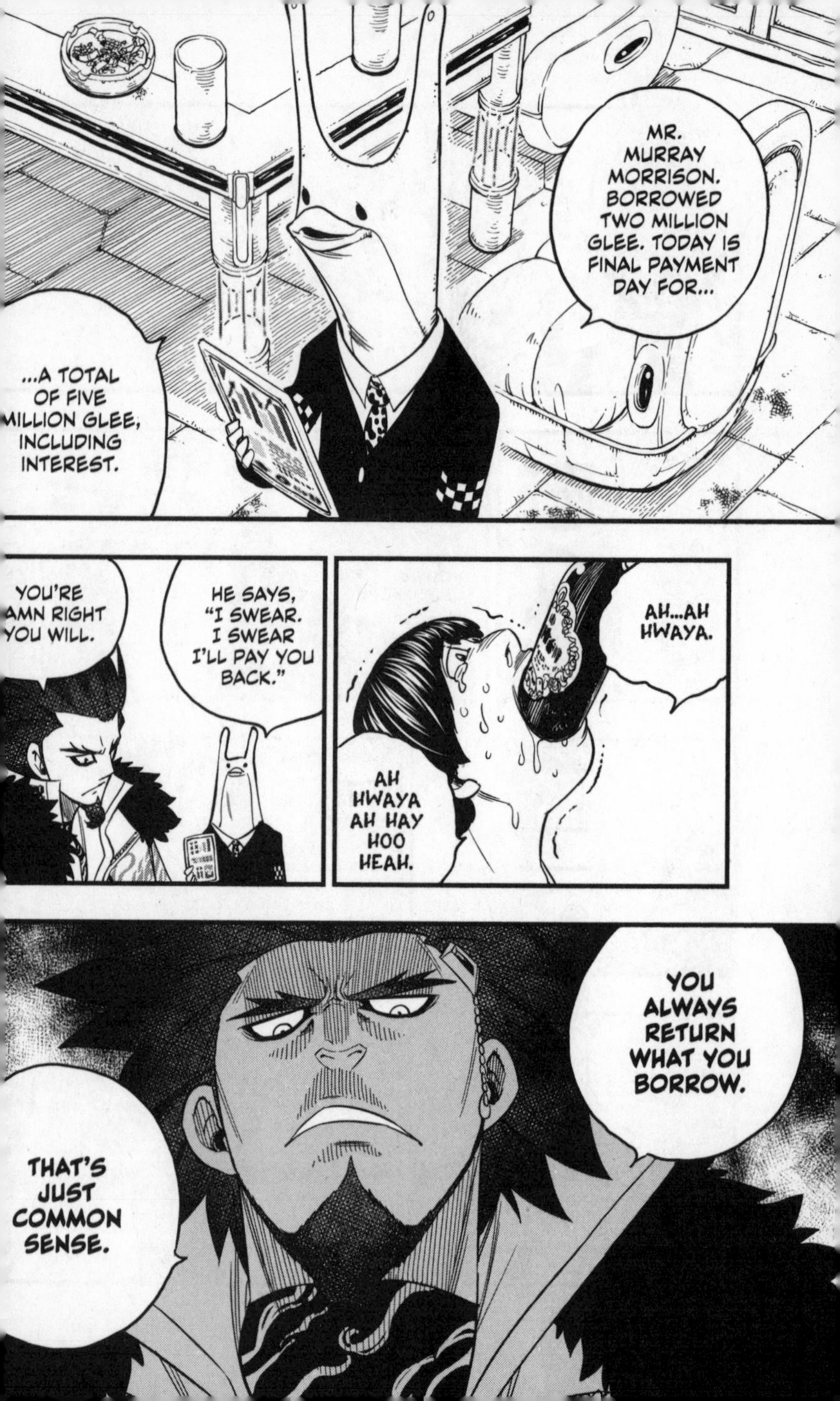
MR. MURRAY MORRISON. BORROWED TWO MILLION GLEE. TODAY IS FINAL PAYMENT DAY FOR...
...A TOTAL OF FIVE MILLION GLEE, INCLUDING INTEREST.
AH...AH HWAYA.
AH HWAYA AH HAY HOO HEAH.
HE SAYS, "I SWEAR. I SWEAR I'LL PAY YOU BACK."
YOU'RE AMN RIGHT YOU WILL.
YOU ALWAYS RETURN WHAT YOU BORROW.
THAT'S JUST COMMON SENSE.

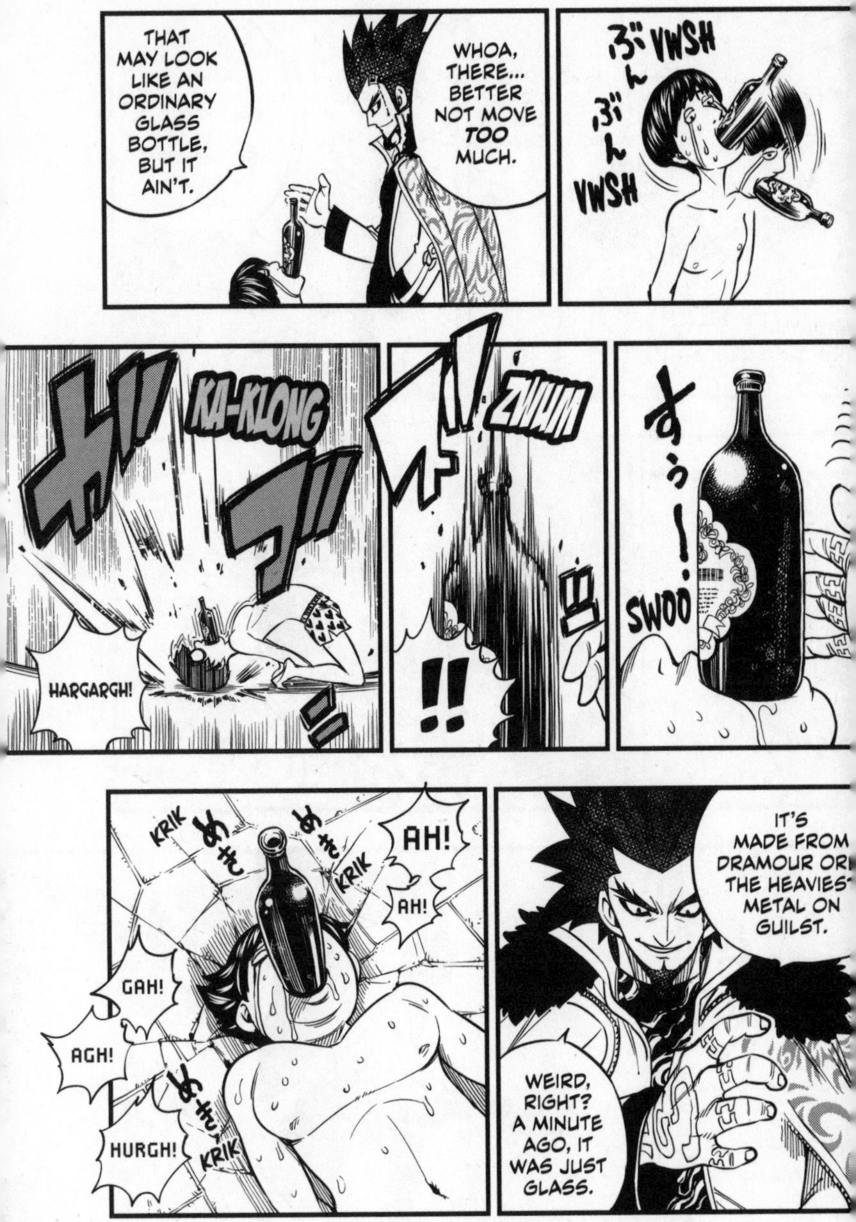
ぶん VWSH
ぶん VWSH
WHOA, THERE... BETTER NOT MOVE *TOO* MUCH.
THAT MAY LOOK LIKE AN ORDINARY GLASS BOTTLE, BUT IT AIN'T.
すぅー! SWOO
ZWUM
!!
KA-KLONG
HARGARGH!
IT'S MADE FROM DRAMOUR OR THE HEAVIES METAL ON GUILST.
WEIRD, RIGHT? A MINUTE AGO, IT WAS JUST GLASS.
めき KRIK
AH!
AH!
めき KRIK
GAH!
AGH!
めき KRIK
HURGH!

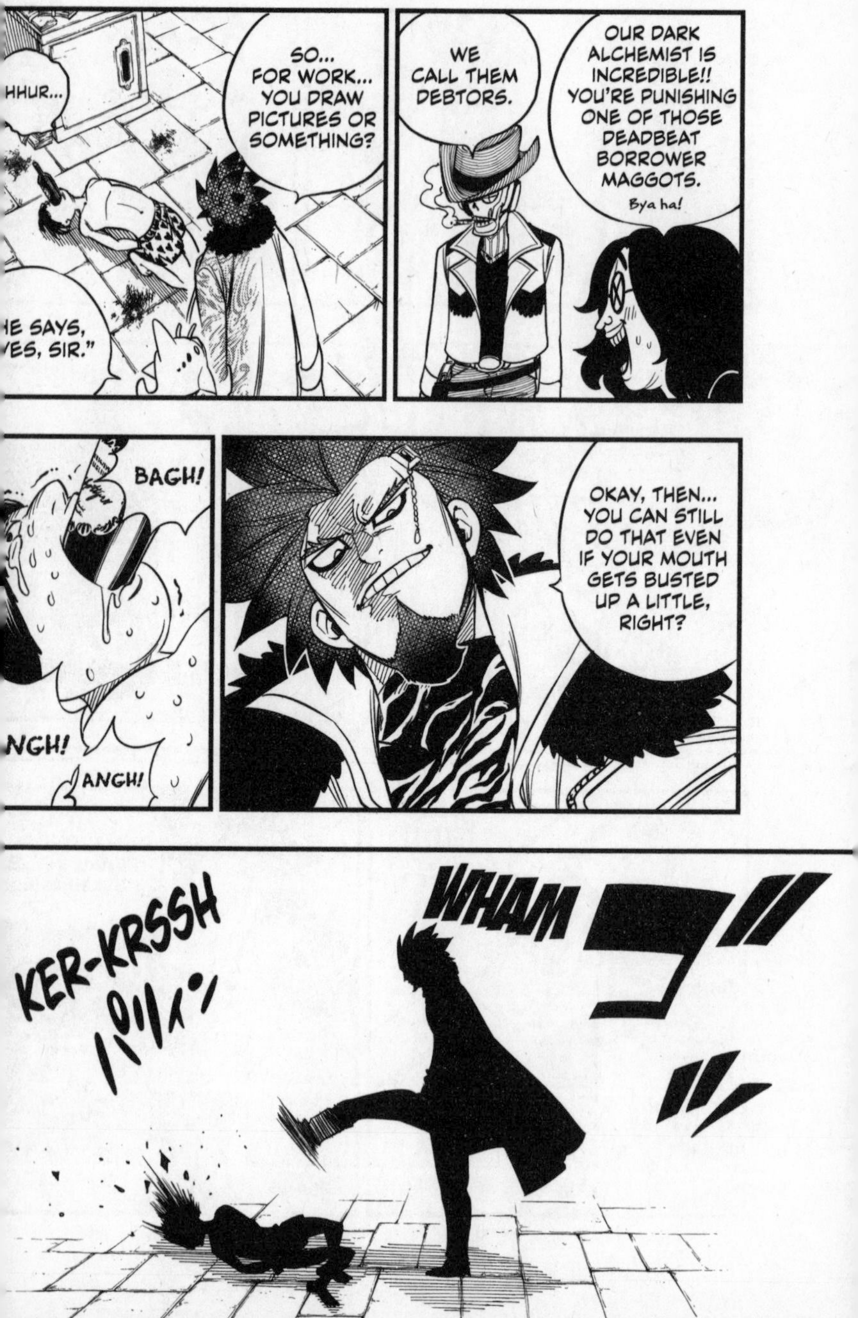
OUR DARK ALCHEMIST IS INCREDIBLE!! YOU'RE PUNISHING ONE OF THOSE DEADBEAT BORROWER MAGGOTS.
Bya ha!
WE CALL THEM DEBTORS.
SO... FOR WORK... YOU DRAW PICTURES OR SOMETHING?
HHUR...
HE SAYS,
YES, SIR."
OKAY, THEN... YOU CAN STILL DO THAT EVEN IF YOUR MOUTH GETS BUSTED UP A LITTLE, RIGHT?
BAGH!
NGH!
ANGH!
WHAM
KER-KRSSH
パリィン

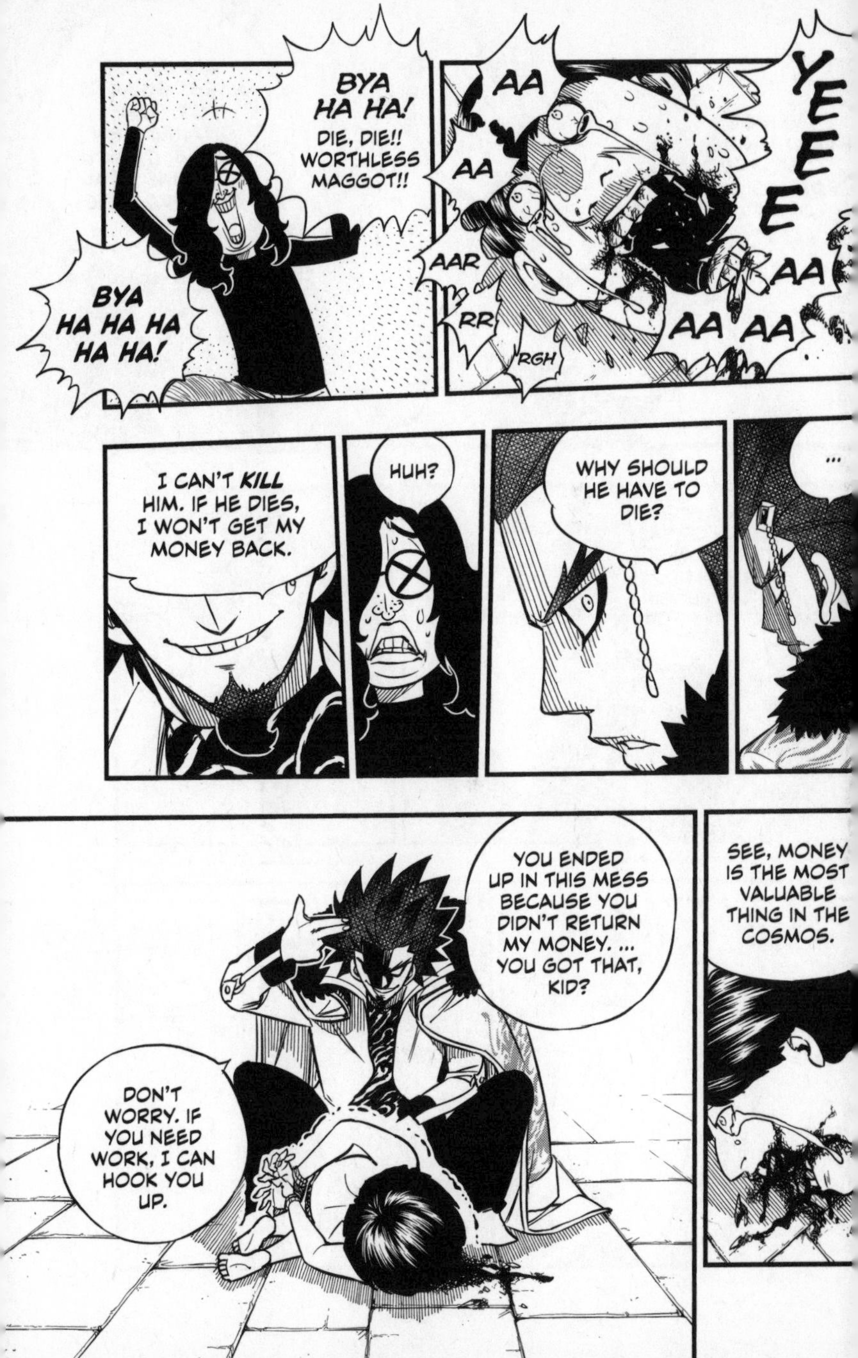
YEEE
E
AA
AA AA
AA
AA
AARRRRGH
BYA HA HA!
DIE, DIE!! WORTHLESS MAGGOT!!
BYA HA HA HA HA HA!
...
WHY SHOULD HE HAVE TO DIE?
HUH?
I CAN'T **KILL** HIM. IF HE DIES, I WON'T GET MY MONEY BACK.
SEE, MONEY IS THE MOST VALUABLE THING IN THE COSMOS.
YOU ENDED UP IN THIS MESS BECAUSE YOU DIDN'T RETURN MY MONEY. ... YOU GOT THAT, KID?
DON'T WORRY. IF YOU NEED WORK, I CAN HOOK YOU UP.

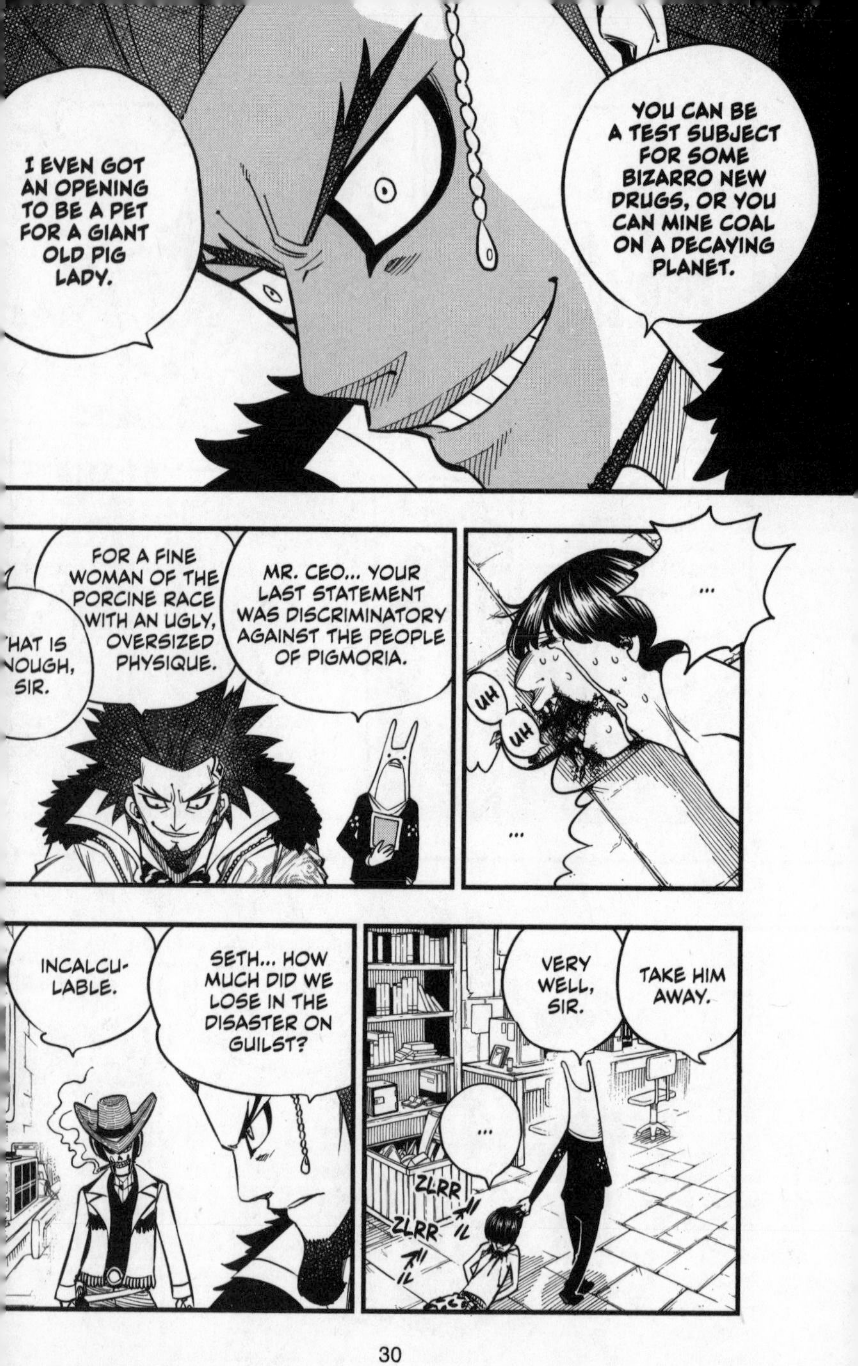
YOU CAN BE A TEST SUBJECT FOR SOME BIZARRO NEW DRUGS, OR YOU CAN MINE COAL ON A DECAYING PLANET.
I EVEN GOT AN OPENING TO BE A PET FOR A GIANT OLD PIG LADY.
...
UH
UH
...
MR. CEO... YOUR LAST STATEMENT WAS DISCRIMINATORY AGAINST THE PEOPLE OF PIGMORIA.
FOR A FINE WOMAN OF THE PORCINE RACE WITH AN UGLY, OVERSIZED PHYSIQUE.
HAT IS NOUGH, SIR.
TAKE HIM AWAY.
VERY WELL, SIR.
...
ZLRR
ZLRR
SETH... HOW MUCH DID WE LOSE IN THE DISASTER ON GUILST?
INCALCU-LABLE.

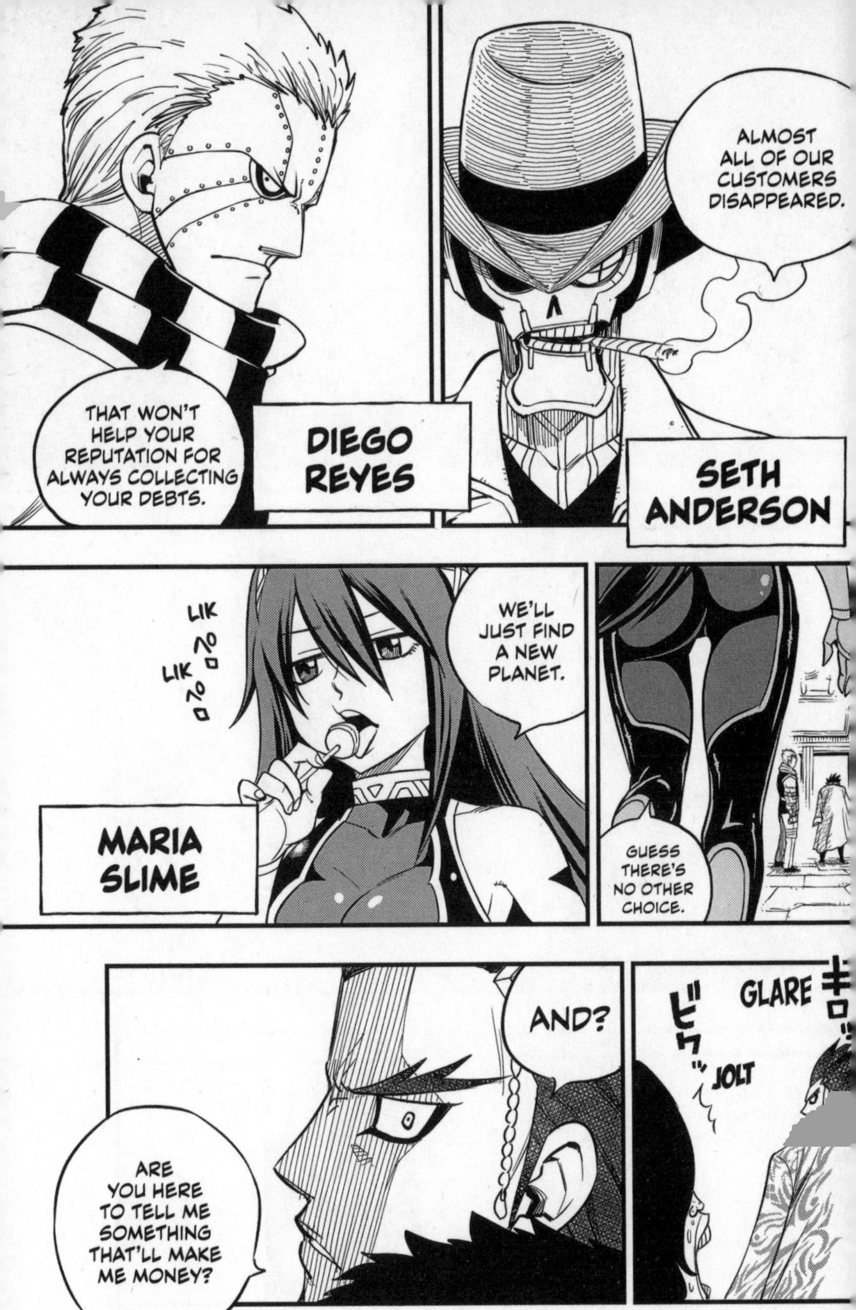

ALMOST ALL OF OUR CUSTOMERS DISAPPEARED.
SETH ANDERSON
THAT WON'T HELP YOUR REPUTATION FOR ALWAYS COLLECTING YOUR DEBTS.
DIEGO REYES
GUESS THERE'S NO OTHER CHOICE.
WE'LL JUST FIND A NEW PLANET.
LIK
LIK
MARIA SLIME
GLARE
JOLT
AND?
ARE YOU HERE TO TELL ME SOMETHING THAT'LL MAKE ME MONEY?

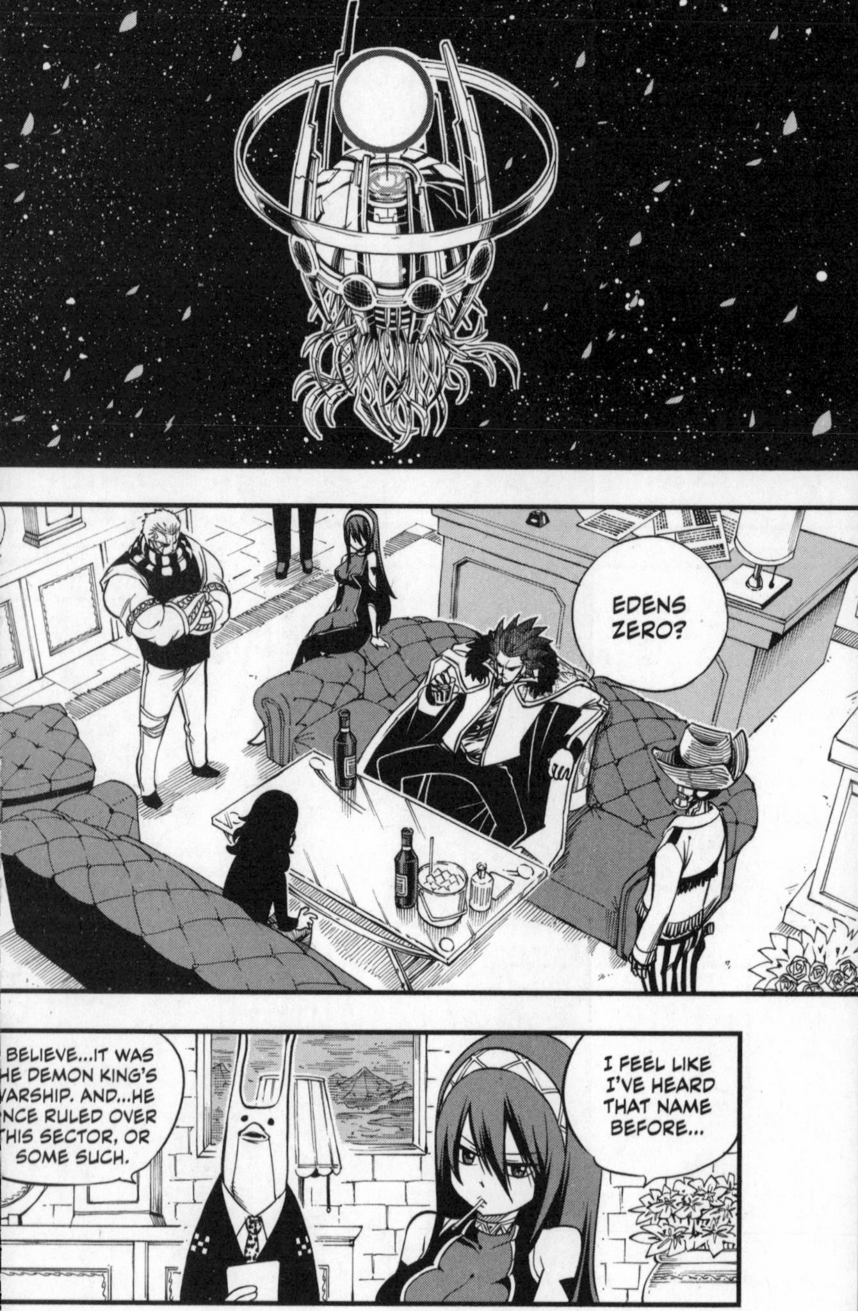
EDENS ZERO?
I FEEL LIKE I'VE HEARD THAT NAME BEFORE...
BELIEVE...IT WAS HE DEMON KING'S VARSHIP. AND...HE NCE RULED OVER THIS SECTOR, OR SOME SUCH.

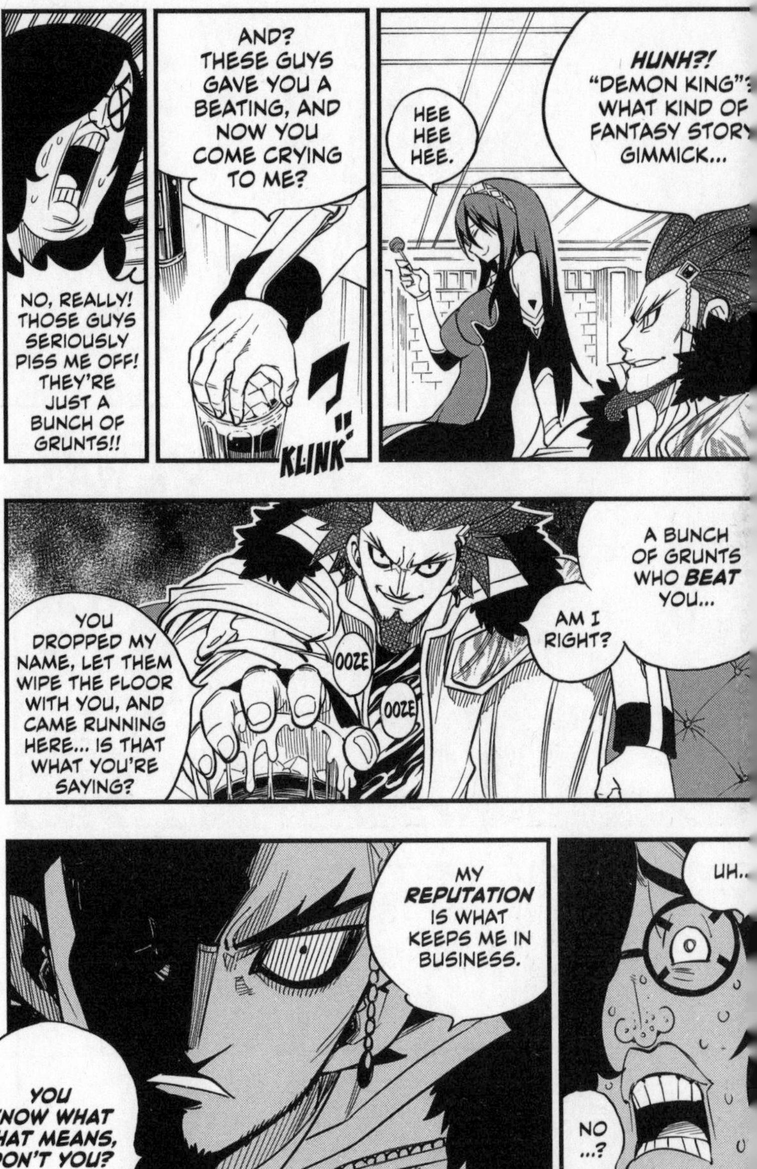
HUNH?! “DEMON KING” WHAT KIND OF FANTASY STORY GIMMICK...
HEE HEE HEE.
AND? THESE GUYS GAVE YOU A BEATING, AND NOW YOU COME CRYING TO ME?
KLINK
NO, REALLY! THOSE GUYS SERIOUSLY PISS ME OFF! THEY'RE JUST A BUNCH OF GRUNTS!!
A BUNCH OF GRUNTS WHO BEAT YOU...
AM I RIGHT?
OOZE
OOZE
YOU DROPPED MY NAME, LET THEM WIPE THE FLOOR WITH YOU, AND CAME RUNNING HERE... IS THAT WHAT YOU'RE SAYING?
UH...
NO ...?
MY REPUTATION IS WHAT KEEPS ME IN BUSINESS.
YOU KNOW WHAT THAT MEANS, DON'T YOU?

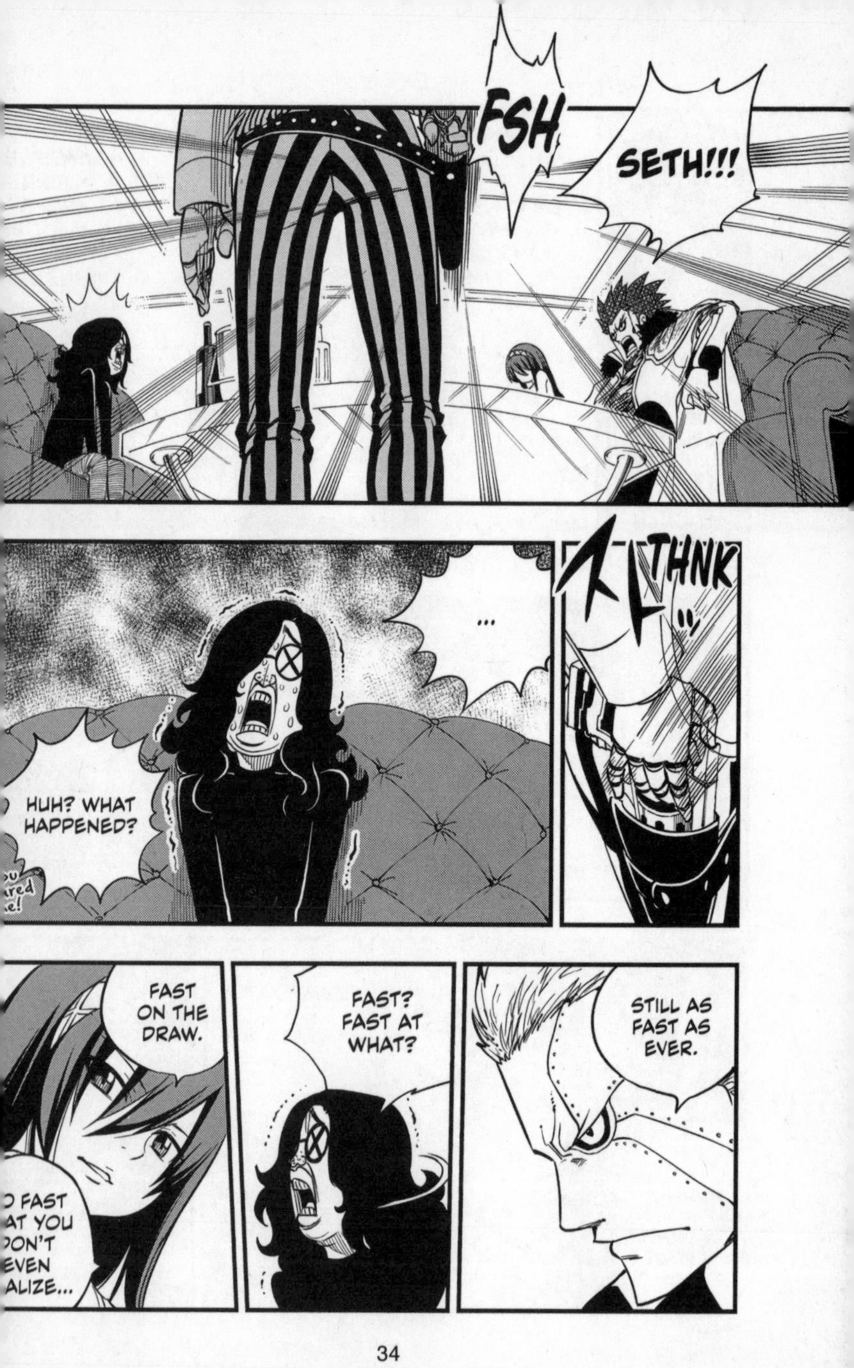
FSH
SETH!!!
THNK
...
HUH? WHAT HAPPENED?
STILL AS FAST AS EVER.
FAST? FAST AT WHAT?
FAST ON THE DRAW.

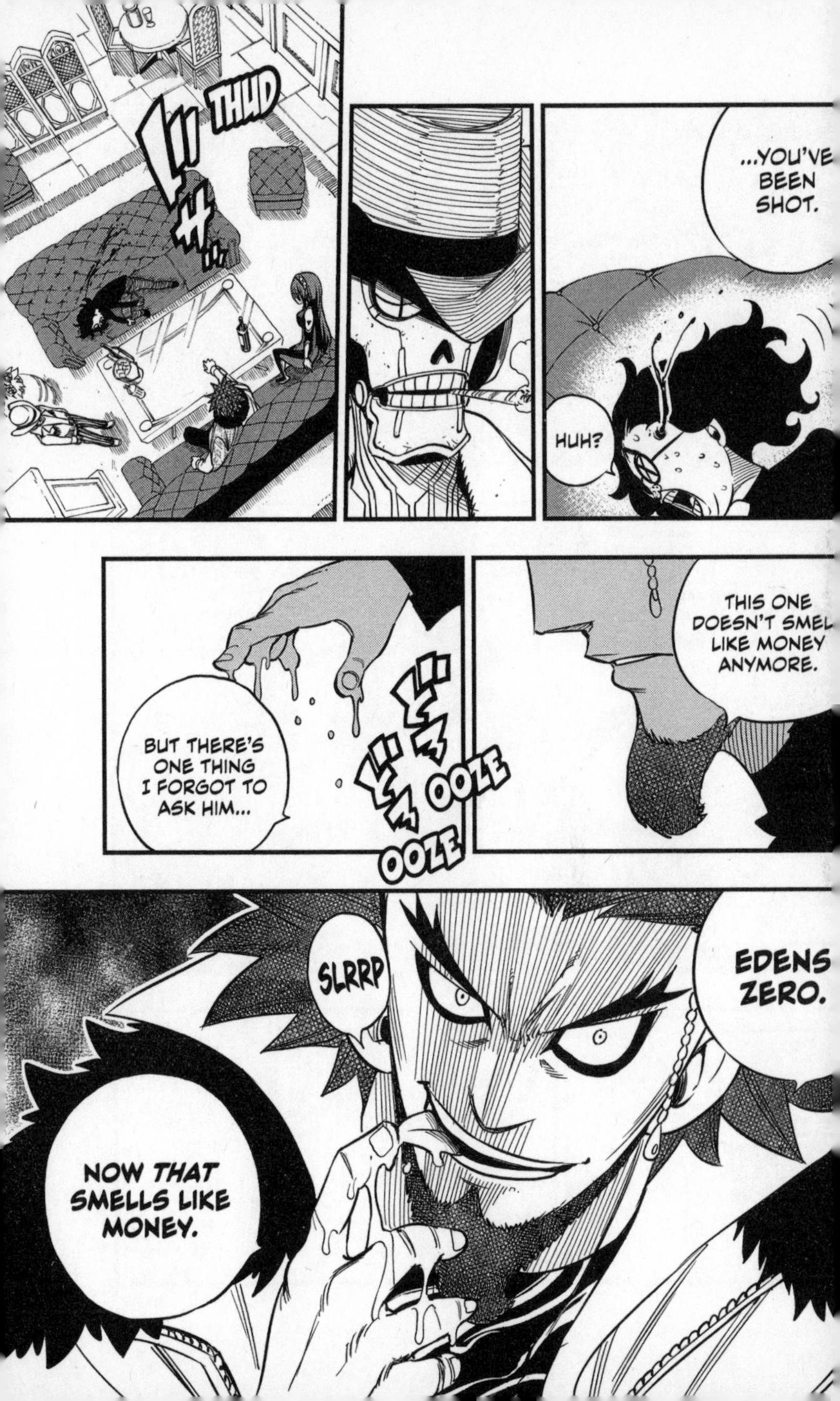
...YOU'VE BEEN SHOT.
HUH?
THUD
THIS ONE DOESN'T SMEL LIKE MONEY ANYMORE.
BUT THERE'S ONE THING I FORGOT TO ASK HIM...
OOZE
OOZE
EDENS ZERO.
SLRRP
NOW *THAT* SMELLS LIKE MONEY.

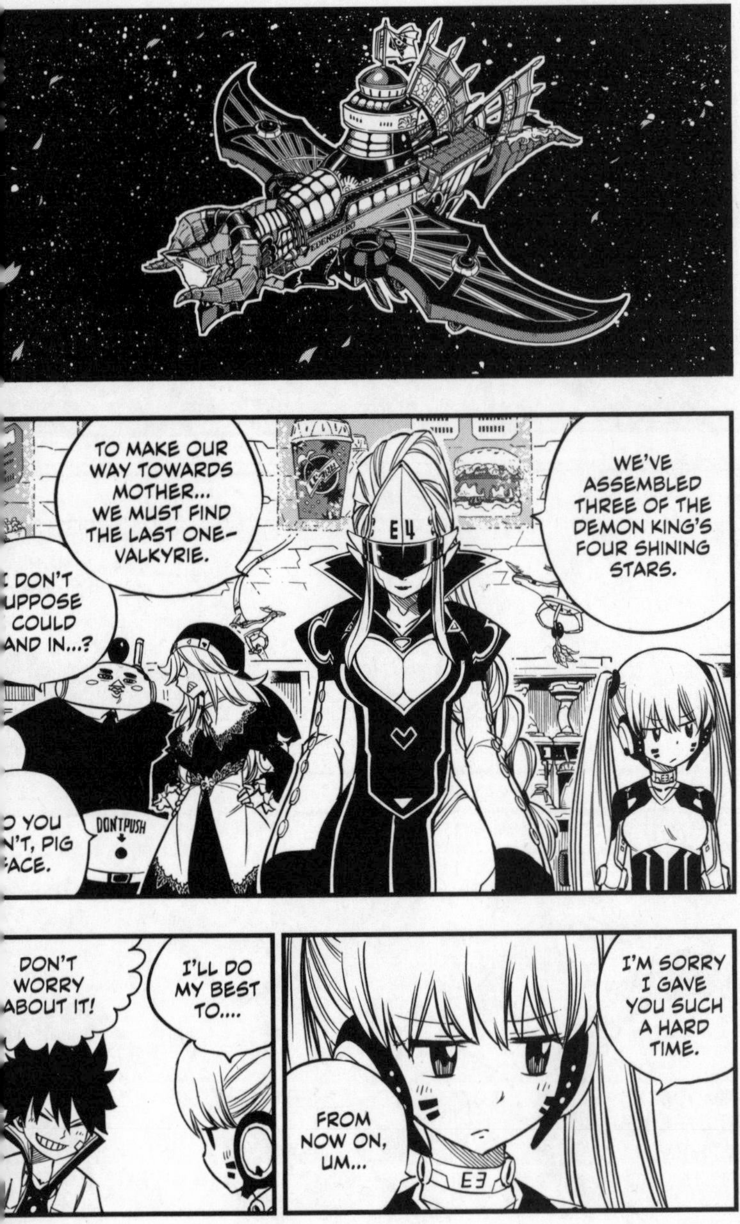
WE'VE ASSEMBLED THREE OF THE DEMON KING'S FOUR SHINING STARS.
TO MAKE OUR WAY TOWARDS MOTHER... WE MUST FIND THE LAST ONE- VALKYRIE.
DON'T UPPOSE COULD AND IN...?
O YOU N'T, PIG FACE.
DONTPUSH
I'M SORRY I GAVE YOU SUCH A HARD TIME.
FROM NOW ON, UM...
I'LL DO MY BEST TO....
DON'T WORRY ABOUT IT!

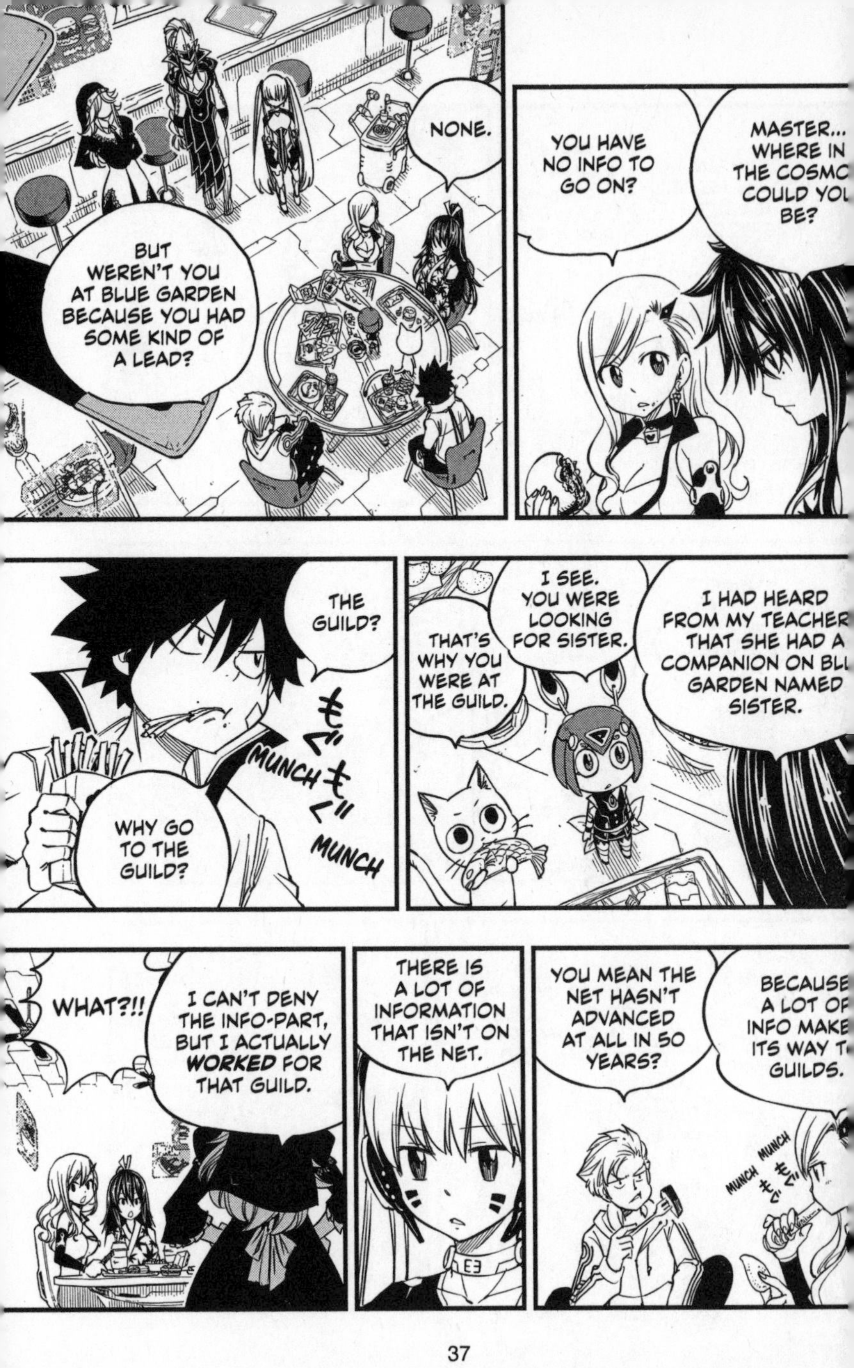
MASTER... WHERE IN THE COSMO COULD YOU BE?
YOU HAVE NO INFO TO GO ON?
NONE.
BUT WEREN'T YOU AT BLUE GARDEN BECAUSE YOU HAD SOME KIND OF A LEAD?
I HAD HEARD FROM MY TEACHER THAT SHE HAD A COMPANION ON BLU GARDEN NAMED SISTER.
I SEE. YOU WERE LOOKING FOR SISTER.
THAT'S WHY YOU WERE AT THE GUILD.
THE GUILD?
もぐ MUNCH
もぐ MUNCH
WHY GO TO THE GUILD?
BECAUSE A LOT OF INFO MAKE ITS WAY T GUILDS.
MUNCH MUNCH もぐ もぐ
YOU MEAN THE NET HASN'T ADVANCED AT ALL IN 50 YEARS?
THERE IS A LOT OF INFORMATION THAT ISN'T ON THE NET.
I CAN'T DENY THE INFO-PART, BUT I ACTUALLY WORKED FOR THAT GUILD.
WHAT?!!

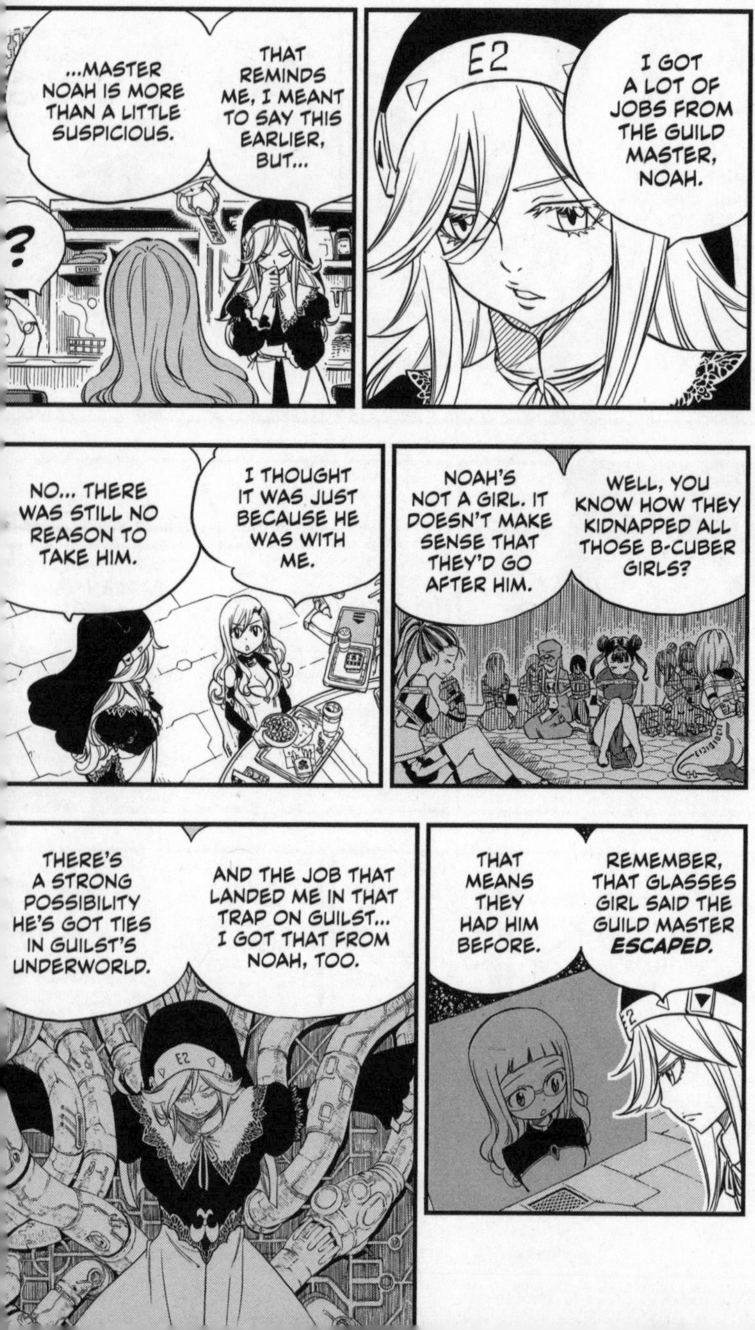
I GOT A LOT OF JOBS FROM THE GUILD MASTER, NOAH.
THAT REMINDS ME, I MEANT TO SAY THIS EARLIER, BUT...
...MASTER NOAH IS MORE THAN A LITTLE SUSPICIOUS.
?
WELL, YOU KNOW HOW THEY KIDNAPPED ALL THOSE B-CUBER GIRLS?
NOAH'S NOT A GIRL. IT DOESN'T MAKE SENSE THAT THEY'D GO AFTER HIM.
I THOUGHT IT WAS JUST BECAUSE HE WAS WITH ME.
NO... THERE WAS STILL NO REASON TO TAKE HIM.
REMEMBER, THAT GLASSES GIRL SAID THE GUILD MASTER *ESCAPED.*
THAT MEANS THEY HAD HIM BEFORE.
AND THE JOB THAT LANDED ME IN THAT TRAP ON GUILST... I GOT THAT FROM NOAH, TOO.
THERE'S A STRONG POSSIBILITY HE'S GOT TIES IN GUILST'S UNDERWORLD.

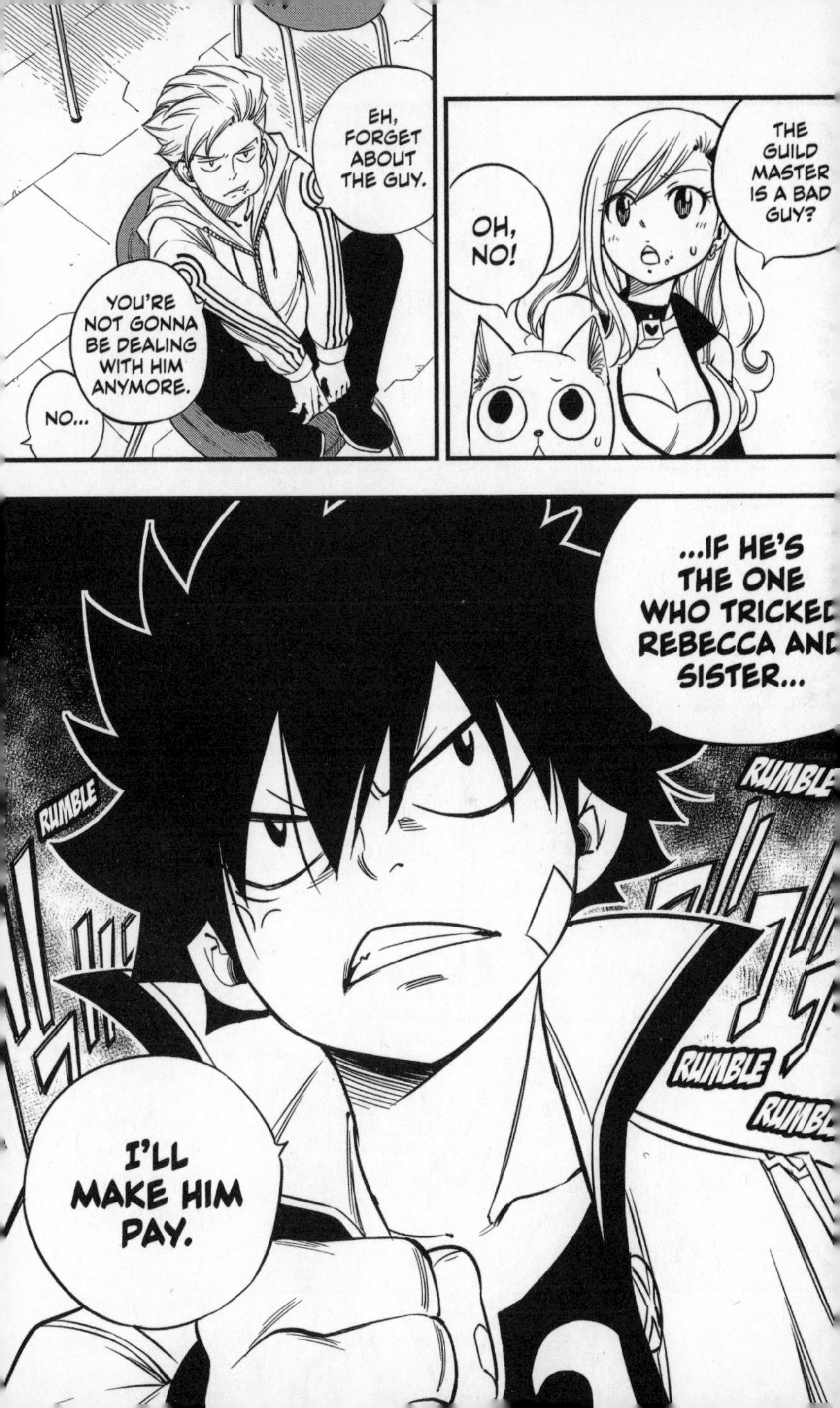
THE GUILD MASTER IS A BAD GUY?
OH, NO!
EH, FORGET ABOUT THE GUY.
YOU'RE NOT GONNA BE DEALING WITH HIM ANYMORE.
NO...
...IF HE'S THE ONE WHO TRICKED REBECCA AND SISTER...
RUMBLE
RUMBLE
RUMBLE
RUMBL
I'LL MAKE HIM PAY.

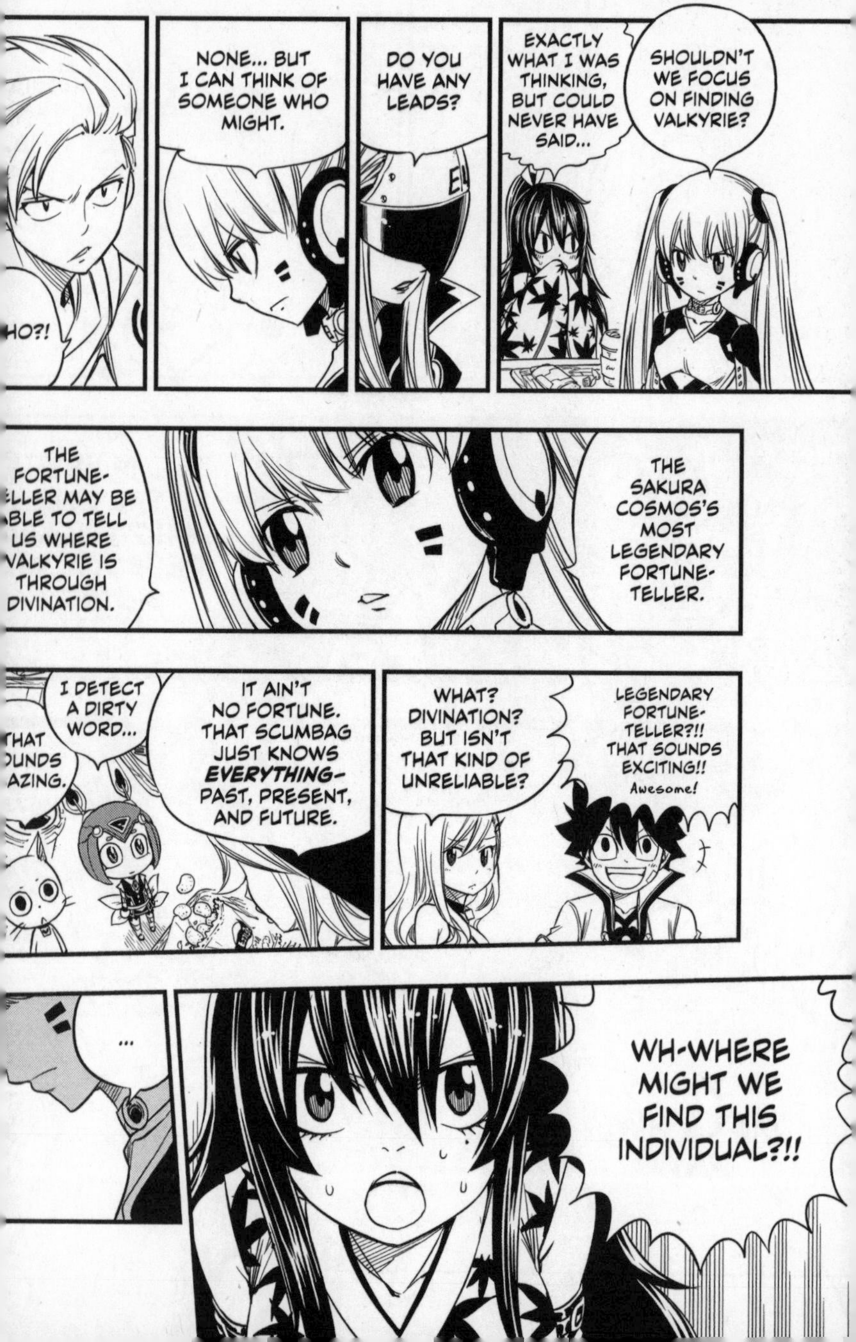
SHOULDN'T WE FOCUS ON FINDING VALKYRIE?
EXACTLY WHAT I WAS THINKING, BUT COULD NEVER HAVE SAID...
DO YOU HAVE ANY LEADS?
NONE... BUT I CAN THINK OF SOMEONE WHO MIGHT.
HO?!
THE SAKURA COSMOS'S MOST LEGENDARY FORTUNE-TELLER.
THE FORTUNE-ELLER MAY BE BLE TO TELL US WHERE VALKYRIE IS THROUGH DIVINATION.
LEGENDARY FORTUNE-TELLER?!! THAT SOUNDS EXCITING!!
Awesome!
WHAT? DIVINATION? BUT ISN'T THAT KIND OF UNRELIABLE?
IT AIN'T NO FORTUNE. THAT SCUMBAG JUST KNOWS ***EVERYTHING***—PAST, PRESENT, AND FUTURE.
I DETECT A DIRTY WORD...
THAT OUNDS AZING.
WH-WHERE MIGHT WE FIND THIS INDIVIDUAL?!!
...

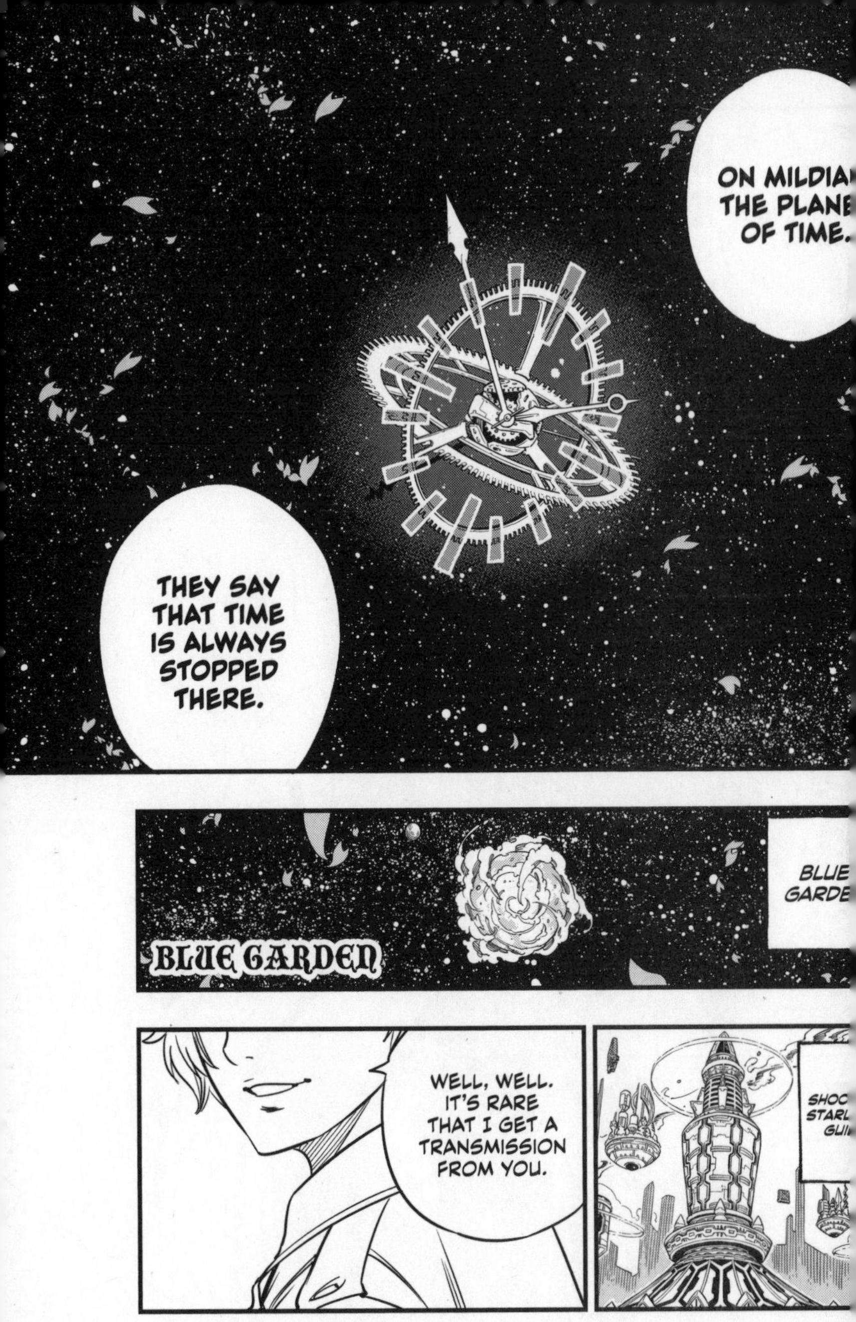
ON MILDIA THE PLANE OF TIME.
THEY SAY THAT TIME IS ALWAYS STOPPED THERE.
BLUE GARDE
BLUE GARDEN
SHOC STARL GUI
WELL, WELL. IT'S RARE THAT I GET A TRANSMISSION FROM YOU.

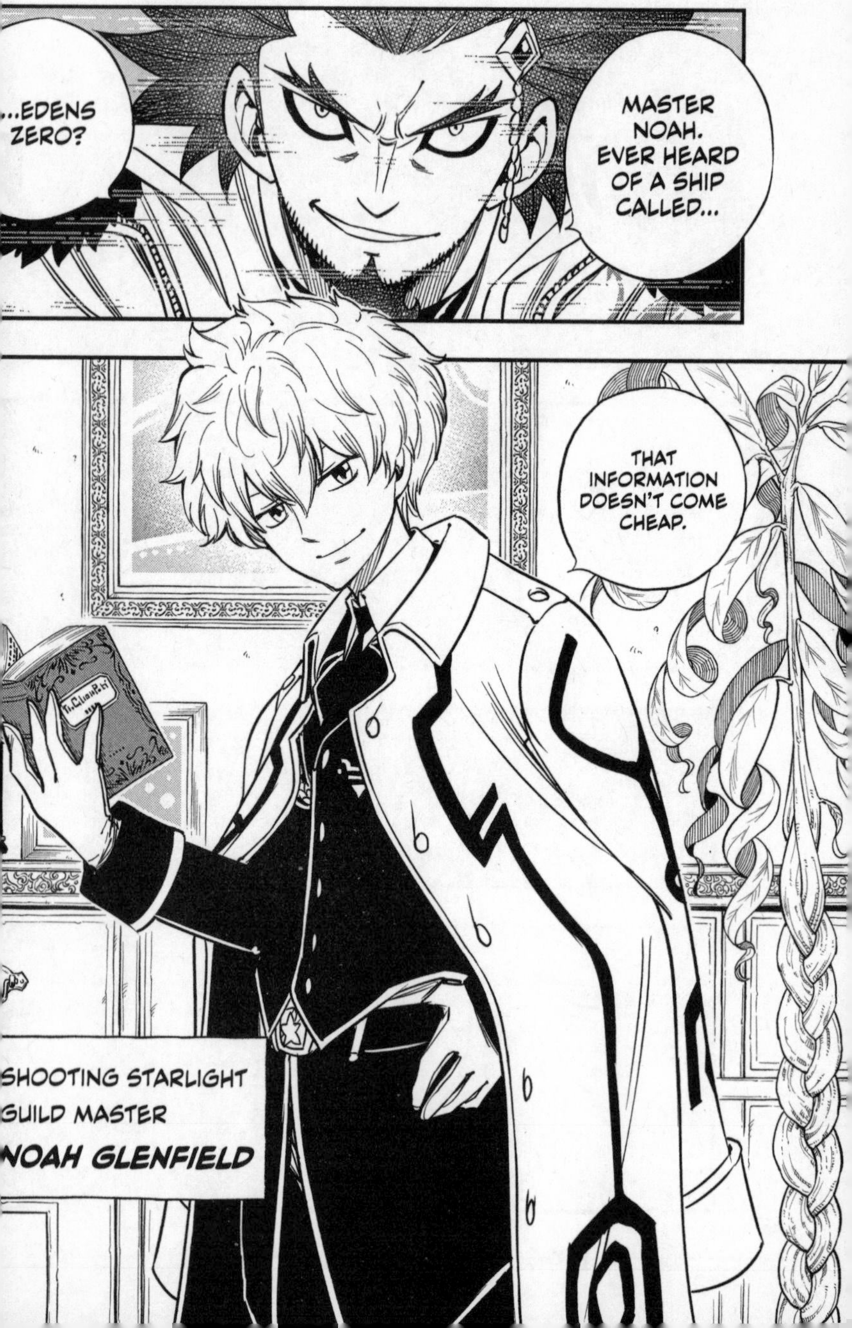
MASTER NOAH. EVER HEARD OF A SHIP CALLED...
...EDENS ZERO?
THAT INFORMATION DOESN'T COME CHEAP.
SHOOTING STARLIGHT GUILD MASTER
NOAH GLENFIELD

EDENS ZERO

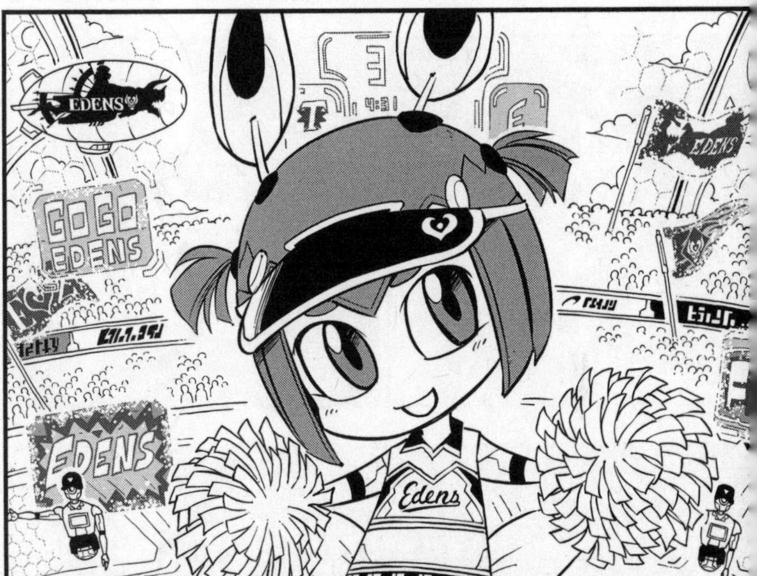
EDENS
EDENS
GO GO EDENS
EDENS
Edens

CHAPTER 44: THE TEMPLE OF KNOWLEDGE

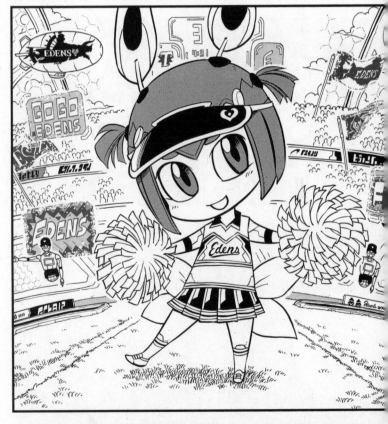

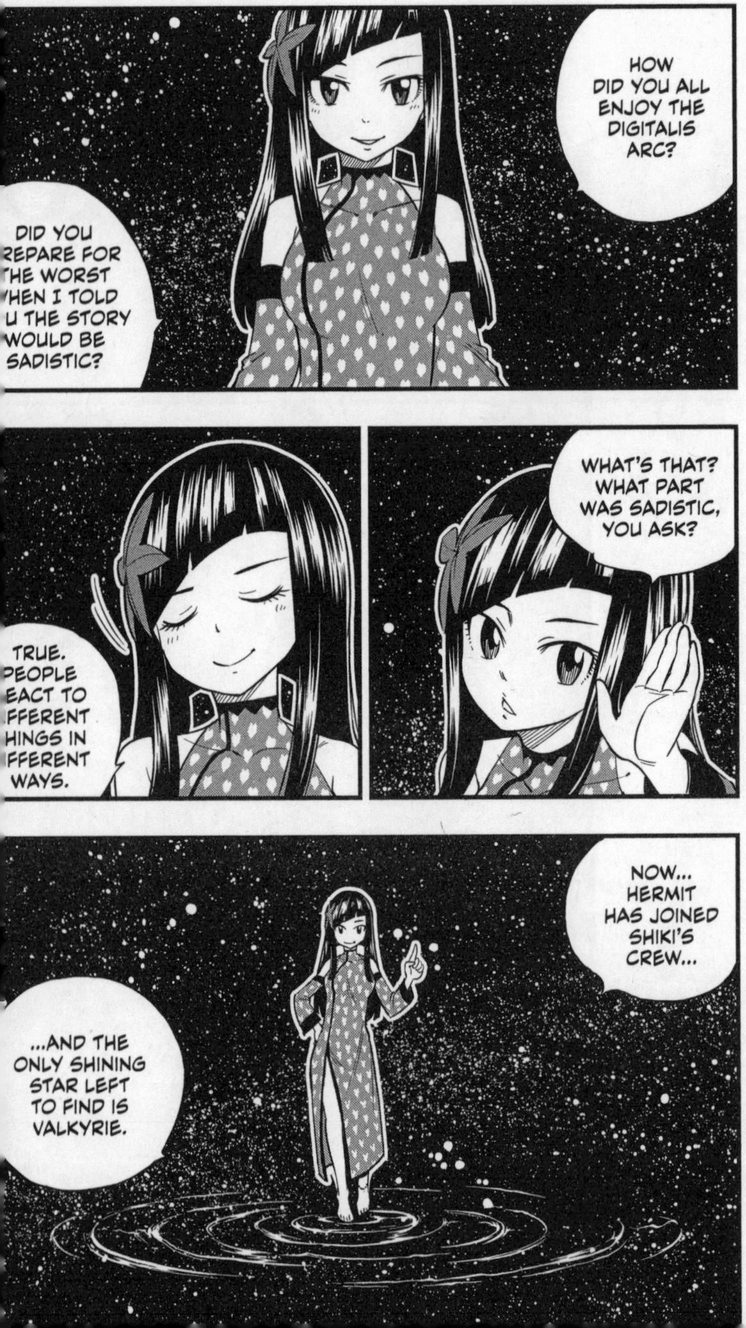
HOW DID YOU ALL ENJOY THE DIGITALIS ARC?
DID YOU REPARE FOR HE WORST HEN I TOLD U THE STORY WOULD BE SADISTIC?
WHAT'S THAT? WHAT PART WAS SADISTIC, YOU ASK?
TRUE. PEOPLE EACT TO FFERENT HINGS IN FFERENT WAYS.
NOW... HERMIT HAS JOINED SHIKI'S CREW...
...AND THE ONLY SHINING STAR LEFT TO FIND IS VALKYRIE.

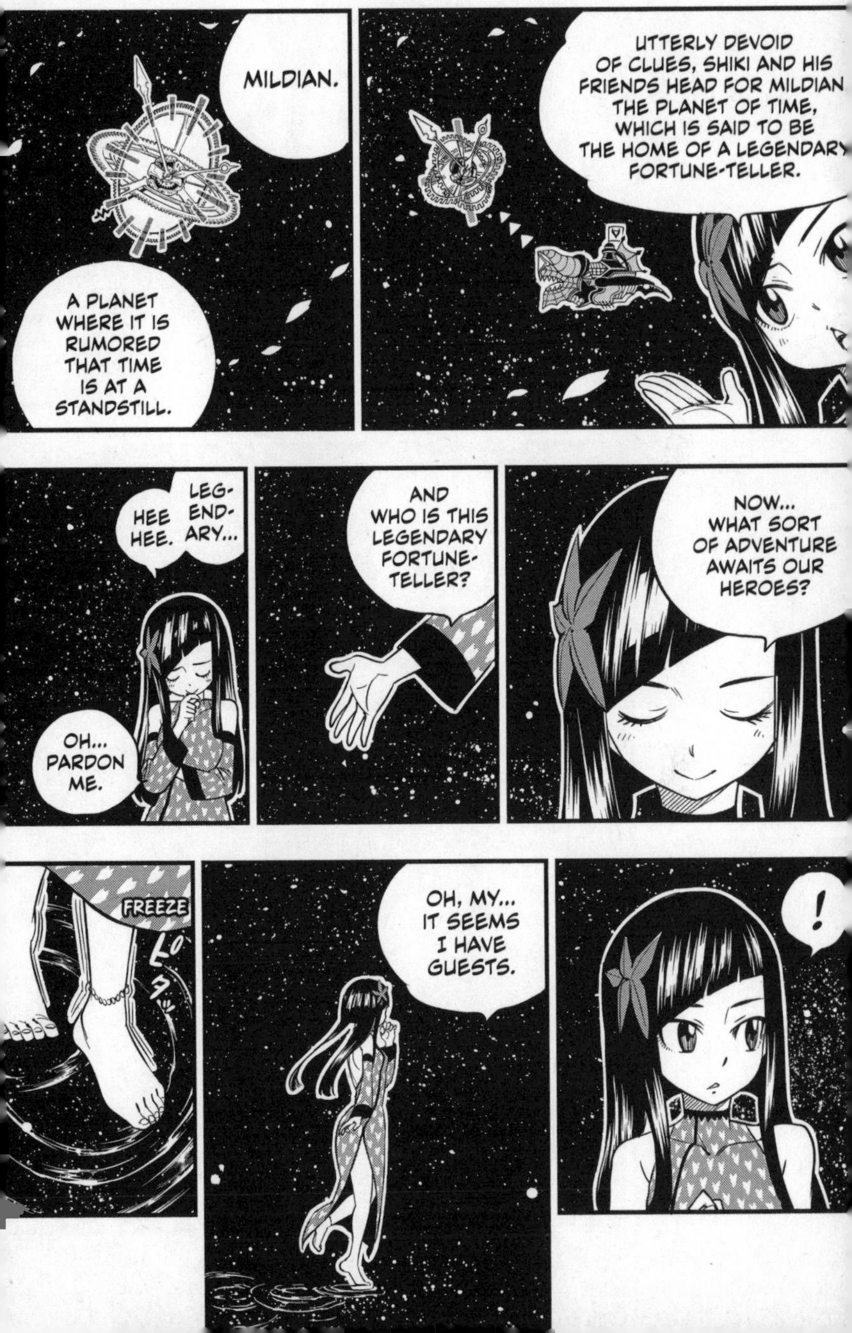
UTTERLY DEVOID OF CLUES, SHIKI AND HIS FRIENDS HEAD FOR MILDIAN THE PLANET OF TIME, WHICH IS SAID TO BE THE HOME OF A LEGENDARY FORTUNE-TELLER.
MILDIAN.
A PLANET WHERE IT IS RUMORED THAT TIME IS AT A STANDSTILL.
NOW... WHAT SORT OF ADVENTURE AWAITS OUR HEROES?
AND WHO IS THIS LEGENDARY FORTUNE-TELLER?
LEG-END-ARY...
HEE HEE.
OH... PARDON ME.
!
OH, MY... IT SEEMS I HAVE GUESTS.
FREEZE

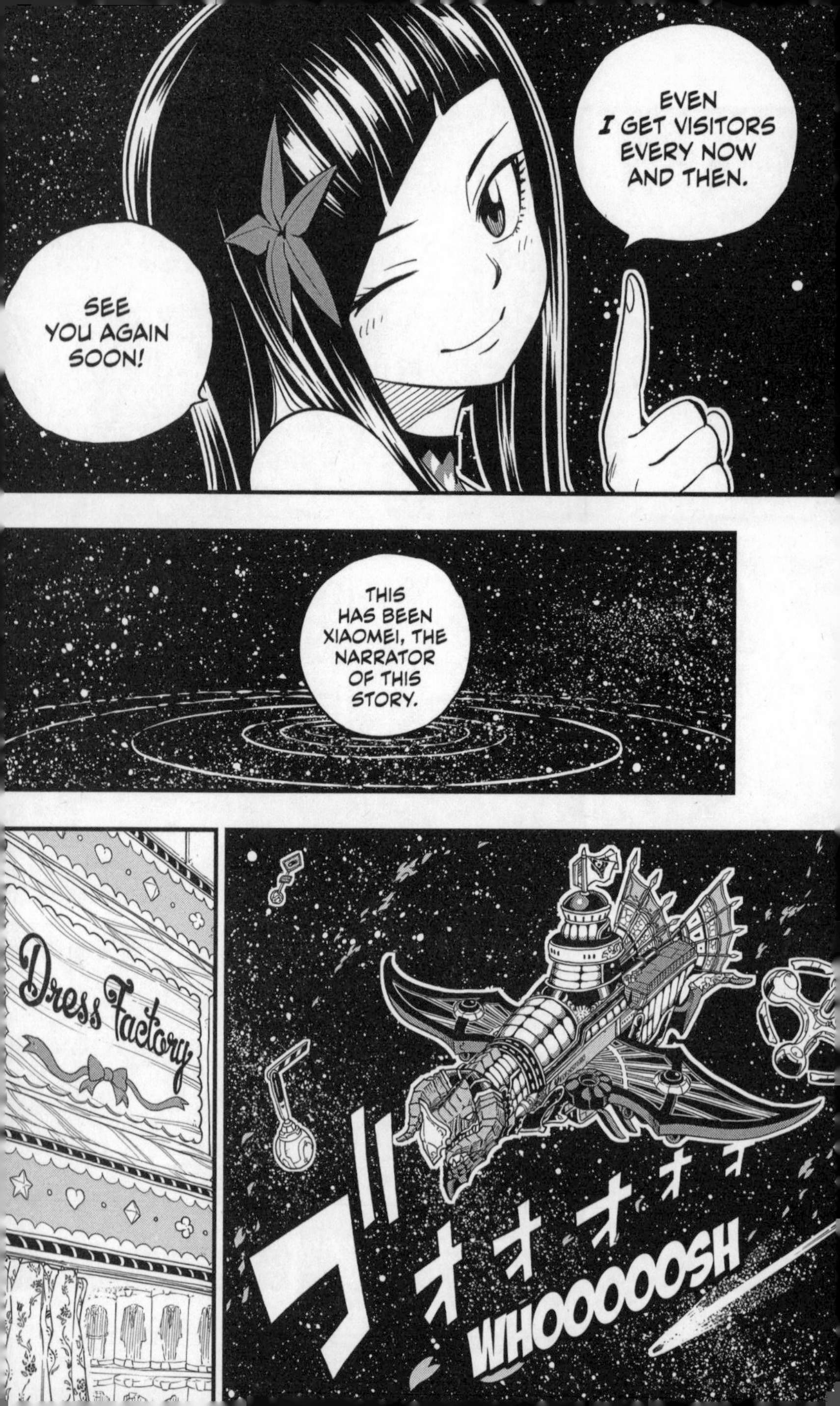
EVEN I GET VISITORS EVERY NOW AND THEN.
SEE YOU AGAIN SOON!
THIS HAS BEEN XIAOMEI, THE NARRATOR OF THIS STORY.
WHOOOOOSH
Dress Factory

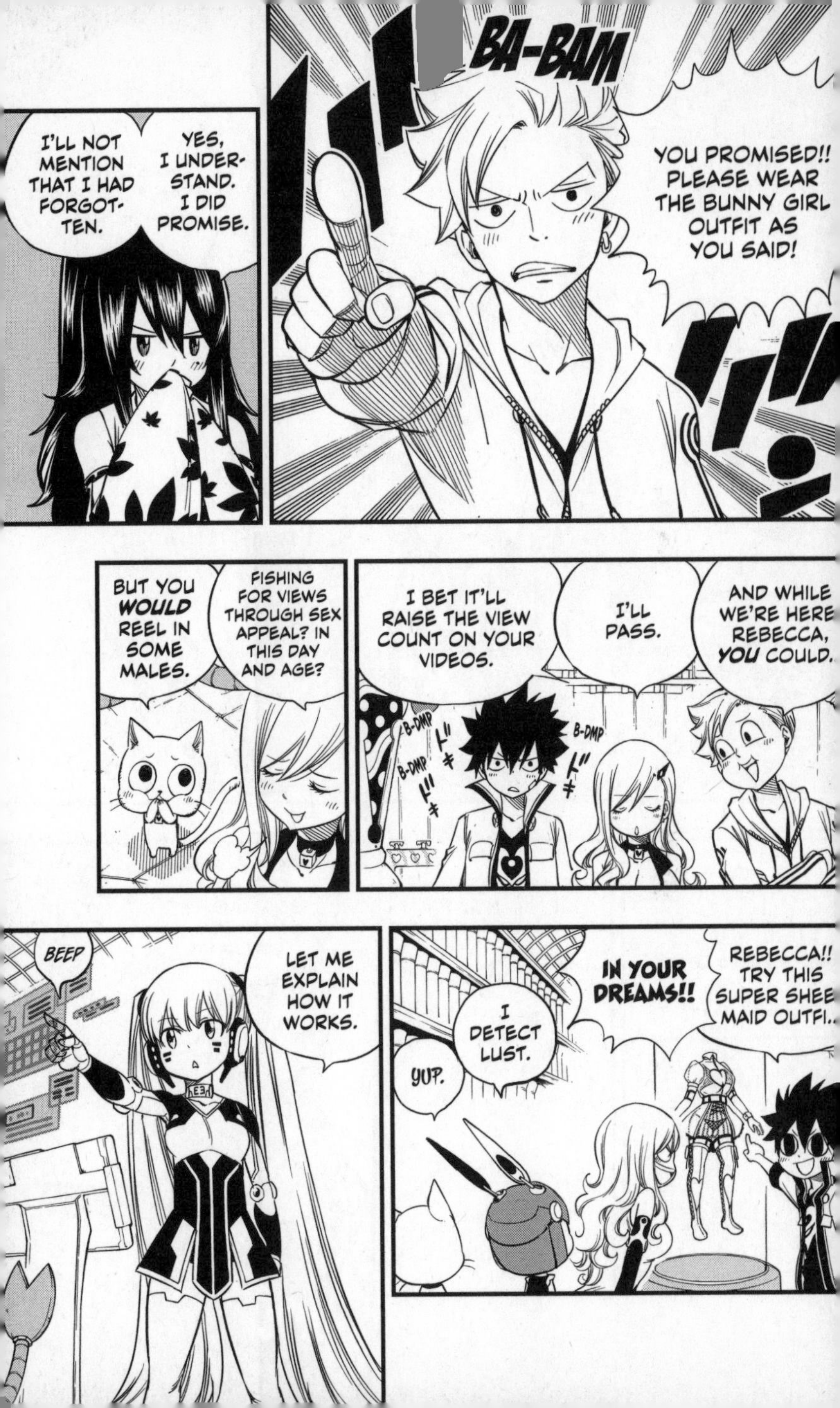
BA-BAM
YOU PROMISED!! PLEASE WEAR THE BUNNY GIRL OUTFIT AS YOU SAID!
YES, I UNDER-STAND. I DID PROMISE.
I'LL NOT MENTION THAT I HAD FORGOT-TEN.
AND WHILE WE'RE HERE REBECCA, **YOU** COULD.
I'LL PASS.
B-DMP
I BET IT'LL RAISE THE VIEW COUNT ON YOUR VIDEOS.
B-DMP
B-DMP
FISHING FOR VIEWS THROUGH SEX APPEAL? IN THIS DAY AND AGE?
BUT YOU ***WOULD*** REEL IN SOME MALES.
REBECCA!! TRY THIS SUPER SHEE MAID OUTFI...
IN YOUR DREAMS!!
I DETECT LUST.
YUP.
LET ME EXPLAIN HOW IT WORKS.
BEEP

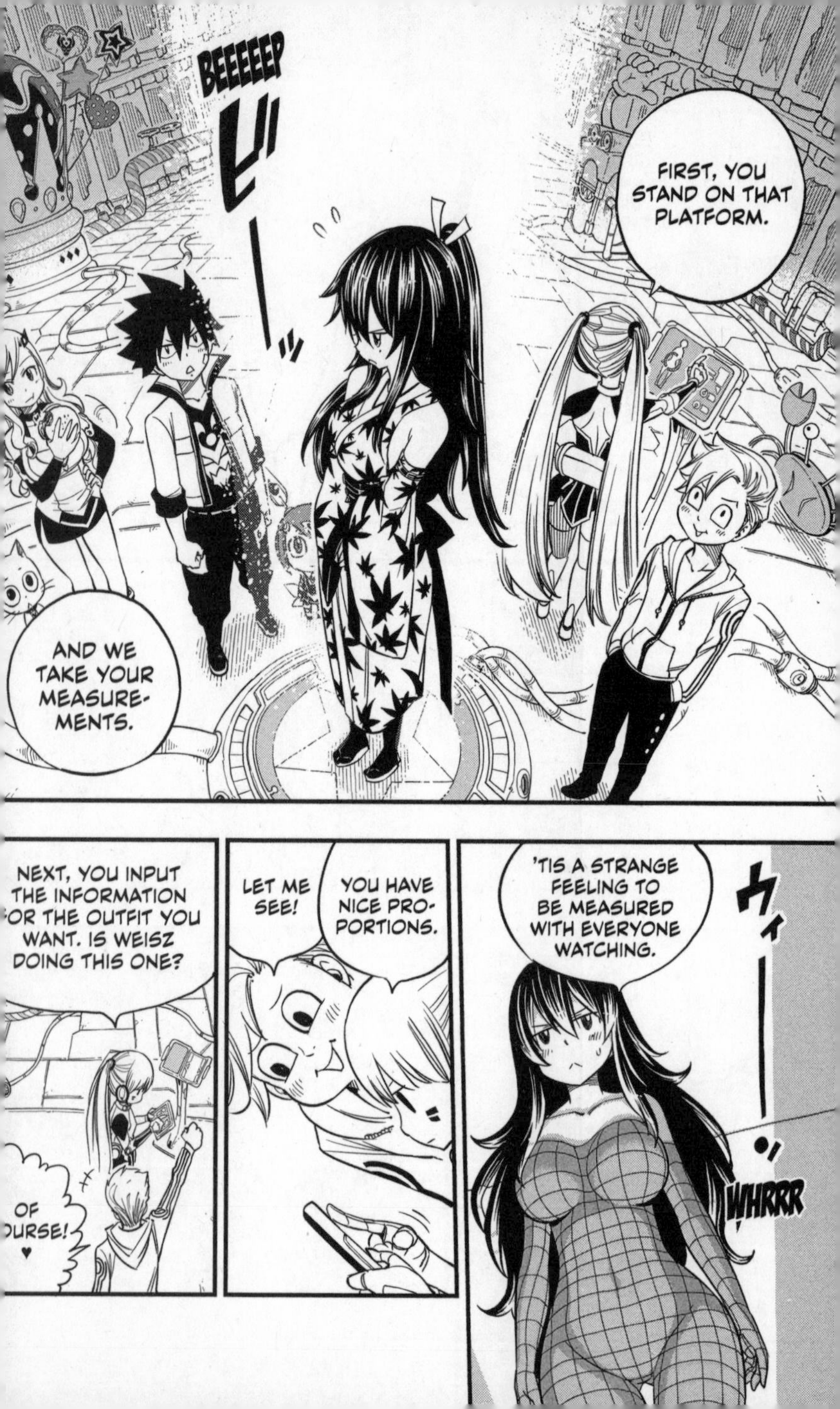
FIRST, YOU STAND ON THAT PLATFORM.
BEEEEEP
AND WE TAKE YOUR MEASURE-MENTS.
'TIS A STRANGE FEELING TO BE MEASURED WITH EVERYONE WATCHING.
WHRRR
YOU HAVE NICE PRO-PORTIONS.
LET ME SEE!
NEXT, YOU INPUT THE INFORMATION 'OR THE OUTFIT YOU WANT. IS WEISZ DOING THIS ONE?
OF OURSE! ♥

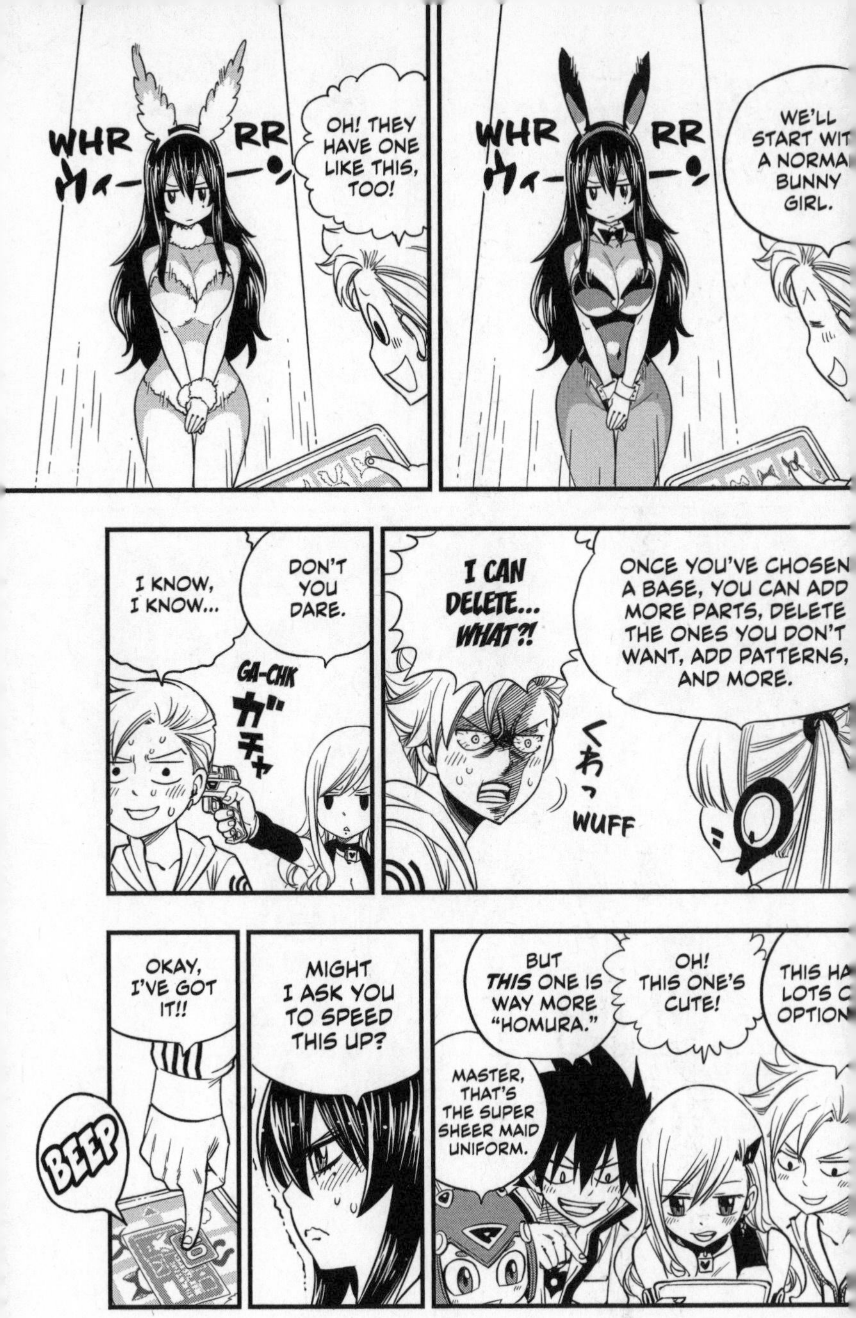
WHR
ウィー
RR
WE'LL START WIT A NORMA BUNNY GIRL.
WHR
ウィー
RR
OH! THEY HAVE ONE LIKE THIS, TOO!
ONCE YOU'VE CHOSEN A BASE, YOU CAN ADD MORE PARTS, DELETE THE ONES YOU DON'T WANT, ADD PATTERNS, AND MORE.
I CAN DELETE... WHAT?!
くわっ
WUFF
DON'T YOU DARE.
I KNOW, I KNOW...
GA-CHK
ガチャ
THIS HA LOTS O OPTION
OH! THIS ONE'S CUTE!
BUT THIS ONE IS WAY MORE "HOMURA."
MASTER, THAT'S THE SUPER SHEER MAID UNIFORM.
MIGHT I ASK YOU TO SPEED THIS UP?
OKAY, I'VE GOT IT!!
BEEP

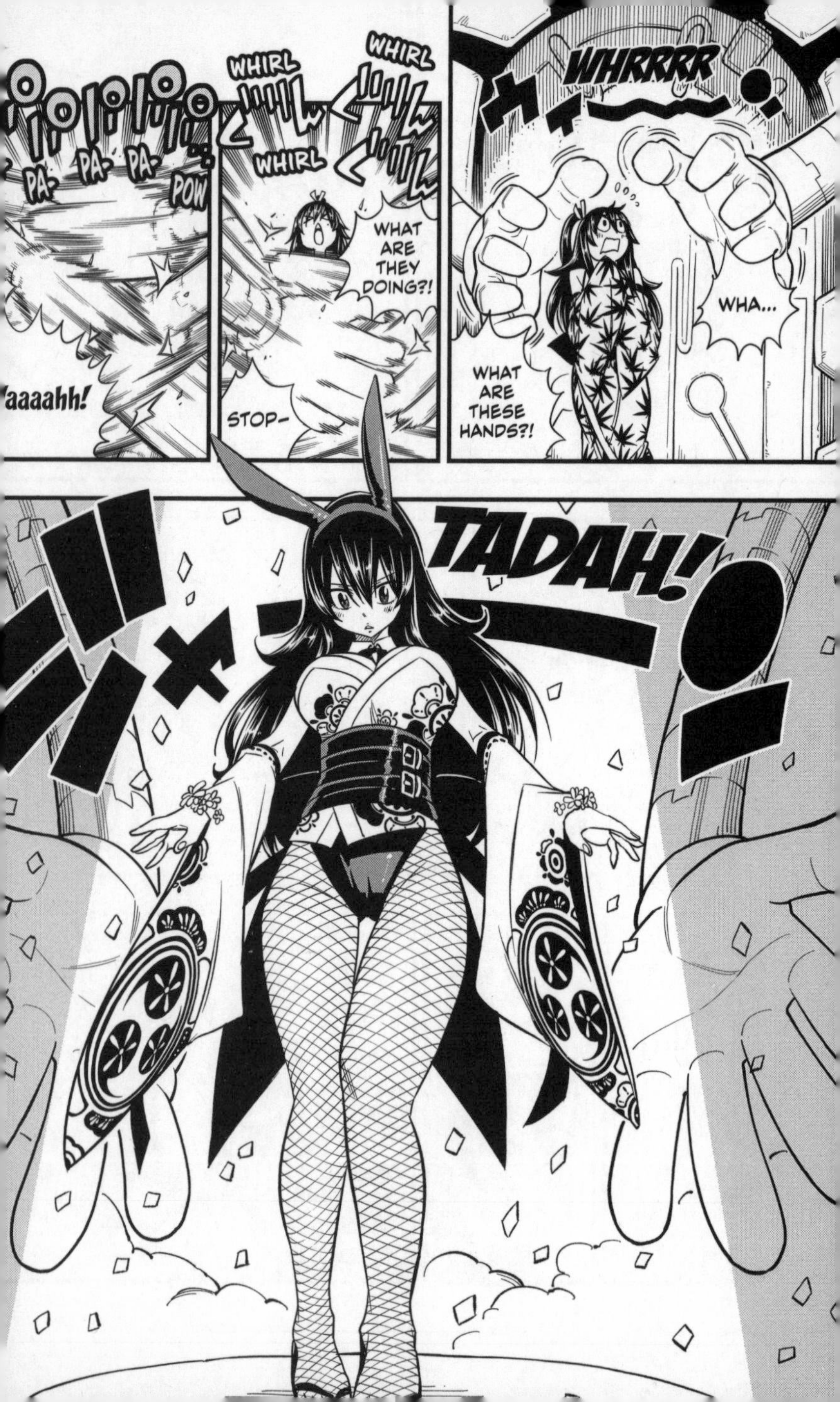
WHRRRR
WHA...
WHAT ARE THESE HANDS?!
WHIRL
WHIRL
WHIRL
WHAT ARE THEY DOING?!
STOP-
PA-
PA-
PA-
POW
aaaahh!
TADAH!

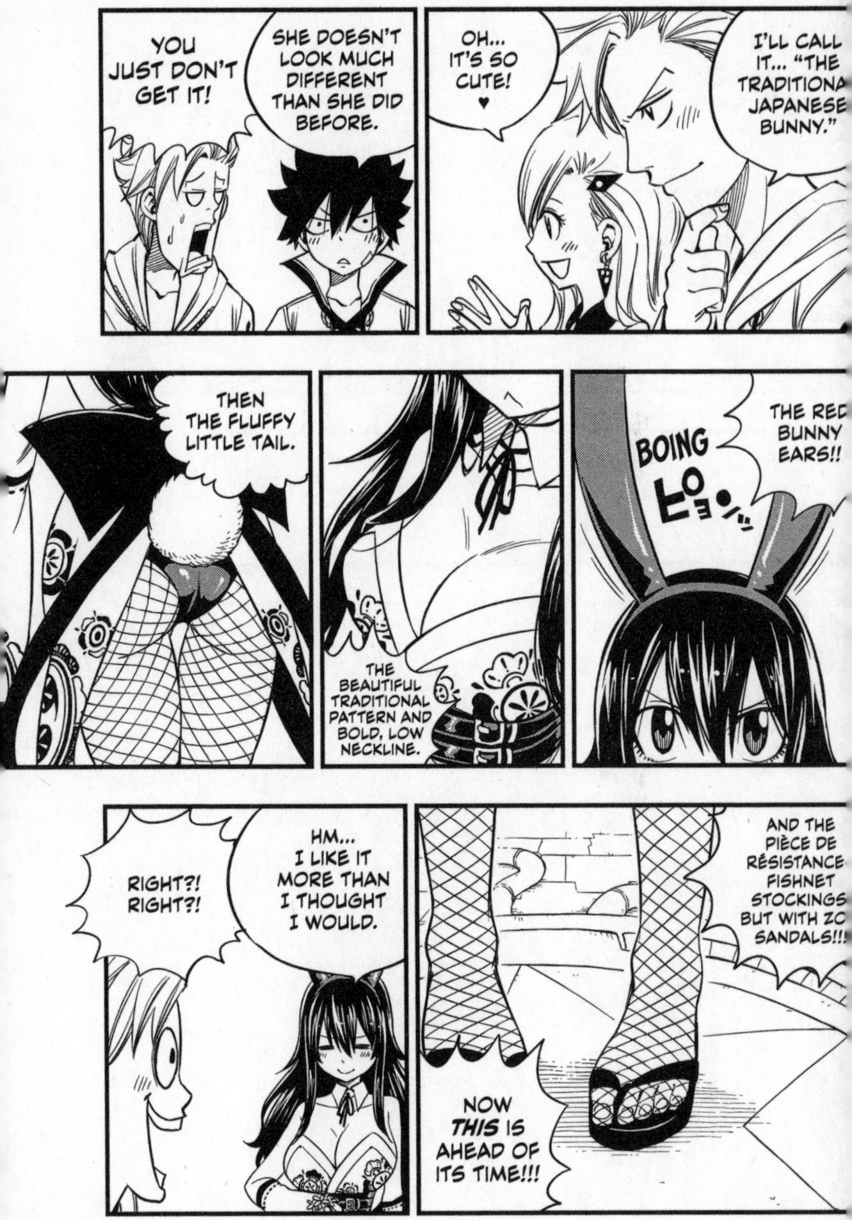

I'LL CALL IT... "THE TRADITIONA JAPANESE BUNNY."
OH... IT'S SO CUTE! ♥
SHE DOESN'T LOOK MUCH DIFFERENT THAN SHE DID BEFORE.
YOU JUST DON'T GET IT!
THE RED BUNNY EARS!!
BOING
ピョンッ
THE BEAUTIFUL TRADITIONAL PATTERN AND BOLD, LOW NECKLINE.
THEN THE FLUFFY LITTLE TAIL.
AND THE PIÈCE DE RÉSISTANCE FISHNET STOCKINGS BUT WITH ZO SANDALS!!!
NOW *THIS* IS AHEAD OF ITS TIME!!!
HM... I LIKE IT MORE THAN I THOUGHT I WOULD.
RIGHT?! RIGHT?!

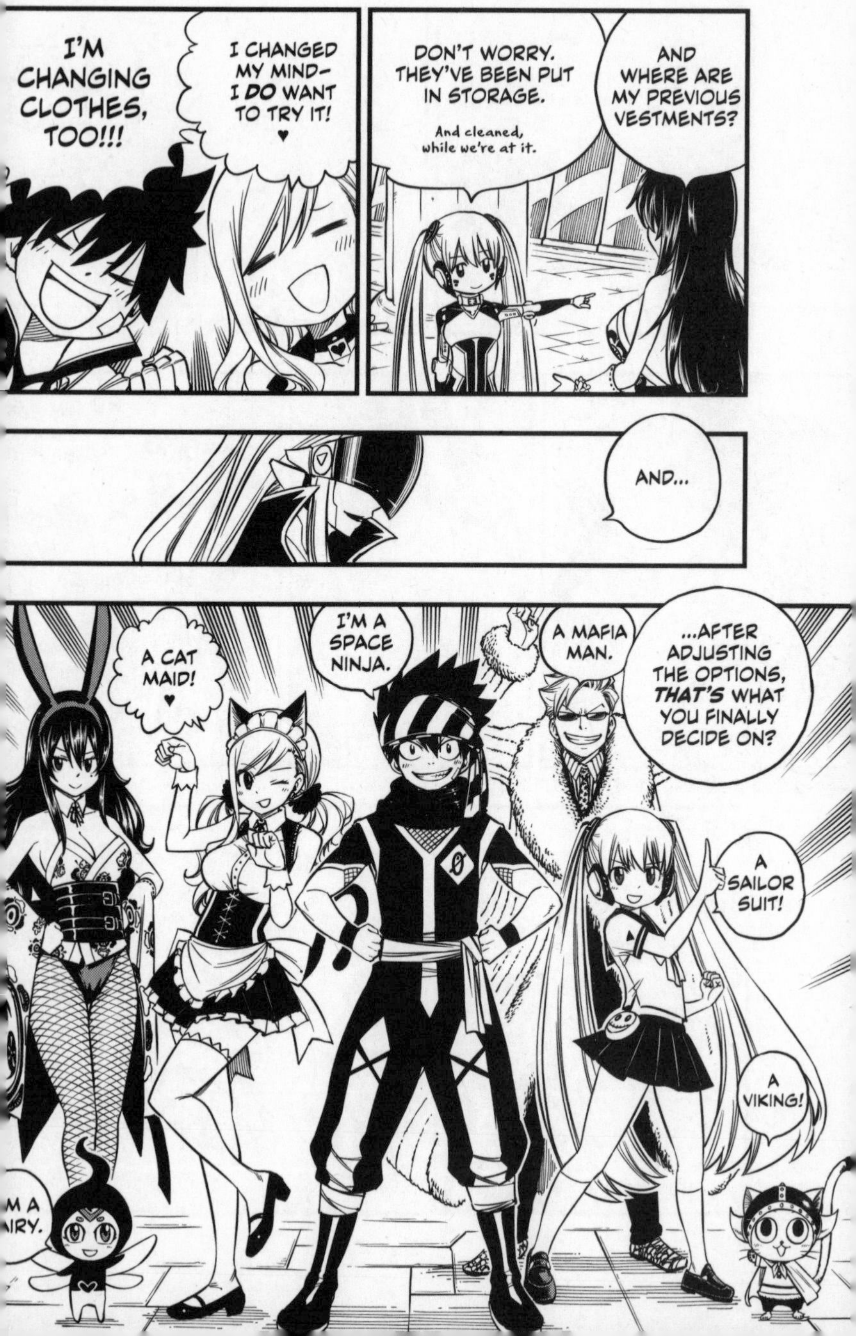
AND WHERE ARE MY PREVIOUS VESTMENTS?
DON'T WORRY. THEY'VE BEEN PUT IN STORAGE.
And cleaned, while we're at it.
I CHANGED MY MIND— I **DO** WANT TO TRY IT! ♥
I'M CHANGING CLOTHES, TOO!!!
AND...
...AFTER ADJUSTING THE OPTIONS, **THAT'S** WHAT YOU FINALLY DECIDE ON?
A MAFIA MAN.
I'M A SPACE NINJA.
A CAT MAID! ♥
A SAILOR SUIT!
A VIKING!
M A IRY.

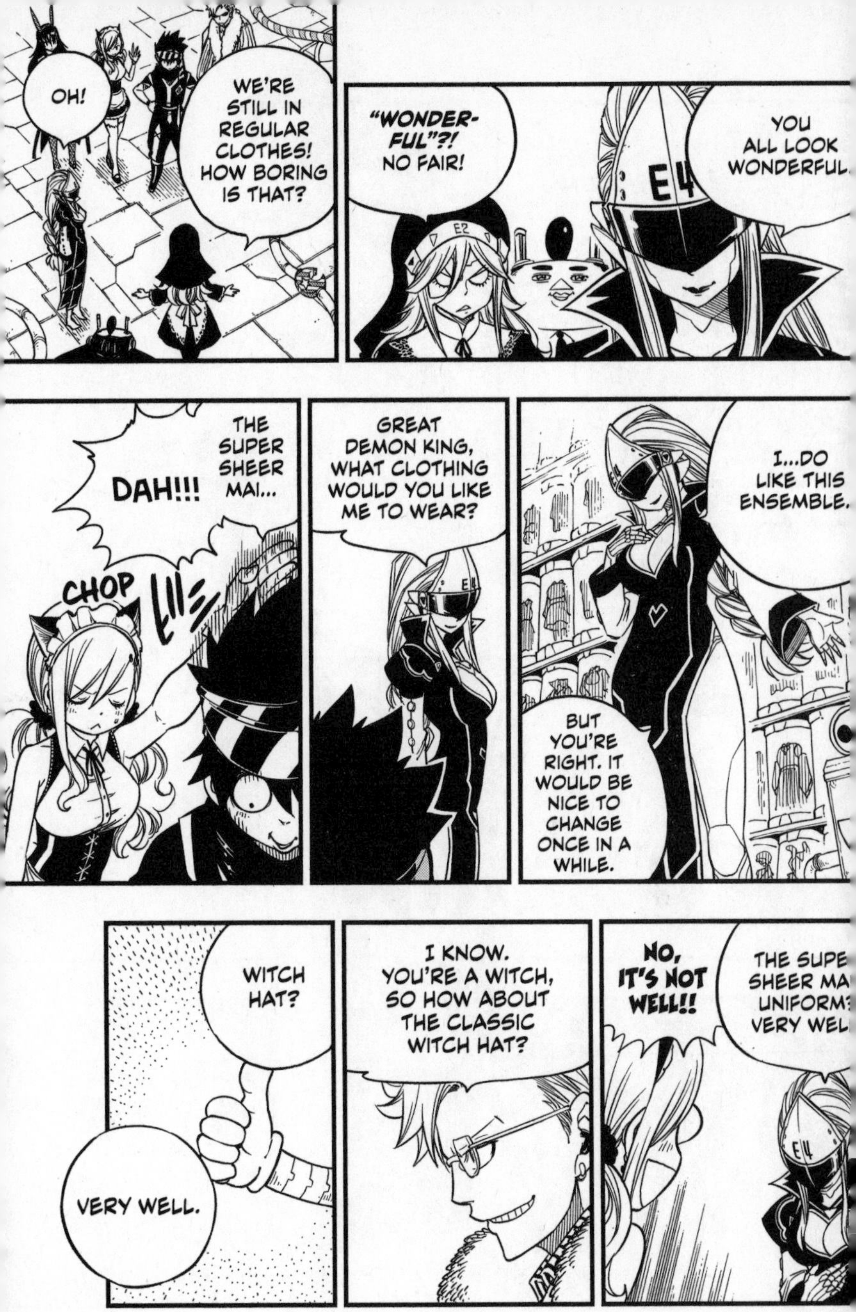
YOU ALL LOOK WONDERFUL.
"WONDERFUL"?! NO FAIR!
WE'RE STILL IN REGULAR CLOTHES! HOW BORING IS THAT?
OH!
I...DO LIKE THIS ENSEMBLE.
BUT YOU'RE RIGHT. IT WOULD BE NICE TO CHANGE ONCE IN A WHILE.
GREAT DEMON KING, WHAT CLOTHING WOULD YOU LIKE ME TO WEAR?
THE SUPER SHEER MAI...
DAH!!!
CHOP
THE SUPE SHEER MA UNIFORM? VERY WEL
NO, IT'S NOT WELL!!
I KNOW. YOU'RE A WITCH, SO HOW ABOUT THE CLASSIC WITCH HAT?
WITCH HAT?
VERY WELL.

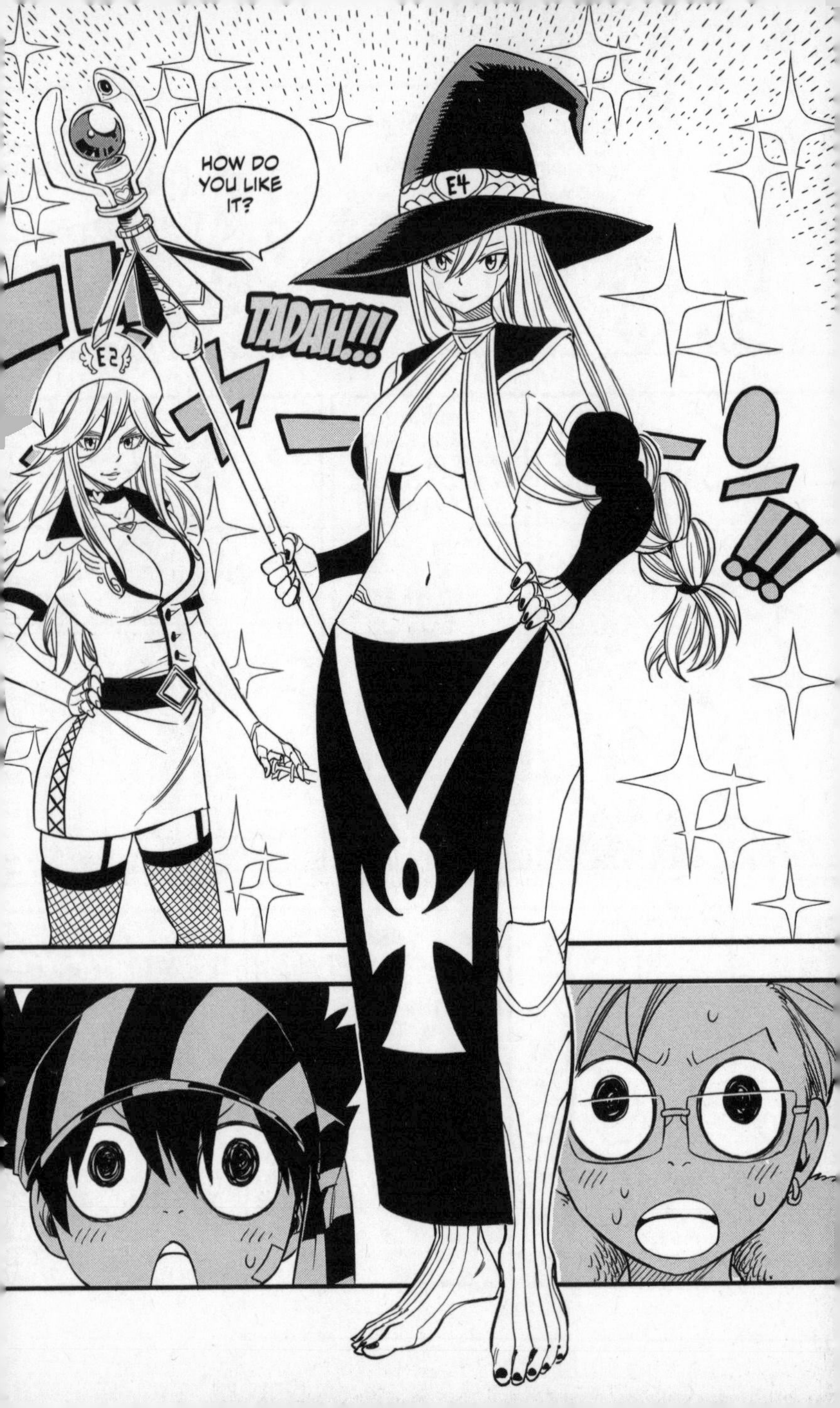
HOW DO YOU LIKE IT?
TADAH!!!

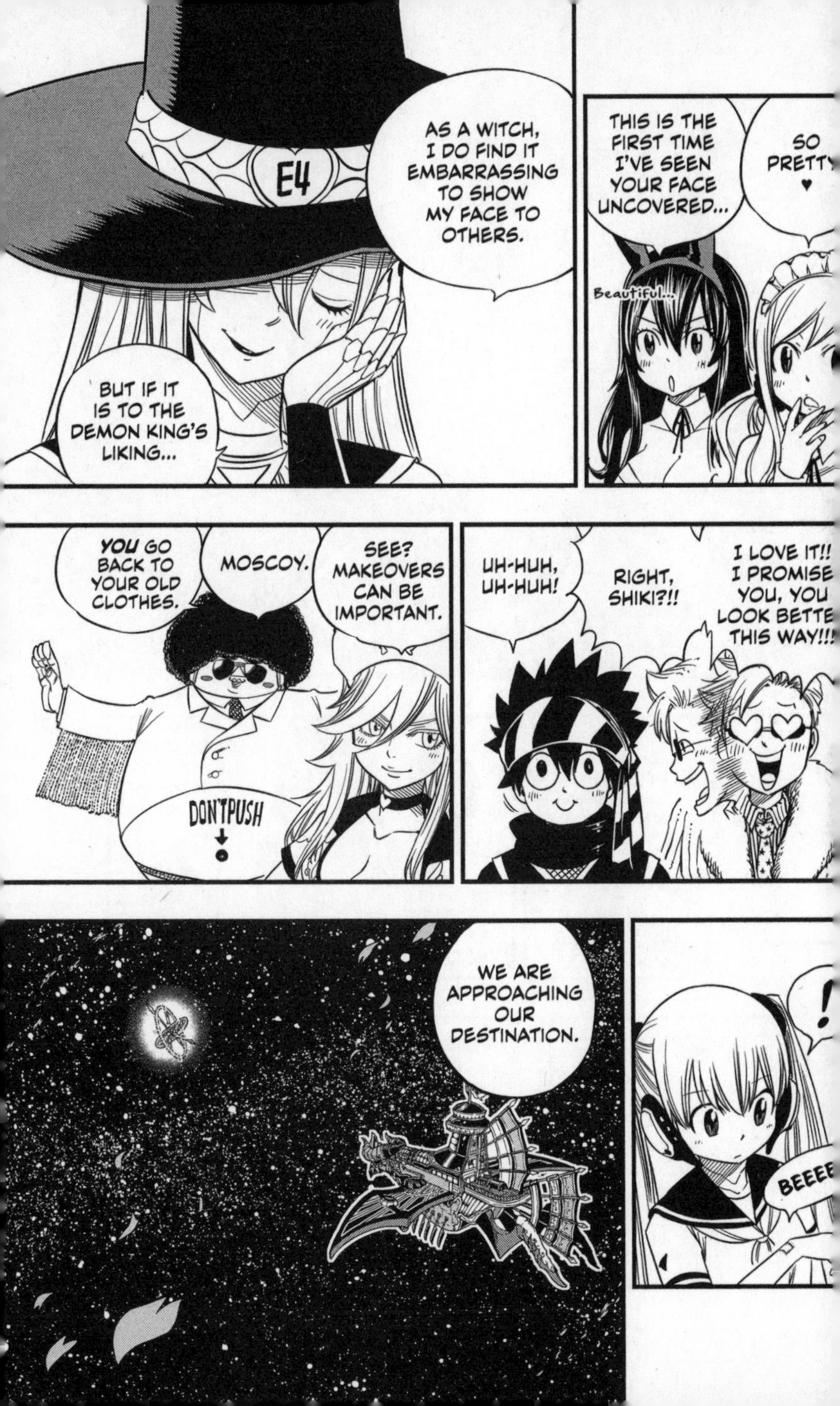
SO PRETTY ♥
THIS IS THE FIRST TIME I'VE SEEN YOUR FACE UNCOVERED...
Beautiful...
AS A WITCH, I DO FIND IT EMBARRASSING TO SHOW MY FACE TO OTHERS.
BUT IF IT IS TO THE DEMON KING'S LIKING...
I LOVE IT!! I PROMISE YOU, YOU LOOK BETTE THIS WAY!!!
RIGHT, SHIKI?!!
UH-HUH, UH-HUH!
SEE? MAKEOVERS CAN BE IMPORTANT.
MOSCOY.
YOU GO BACK TO YOUR OLD CLOTHES.
DON'T PUSH
!
BEEEE
WE ARE APPROACHING OUR DESTINATION.

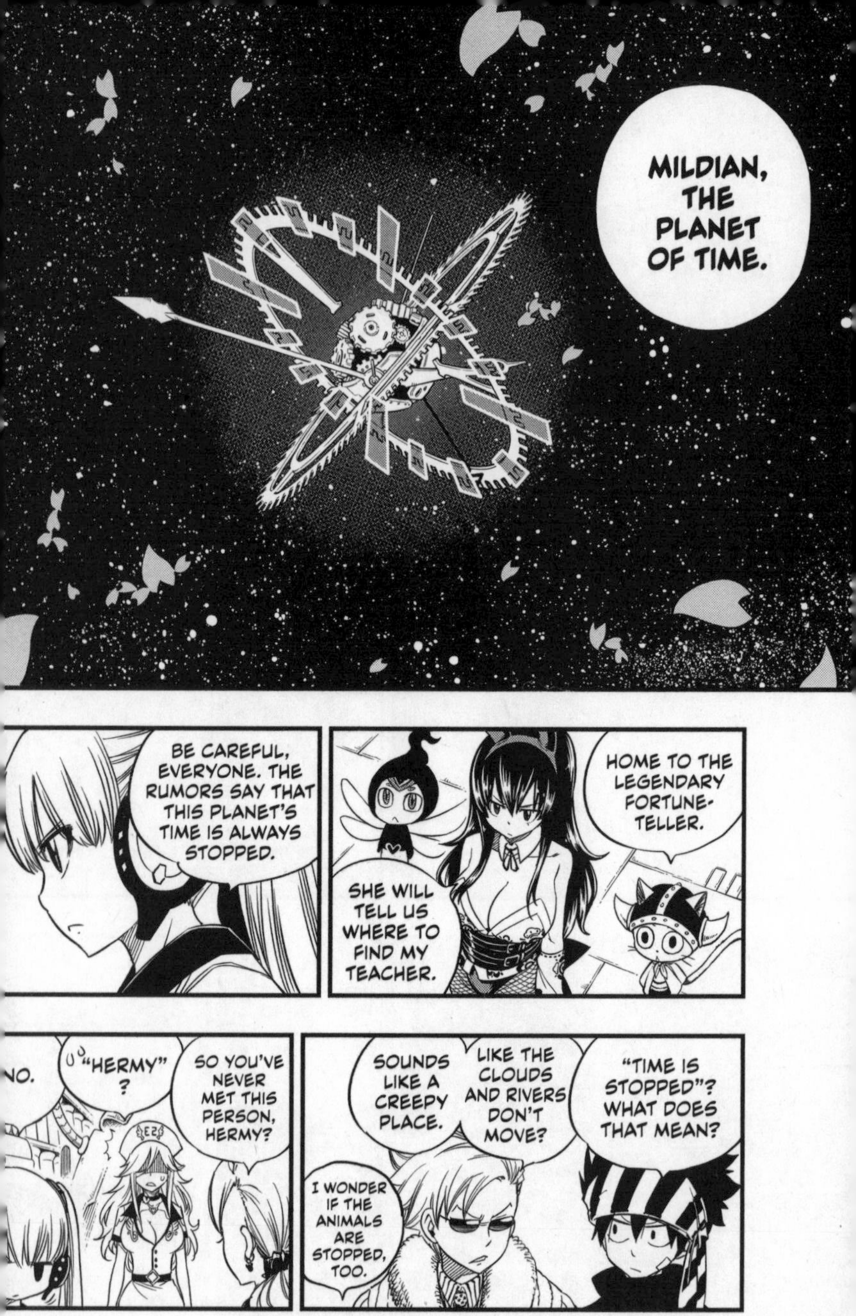
MILDIAN, THE PLANET OF TIME.
HOME TO THE LEGENDARY FORTUNE-TELLER.
SHE WILL TELL US WHERE TO FIND MY TEACHER.
BE CAREFUL, EVERYONE. THE RUMORS SAY THAT THIS PLANET'S TIME IS ALWAYS STOPPED.
"TIME IS STOPPED"? WHAT DOES THAT MEAN?
LIKE THE CLOUDS AND RIVERS DON'T MOVE?
SOUNDS LIKE A CREEPY PLACE.
I WONDER IF THE ANIMALS ARE STOPPED, TOO.
SO YOU'VE NEVER MET THIS PERSON, HERMY?
"HERMY"?
NO.

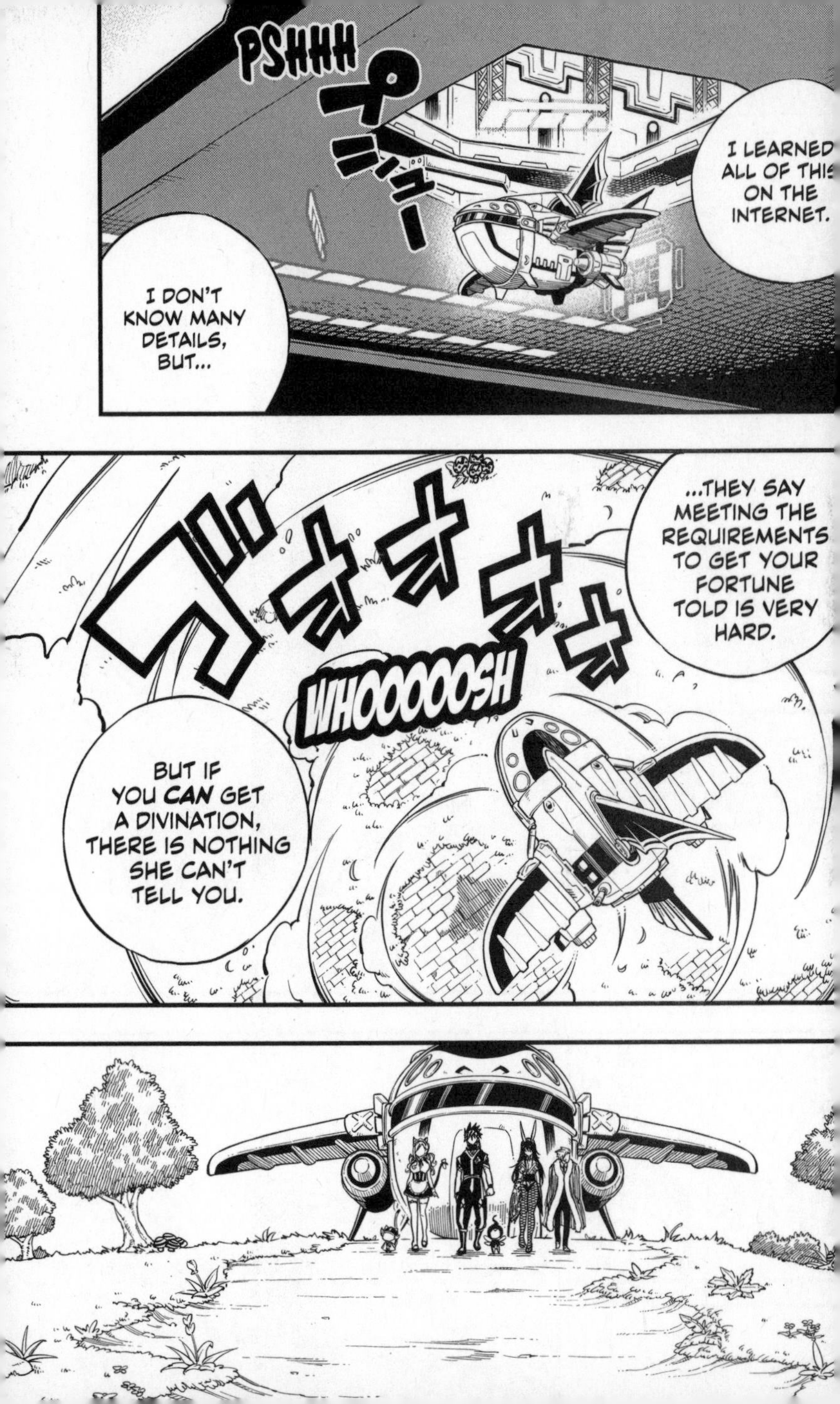

I LEARNED ALL OF THIS ON THE INTERNET.
PSHHH
プシュー
I DON'T KNOW MANY DETAILS, BUT...
...THEY SAY MEETING THE REQUIREMENTS TO GET YOUR FORTUNE TOLD IS VERY HARD.
ゴォォォォ
WHOOOOOSH
BUT IF YOU **CAN** GET A DIVINATION, THERE IS NOTHING SHE CAN'T TELL YOU.

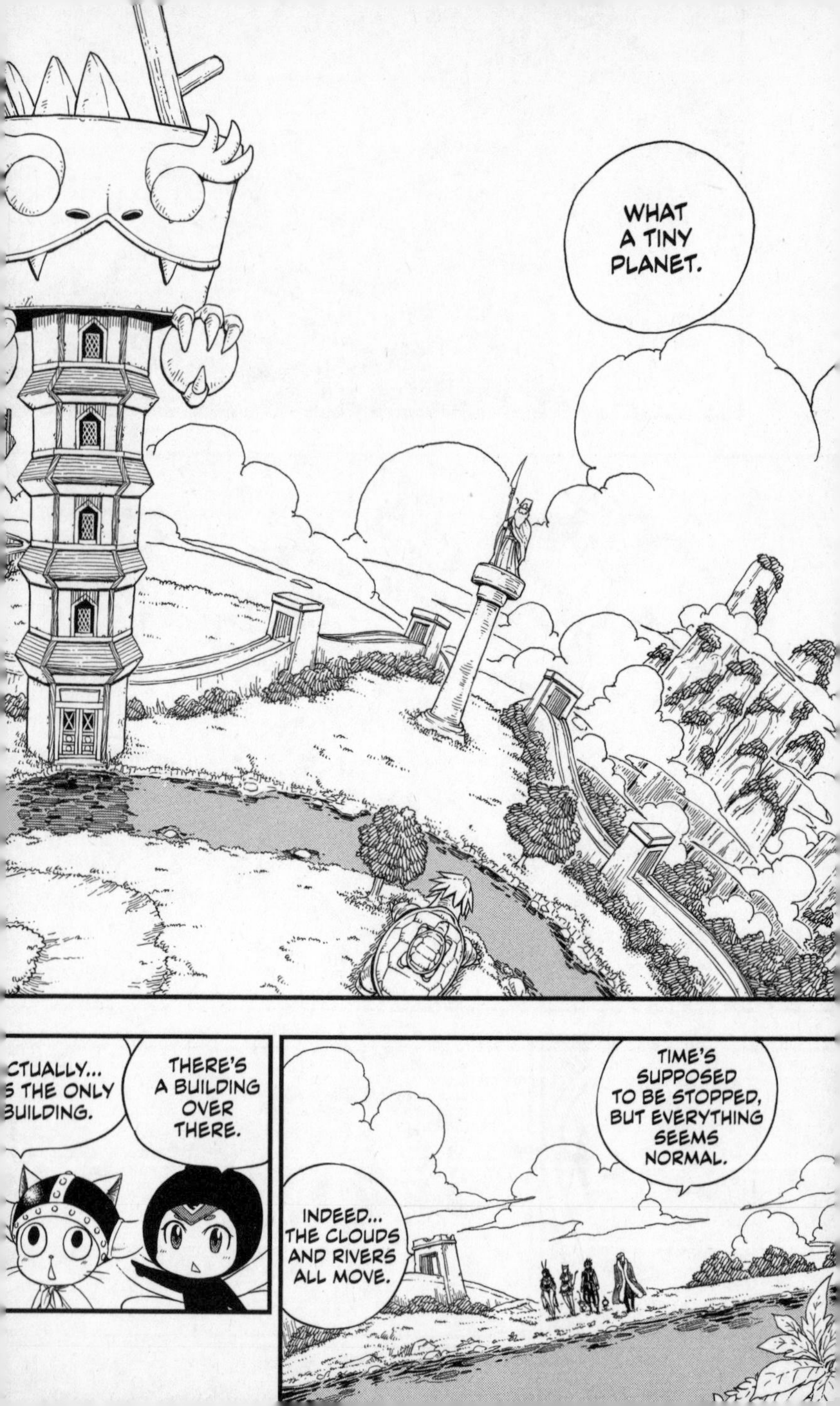
WHAT A TINY PLANET.
TIME'S SUPPOSED TO BE STOPPED, BUT EVERYTHING SEEMS NORMAL.
INDEED... THE CLOUDS AND RIVERS ALL MOVE.
THERE'S A BUILDING OVER THERE.
CTUALLY... S THE ONLY BUILDING.

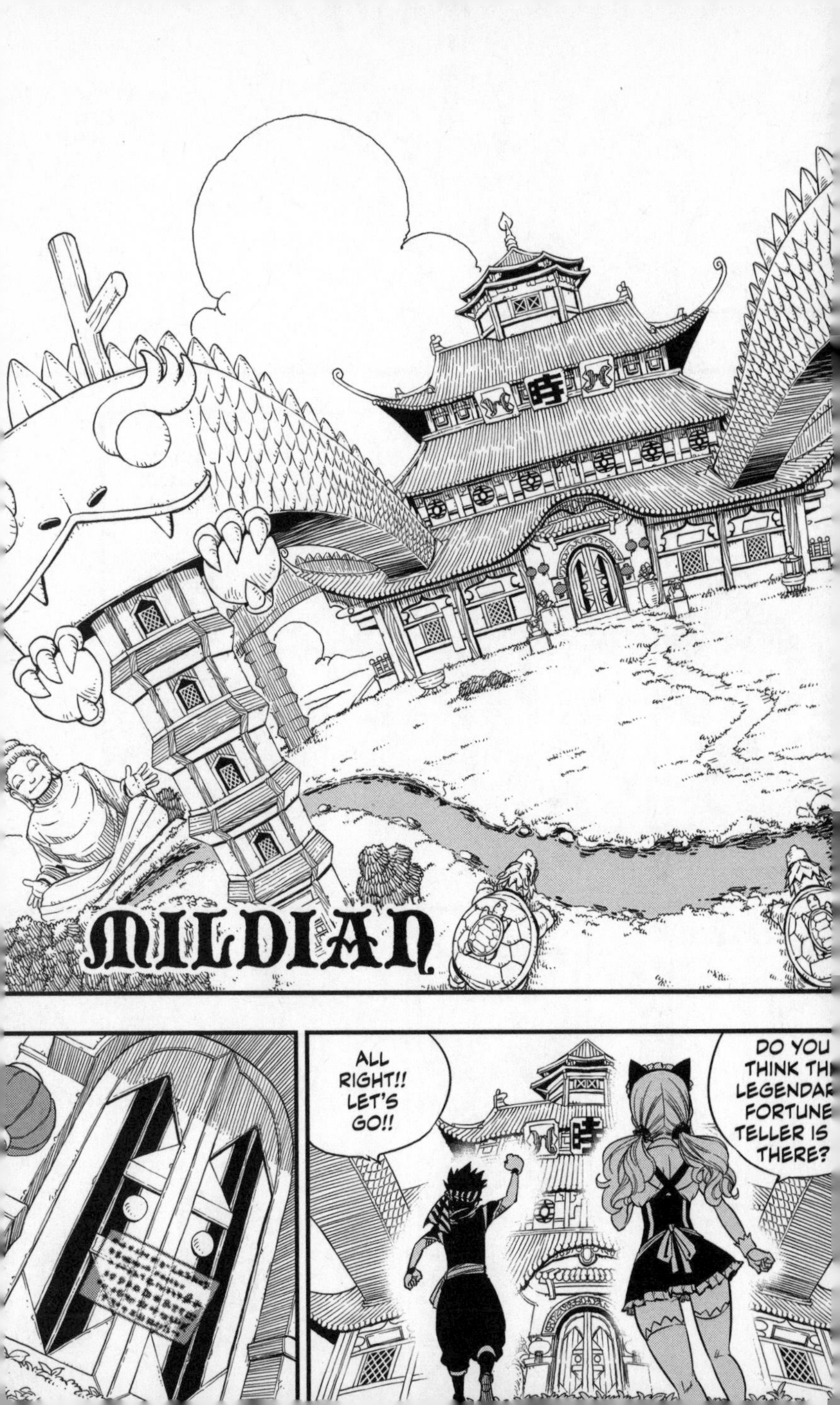
時
MILDIAN
DO YOU THINK TH LEGENDAR FORTUNE TELLER IS THERE?
ALL RIGHT!! LET'S GO!!

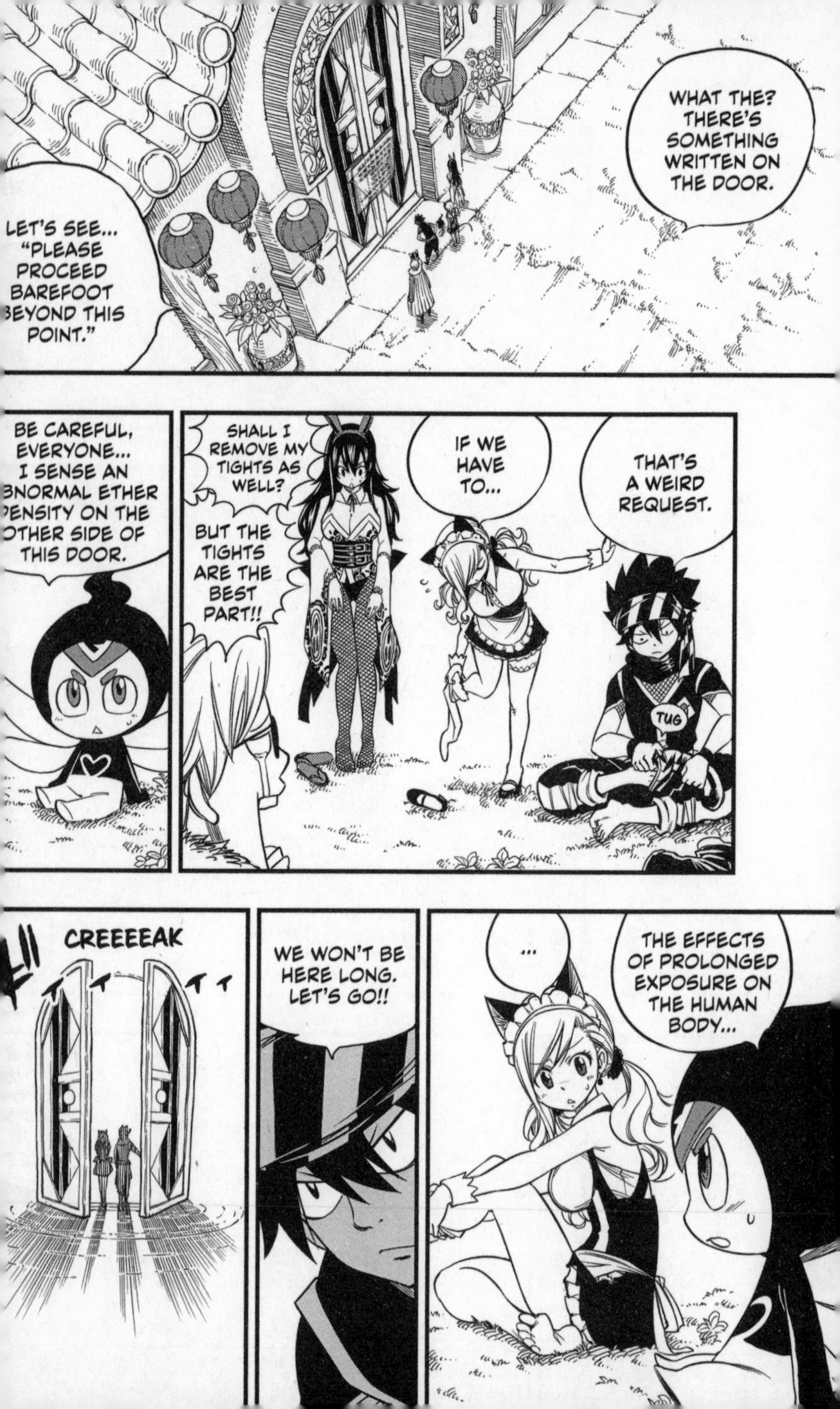
WHAT THE? THERE'S SOMETHING WRITTEN ON THE DOOR.
LET'S SEE... "PLEASE PROCEED BAREFOOT BEYOND THIS POINT."
THAT'S A WEIRD REQUEST.
TUG
IF WE HAVE TO...
SHALL I REMOVE MY TIGHTS AS WELL?
BUT THE TIGHTS ARE THE BEST PART!!
BE CAREFUL, EVERYONE... I SENSE AN ABNORMAL ETHER DENSITY ON THE OTHER SIDE OF THIS DOOR.
THE EFFECTS OF PROLONGED EXPOSURE ON THE HUMAN BODY...
...
WE WON'T BE HERE LONG. LET'S GO!!
CREEEEAK

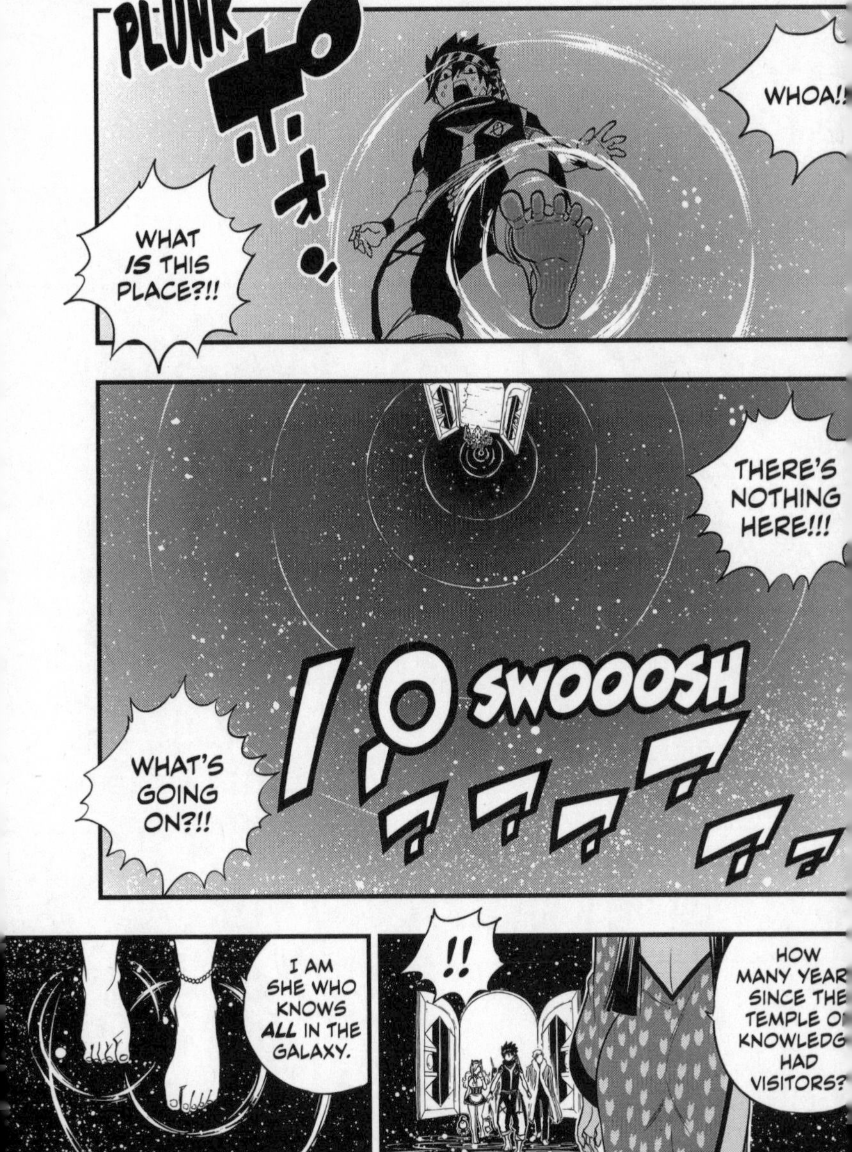
WHOA!!
PLUNK
WHAT IS THIS PLACE?!!
THERE'S NOTHING HERE!!!
SWOOOSH
WHAT'S GOING ON?!!
HOW MANY YEAR SINCE THE TEMPLE O KNOWLEDG HAD VISITORS?
!!
I AM SHE WHO KNOWS ALL IN THE GALAXY.

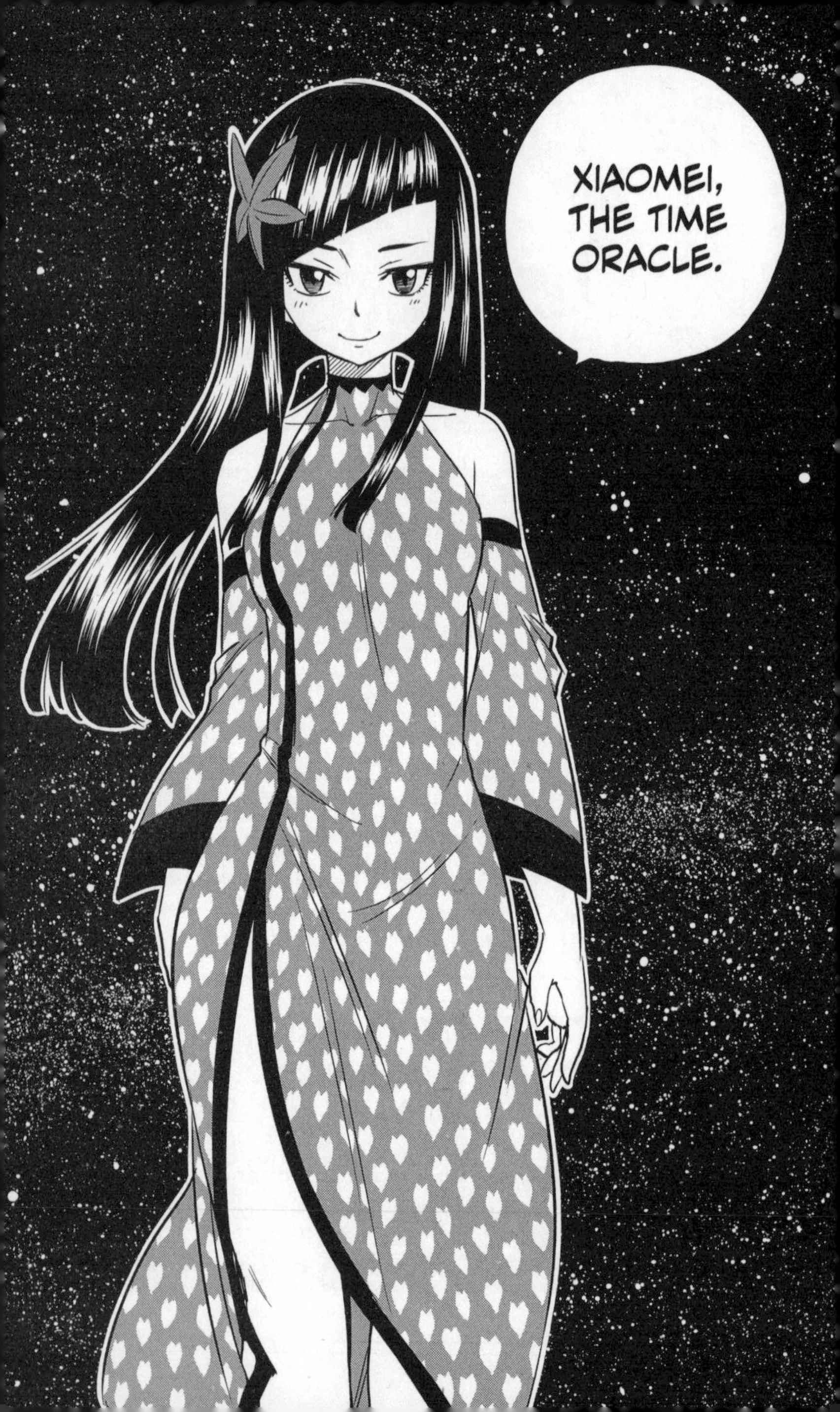
XIAOMEI, THE TIME ORACLE.

EDENS ZERO

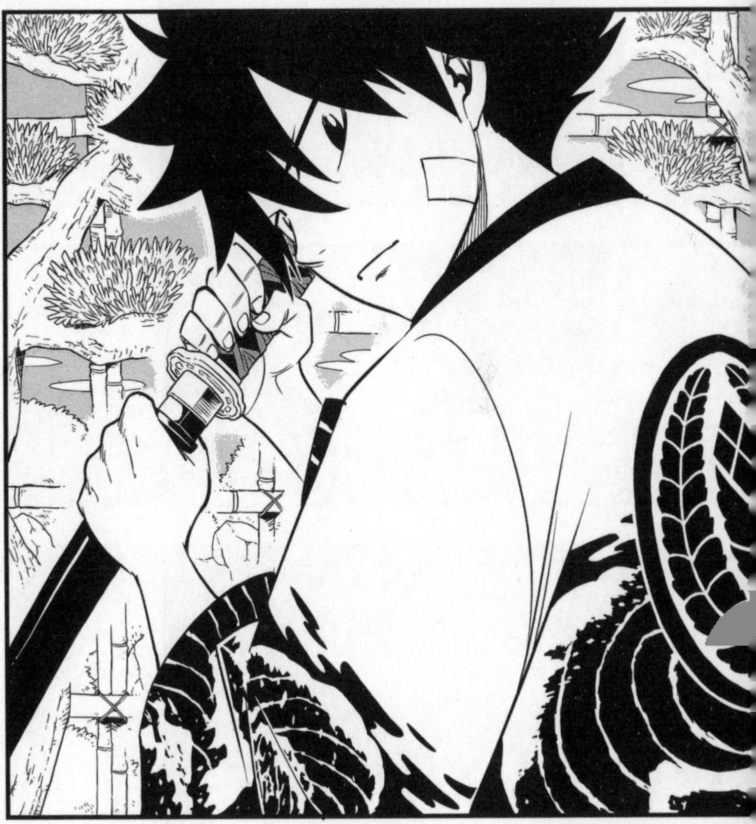

CHAPTER 45: THE BATTLE COLISEUM

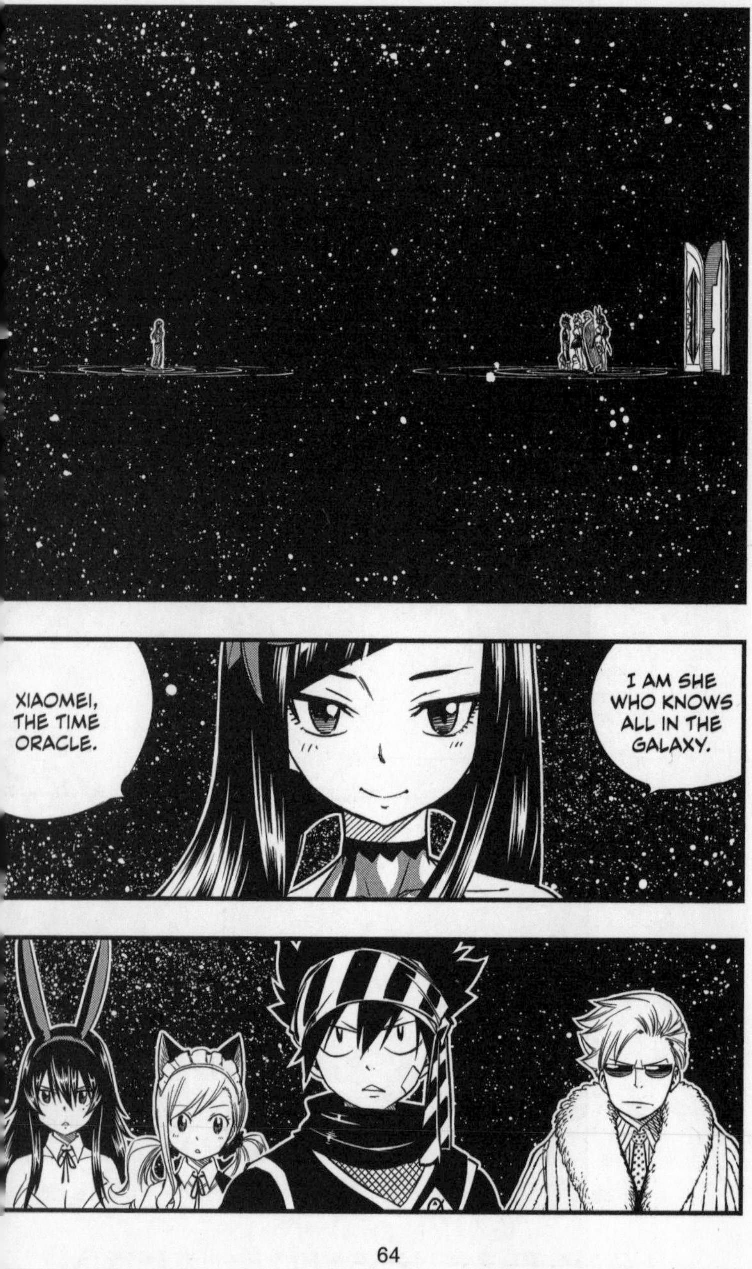
I AM SHE WHO KNOWS ALL IN THE GALAXY.
XIAOMEI, THE TIME ORACLE.

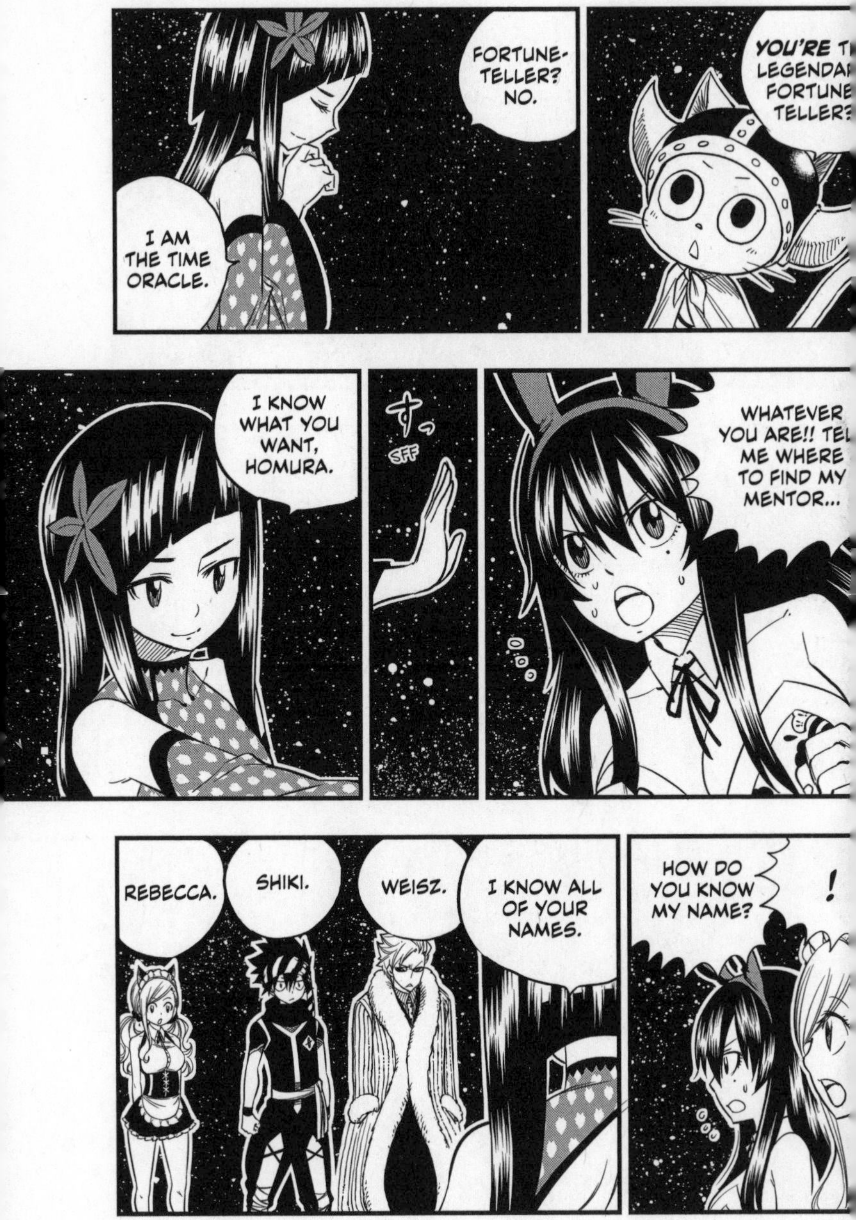
YOU'RE T
LEGENDAR
FORTUNE
TELLER?
FORTUNE-TELLER? NO.
I AM THE TIME ORACLE.
WHATEVER YOU ARE!! TEL
ME WHERE TO FIND MY MENTOR...
すっ
SFF
I KNOW WHAT YOU WANT, HOMURA.
HOW DO YOU KNOW MY NAME?
!
I KNOW ALL OF YOUR NAMES.
WEISZ.
SHIKI.
REBECCA.

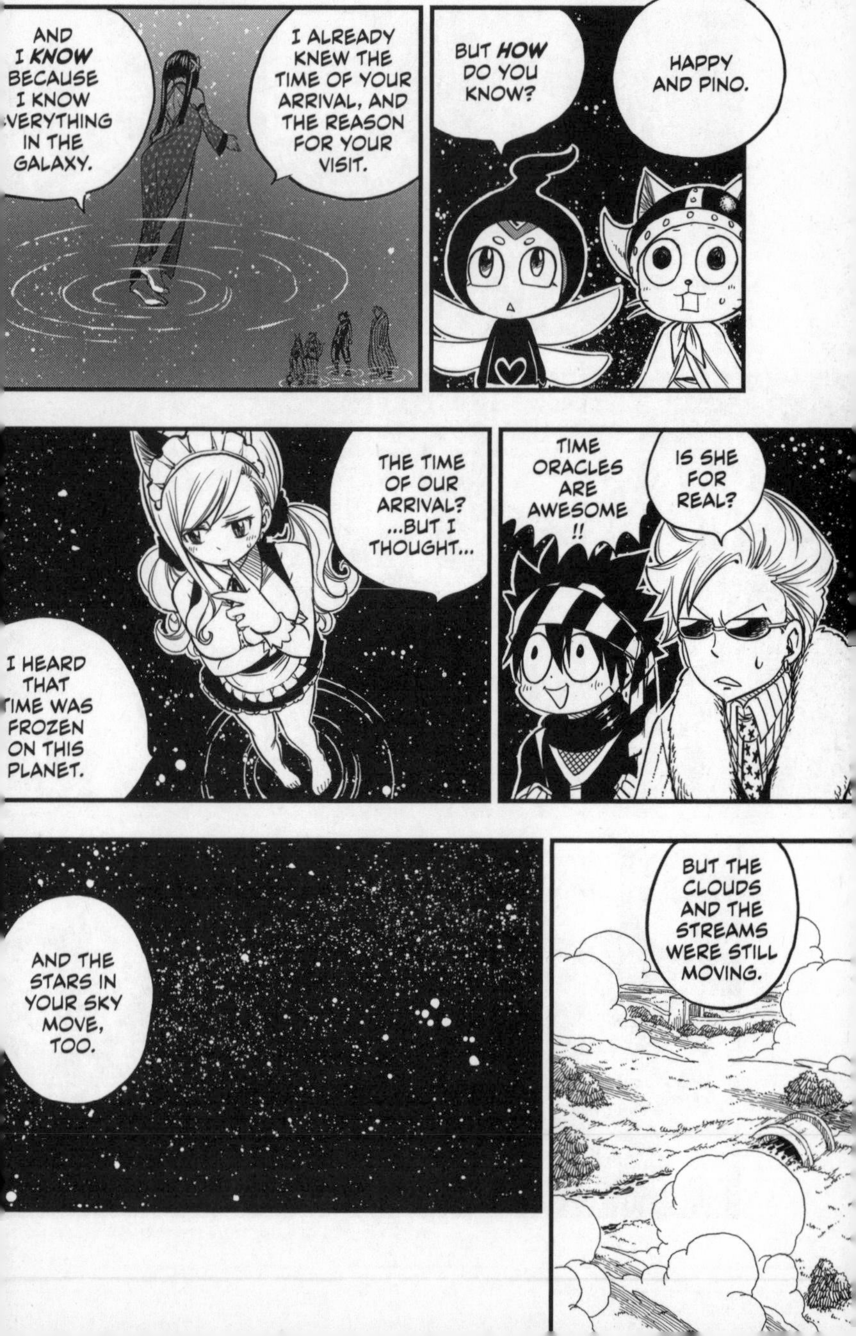
HAPPY AND PINO.
BUT HOW DO YOU KNOW?
I ALREADY KNEW THE TIME OF YOUR ARRIVAL, AND THE REASON FOR YOUR VISIT.
AND I KNOW BECAUSE I KNOW VERYTHING IN THE GALAXY.
IS SHE FOR REAL?
TIME ORACLES ARE AWESOME !!
THE TIME OF OUR ARRIVAL? ...BUT I THOUGHT...
I HEARD THAT IME WAS FROZEN ON THIS PLANET.
BUT THE CLOUDS AND THE STREAMS WERE STILL MOVING.
AND THE STARS IN YOUR SKY MOVE, TOO.

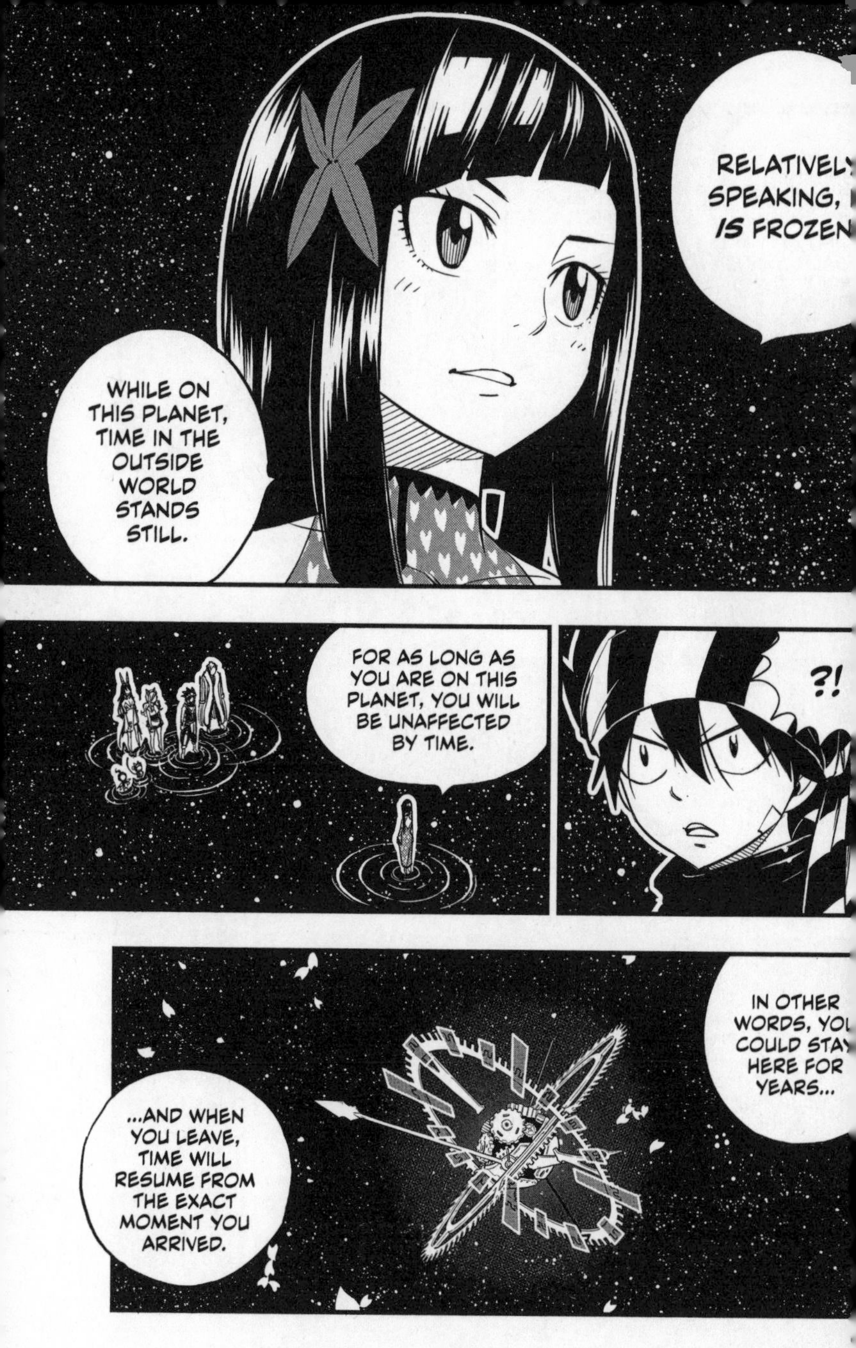
RELATIVELY SPEAKING, IS FROZEN
WHILE ON THIS PLANET, TIME IN THE OUTSIDE WORLD STANDS STILL.
?!
FOR AS LONG AS YOU ARE ON THIS PLANET, YOU WILL BE UNAFFECTED BY TIME.
IN OTHER WORDS, YOU COULD STAY HERE FOR YEARS...
...AND WHEN YOU LEAVE, TIME WILL RESUME FROM THE EXACT MOMENT YOU ARRIVED.

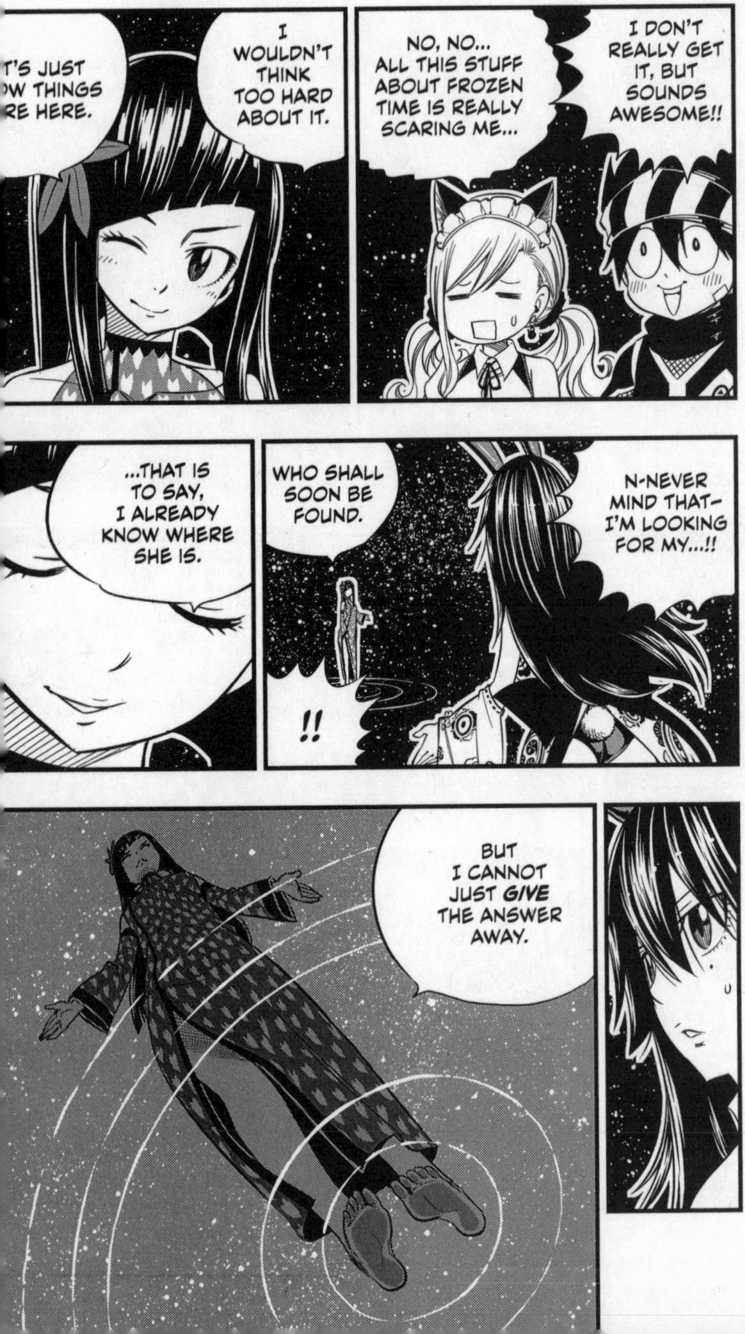
I DON'T REALLY GET IT, BUT SOUNDS AWESOME!!
NO, NO... ALL THIS STUFF ABOUT FROZEN TIME IS REALLY SCARING ME...
I WOULDN'T THINK TOO HARD ABOUT IT.
T'S JUST OW THINGS RE HERE.
N-NEVER MIND THAT— I'M LOOKING FOR MY...!!
WHO SHALL SOON BE FOUND.
!!
...THAT IS TO SAY, I ALREADY KNOW WHERE SHE IS.
BUT I CANNOT JUST *GIVE* THE ANSWER AWAY.

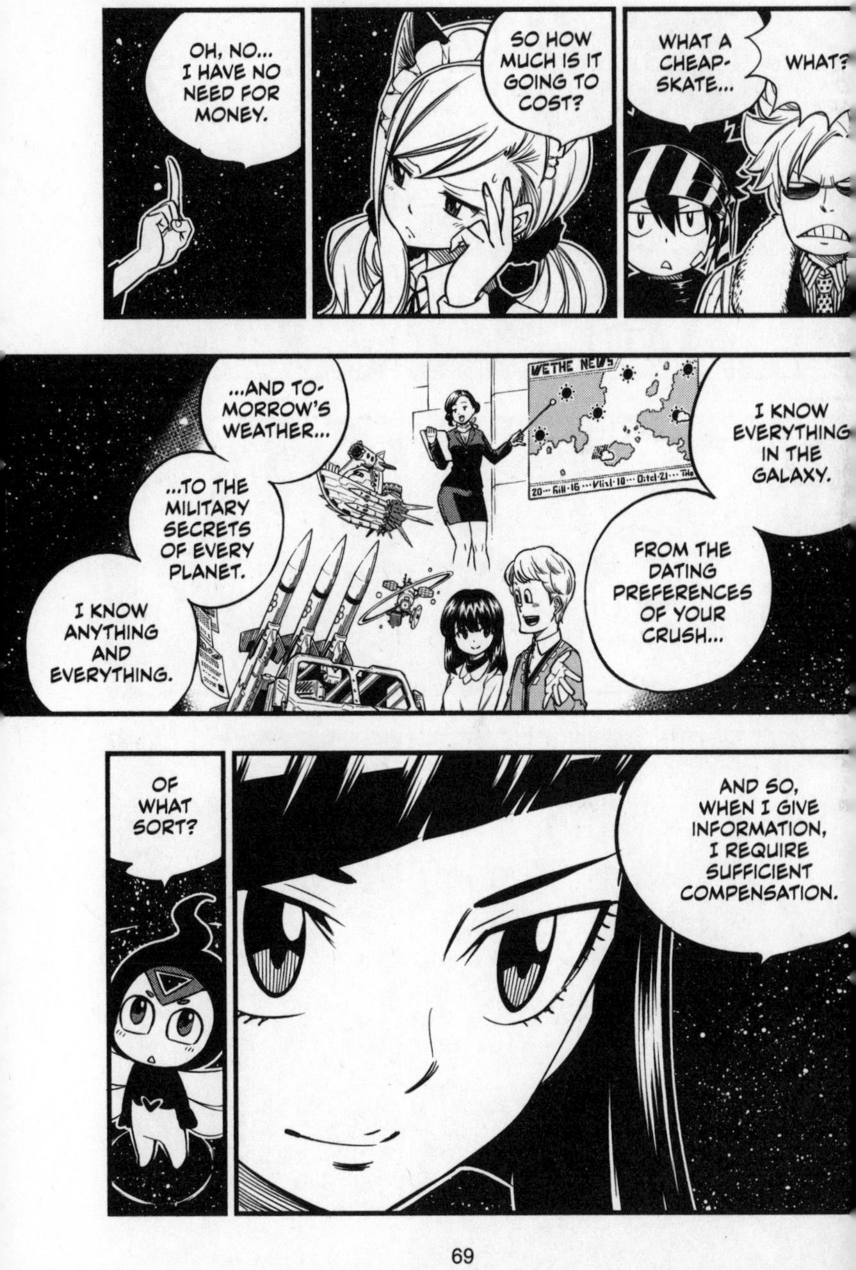
WHAT?
WHAT A CHEAPSKATE...
SO HOW MUCH IS IT GOING TO COST?
OH, NO... I HAVE NO NEED FOR MONEY.
I KNOW EVERYTHING IN THE GALAXY.
FROM THE DATING PREFERENCES OF YOUR CRUSH...
...AND TOMORROW'S WEATHER...
...TO THE MILITARY SECRETS OF EVERY PLANET.
I KNOW ANYTHING AND EVERYTHING.
AND SO, WHEN I GIVE INFORMATION, I REQUIRE SUFFICIENT COMPENSATION.
OF WHAT SORT?

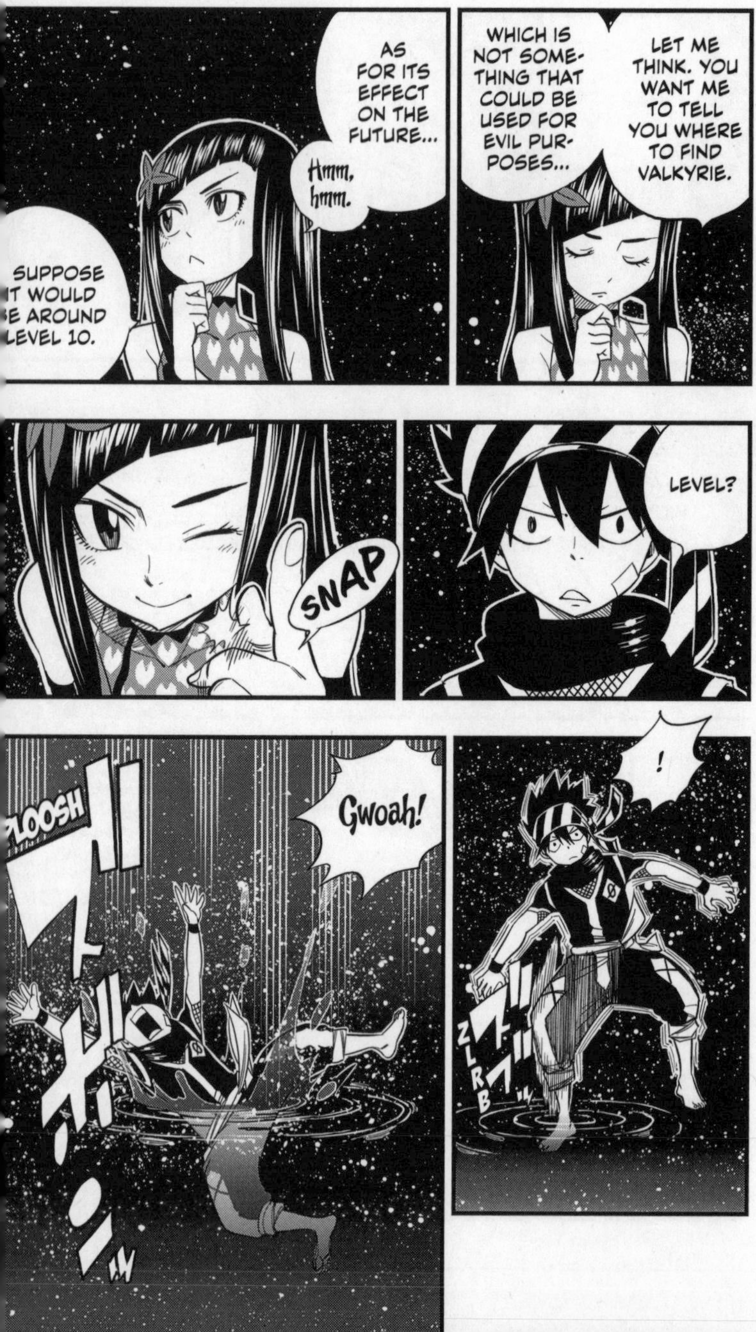
LET ME THINK. YOU WANT ME TO TELL YOU WHERE TO FIND VALKYRIE.
WHICH IS NOT SOMETHING THAT COULD BE USED FOR EVIL PURPOSES...
AS FOR ITS EFFECT ON THE FUTURE...
Hmm, hmm.
SUPPOSE IT WOULD BE AROUND LEVEL 10.
LEVEL?
SNAP
!
ZLRB
Gwoah!
PLOOSH

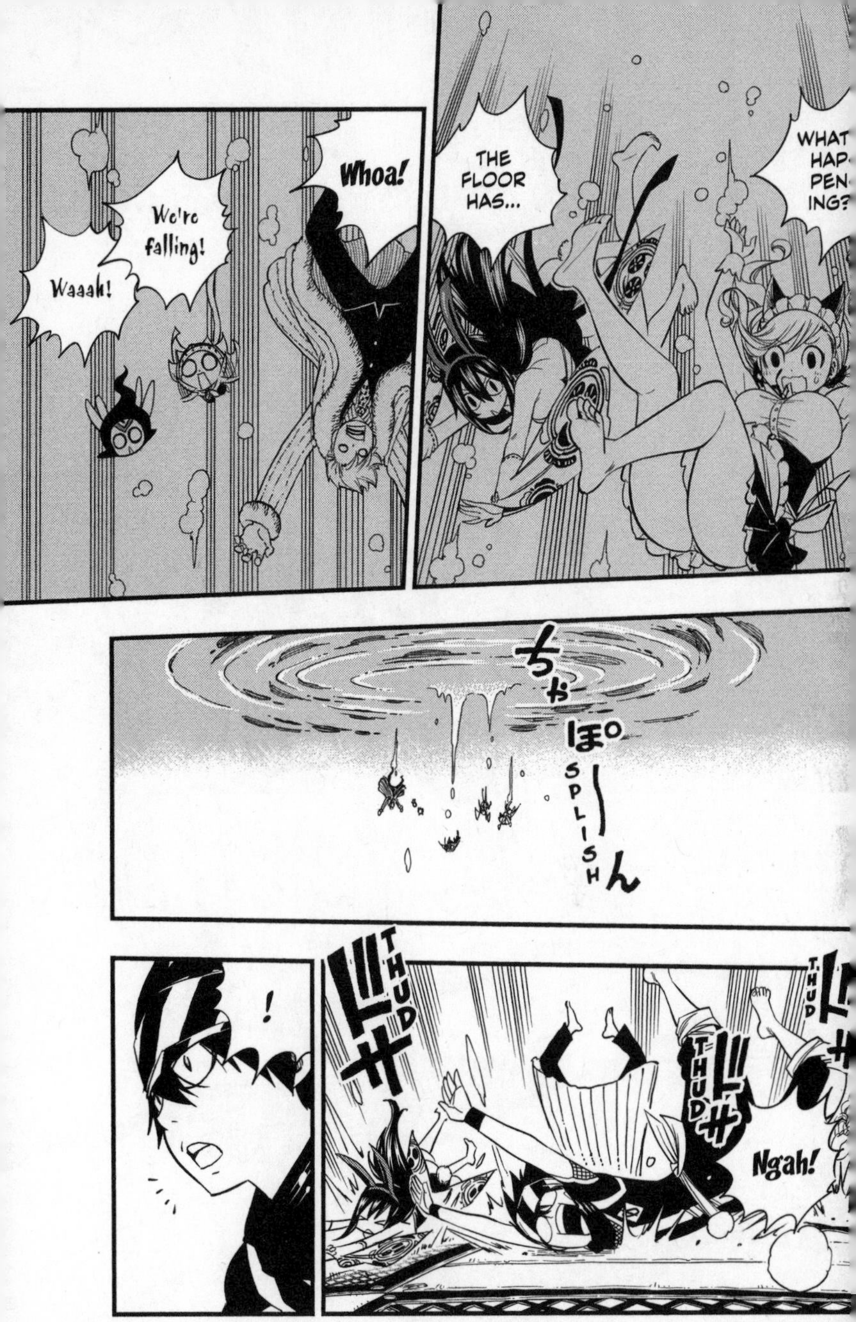
WHAT HAP-PEN-ING?
THE FLOOR HAS...
Whoa!
We're falling!
Waaah!
SPLISH
THUD
THUD
Ngah!
THUD
!

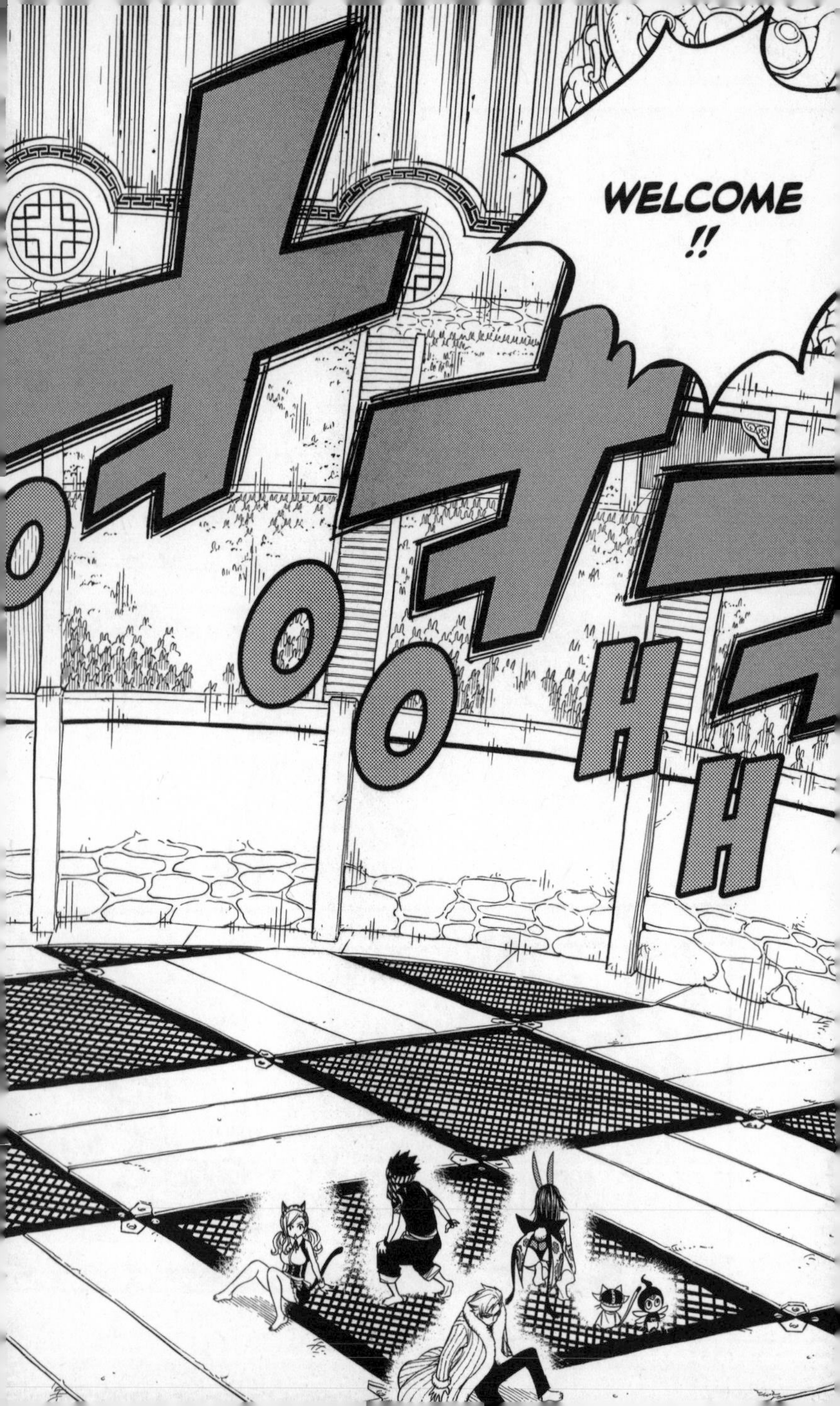
WELCOME!!
OOOHH

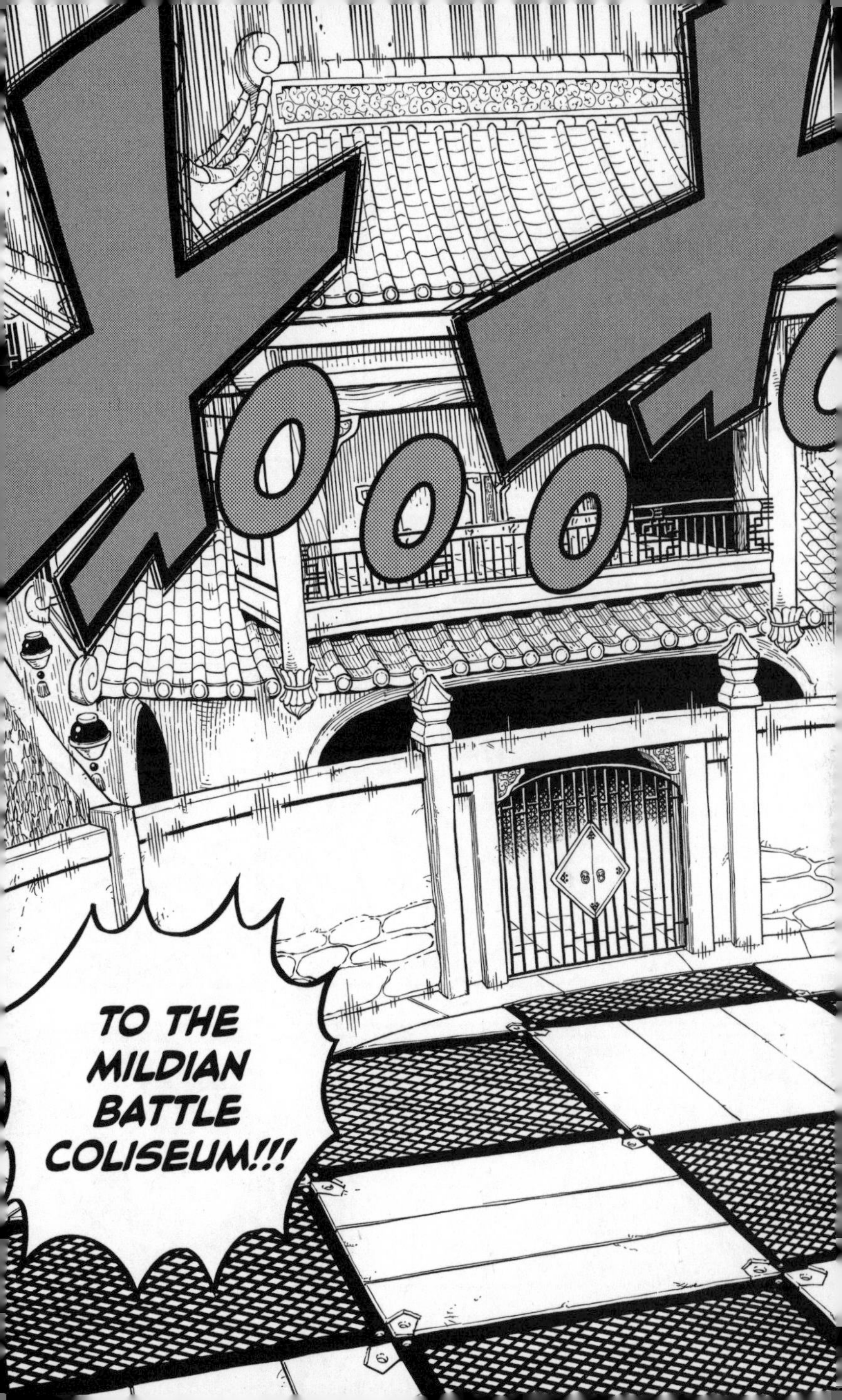
WOOOO
TO THE MILDIAN BATTLE COLISEUM!!!

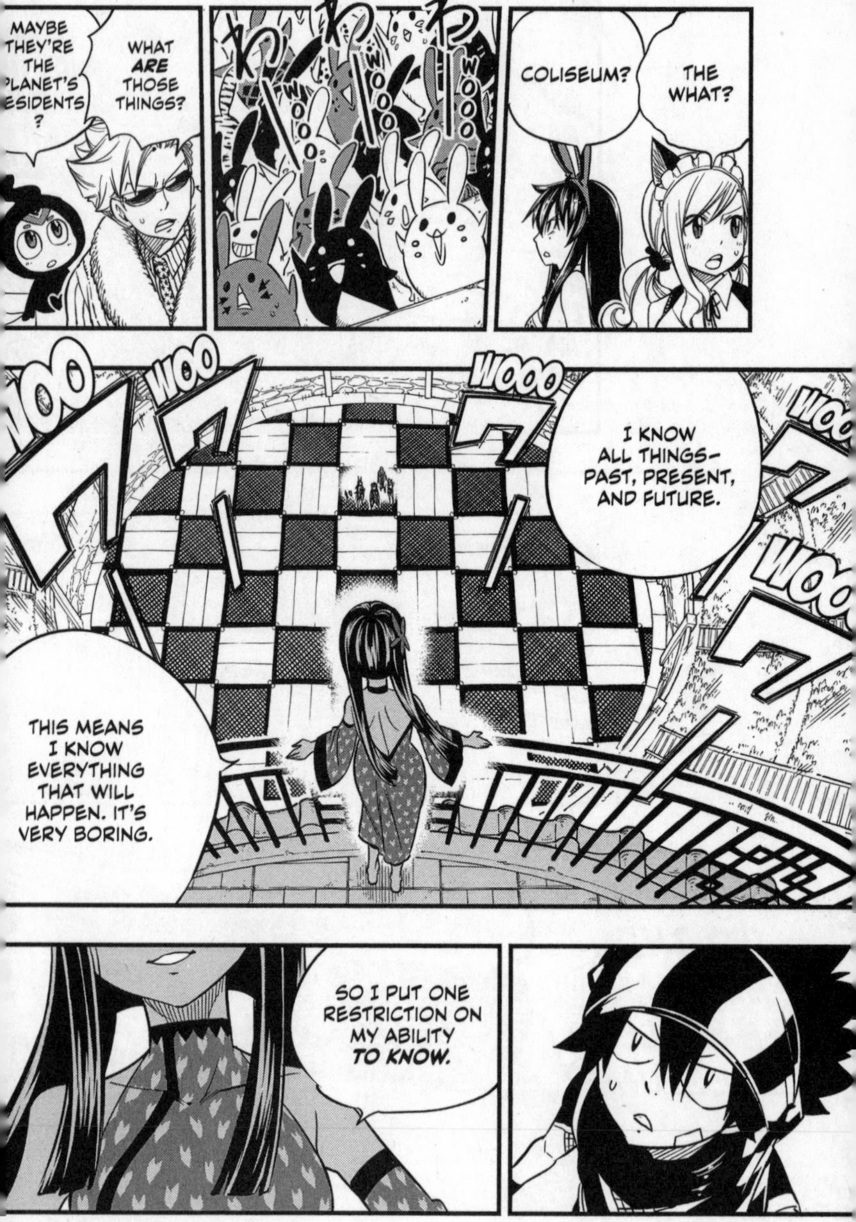
THE WHAT?
COLISEUM?
わ わ わ
WOOOO
WOOO
WOOO
WHAT *ARE* THOSE THINGS?
MAYBE THEY'RE THE LANET'S ESIDENTS ?
WOOO
WOO
WOO
WOO
WOO
I KNOW ALL THINGS– PAST, PRESENT, AND FUTURE.
THIS MEANS I KNOW EVERYTHING THAT WILL HAPPEN. IT'S VERY BORING.
SO I PUT ONE RESTRICTION ON MY ABILITY *TO KNOW.*

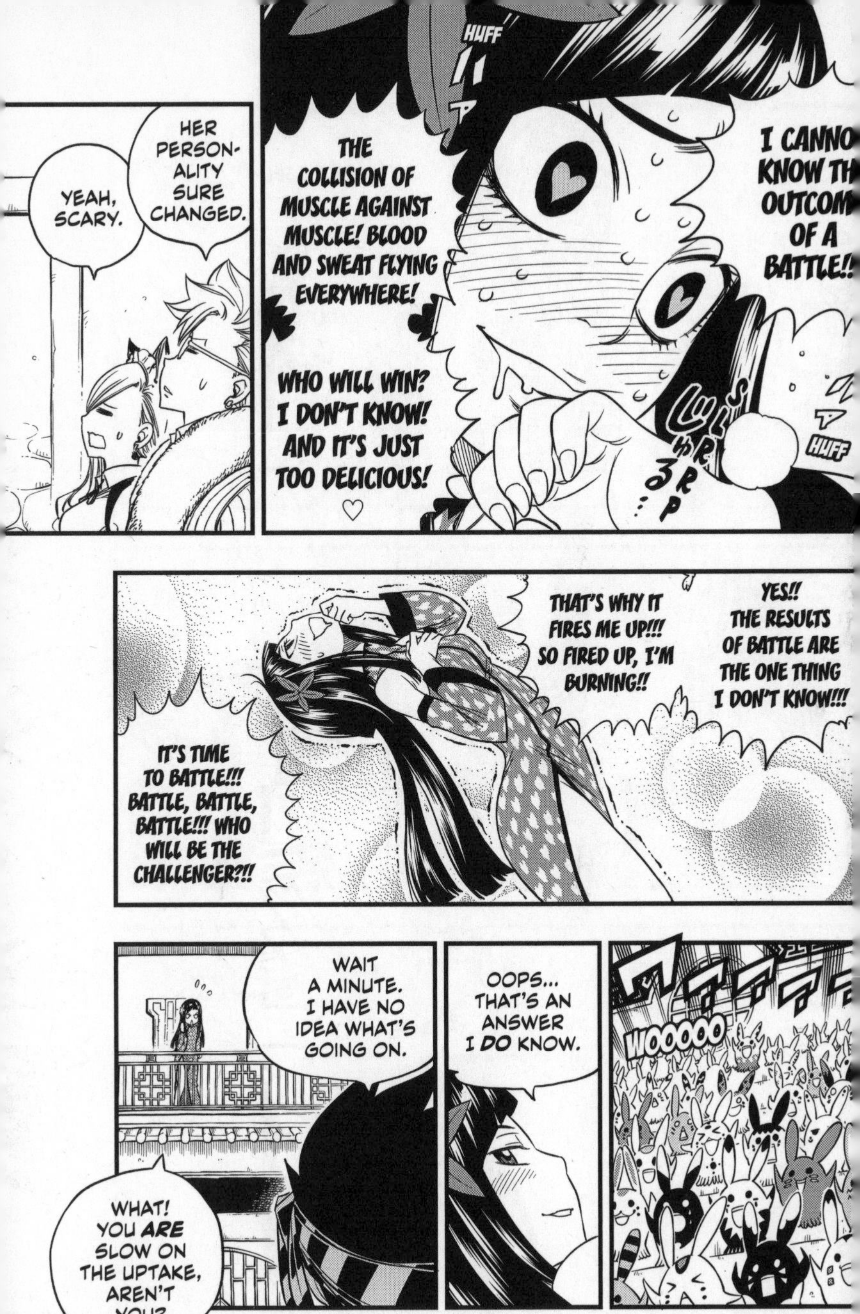
HUFF
I CANNO
KNOW TH
OUTCOM
OF A
BATTLE!!
THE COLLISION OF MUSCLE AGAINST MUSCLE! BLOOD AND SWEAT FLYING EVERYWHERE!
WHO WILL WIN? I DON'T KNOW! AND IT'S JUST TOO DELICIOUS! ♡
SLURRP
HUFF
HER PERSON-ALITY SURE CHANGED.
YEAH, SCARY.
YES!! THE RESULTS OF BATTLE ARE THE ONE THING I DON'T KNOW!!!
THAT'S WHY IT FIRES ME UP!!! SO FIRED UP, I'M BURNING!!
IT'S TIME TO BATTLE!!! BATTLE, BATTLE, BATTLE!!! WHO WILL BE THE CHALLENGER?!!
WOOOOO
OOPS... THAT'S AN ANSWER I DO KNOW.
WAIT A MINUTE. I HAVE NO IDEA WHAT'S GOING ON.
WHAT! YOU ARE SLOW ON THE UPTAKE, AREN'T YOU?

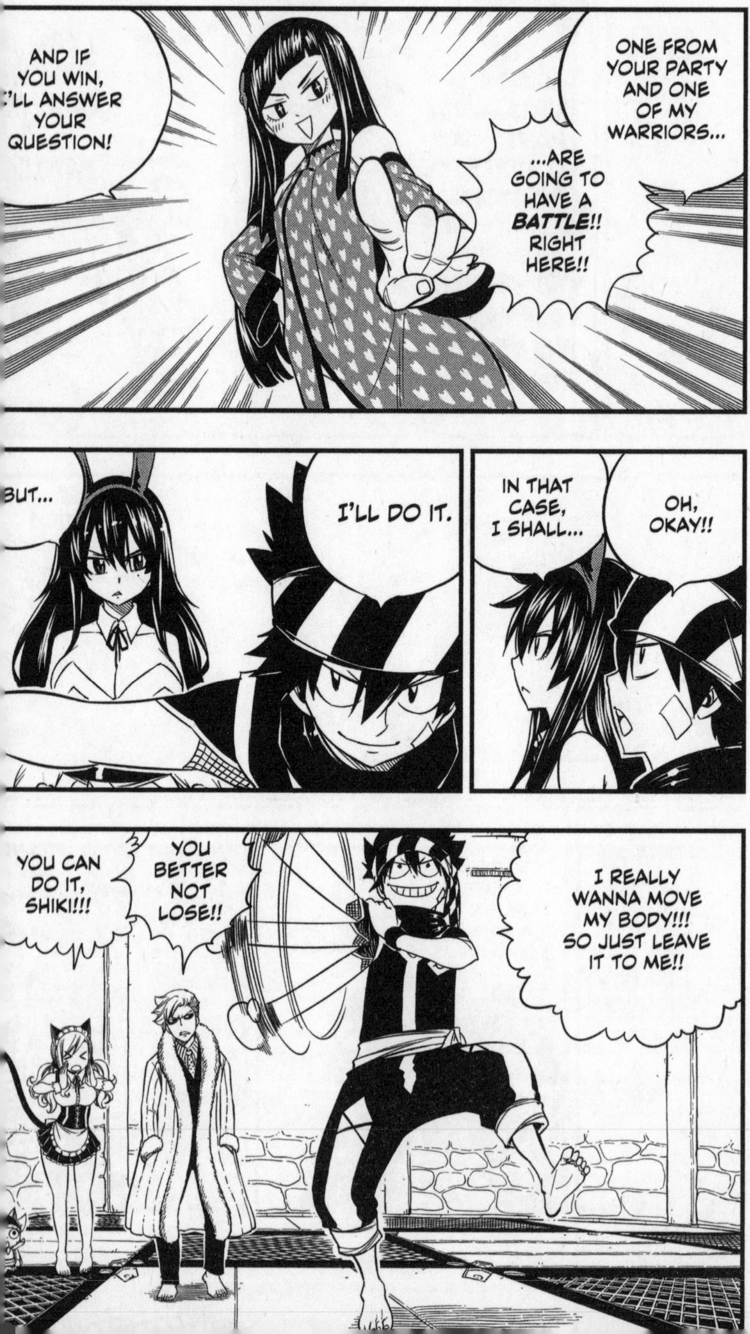
ONE FROM YOUR PARTY AND ONE OF MY WARRIORS...
...ARE GOING TO HAVE A *BATTLE*!! RIGHT HERE!!
AND IF YOU WIN, I'LL ANSWER YOUR QUESTION!
OH, OKAY!!
IN THAT CASE, I SHALL...
I'LL DO IT.
BUT...
I REALLY WANNA MOVE MY BODY!!! SO JUST LEAVE IT TO ME!!
YOU BETTER NOT LOSE!!
YOU CAN DO IT, SHIKI!!!

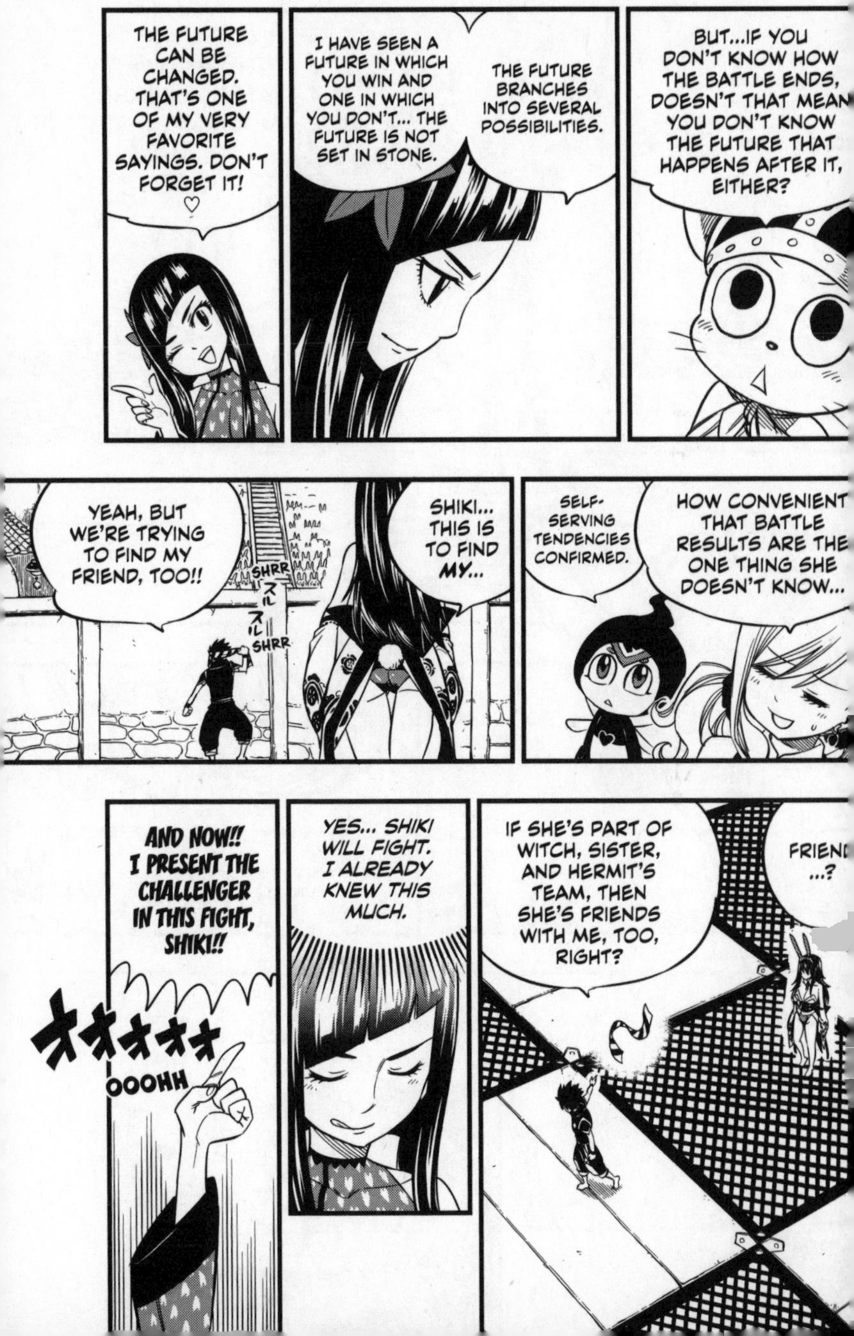
BUT...IF YOU DON'T KNOW HOW THE BATTLE ENDS, DOESN'T THAT MEAN YOU DON'T KNOW THE FUTURE THAT HAPPENS AFTER IT, EITHER?
THE FUTURE BRANCHES INTO SEVERAL POSSIBILITIES.
I HAVE SEEN A FUTURE IN WHICH YOU WIN AND ONE IN WHICH YOU DON'T... THE FUTURE IS NOT SET IN STONE.
THE FUTURE CAN BE CHANGED. THAT'S ONE OF MY VERY FAVORITE SAYINGS. DON'T FORGET IT! ♡
HOW CONVENIENT THAT BATTLE RESULTS ARE THE ONE THING SHE DOESN'T KNOW...
SELF-SERVING TENDENCIES CONFIRMED.
SHIKI... THIS IS TO FIND *MY*...
YEAH, BUT WE'RE TRYING TO FIND MY FRIEND, TOO!!
SHRR スル スル SHRR
FRIEN ...?
IF SHE'S PART OF WITCH, SISTER, AND HERMIT'S TEAM, THEN SHE'S FRIENDS WITH ME, TOO, RIGHT?
YES... SHIKI WILL FIGHT. I ALREADY KNEW THIS MUCH.
AND NOW!! I PRESENT THE CHALLENGER IN THIS FIGHT, SHIKI!!
オオオオオ OOOHH

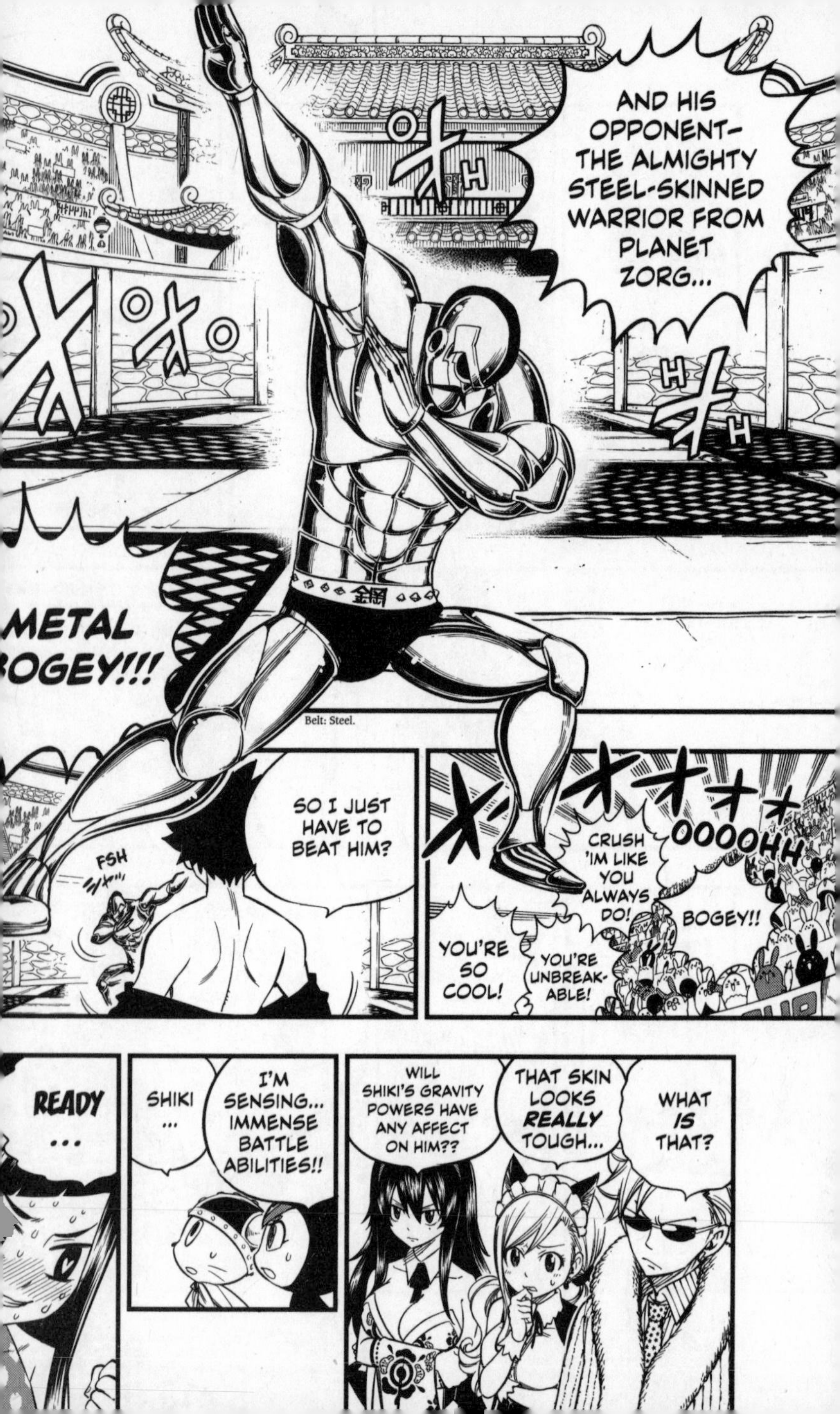
AND HIS OPPONENT— THE ALMIGHTY STEEL-SKINNED WARRIOR FROM PLANET ZORG...
METAL BOGEY!!!
Belt: Steel.
OOOOHH
CRUSH 'EM LIKE YOU ALWAYS DO!
BOGEY!!
YOU'RE UNBREAKABLE!
YOU'RE SO COOL!
SO I JUST HAVE TO BEAT HIM?
FSH
WHAT *IS* THAT?
THAT SKIN LOOKS *REALLY* TOUGH...
WILL SHIKI'S GRAVITY POWERS HAVE ANY AFFECT ON HIM??
I'M SENSING... IMMENSE BATTLE ABILITIES!!
SHIKI...
READY...

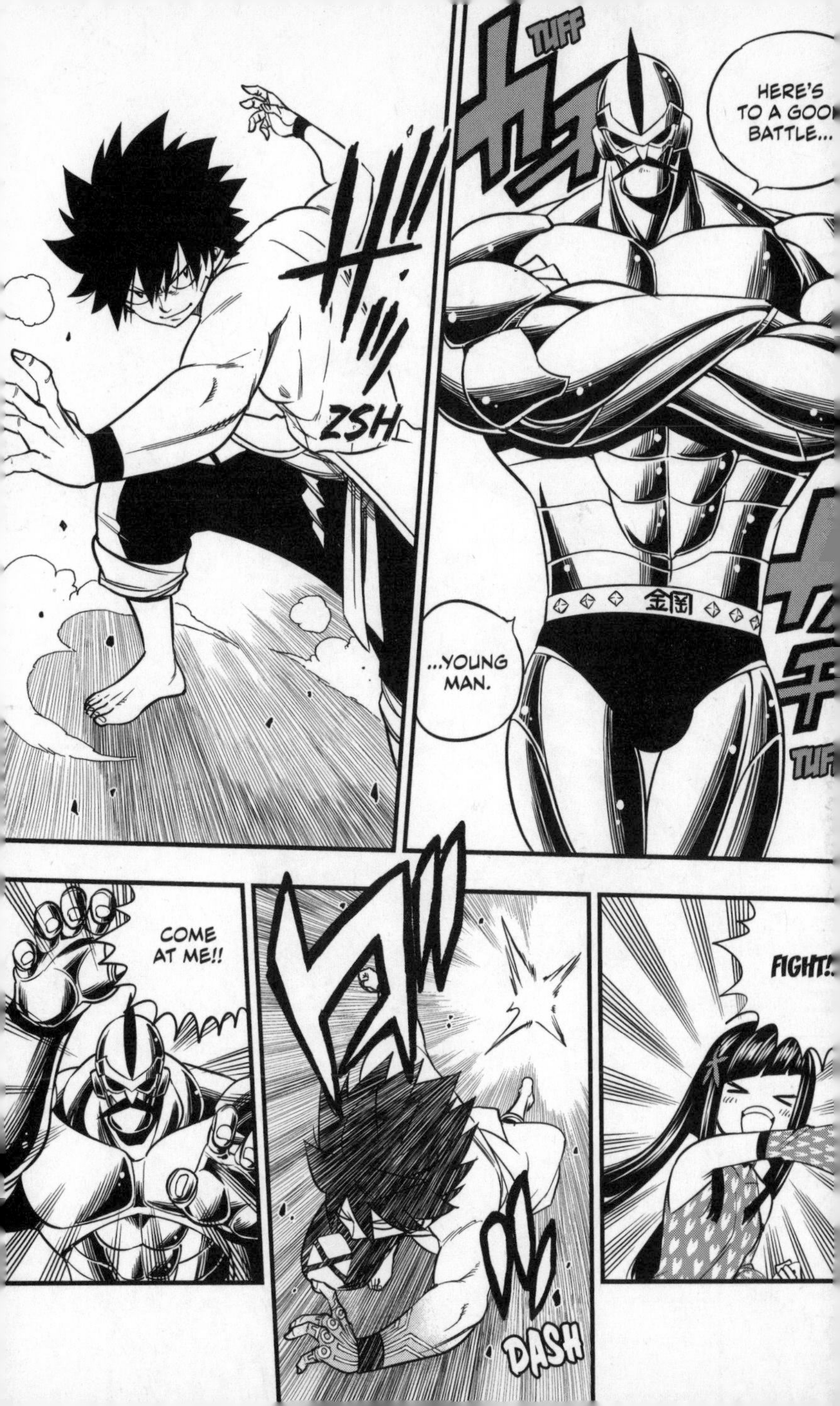

TUFF
HERE'S TO A GOO
BATTLE...
...YOUNG MAN.
TUF
ZSH
FIGHT!!
DASH
COME AT ME!!

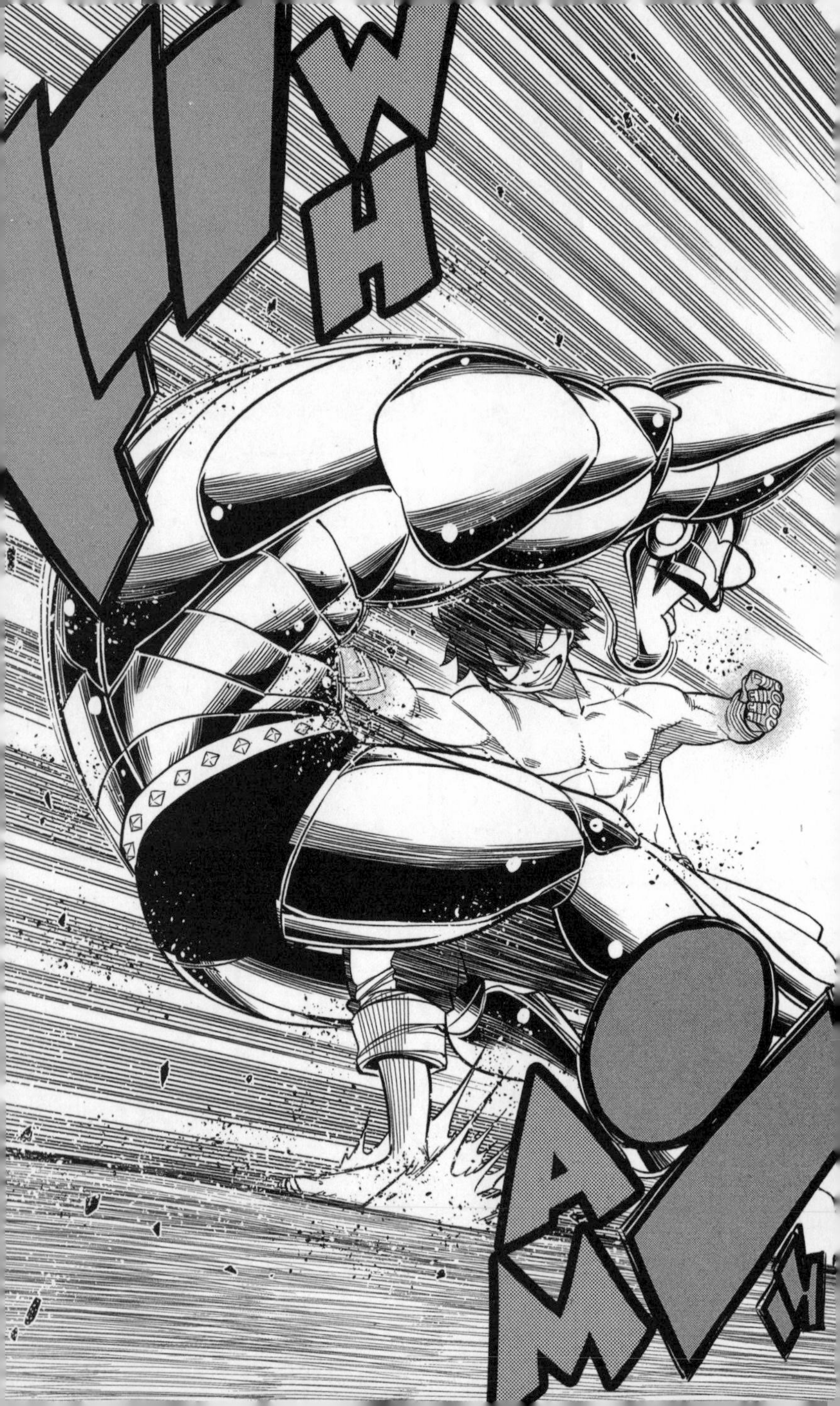
WHAM!!

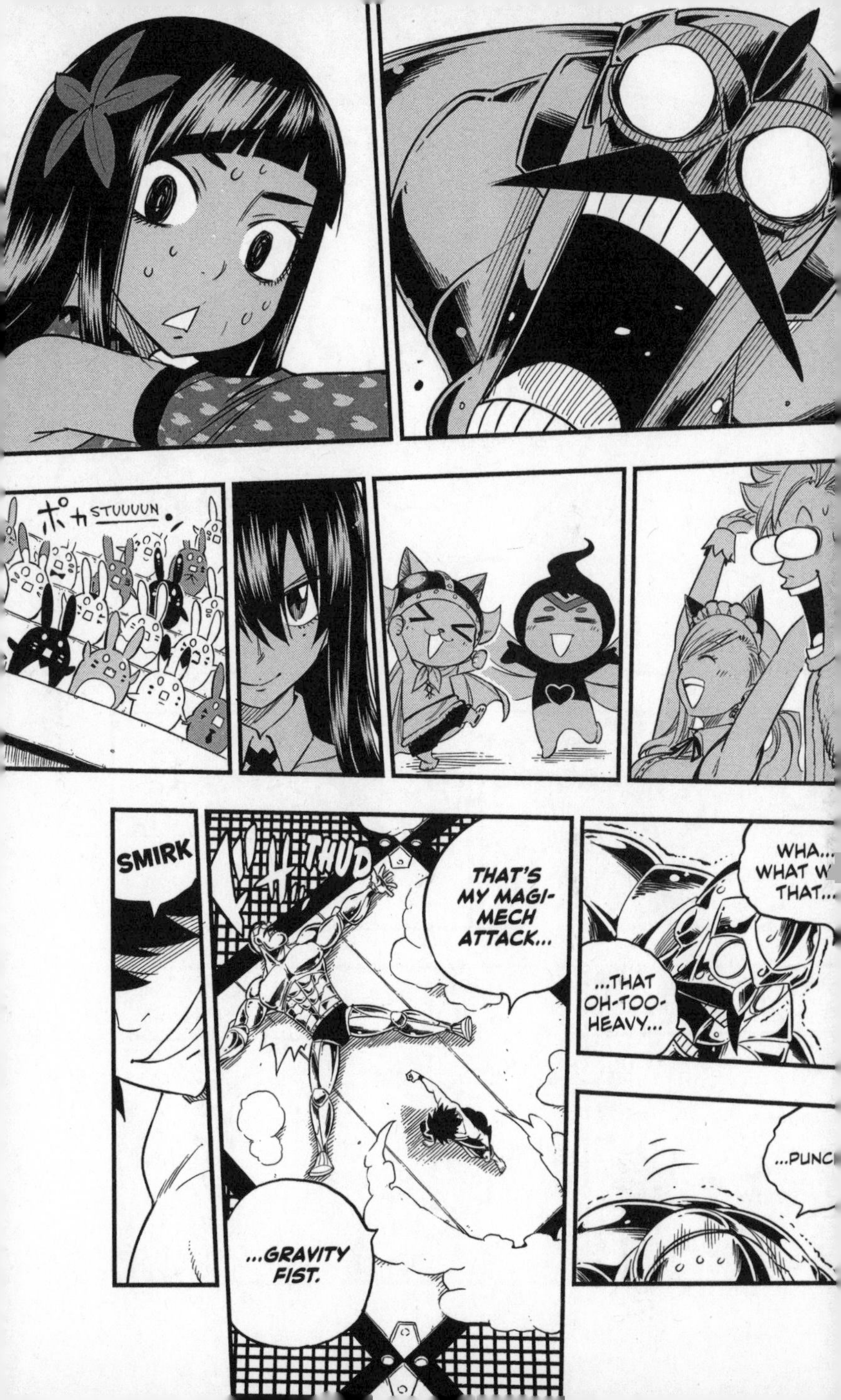
ポカ STUUUUN
WHA... WHAT W THAT...
...THAT OH-TOO-HEAVY...
...PUNC
THUD
THAT'S MY MAGI-MECH ATTACK...
...GRAVITY FIST.
SMIRK

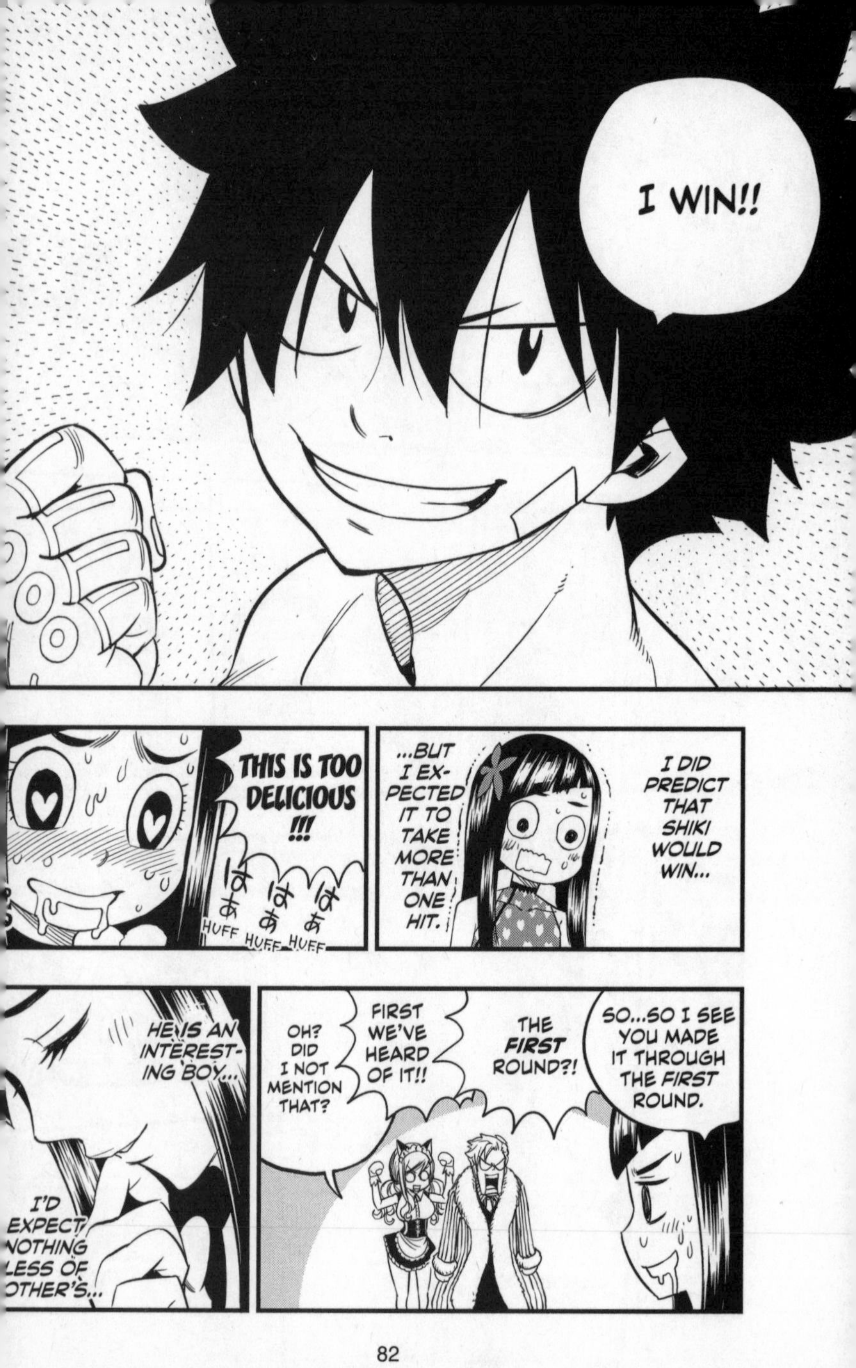

I WIN!!
I DID PREDICT THAT SHIKI WOULD WIN...
...BUT I EXPECTED IT TO TAKE MORE THAN ONE HIT.
THIS IS TOO DELICIOUS!!!
はあ HUFF
はあ HUFF
はあ HUFF
SO...SO I SEE YOU MADE IT THROUGH THE FIRST ROUND.
THE FIRST ROUND?!
FIRST WE'VE HEARD OF IT!!
OH? DID I NOT MENTION THAT?
HE IS AN INTERESTING BOY...
I'D EXPECT NOTHING LESS OF OTHER'S...

EDENS ZERO

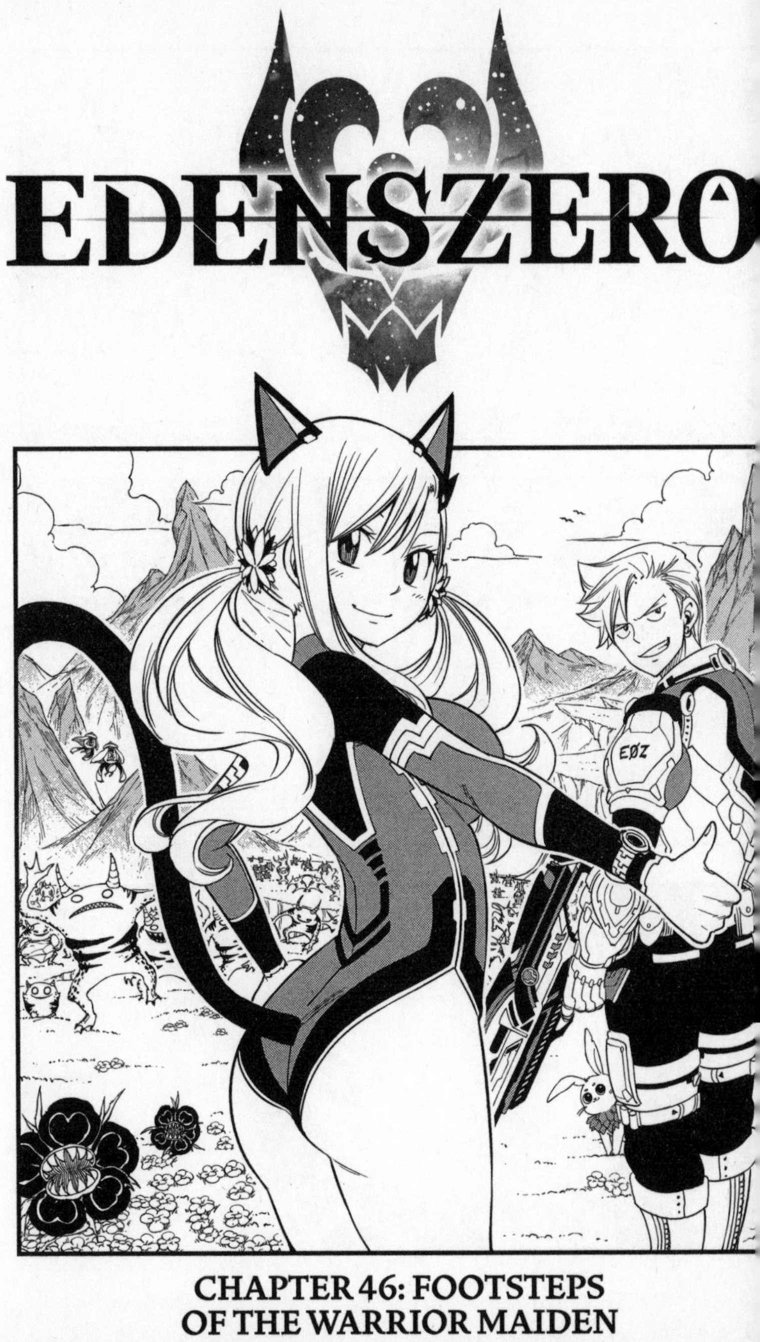
EØZ

CHAPTER 46: FOOTSTEPS OF THE WARRIOR MAIDEN

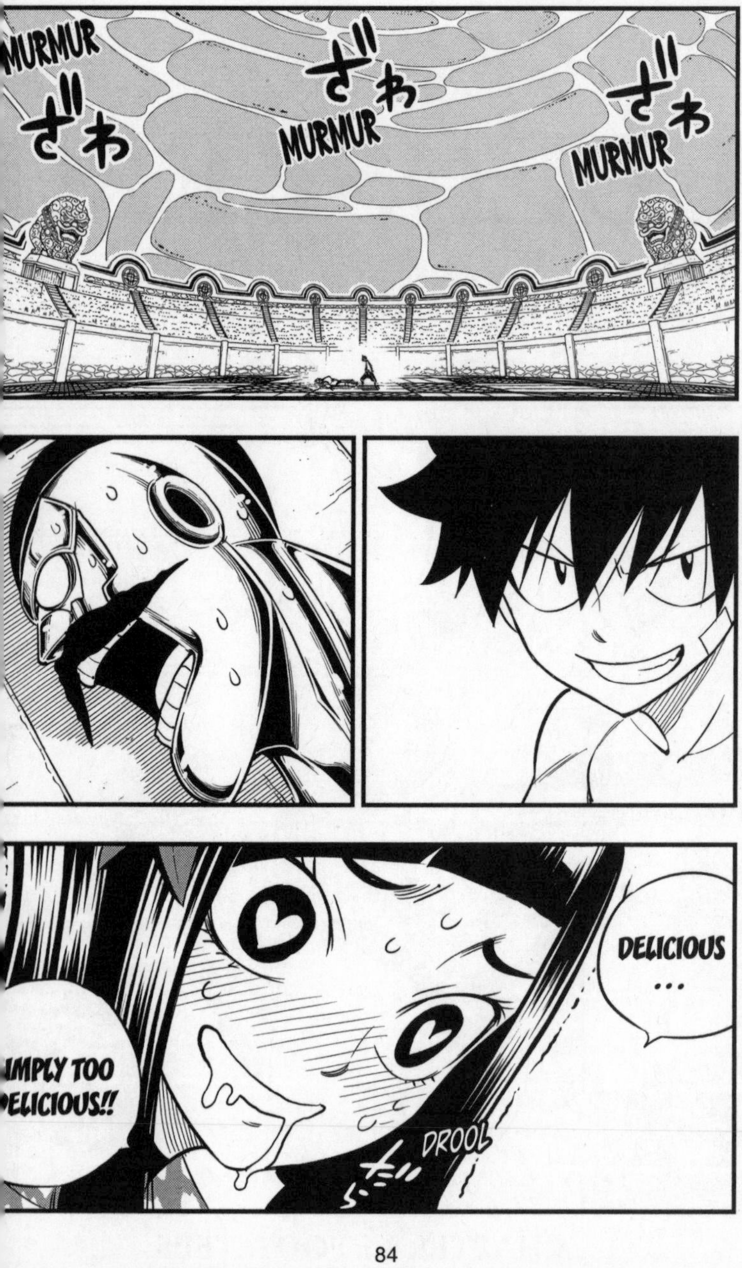
ざわ
MURMUR
ざわ
MURMUR
MURMUR
ざわ
DELICIOUS ...
IMPLY TOO
ELICIOUS!!
DROOL

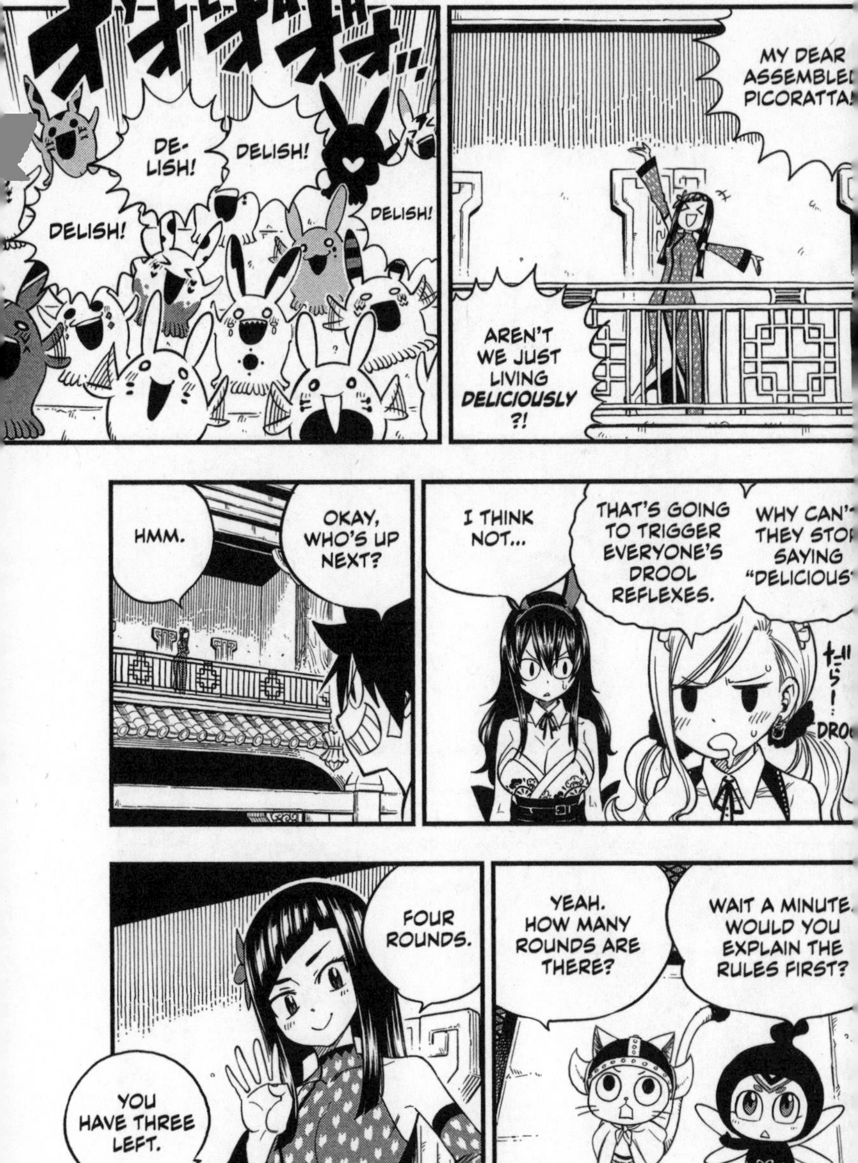
MY DEAR ASSEMBLED PICORATTA!
AREN'T WE JUST LIVING *DELICIOUSLY* ?!
YEAH
DE-LISH!
DELISH!
DELISH!
DELISH!
WHY CAN'T THEY STOP SAYING "DELICIOUS"
THAT'S GOING TO TRIGGER EVERYONE'S DROOL REFLEXES.
I THINK NOT...
DRO
OKAY, WHO'S UP NEXT?
HMM.
WAIT A MINUTE. WOULD YOU EXPLAIN THE RULES FIRST?
YEAH. HOW MANY ROUNDS ARE THERE?
FOUR ROUNDS.
YOU HAVE THREE LEFT.

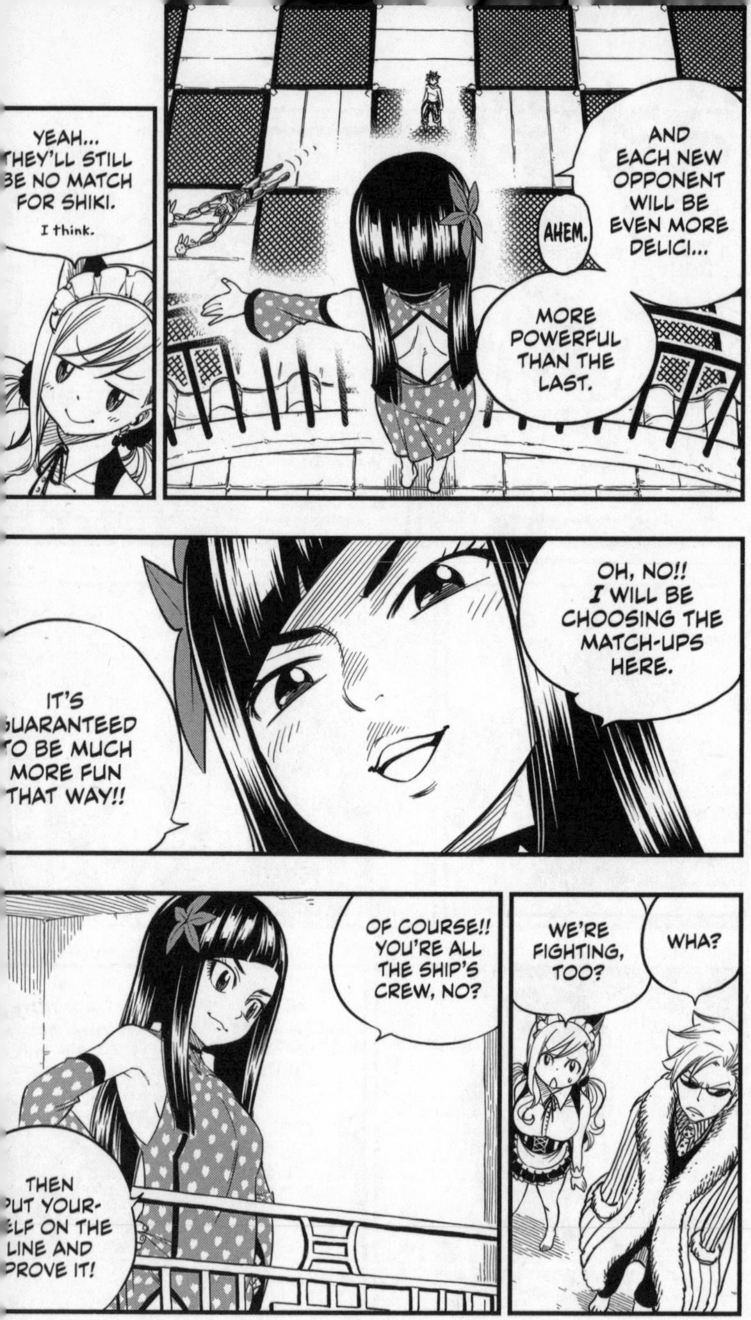
AND EACH NEW OPPONENT WILL BE EVEN MORE DELICI...
AHEM.
MORE POWERFUL THAN THE LAST.
YEAH... THEY'LL STILL BE NO MATCH FOR SHIKI.
I think.
OH, NO!! *I* WILL BE CHOOSING THE MATCH-UPS HERE.
IT'S GUARANTEED TO BE MUCH MORE FUN THAT WAY!!
WHA?
WE'RE FIGHTING, TOO?
OF COURSE!! YOU'RE ALL THE SHIP'S CREW, NO?
THEN PUT YOUR-SELF ON THE LINE AND PROVE IT!

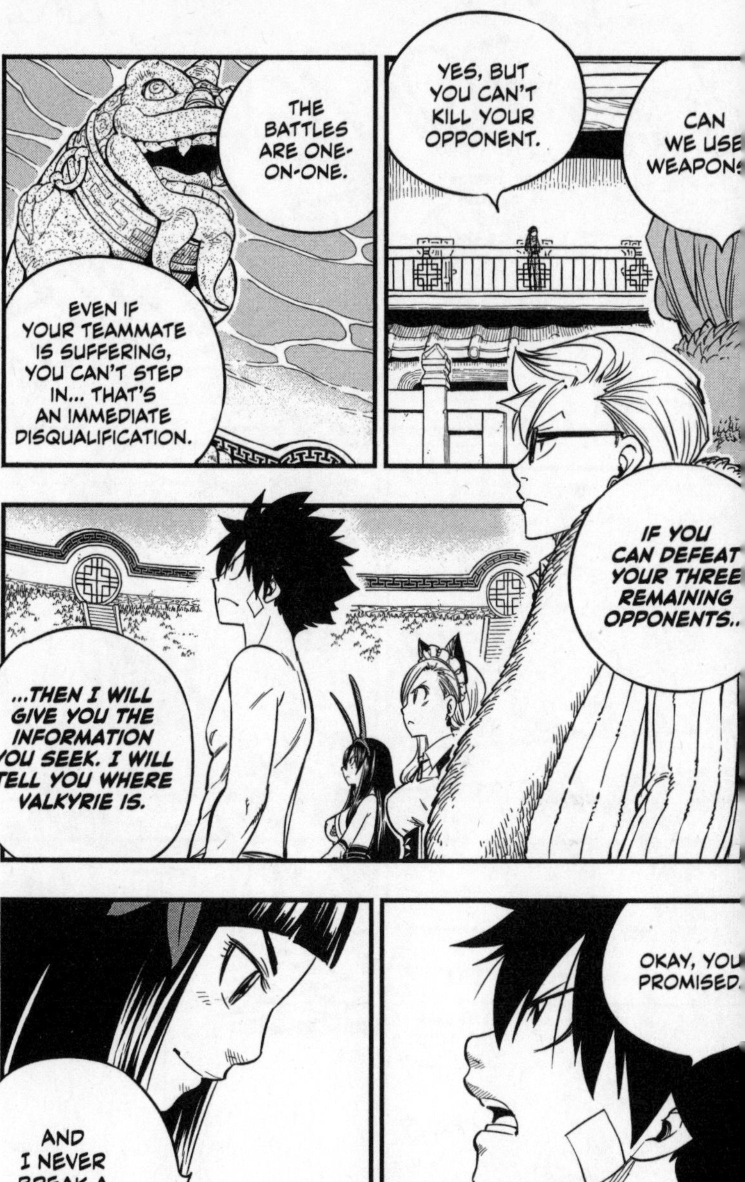

CAN WE USE WEAPON
YES, BUT YOU CAN'T KILL YOUR OPPONENT.
THE BATTLES ARE ONE-ON-ONE.
EVEN IF YOUR TEAMMATE IS SUFFERING, YOU CAN'T STEP IN... THAT'S AN IMMEDIATE DISQUALIFICATION.
IF YOU CAN DEFEAT YOUR THREE REMAINING OPPONENTS..
...THEN I WILL GIVE YOU THE INFORMATION YOU SEEK. I WILL TELL YOU WHERE VALKYRIE IS.
OKAY, YOU PROMISED.
AND I NEVER BREAK A PROMISE.

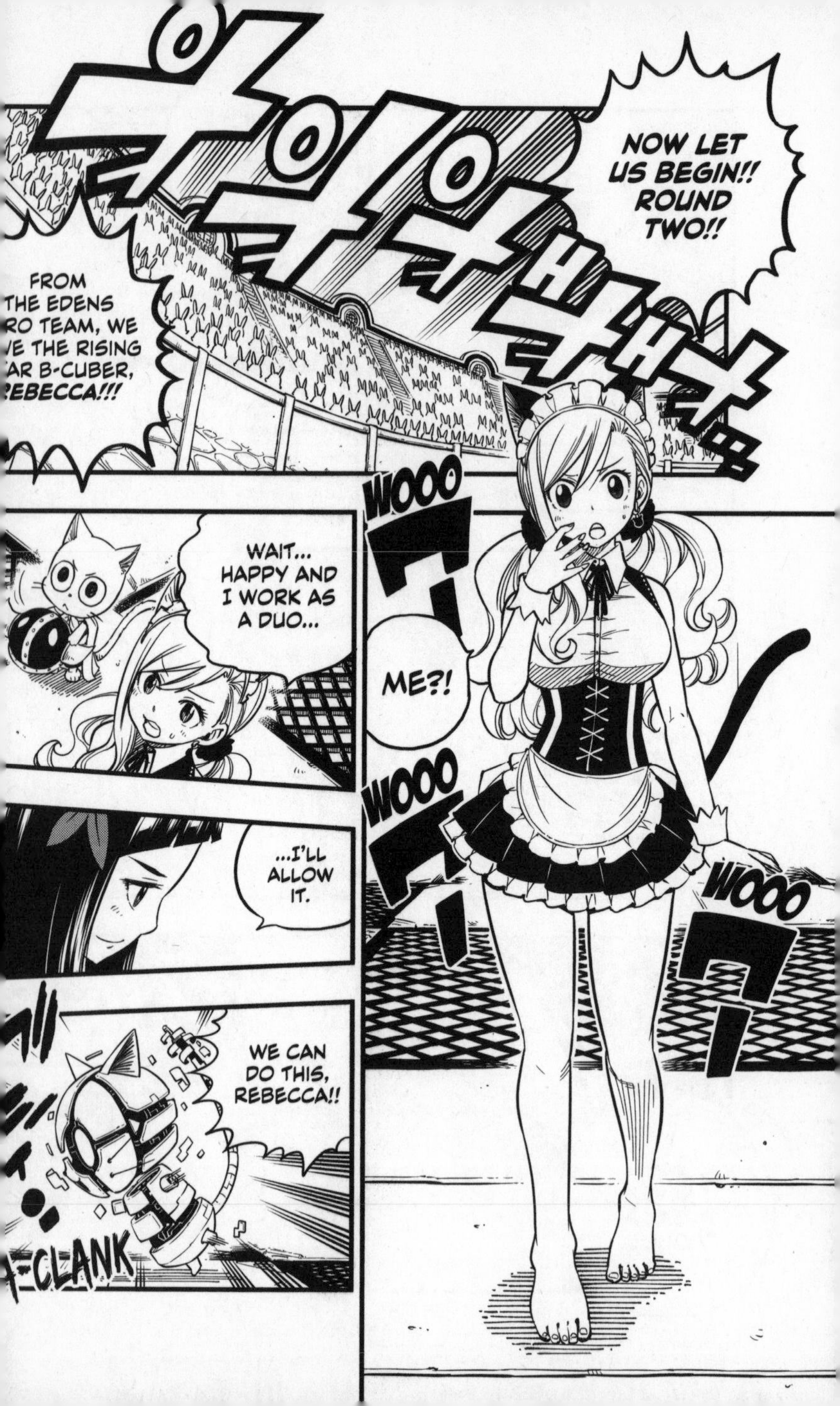
NOW LET US BEGIN!! ROUND TWO!!
FROM THE EDENS
RO TEAM, WE
VE THE RISING
AR B-CUBER,
EBECCA!!!
WOOO
ME?!
WOOO
WOOO
WAIT... HAPPY AND I WORK AS A DUO...
...I'LL ALLOW IT.
WE CAN DO THIS, REBECCA!!
CLANK

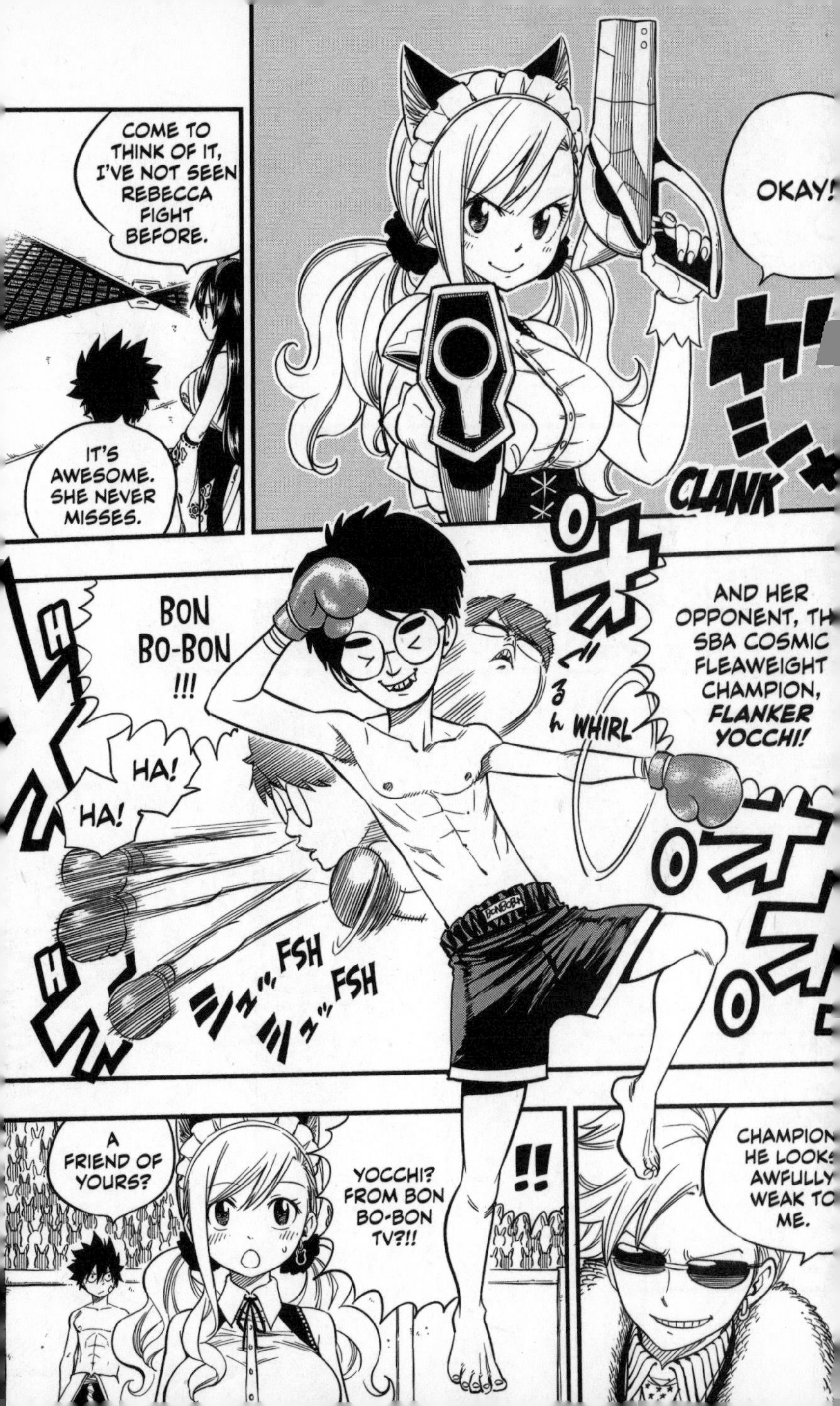
OKAY!
CLANK
COME TO THINK OF IT, I'VE NOT SEEN REBECCA FIGHT BEFORE.
IT'S AWESOME. SHE NEVER MISSES.
AND HER OPPONENT, TH SBA COSMIC FLEAWEIGHT CHAMPION, FLANKER YOCCHI!
WHIRL
BON BO-BON !!!
HA!
HA!
FSH
FSH
CHAMPION HE LOOKS AWFULLY WEAK TO ME.
!!
YOCCHI? FROM BON BO-BON TV?!!
A FRIEND OF YOURS?

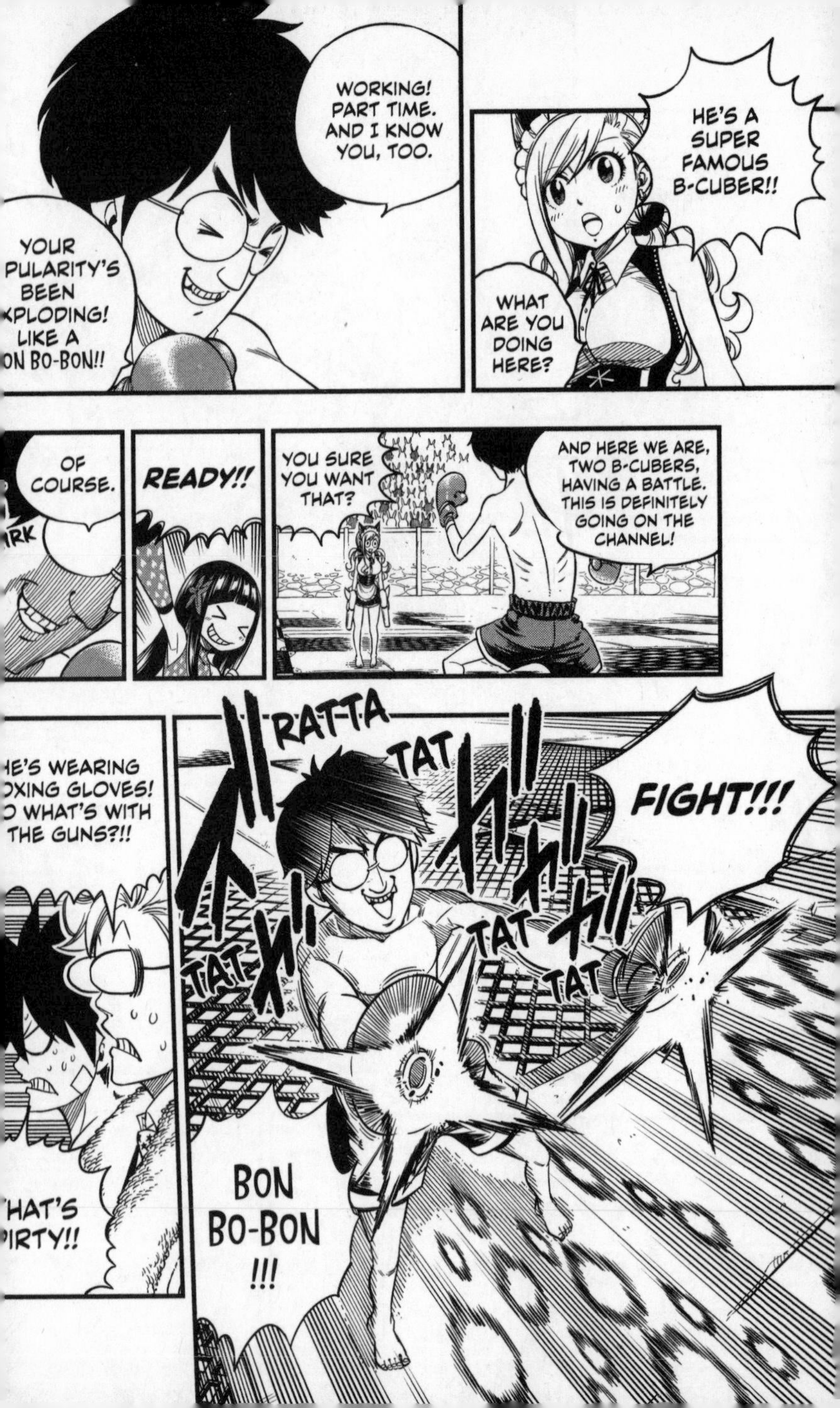
HE'S A SUPER FAMOUS B-CUBER!!
WHAT ARE YOU DOING HERE?
WORKING! PART TIME. AND I KNOW YOU, TOO.
YOUR PULARITY'S BEEN XPLODING! LIKE A ON BO-BON!!
AND HERE WE ARE, TWO B-CUBERS, HAVING A BATTLE. THIS IS DEFINITELY GOING ON THE CHANNEL!
YOU SURE YOU WANT THAT?
READY!!
OF COURSE.
RK
FIGHT!!!
RATTA TAT
TAT
TAT
TAT
TAT
BON BO-BON !!!
E'S WEARING OXING GLOVES! O WHAT'S WITH THE GUNS?!!
HAT'S IRTY!!

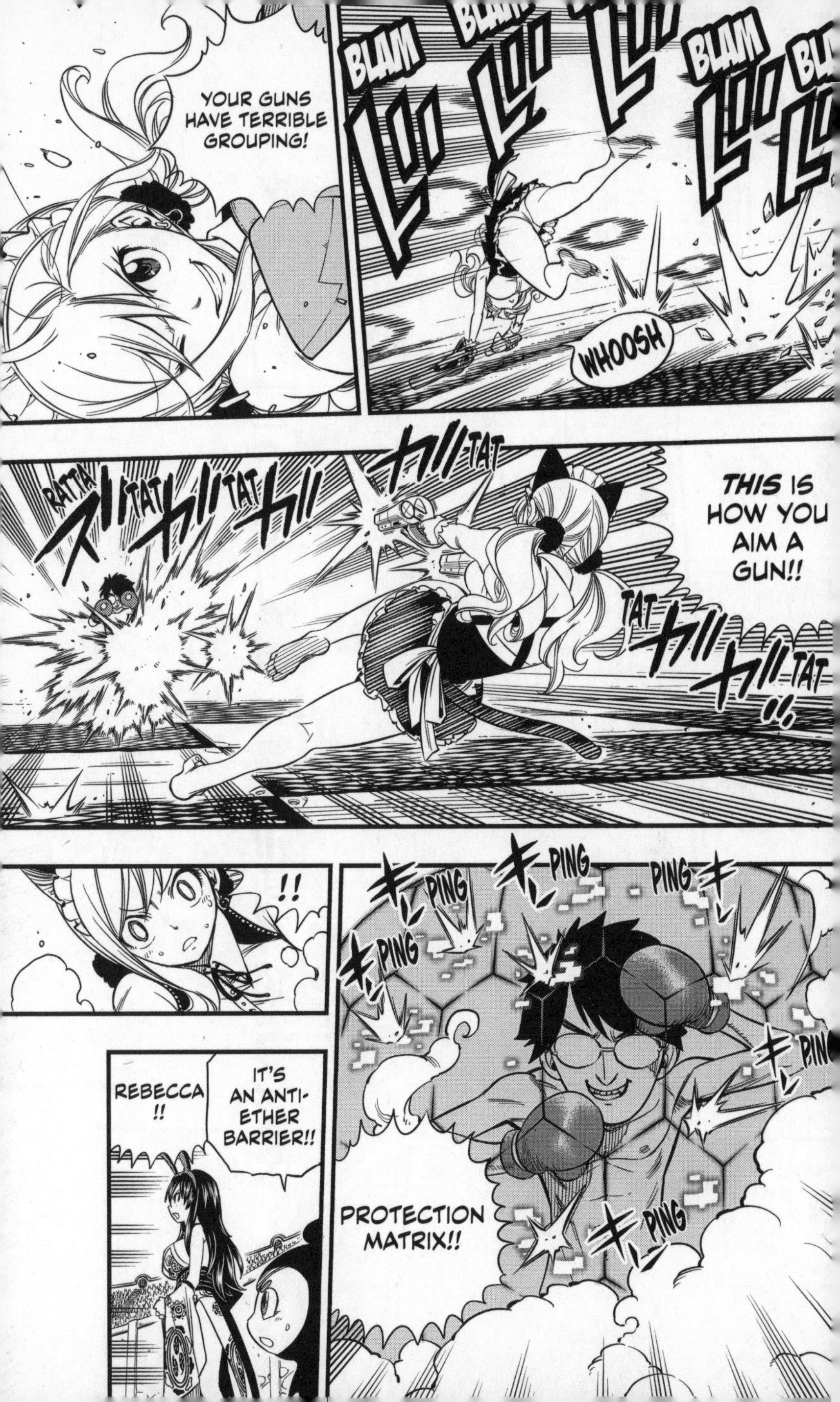
BLAM
BLAM
BLAM
WHOOSH
YOUR GUNS HAVE TERRIBLE GROUPING!
TAT
THIS IS HOW YOU AIM A GUN!!
TAT
TAT
TAT
TAT
RATTA
PING
PING
PING
PING
PING
PING
PROTECTION MATRIX!!
!!
IT'S AN ANTI-ETHER BARRIER!!
REBECCA!!

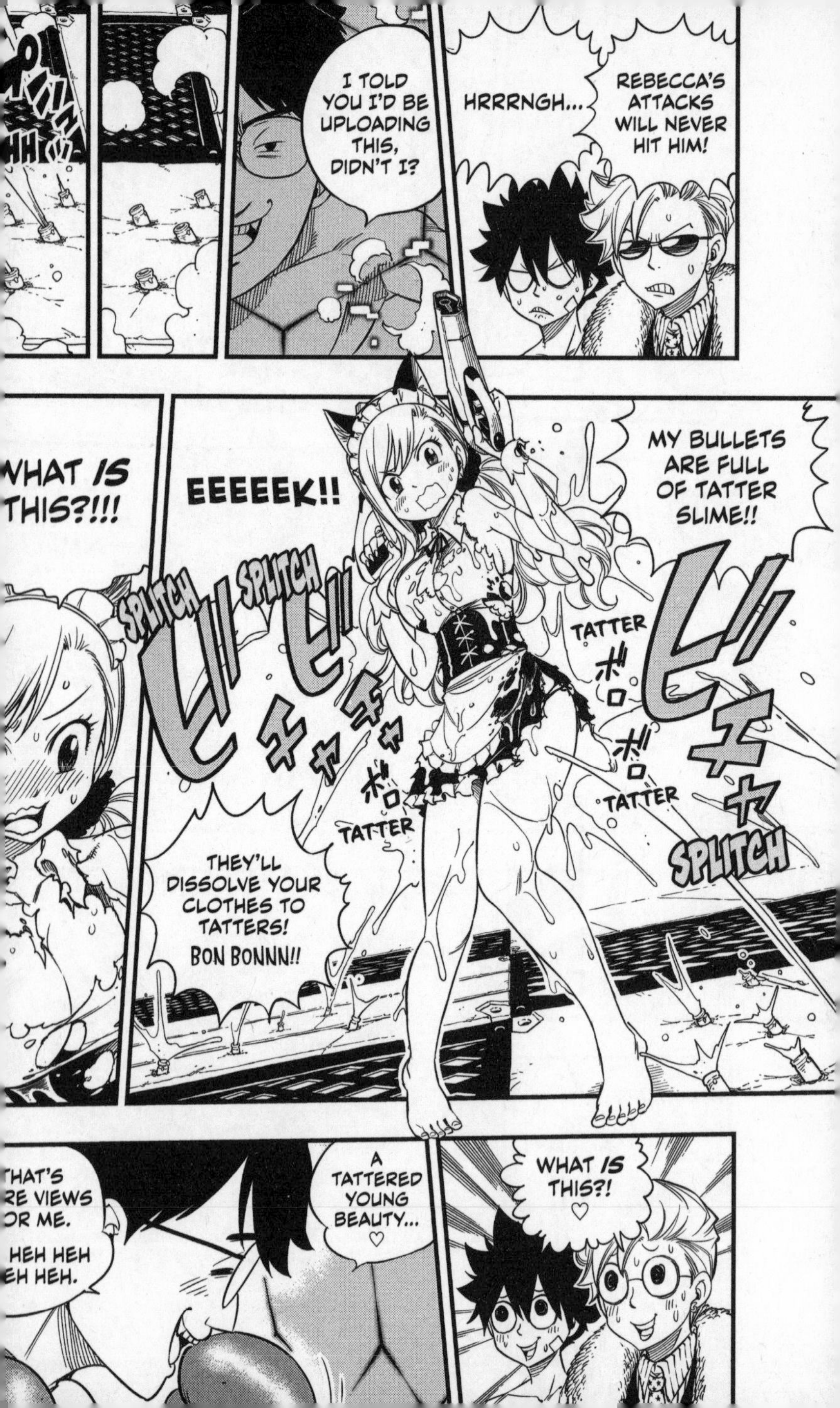

REBECCA'S ATTACKS WILL NEVER HIT HIM!
HRRRNGH...
I TOLD YOU I'D BE UPLOADING THIS, DIDN'T I?
MY BULLETS ARE FULL OF TATTER SLIME!!
EEEEEK!!
TATTER
TATTER
SPLITCH
SPLITCH
SPLITCH
TATTER
THEY'LL DISSOLVE YOUR CLOTHES TO TATTERS!
BON BONNN!!
WHAT IS THIS?!!!
WHAT IS THIS?! ♡
A TATTERED YOUNG BEAUTY... ♡
THAT'S
RE VIEWS
OR ME.
HEH HEH
EH HEH.

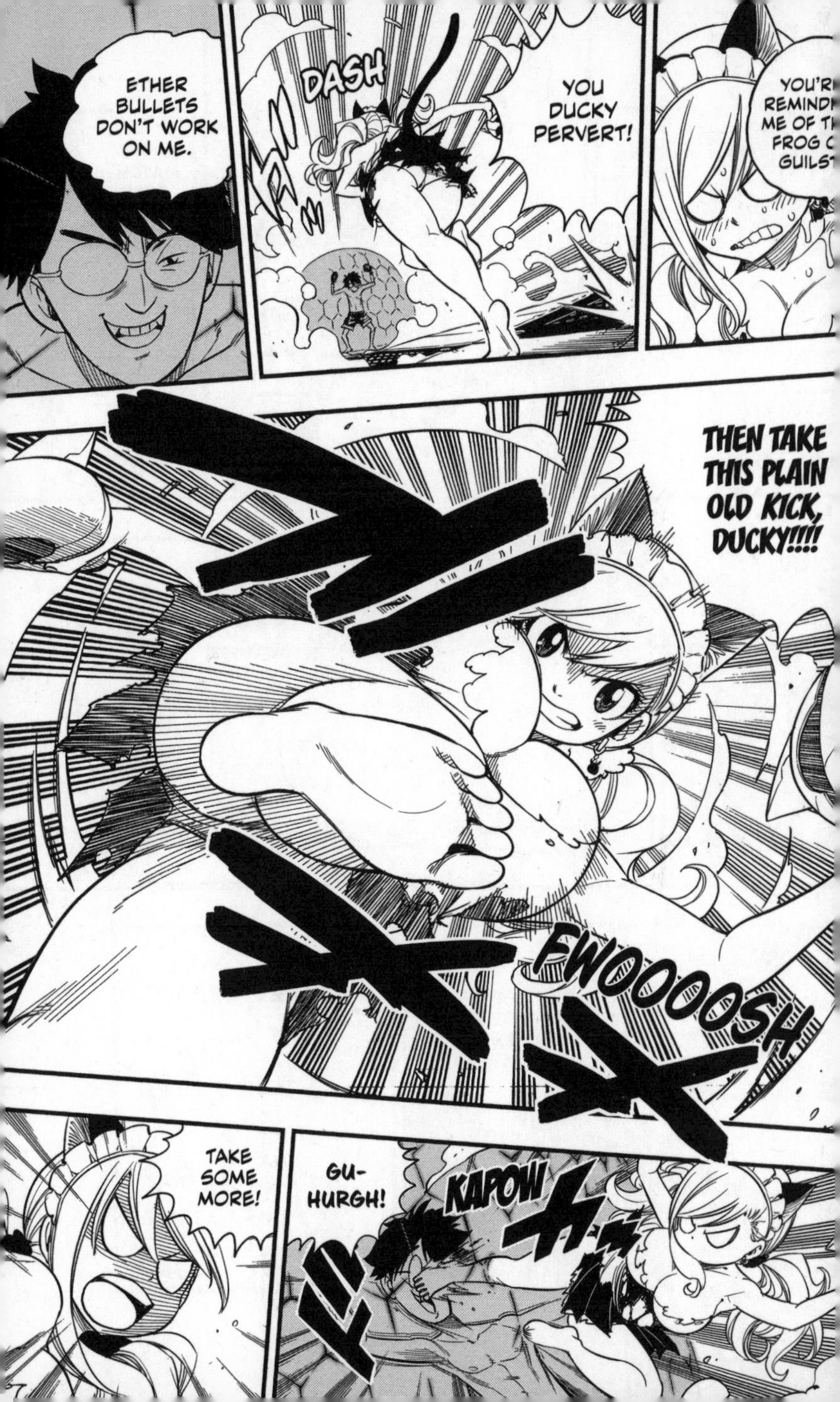
YOU'R REMIND ME OF T FROG G GUILS
DASH
YOU DUCKY PERVERT!
ETHER BULLETS DON'T WORK ON ME.
THEN TAKE THIS PLAIN OLD KICK, DUCKY!!!!
FWOOOOSH
GU-HURGH!
KAPOW
TAKE SOME MORE!

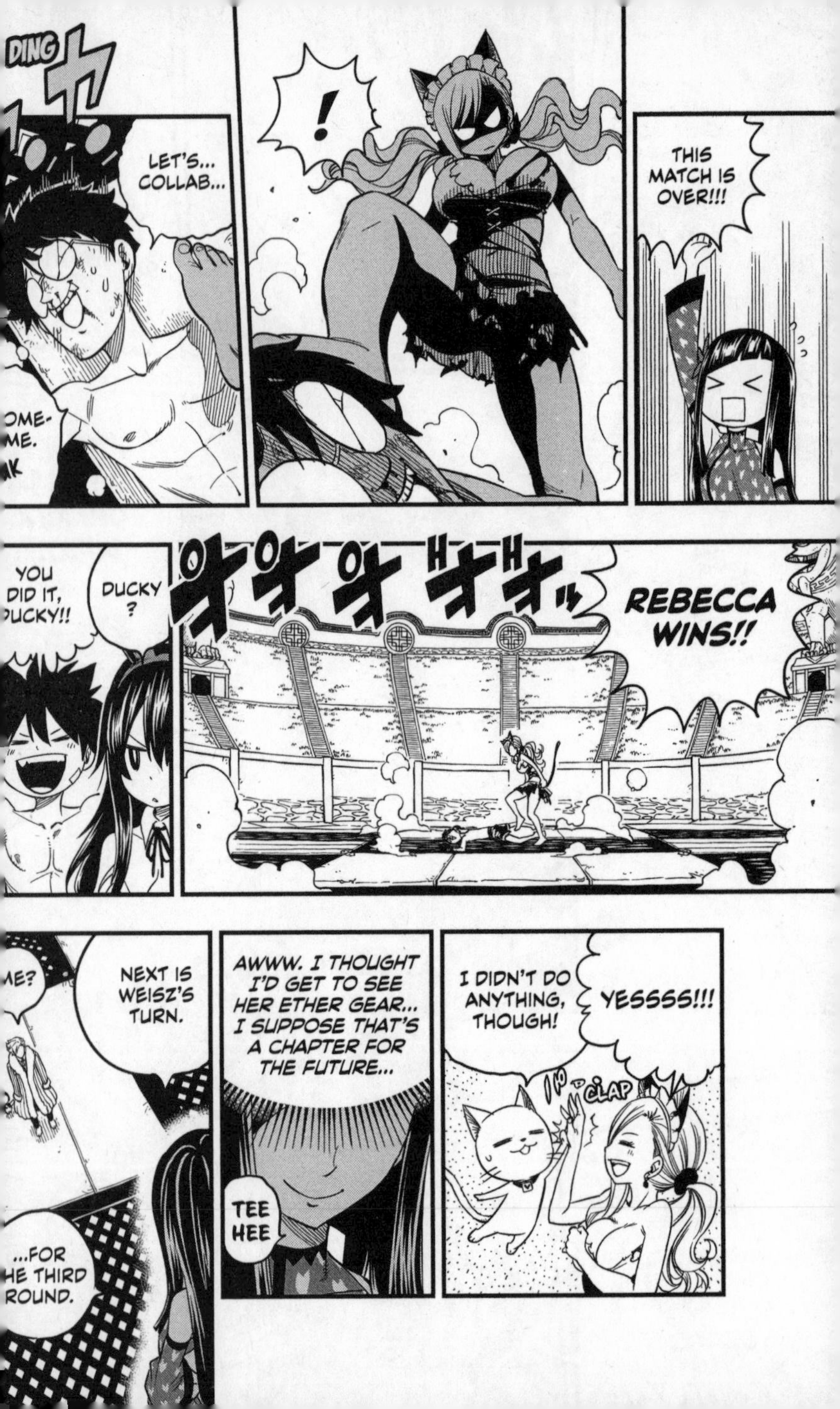
THIS MATCH IS OVER!!!
!
DING
LET'S... COLLAB...
OME-
ME.
AK
REBECCA WINS!!
DUCKY ?
YOU DID IT, UCKY!!
YESSSS!!!
I DIDN'T DO ANYTHING, THOUGH!
CLAP
AWWW. I THOUGHT I'D GET TO SEE HER ETHER GEAR... I SUPPOSE THAT'S A CHAPTER FOR THE FUTURE...
TEE HEE
ME?
NEXT IS WEISZ'S TURN.
...FOR HE THIRD ROUND.

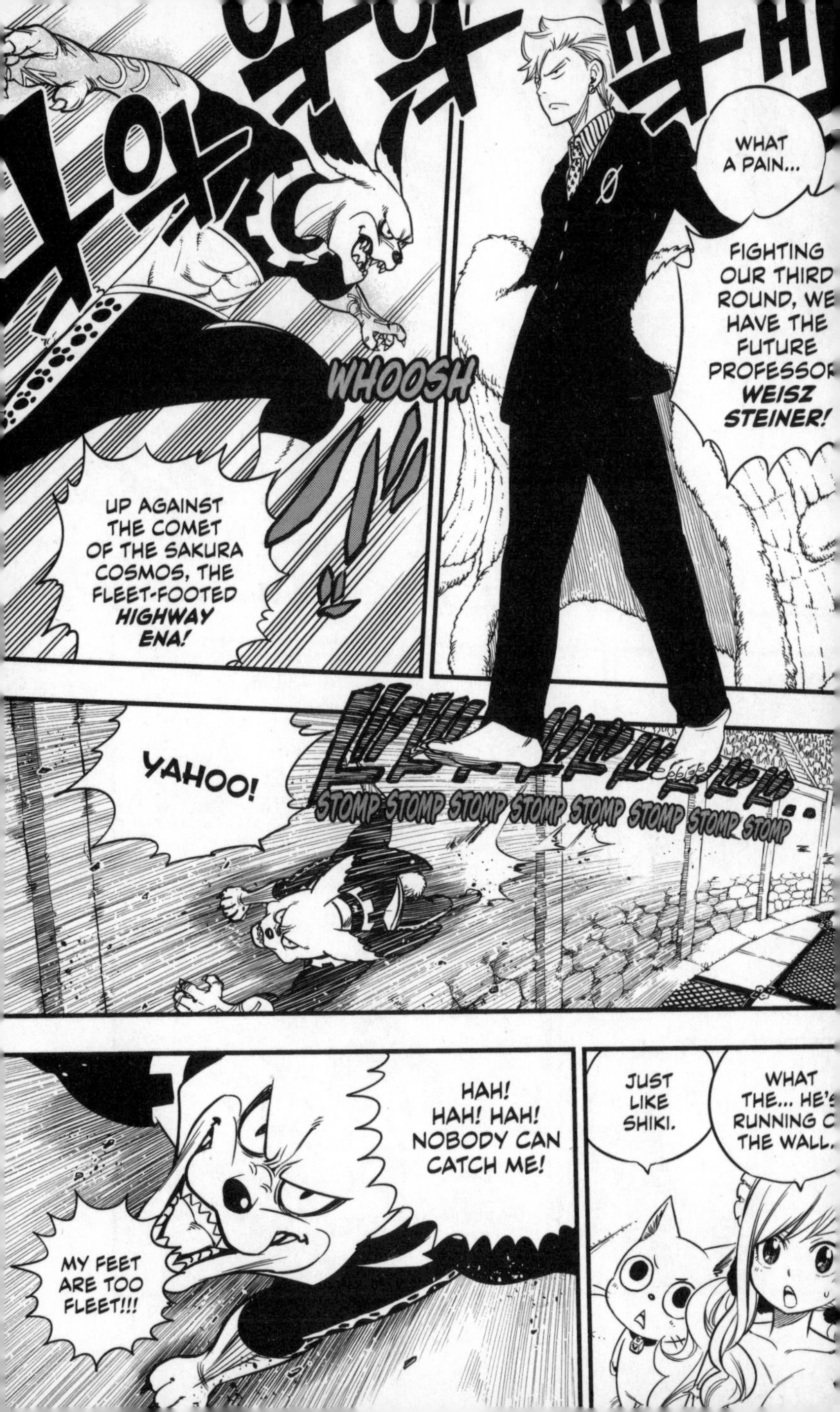
WHAT A PAIN...
FIGHTING OUR THIRD ROUND, WE HAVE THE FUTURE PROFESSOR WEISZ STEINER!
WHOOSH
UP AGAINST THE COMET OF THE SAKURA COSMOS, THE FLEET-FOOTED HIGHWAY ENA!
YAHOO!
STOMP STOMP STOMP STOMP STOMP STOMP STOMP STOMP
WHAT THE... HE'S RUNNING O THE WALL.
JUST LIKE SHIKI.
HAH! HAH! HAH! NOBODY CAN CATCH ME!
MY FEET ARE TOO FLEET!!!

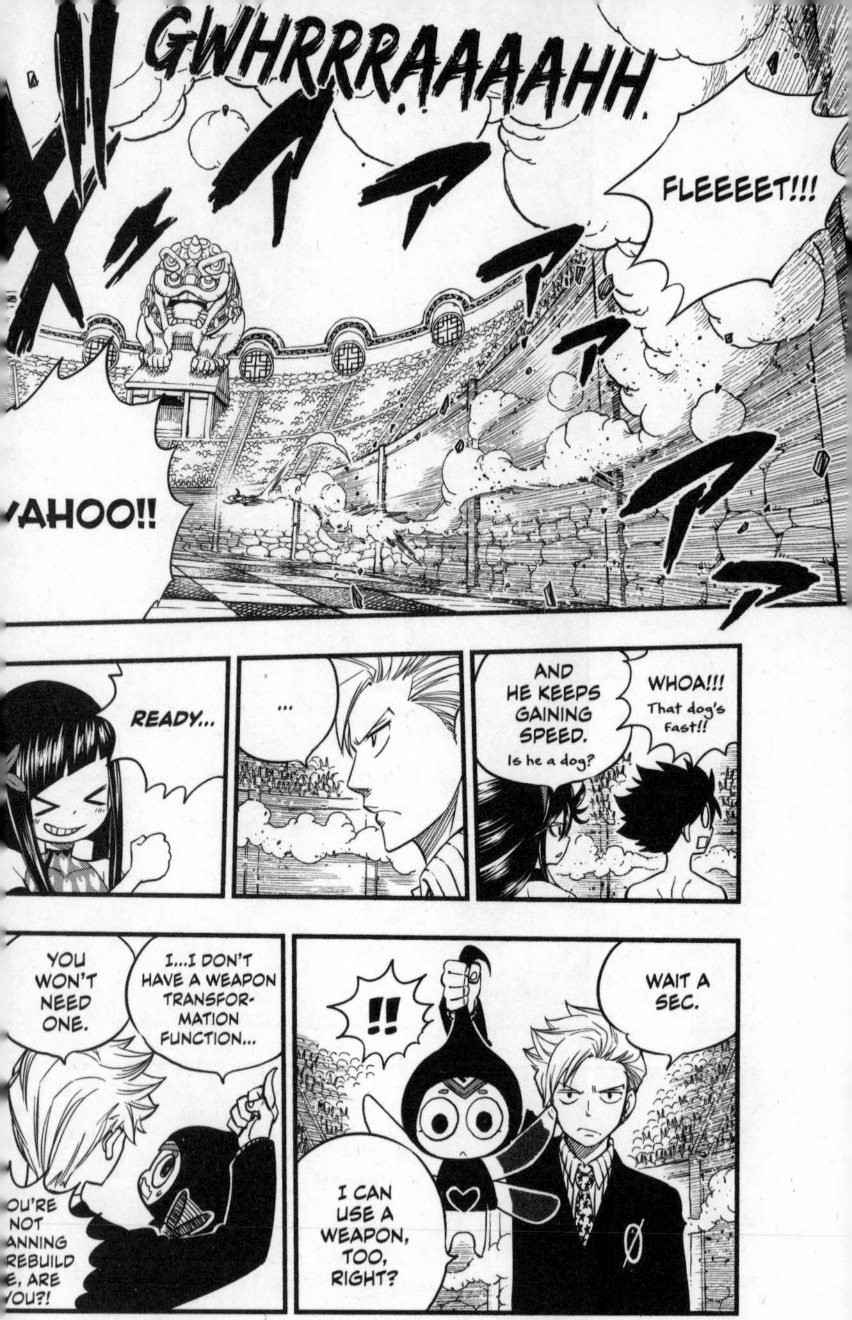

GWHRRRAAAAHH
FLEEEEET!!!
AHOO!!
WHOA!!! That dog's fast!!
AND HE KEEPS GAINING SPEED. Is he a dog?
...
READY...
WAIT A SEC.
!!
I CAN USE A WEAPON, TOO, RIGHT?
I...I DON'T HAVE A WEAPON TRANSFORMATION FUNCTION...
YOU WON'T NEED ONE.
OU'RE NOT ANNING REBUILD E, ARE YOU?!

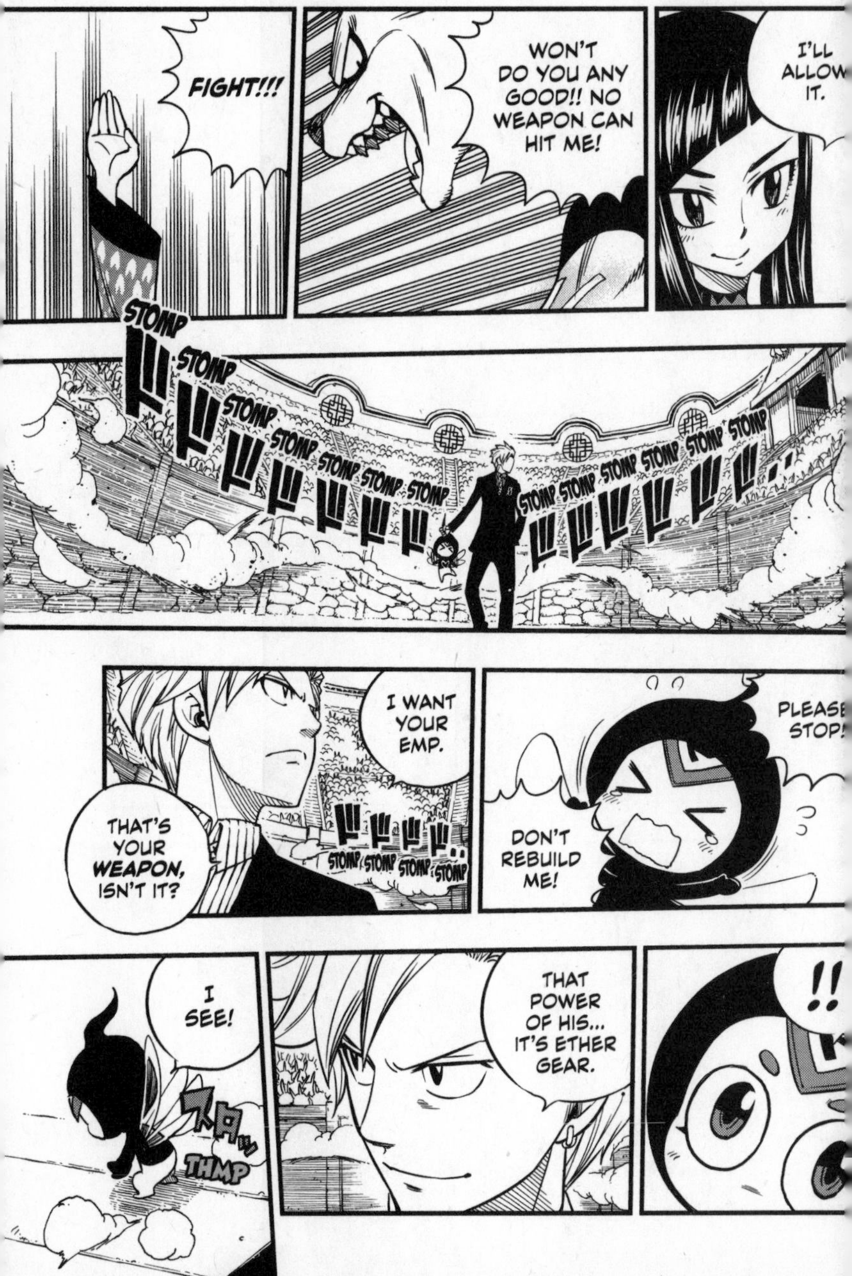
I'LL ALLOW IT.
WON'T DO YOU ANY GOOD!! NO WEAPON CAN HIT ME!
FIGHT!!!
STOMP STOMP STOMP STOMP STOMP STOMP STOMP
STOMP STOMP STOMP STOMP STOMP STOMP STOMP
PLEASE STOP!
DON'T REBUILD ME!
I WANT YOUR EMP.
THAT'S YOUR WEAPON, ISN'T IT?
STOMP STOMP STOMP STOMP
!!
THAT POWER OF HIS... IT'S ETHER GEAR.
I SEE!
THMP

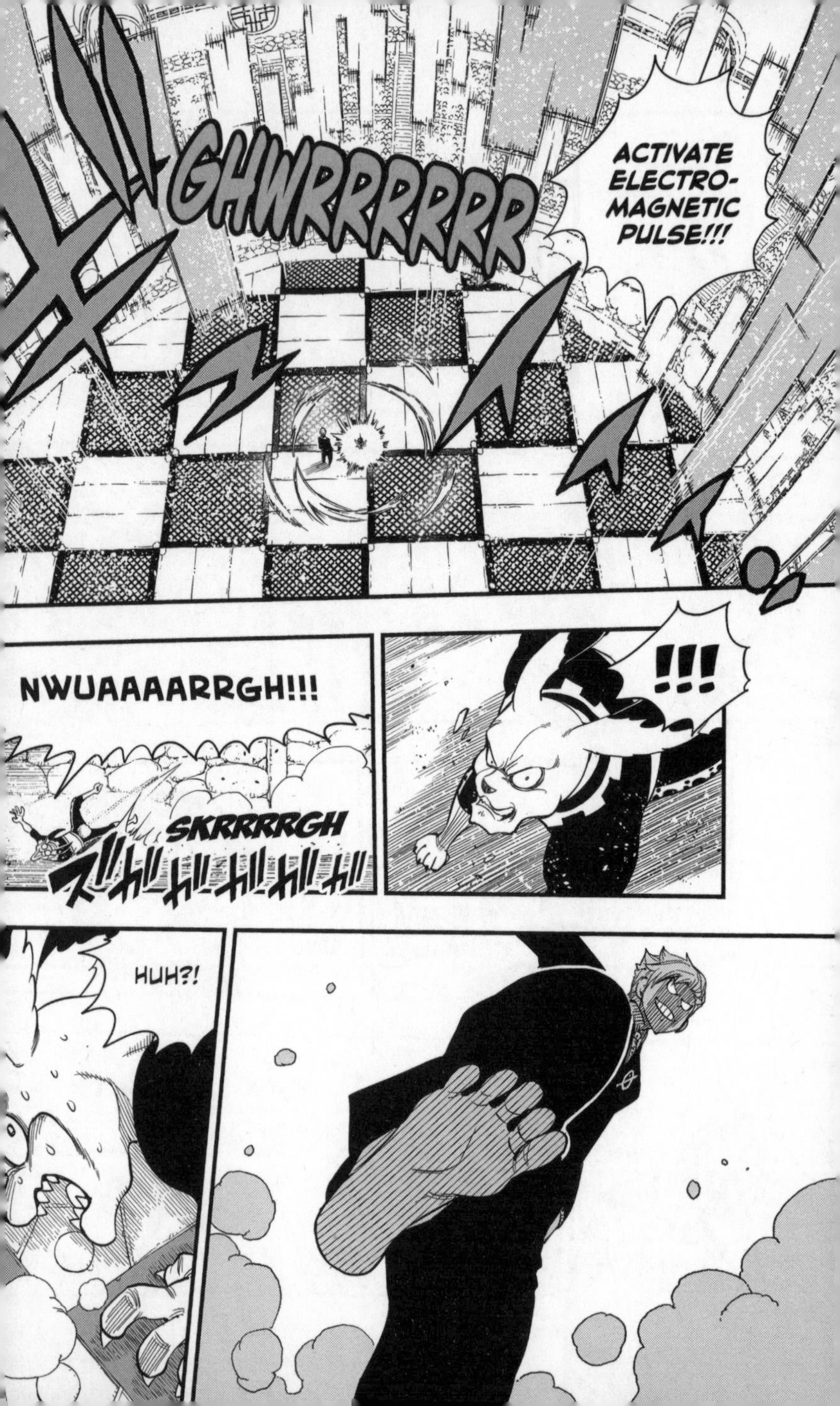
ACTIVATE ELECTRO-MAGNETIC PULSE!!!
GHWRRRRRRR
!!!
NWUAAAARRGH!!!
SKRRRRGH
ズガガガガガ
HUH?!

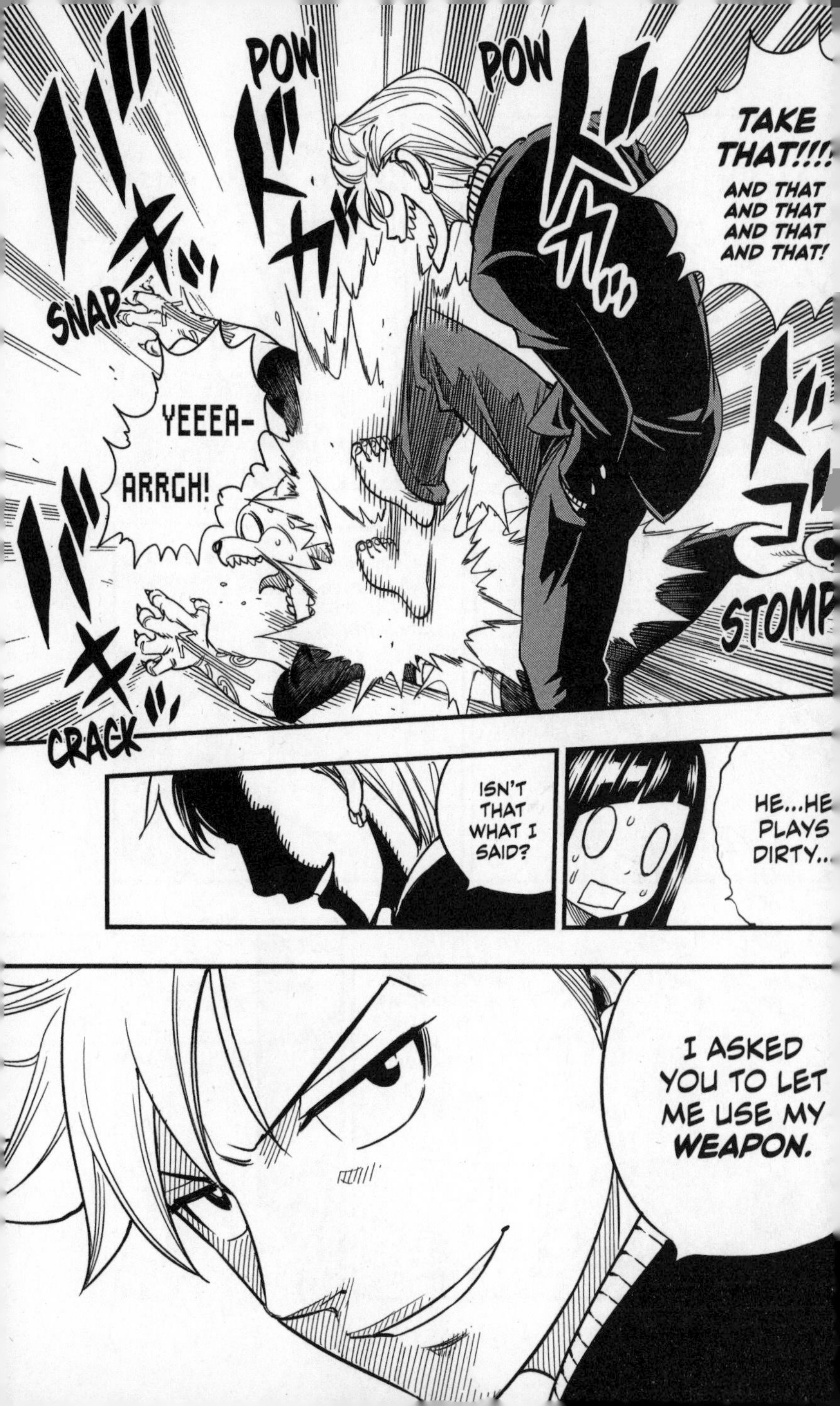

TAKE THAT!!!!
AND THAT AND THAT AND THAT AND THAT!
POW
POW
SNAP
YEEEA- ARRGH!
STOMP
CRACK
HE...HE PLAYS DIRTY...
ISN'T THAT WHAT I SAID?
I ASKED YOU TO LET ME USE MY **WEAPON.**

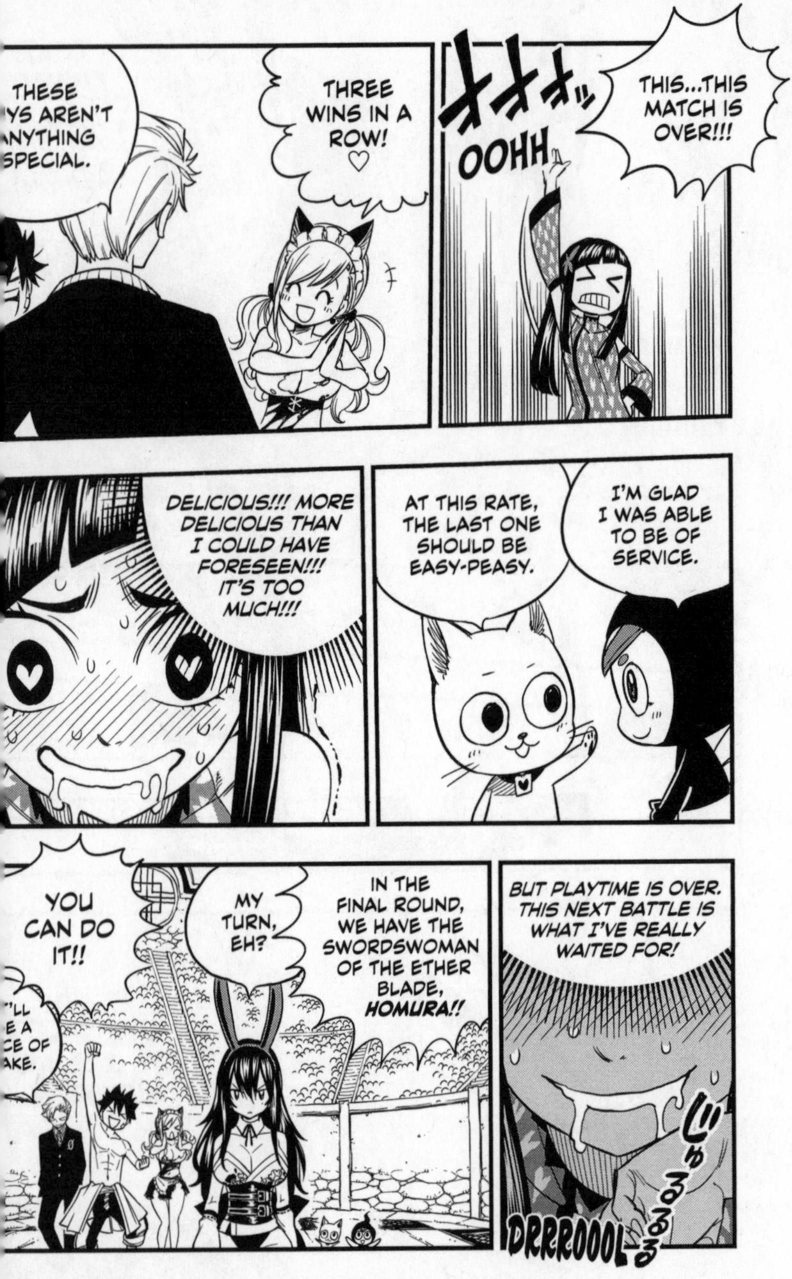
OOHH
THIS...THIS MATCH IS OVER!!!
THREE WINS IN A ROW! ♡
THESE
YS AREN'T
NYTHING
SPECIAL.
I'M GLAD I WAS ABLE TO BE OF SERVICE.
AT THIS RATE, THE LAST ONE SHOULD BE EASY-PEASY.
DELICIOUS!!! MORE DELICIOUS THAN I COULD HAVE FORESEEN!!! IT'S TOO MUCH!!!
BUT PLAYTIME IS OVER. THIS NEXT BATTLE IS WHAT I'VE REALLY WAITED FOR!
DRRROOOL
IN THE FINAL ROUND, WE HAVE THE SWORDSWOMAN OF THE ETHER BLADE, HOMURA!!
MY TURN, EH?
YOU CAN DO IT!!
'LL
E A
CE OF
AKE.

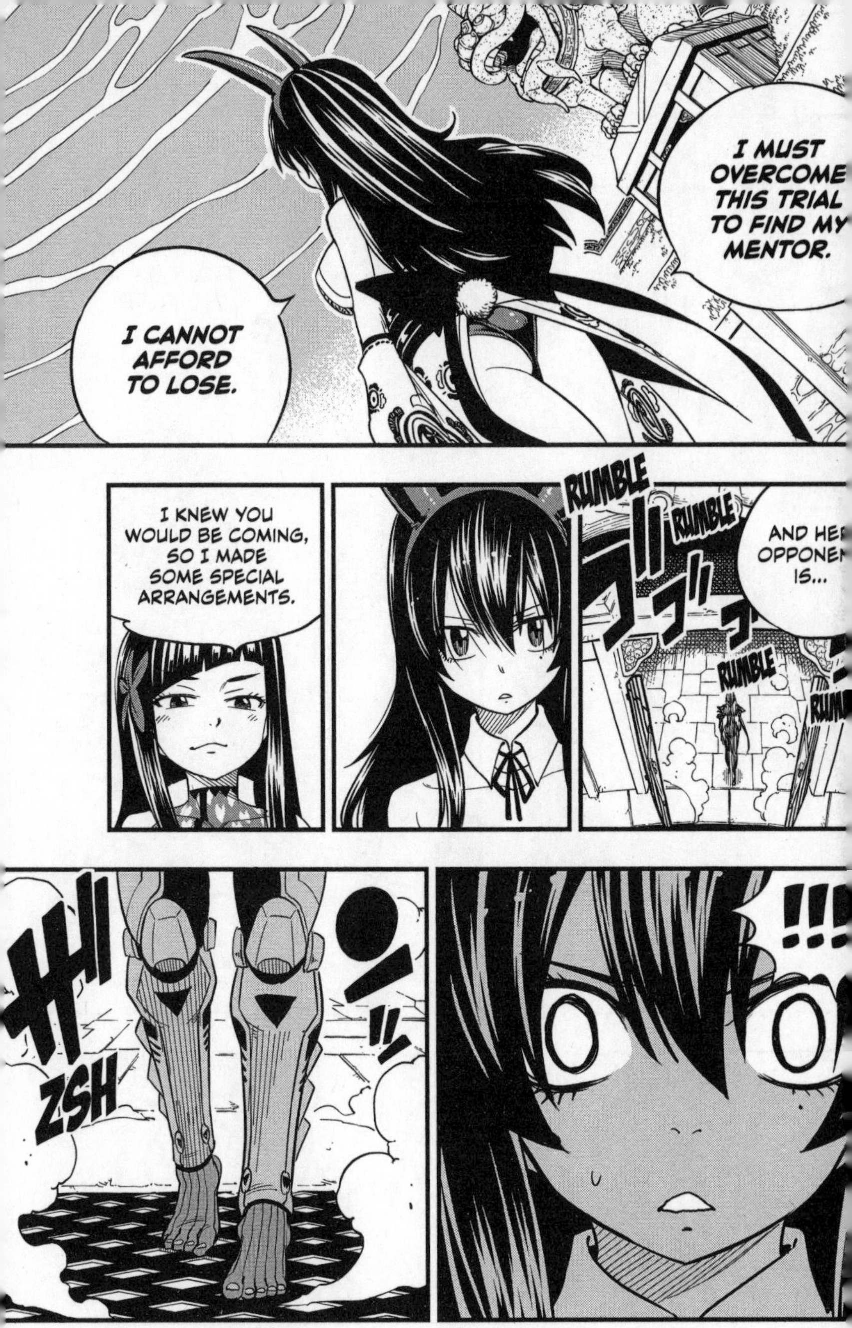
I MUST OVERCOME THIS TRIAL TO FIND MY MENTOR.
I CANNOT AFFORD TO LOSE.
RUMBLE
RUMBLE
AND HE
OPPONE
IS...
RUMBLE
I KNEW YOU WOULD BE COMING, SO I MADE SOME SPECIAL ARRANGEMENTS.
!!!
!!
ZSH

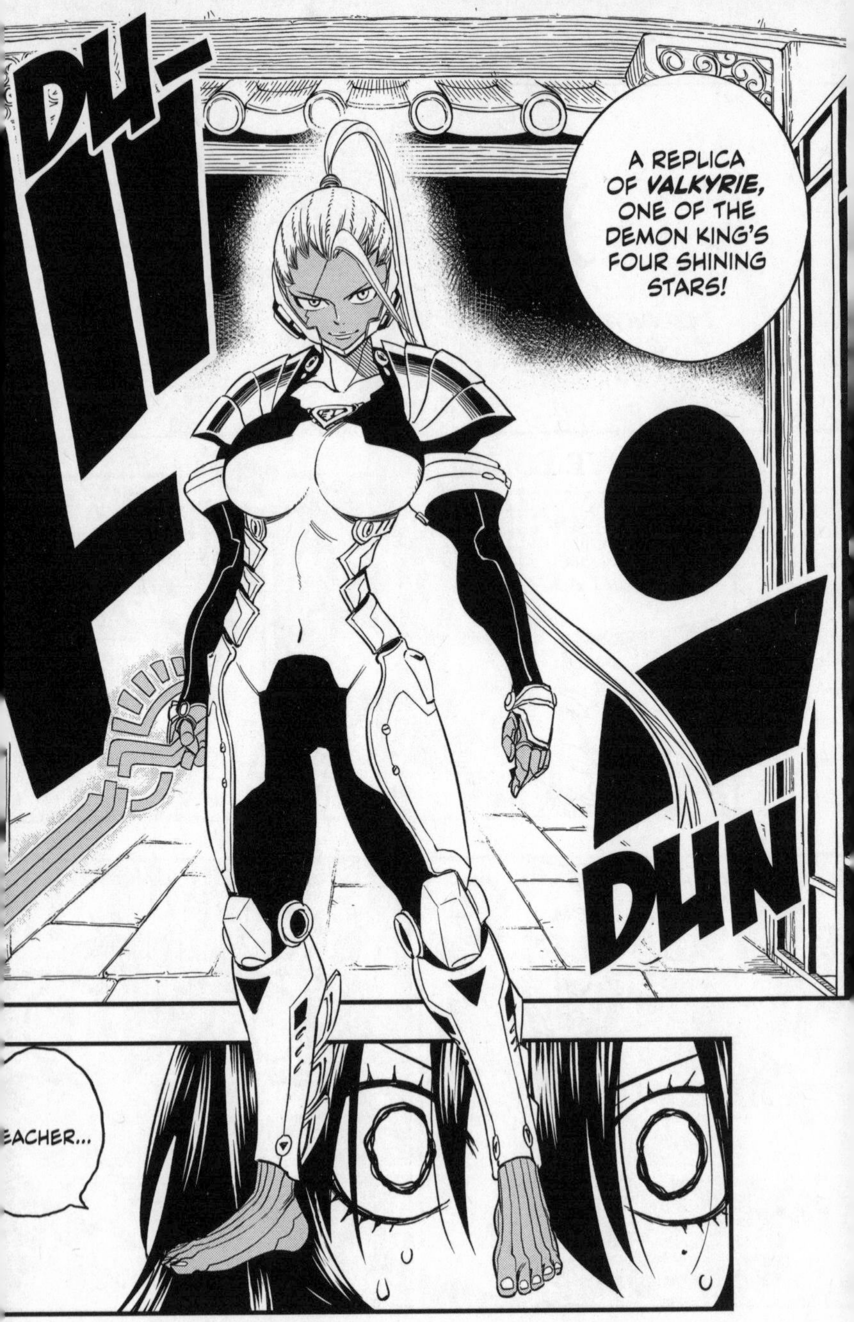
A REPLICA OF VALKYRIE, ONE OF THE DEMON KING'S FOUR SHINING STARS!
DUH-
DUN
EACHER...

EDENSZERO

CHAPTER 47: WORDS WILL GIVE YOU STRENGTH

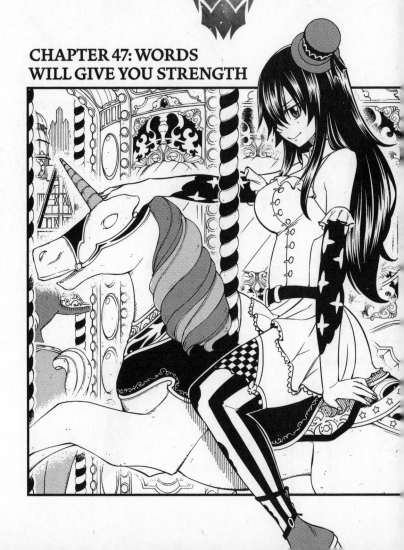

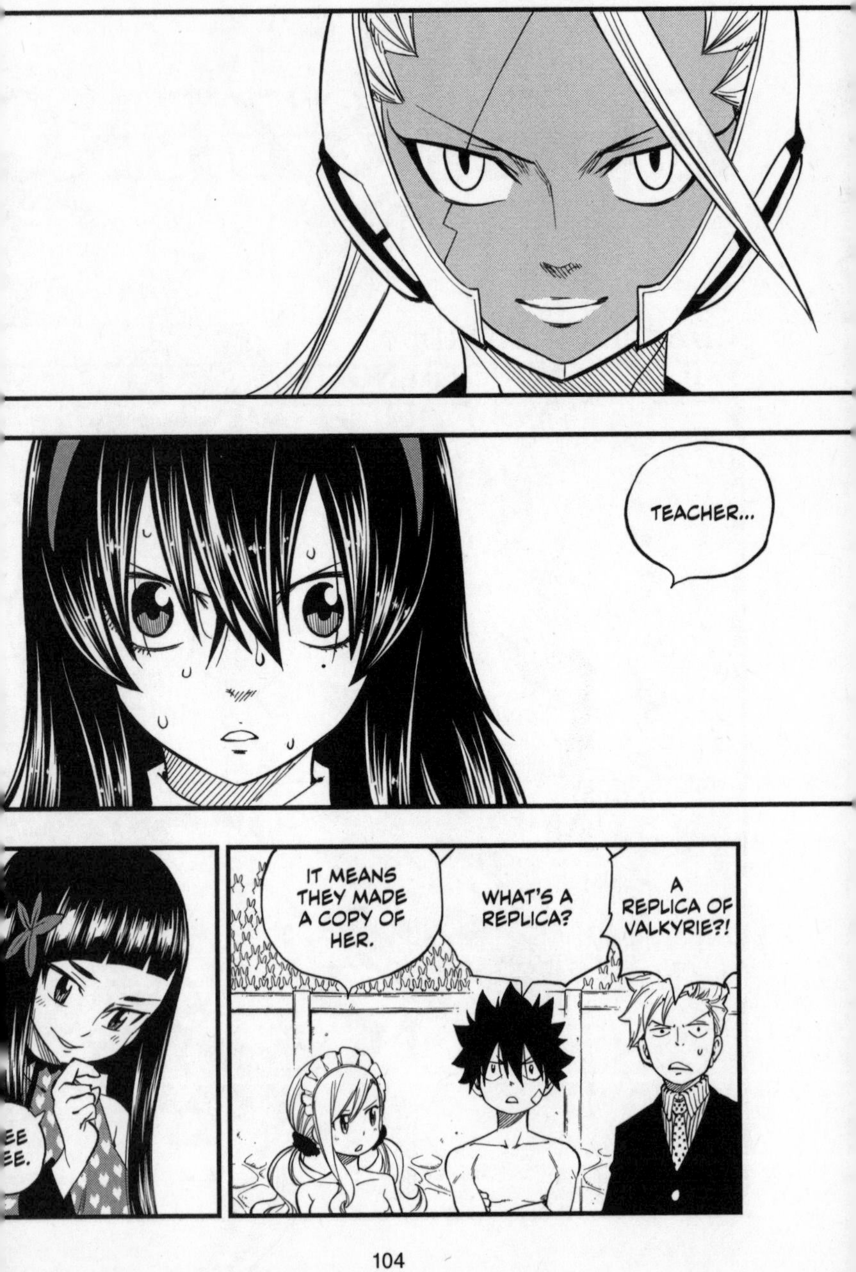
TEACHER...
A REPLICA OF VALKYRIE?!
WHAT'S A REPLICA?
IT MEANS THEY MADE A COPY OF HER.

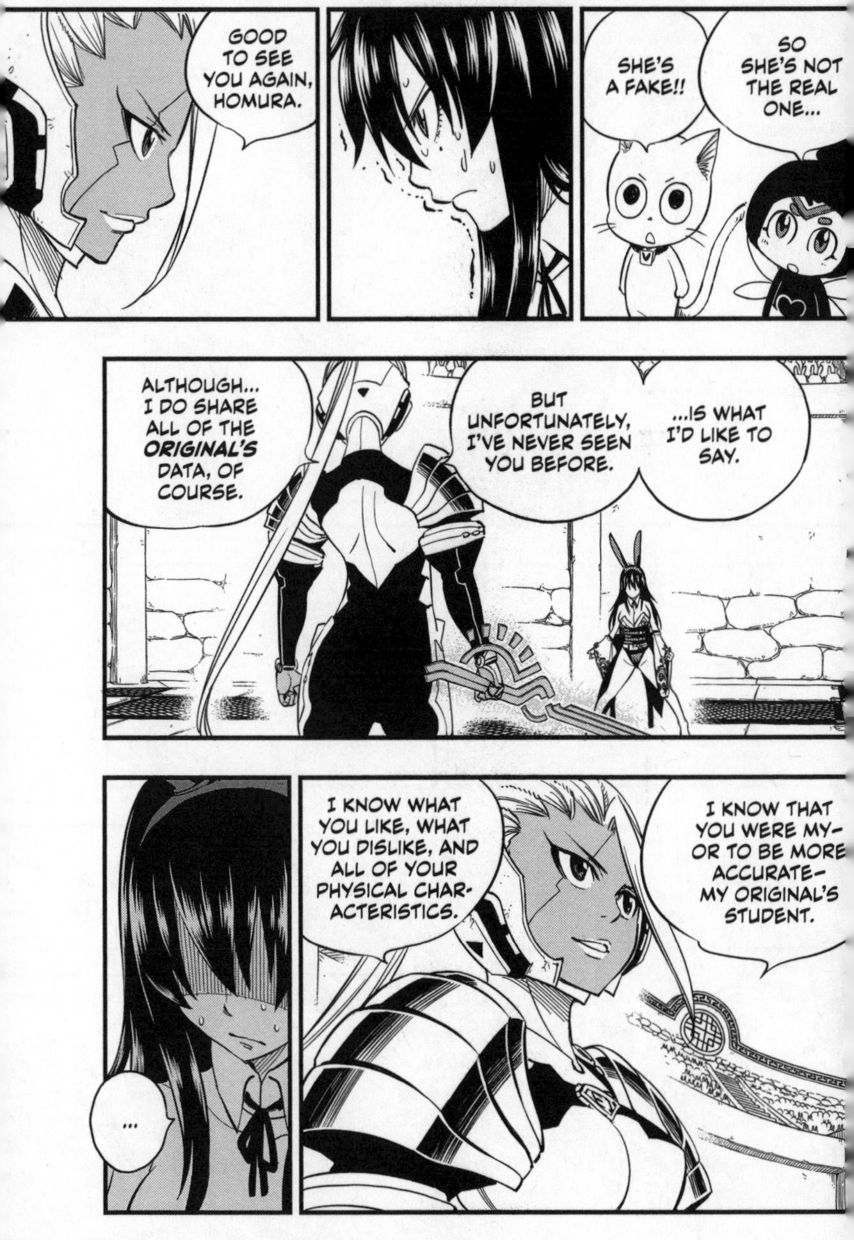
SO SHE'S NOT THE REAL ONE...
SHE'S A FAKE!!
GOOD TO SEE YOU AGAIN, HOMURA.
BUT UNFORTUNATELY, I'VE NEVER SEEN YOU BEFORE.
...IS WHAT I'D LIKE TO SAY.
ALTHOUGH... I DO SHARE ALL OF THE ***ORIGINAL'S*** DATA, OF COURSE.
I KNOW THAT YOU WERE MY— OR TO BE MORE ACCURATE— MY ORIGINAL'S STUDENT.
I KNOW WHAT YOU LIKE, WHAT YOU DISLIKE, AND ALL OF YOUR PHYSICAL CHAR-ACTERISTICS.
...

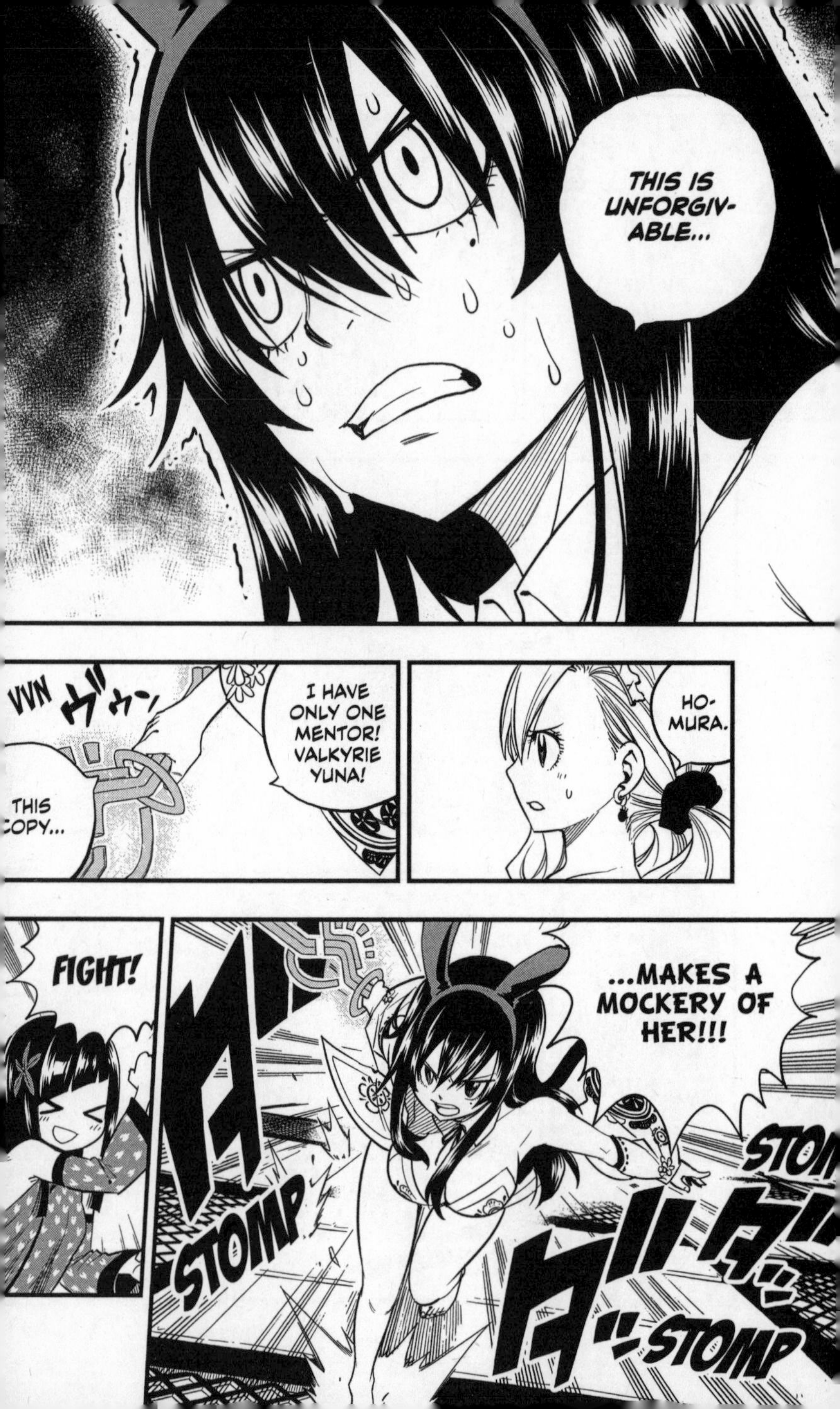
THIS IS UNFORGIV-ABLE...
HO-MURA.
I HAVE ONLY ONE MENTOR! VALKYRIE YUNA!
VVN
THIS COPY...
...MAKES A MOCKERY OF HER!!!
STOM
STOMP
STOMP
FIGHT!

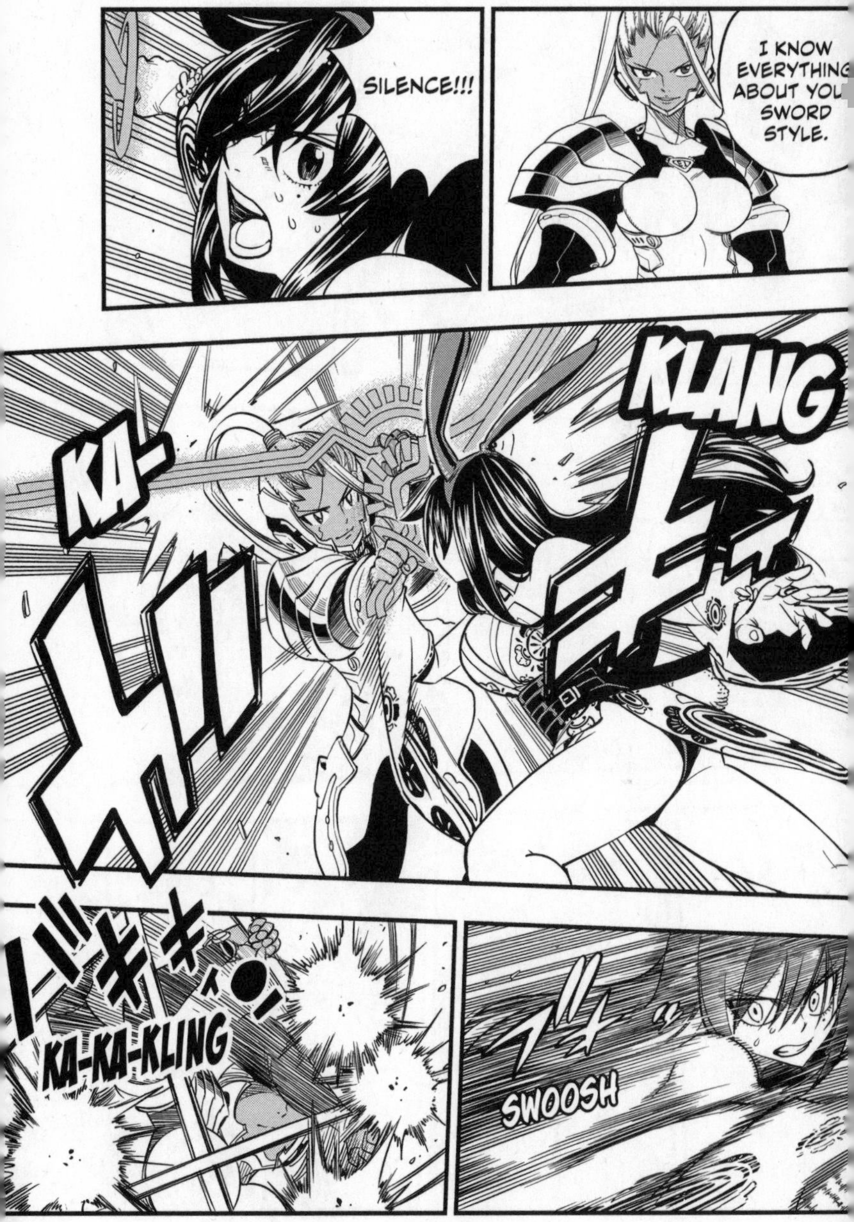
I KNOW EVERYTHING ABOUT YOU SWORD STYLE.
SILENCE!!!
KLANG
KA-
SWOOSH
KA-KA-KLING

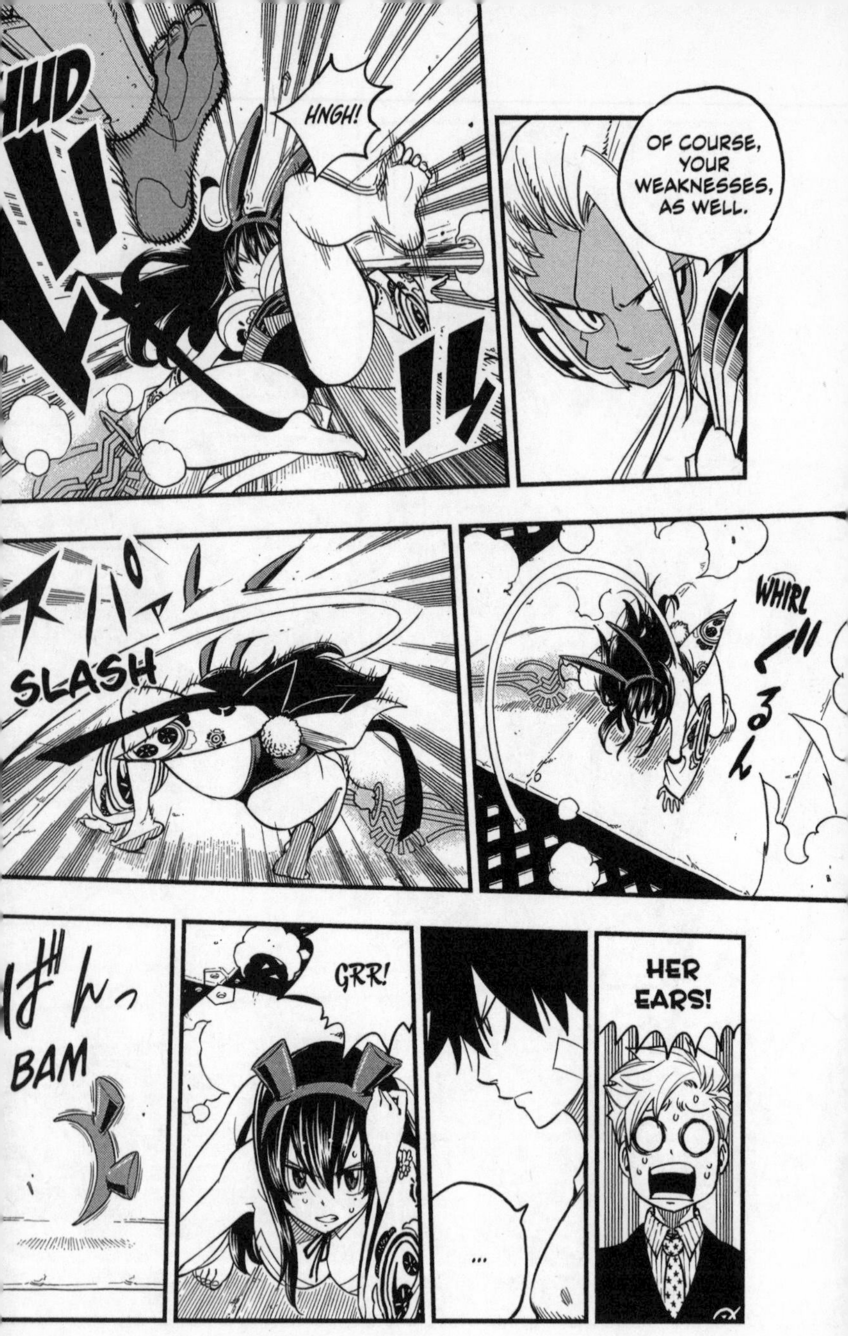
OF COURSE, YOUR WEAKNESSES, AS WELL.
HNGH!
WHIRL
SLASH
HER EARS!
...
GRR!
ばんっ
BAM

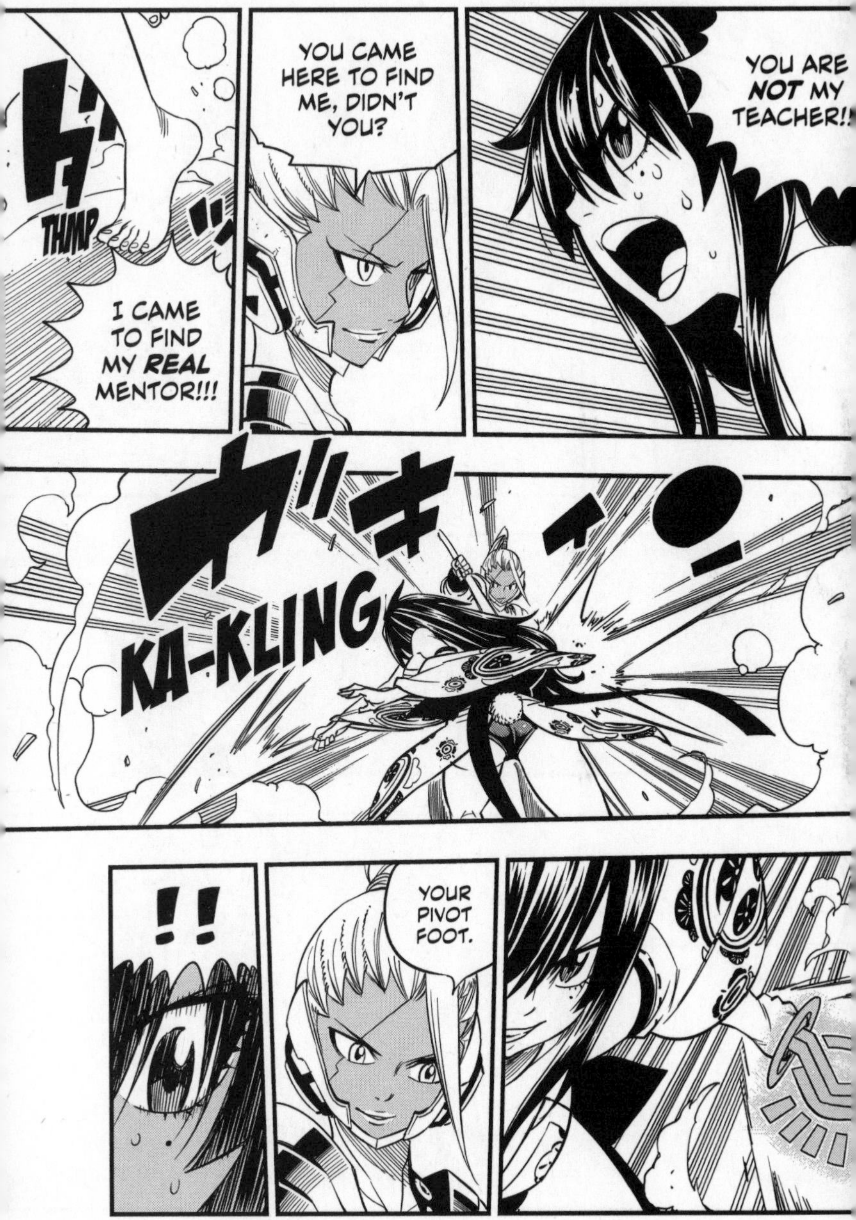
YOU ARE NOT MY TEACHER!!
YOU CAME HERE TO FIND ME, DIDN'T YOU?
THMP
I CAME TO FIND MY REAL MENTOR!!!
KA-KLING
YOUR PIVOT FOOT.
!!

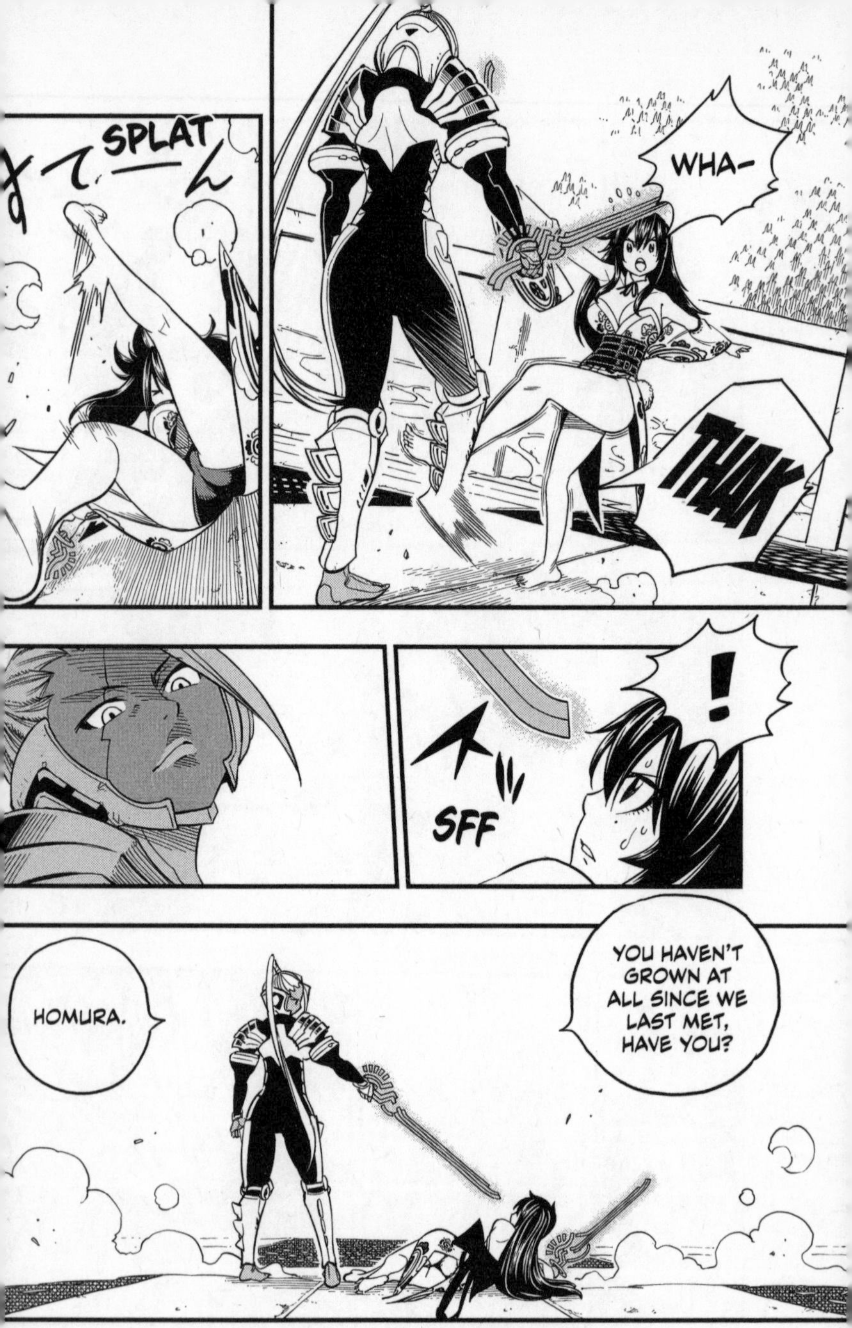
WHA-
THAK
すて
SPLAT
ん
!
SFF
YOU HAVEN'T GROWN AT ALL SINCE WE LAST MET, HAVE YOU?
HOMURA.

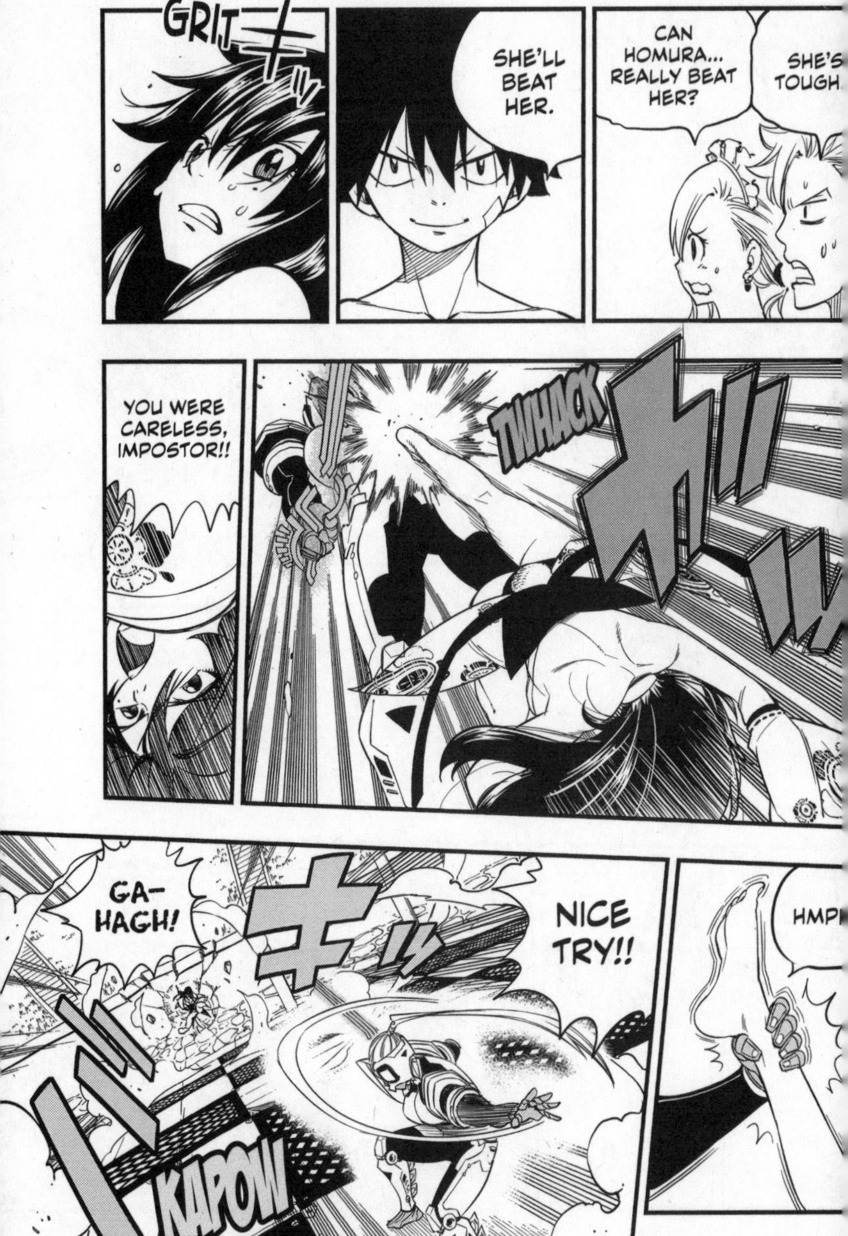
SHE'S TOUGH.
CAN HOMURA... REALLY BEAT HER?
SHE'LL BEAT HER.
GRIT
TWHACK
YOU WERE CARELESS, IMPOSTOR!!
HMP
NICE TRY!!
GA-HAGH!
KAPOW

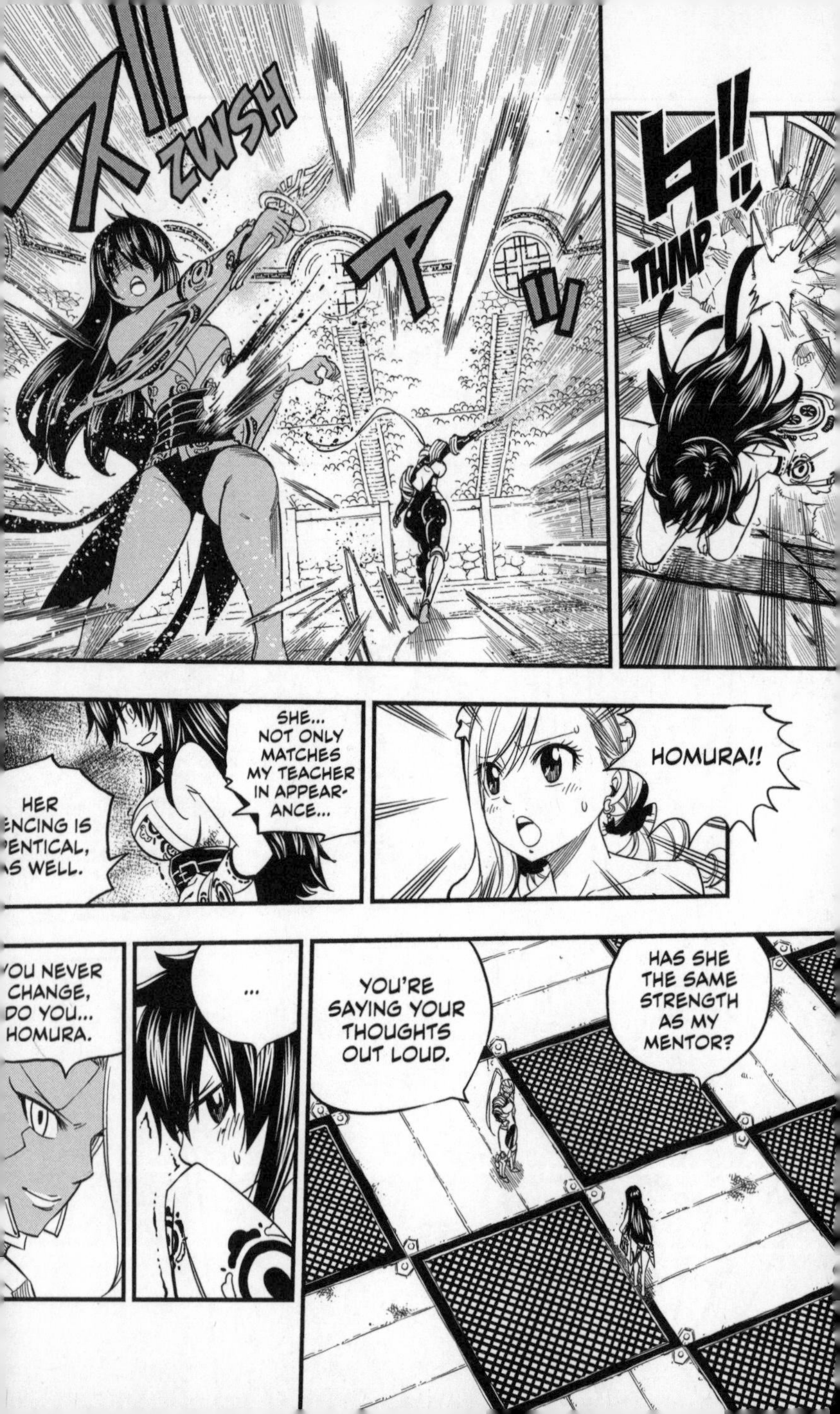
THMP
ZWSH
HOMURA!!
SHE... NOT ONLY MATCHES MY TEACHER IN APPEARANCE...
HER ENCING IS ENTICAL, S WELL.
HAS SHE THE SAME STRENGTH AS MY MENTOR?
YOU'RE SAYING YOUR THOUGHTS OUT LOUD.
...
OU NEVER CHANGE, DO YOU... HOMURA.

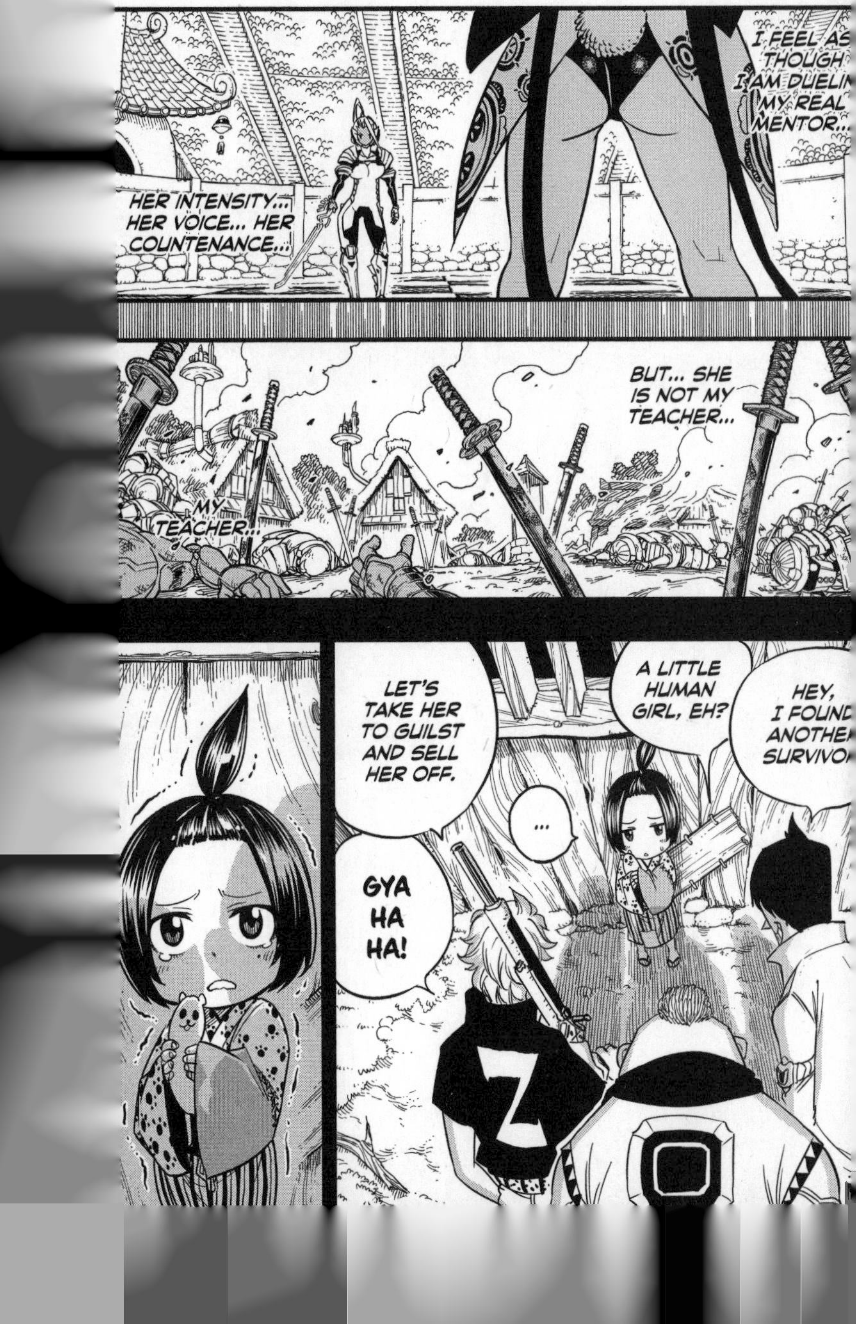

I FEEL AS THOUGH I AM DUELIN MY REAL MENTOR...
HER INTENSITY... HER VOICE... HER COUNTENANCE...
BUT... SHE IS NOT MY TEACHER...
MY TEACHER...
HEY, I FOUND ANOTHE SURVIVO
A LITTLE HUMAN GIRL, EH?
LET'S TAKE HER TO GUILST AND SELL HER OFF.
...
GYA HA HA!

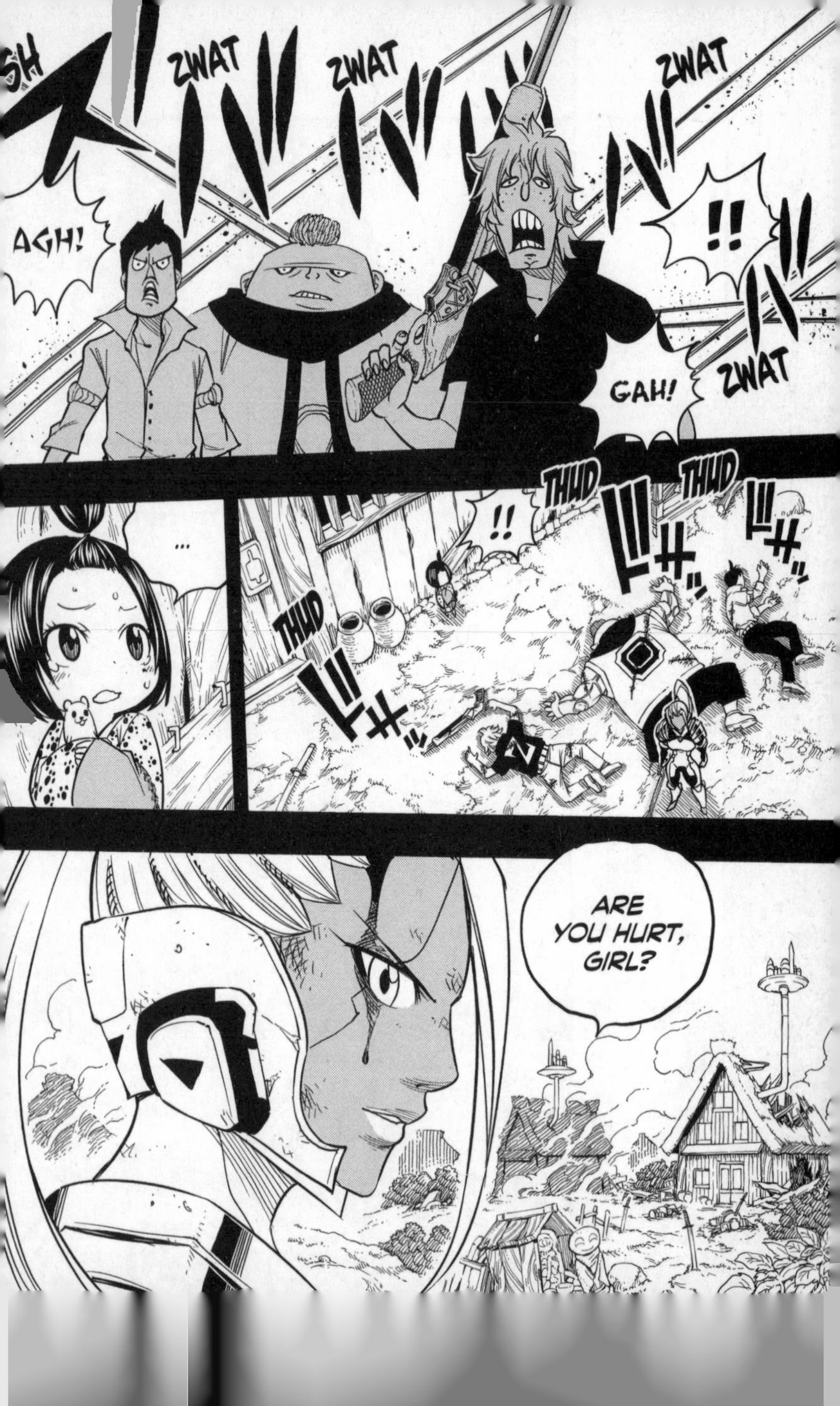

ZWAT
!!
ZWAT
GAH!
ZWAT
ZWAT
SH
AGH!
THUD
THUD
!!
THUD
...
ARE YOU HURT, GIRL?

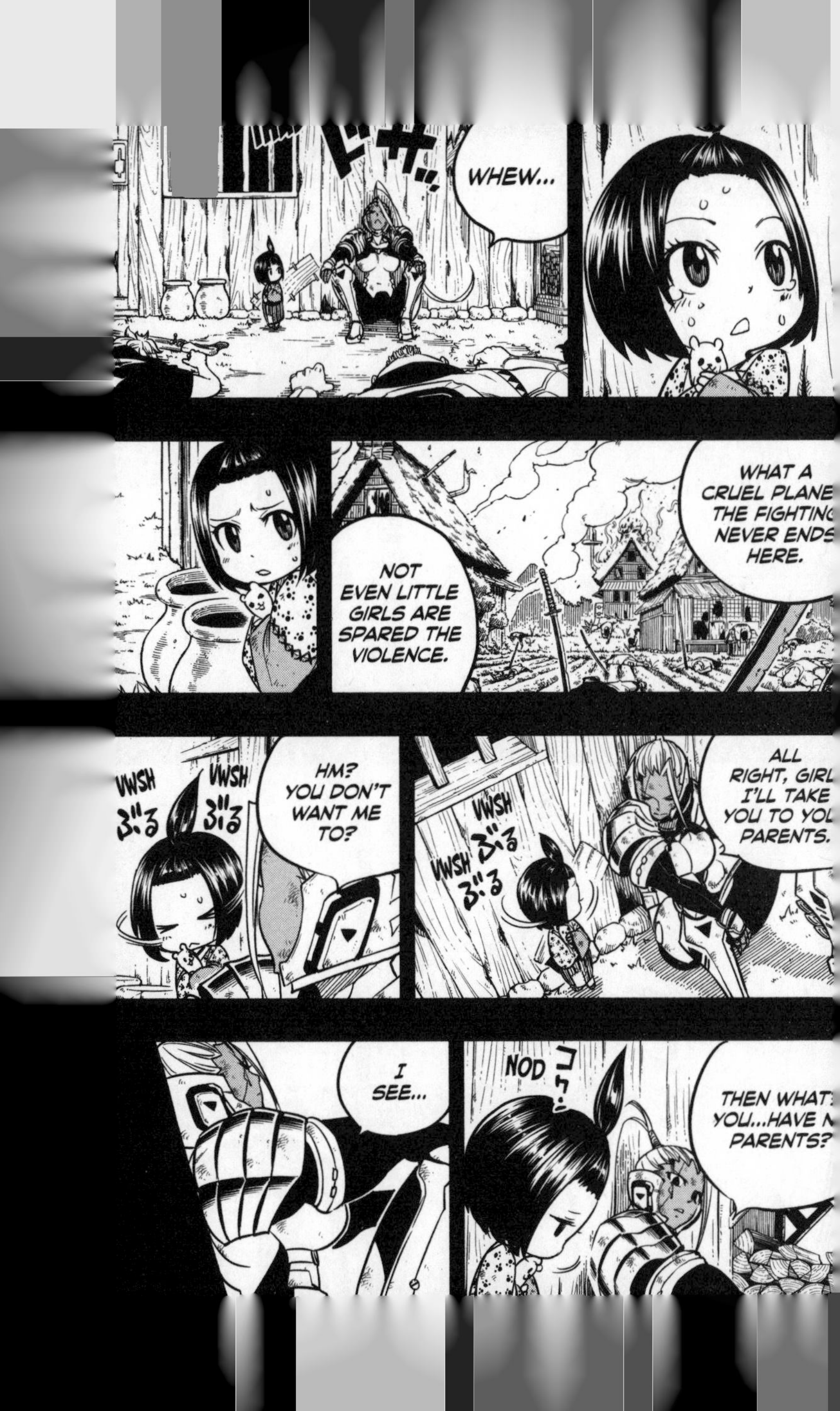
WHEW...
WHAT A CRUEL PLANE THE FIGHTIN NEVER ENDS HERE.
NOT EVEN LITTLE GIRLS ARE SPARED THE VIOLENCE.
ALL RIGHT, GIRL I'LL TAKE YOU TO YO PARENTS.
VWSH ぶる
VWSH ぶる
HM? YOU DON'T WANT ME TO?
VWSH ぶる
VWSH ぶる
THEN WHAT YOU...HAVE N PARENTS?
NOD コク
I SEE...

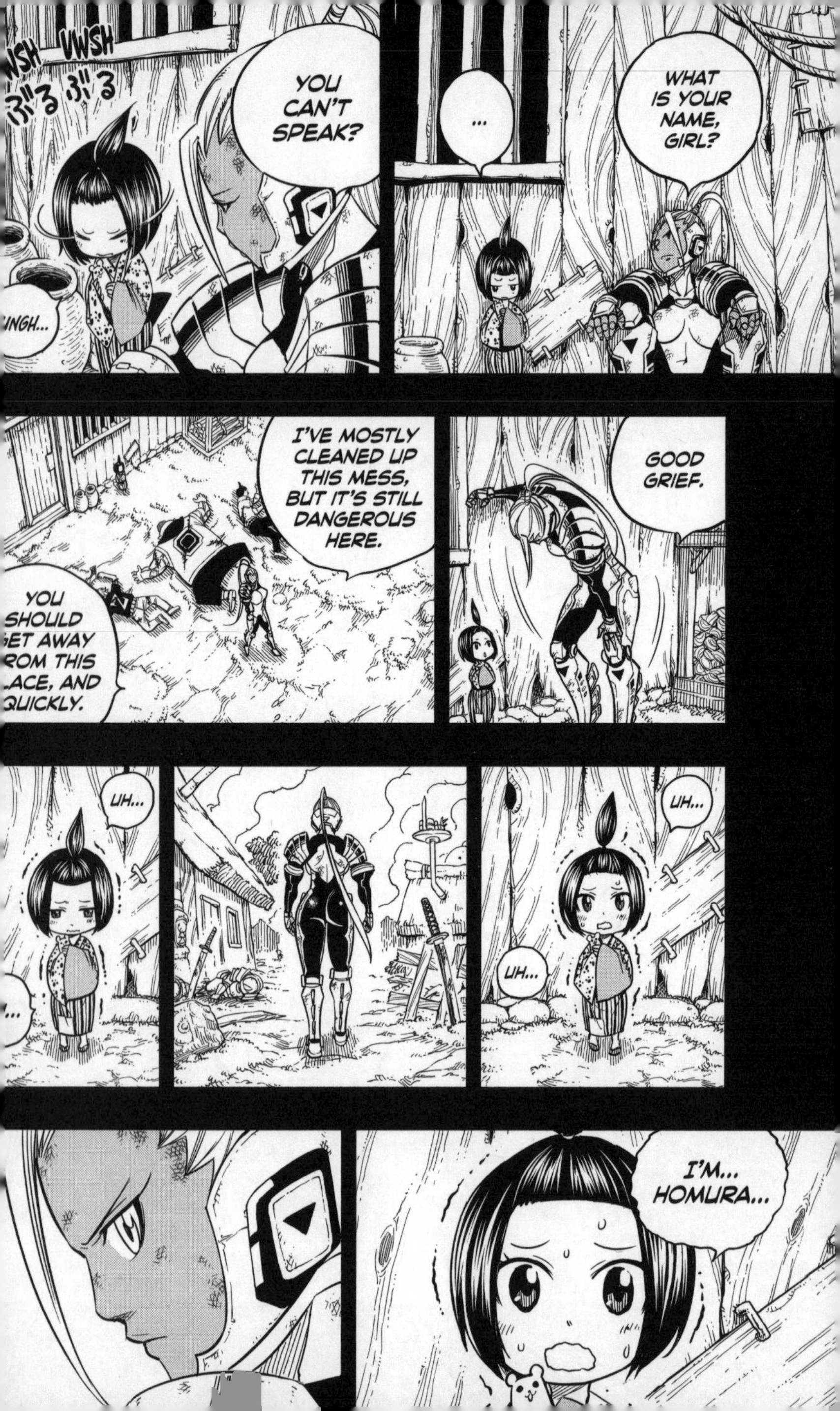
WHAT IS YOUR NAME, GIRL?
...
YOU CAN'T SPEAK?
WSH VWSH
ぶるぶる
NGH...
GOOD GRIEF.
I'VE MOSTLY CLEANED UP THIS MESS, BUT IT'S STILL DANGEROUS HERE.
YOU SHOULD ET AWAY ROM THIS LACE, AND QUICKLY.
UH...
UH...
UH...
...
I'M... HOMURA...

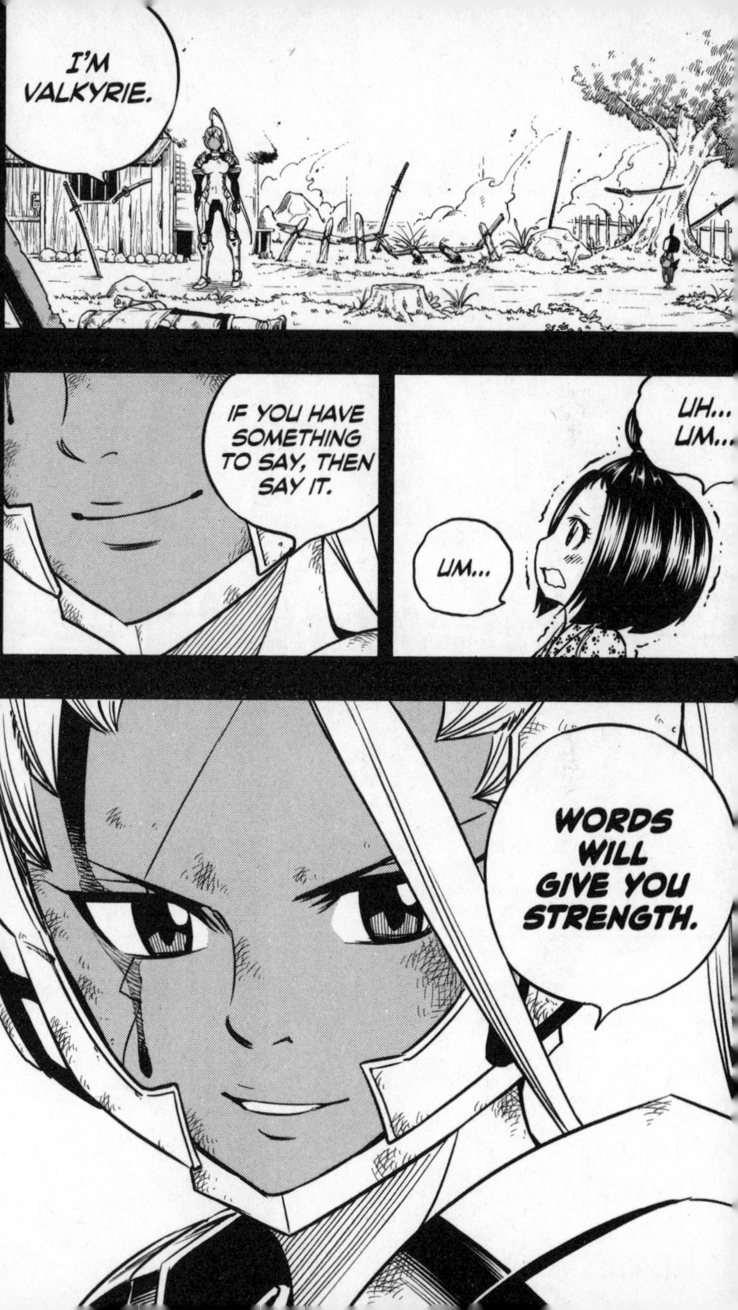
I'M VALKYRIE.
UH... UM...
UM...
IF YOU HAVE SOMETHING TO SAY, THEN SAY IT.
WORDS WILL GIVE YOU STRENGTH.

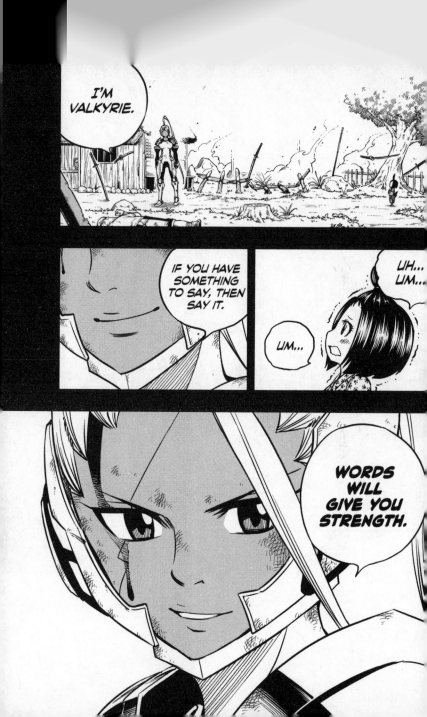

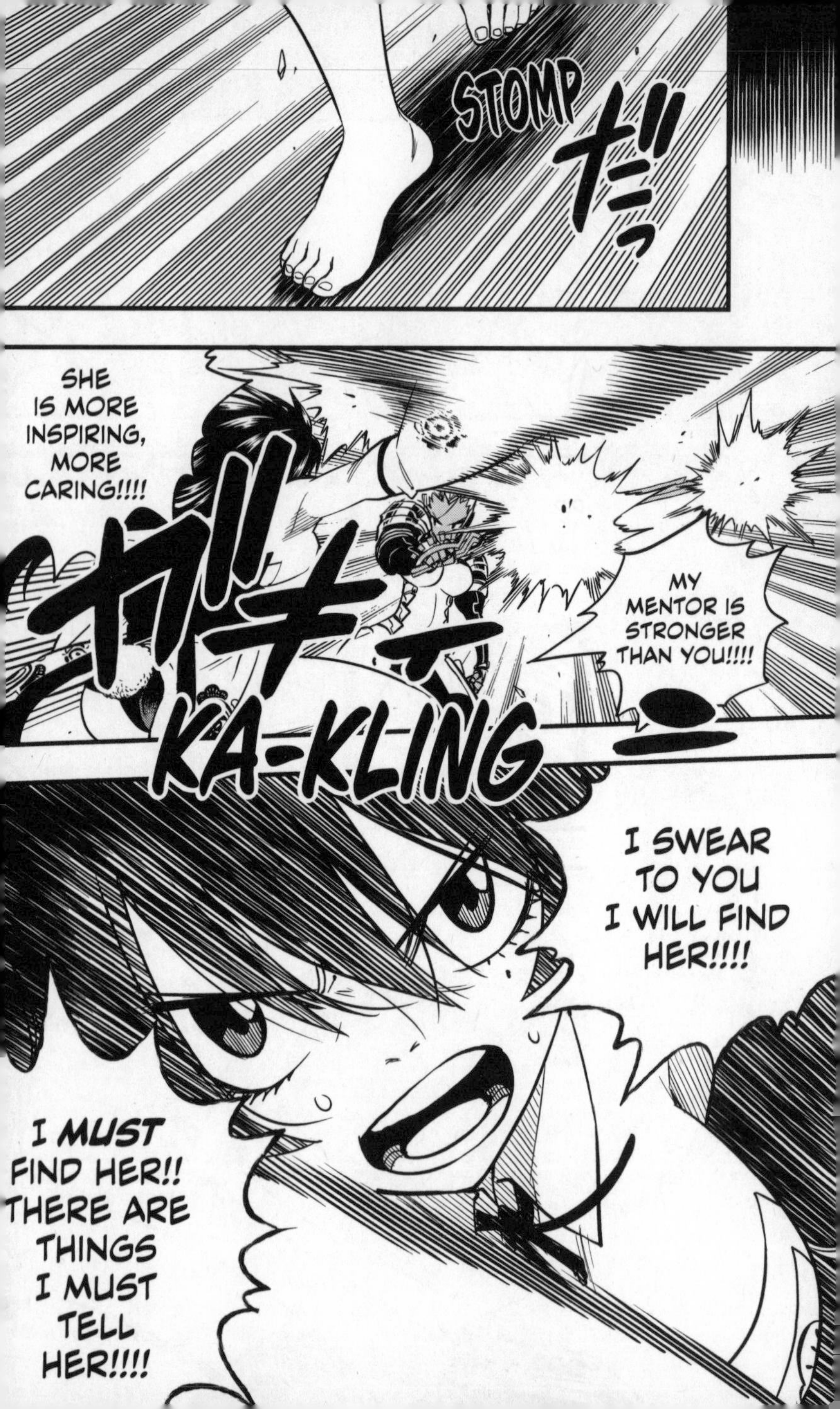

STOMP
ダッ
MY MENTOR IS STRONGER THAN YOU!!!!
SHE IS MORE INSPIRING, MORE CARING!!!!
ガキィ
KA-KLING
I SWEAR TO YOU I WILL FIND HER!!!!
I *MUST* FIND HER!! THERE ARE THINGS I MUST TELL HER!!!!

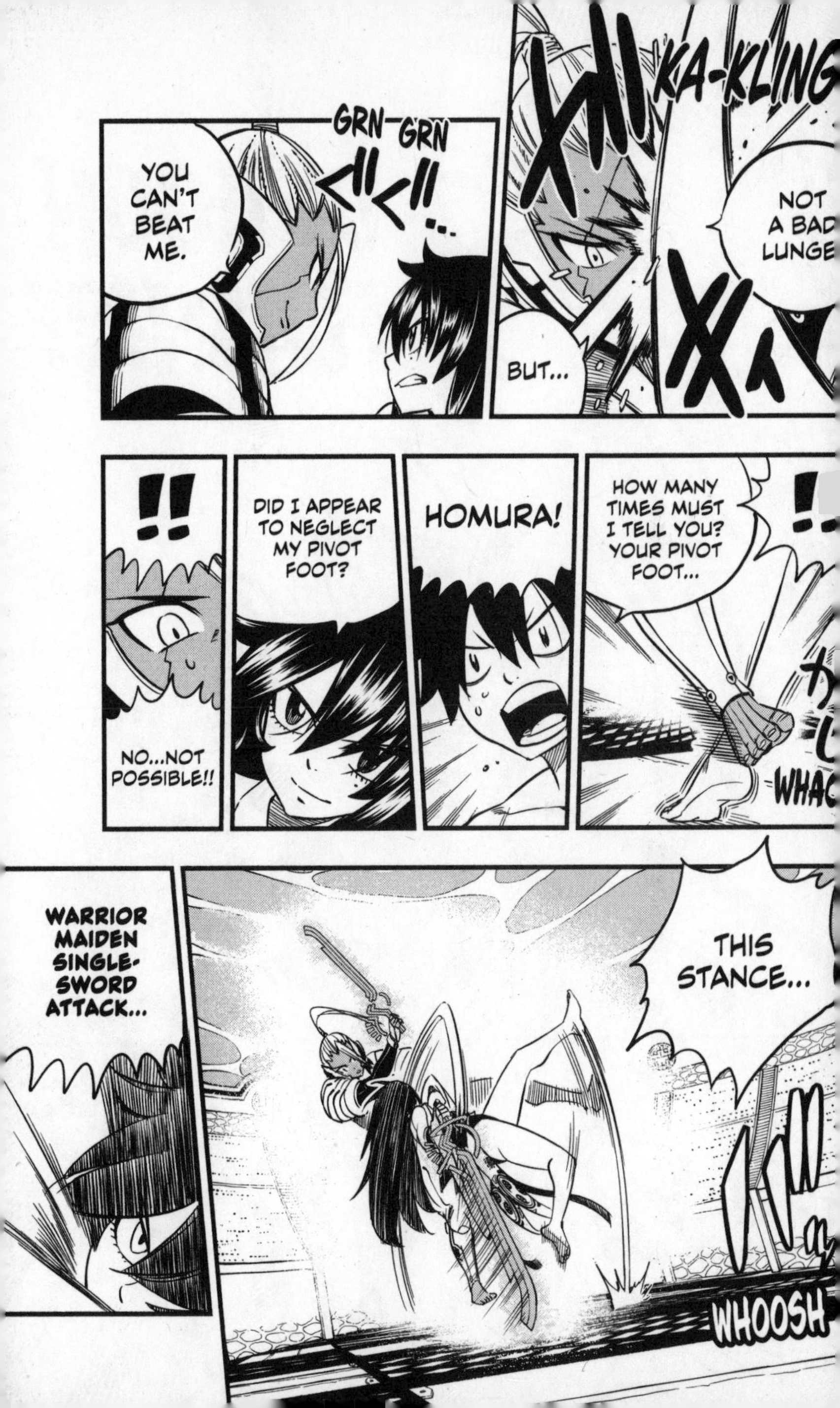
KA-KLING
NOT A BAD LUNGE
BUT...
GRN GRN
YOU CAN'T BEAT ME.
!!
HOW MANY TIMES MUST I TELL YOU? YOUR PIVOT FOOT...
WHAC
HOMURA!
DID I APPEAR TO NEGLECT MY PIVOT FOOT?
!!
NO...NOT POSSIBLE!!
THIS STANCE...
WHOOSH
WARRIOR MAIDEN SINGLE-SWORD ATTACK...

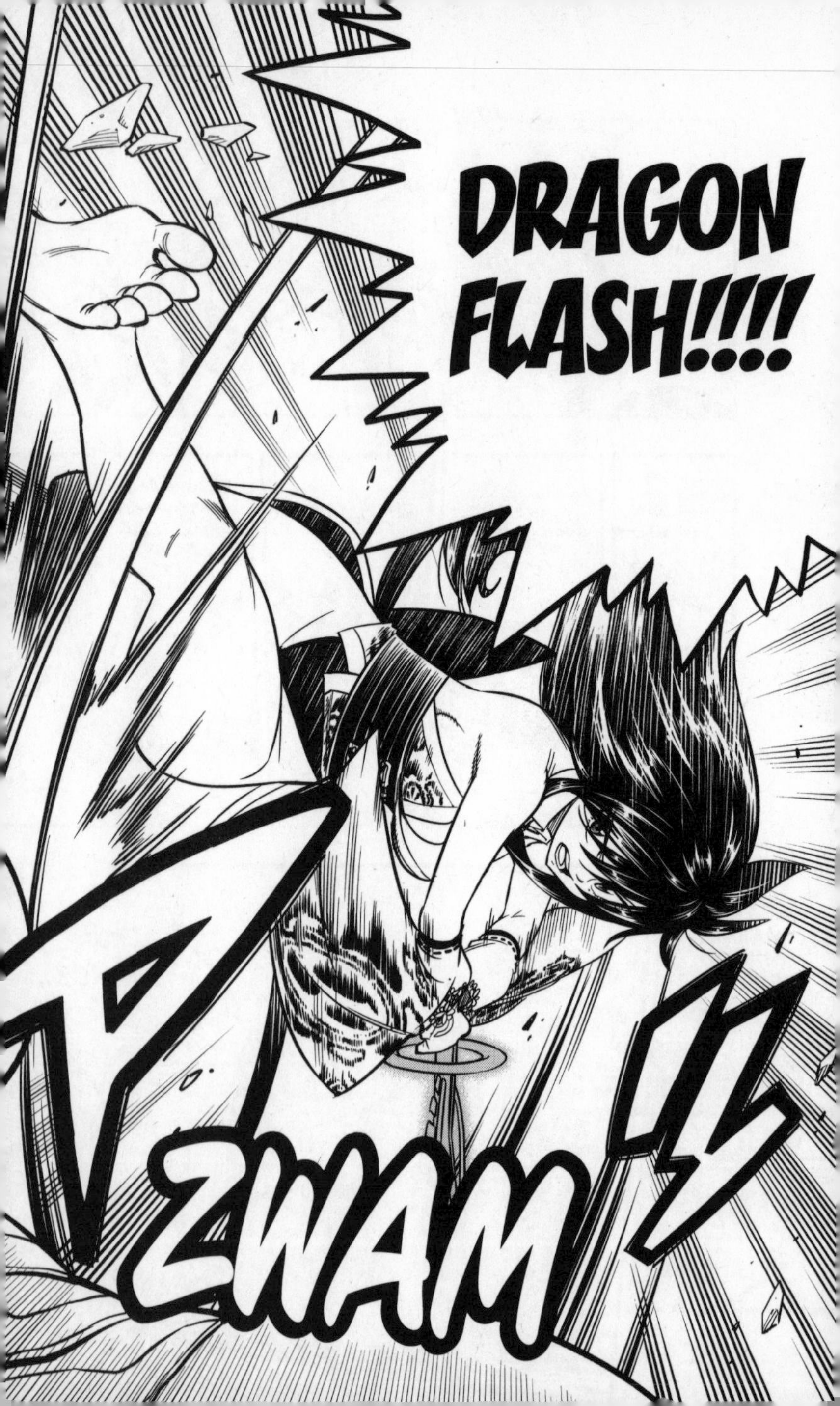
DRAGON FLASH!!!!
ZWAM !!

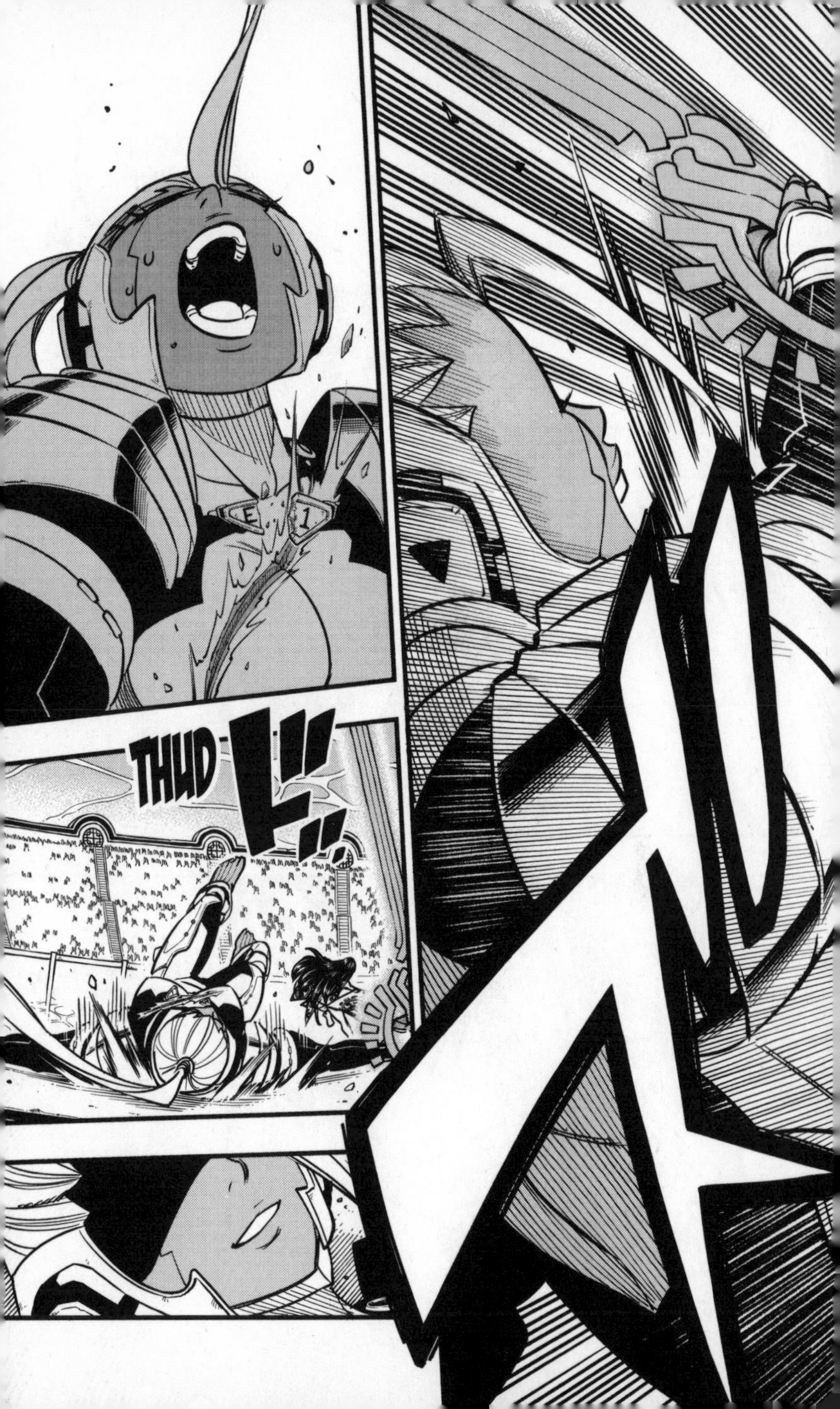
THUD!!

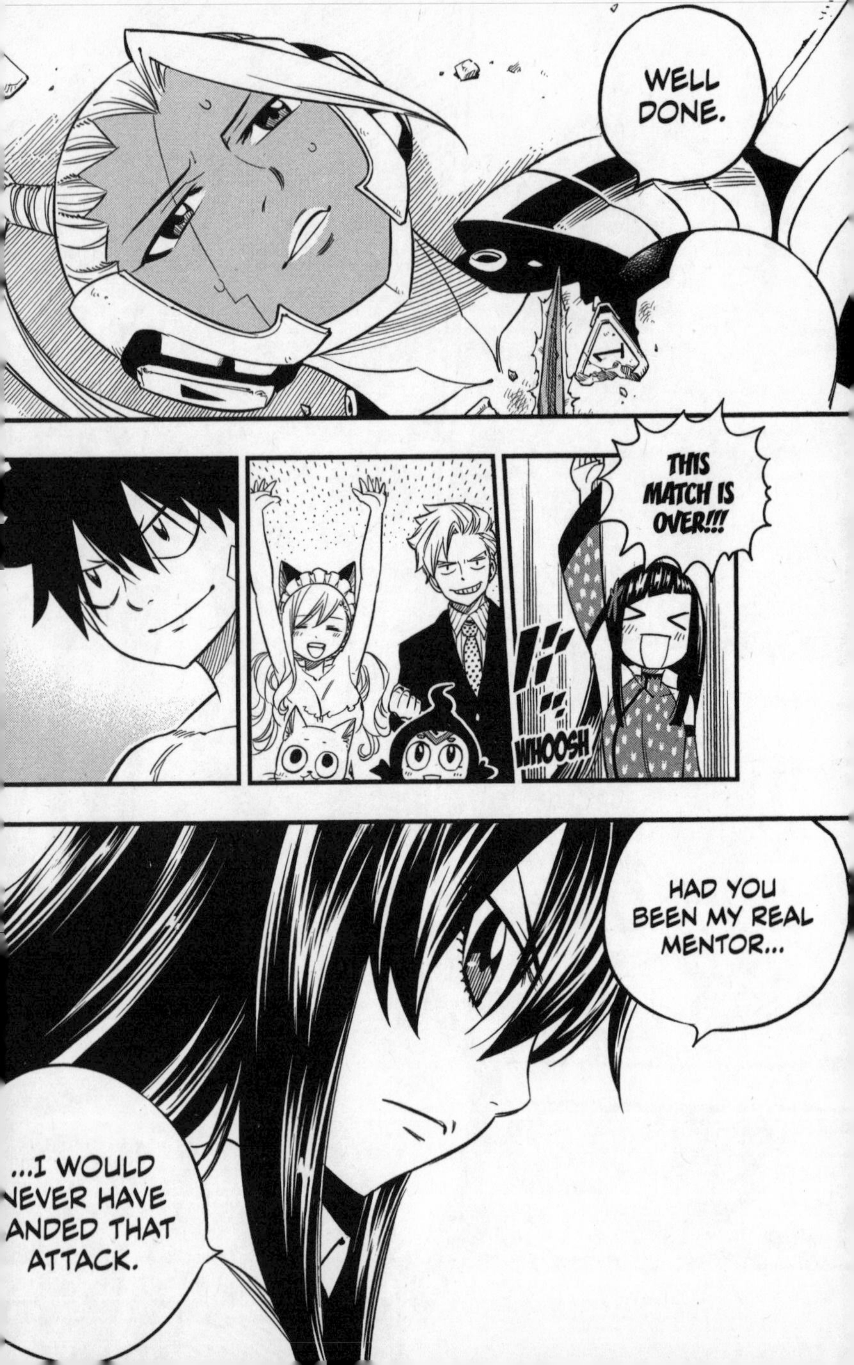
WELL DONE.
THIS MATCH IS OVER!!!
WHOOSH
HAD YOU BEEN MY REAL MENTOR...
...I WOULD NEVER HAVE LANDED THAT ATTACK.

EDENS ZERO

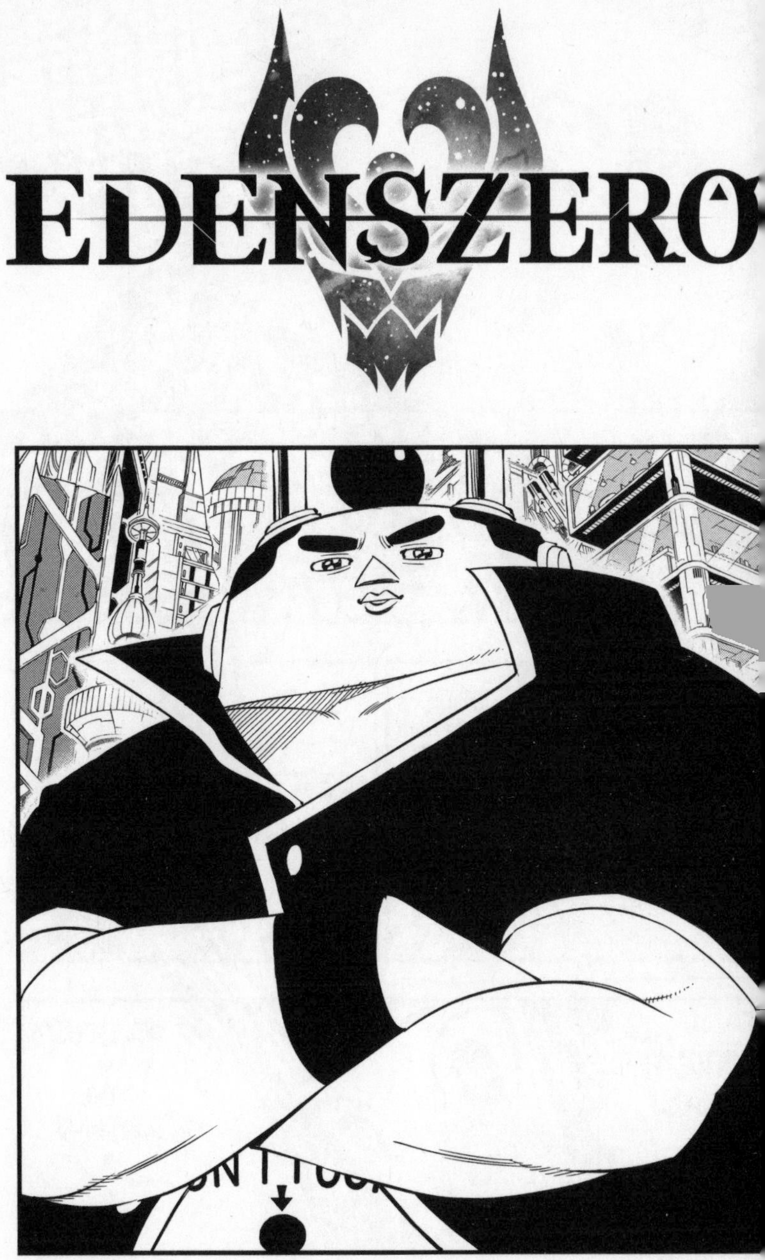

CHAPTER 48: FROM THE PLANET OF ETERNITY

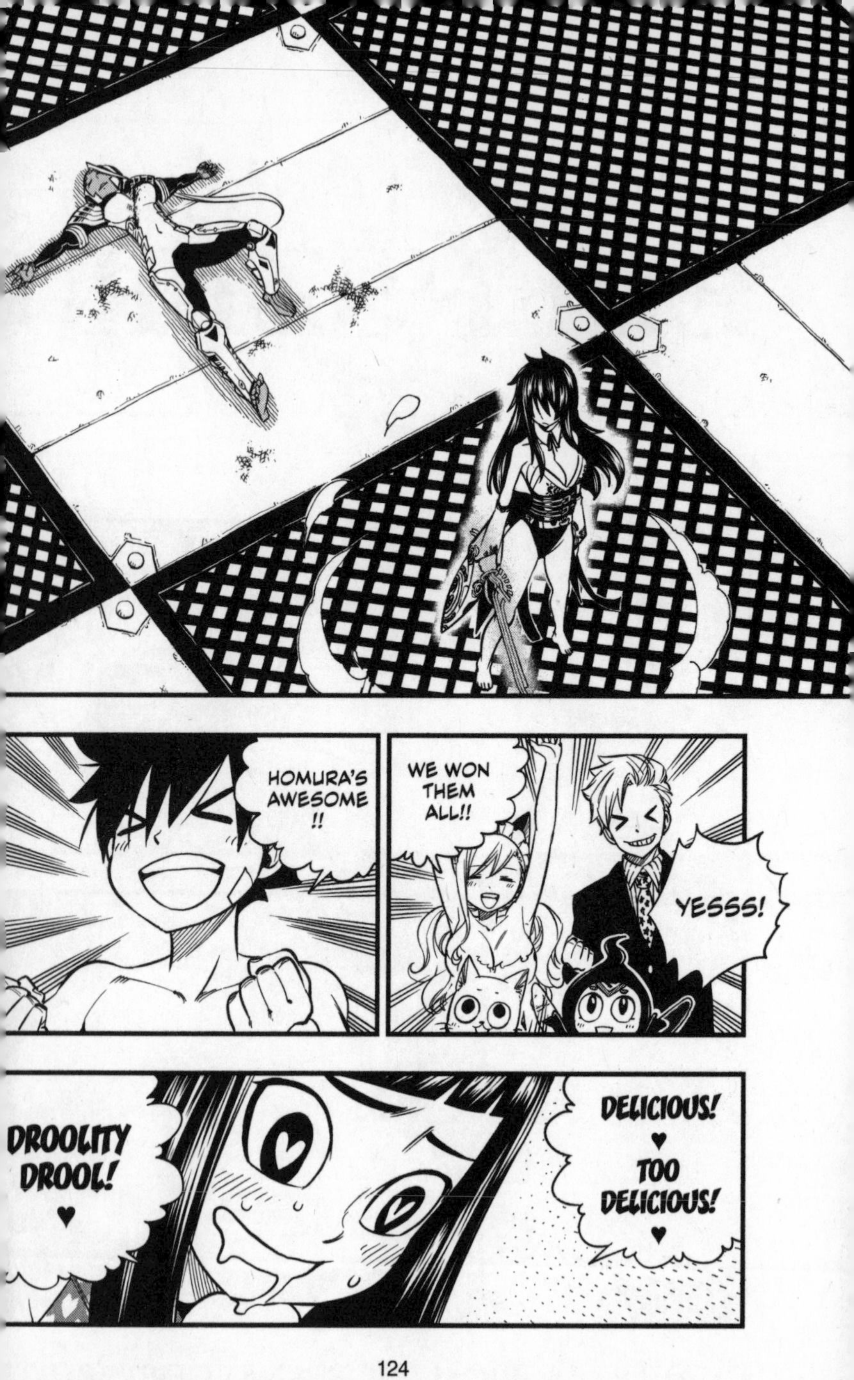
WE WON THEM ALL!!
YESSS!
HOMURA'S AWESOME !!
DELICIOUS! ♥ TOO DELICIOUS! ♥
DROOLITY DROOL! ♥

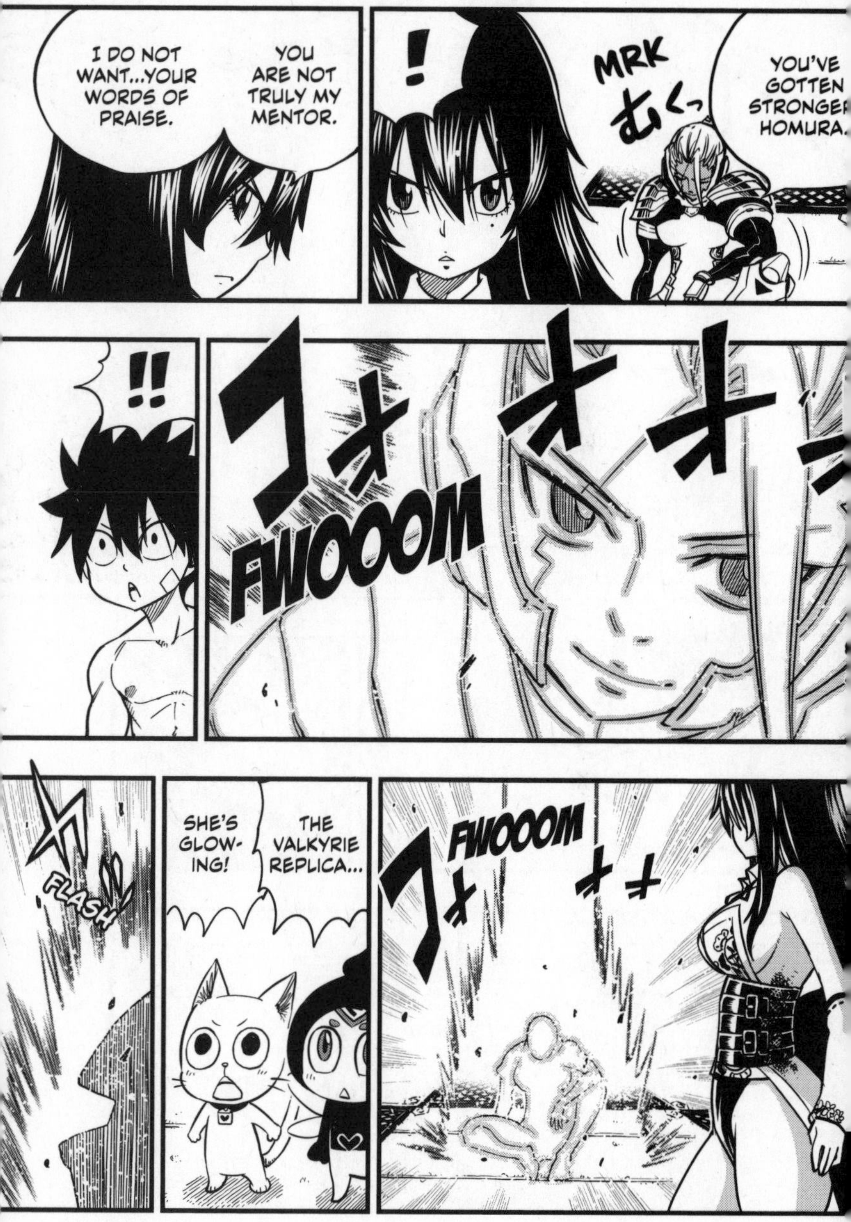

YOU'VE GOTTEN STRONGER HOMURA.
MRK
むくっ
!
YOU ARE NOT TRULY MY MENTOR.
I DO NOT WANT...YOUR WORDS OF PRAISE.
フォオオ
FWOOOM
!!
フォォ
FWOOOM
THE VALKYRIE REPLICA...
SHE'S GLOWING-ING!
FLASH

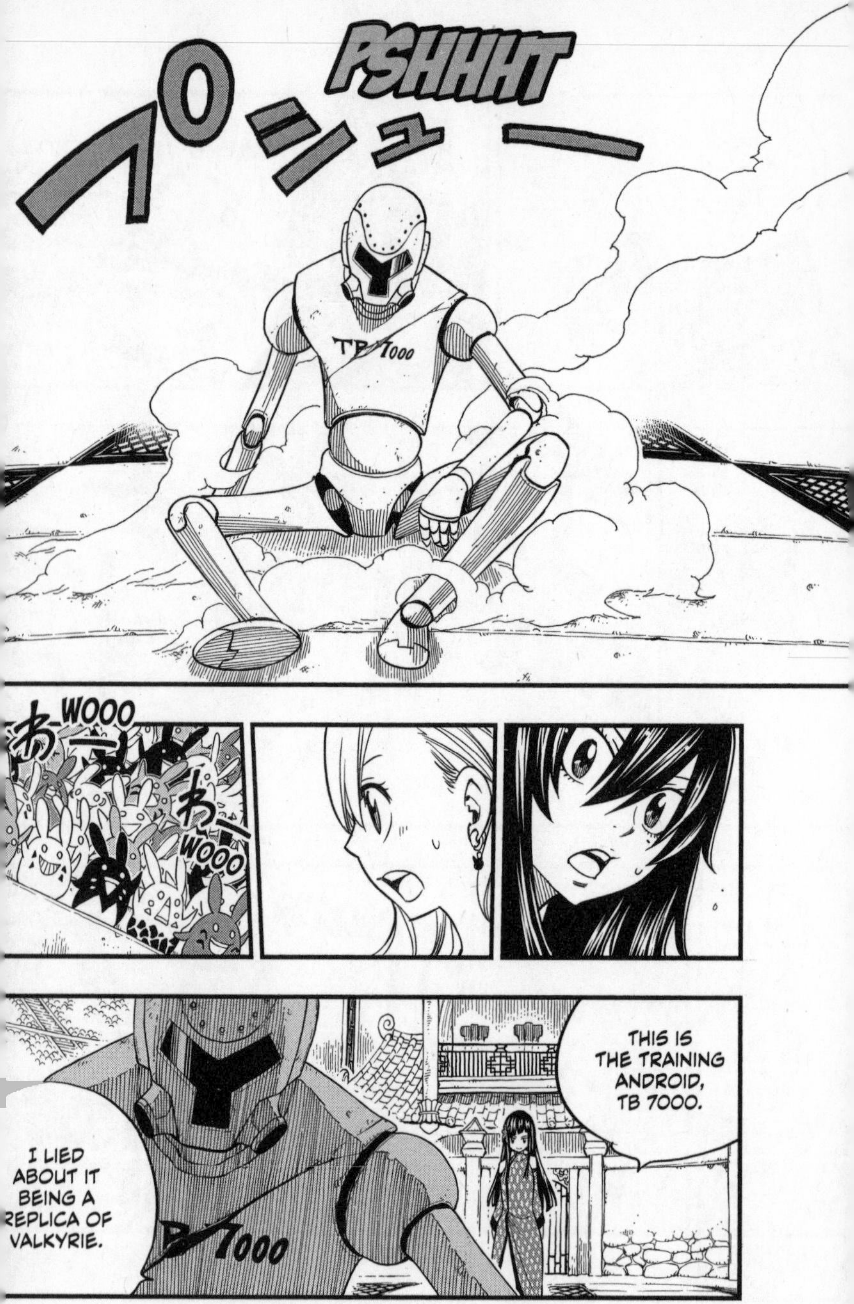
プシュー
PSHHHT
TB 7000
あー WOOO
わー WOOO
THIS IS THE TRAINING ANDROID, TB 7000.
I LIED ABOUT IT BEING A REPLICA OF VALKYRIE.

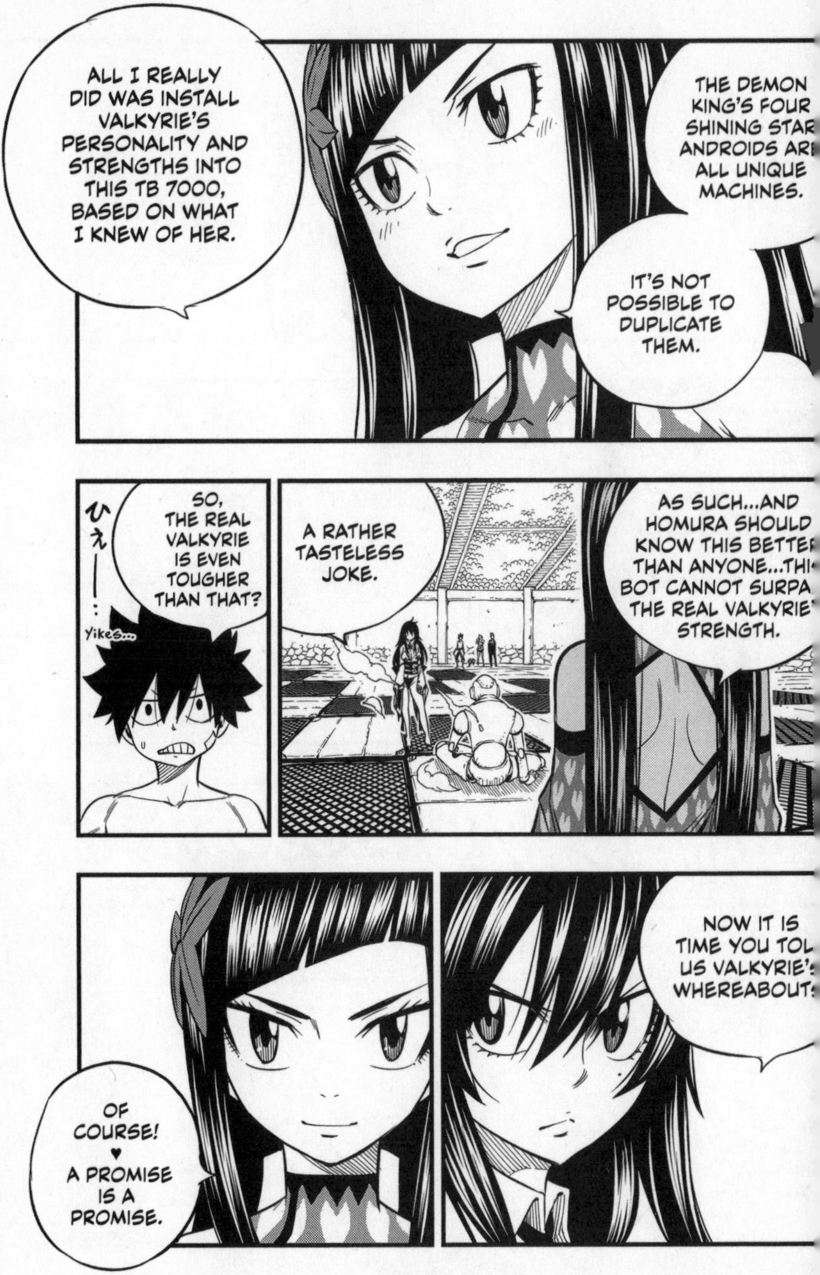
ALL I REALLY DID WAS INSTALL VALKYRIE'S PERSONALITY AND STRENGTHS INTO THIS TB 7000, BASED ON WHAT I KNEW OF HER.
THE DEMON KING'S FOUR SHINING STAR ANDROIDS AR ALL UNIQUE MACHINES.
IT'S NOT POSSIBLE TO DUPLICATE THEM.
AS SUCH...AND HOMURA SHOULD KNOW THIS BETTER THAN ANYONE...THI BOT CANNOT SURPA THE REAL VALKYRIE' STRENGTH.
A RATHER TASTELESS JOKE.
SO, THE REAL VALKYRIE IS EVEN TOUGHER THAN THAT?
ひぇー…
Yikes...
NOW IT IS TIME YOU TOL US VALKYRIE'S WHEREABOUT
OF COURSE! ♥ A PROMISE IS A PROMISE.

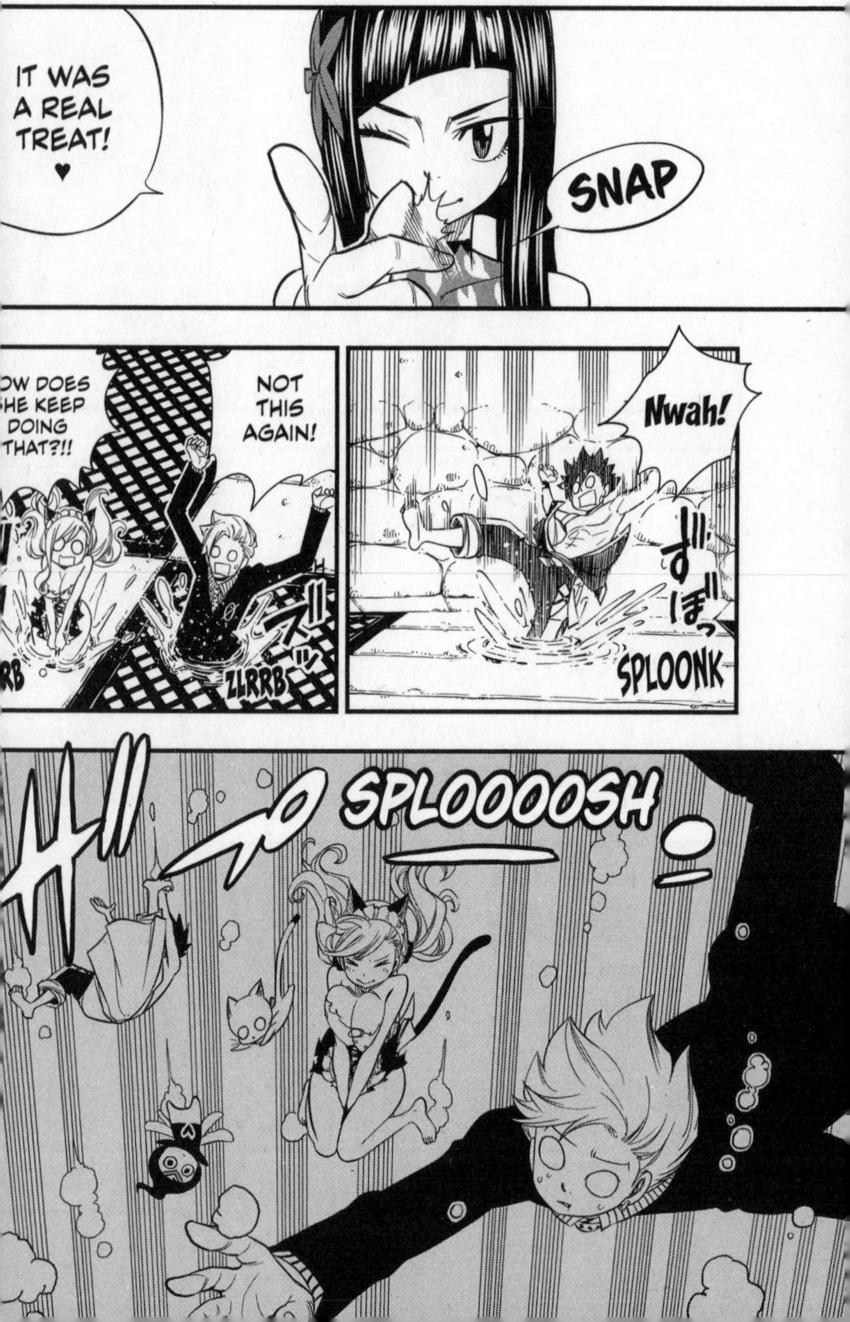
IT WAS A REAL TREAT! ♥
SNAP
Nwah!
ずぼっ
SPLOONK
NOT THIS AGAIN!
OW DOES HE KEEP DOING THAT?!!
ズッ
ZLRRB
RB
SPLOOOOSH

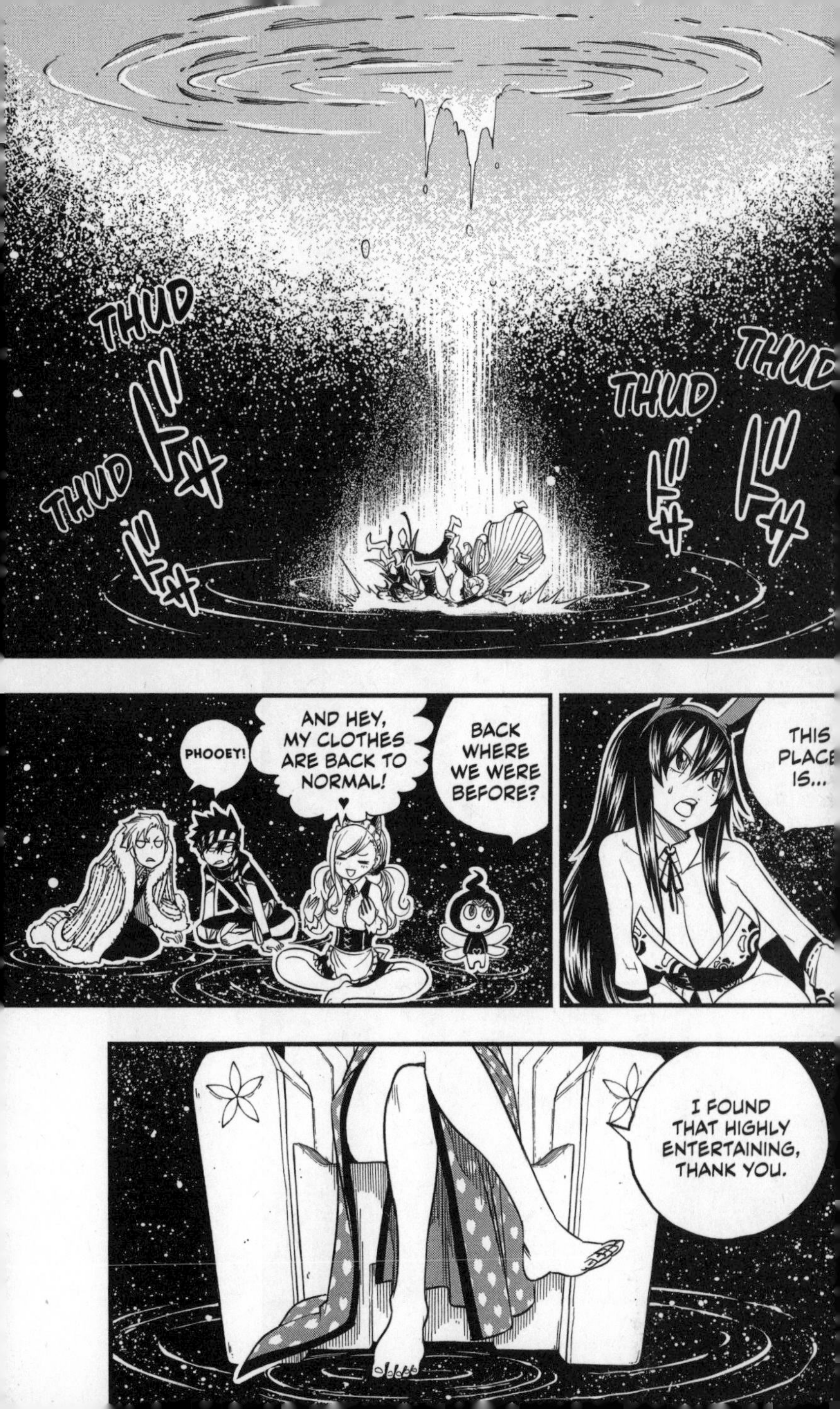
THUD
THUD
THUD
THUD
THIS PLACE IS...
BACK WHERE WE WERE BEFORE?
AND HEY, MY CLOTHES ARE BACK TO NORMAL!
PHOOEY!
I FOUND THAT HIGHLY ENTERTAINING, THANK YOU.

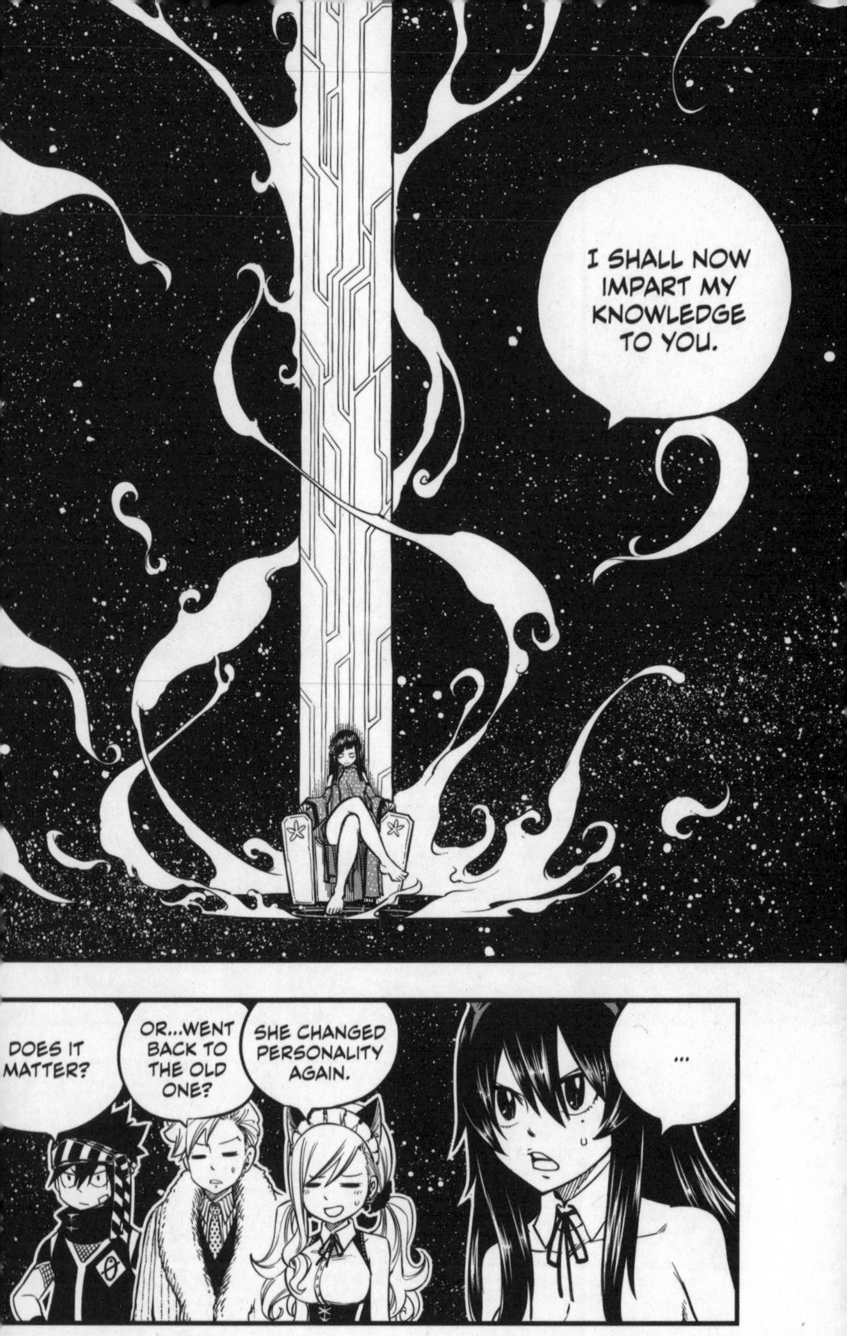
I SHALL NOW IMPART MY KNOWLEDGE TO YOU.
...
SHE CHANGED PERSONALITY AGAIN.
OR...WENT BACK TO THE OLD ONE?
DOES IT MATTER?

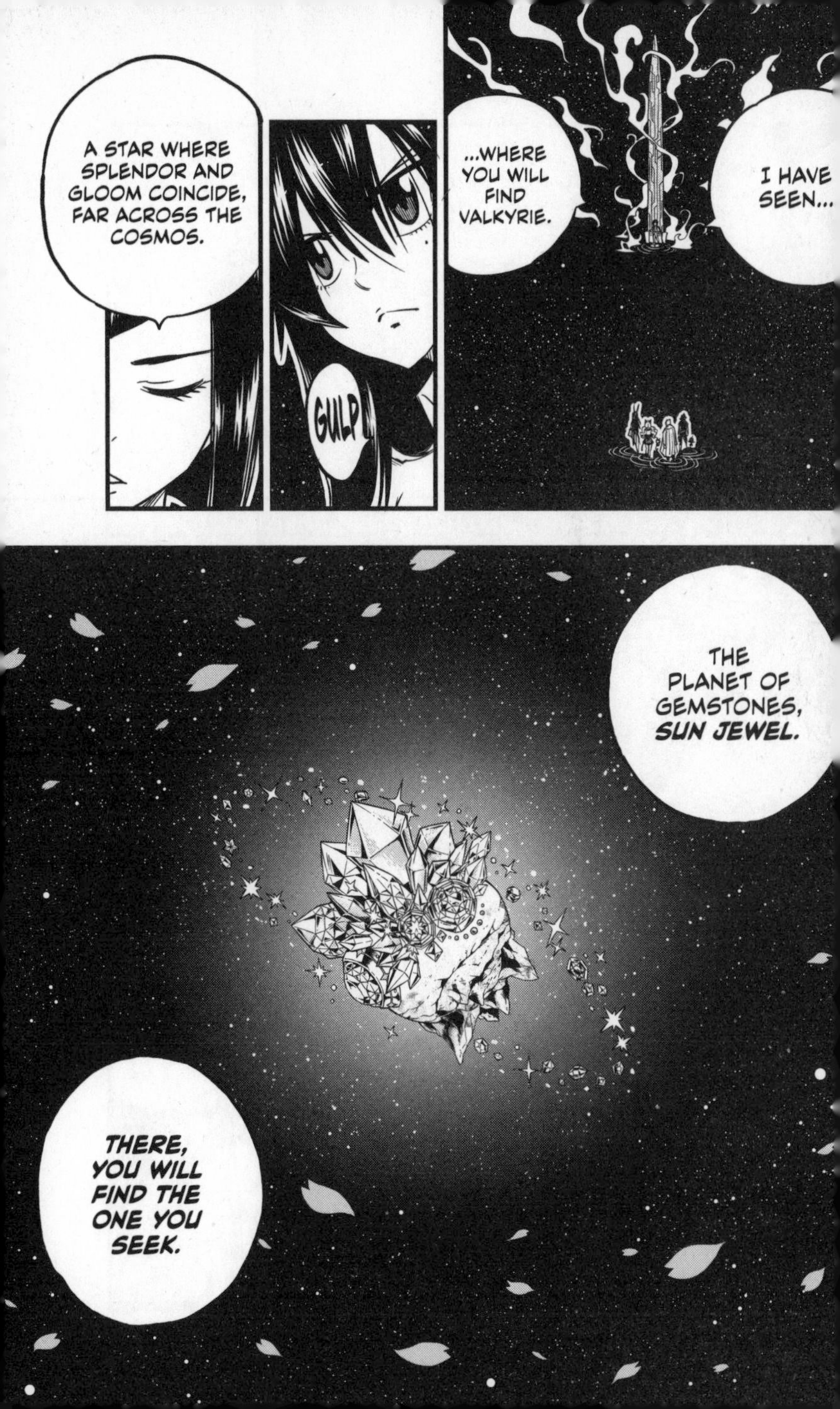
I HAVE SEEN...
...WHERE YOU WILL FIND VALKYRIE.
GULP
A STAR WHERE SPLENDOR AND GLOOM COINCIDE, FAR ACROSS THE COSMOS.
THE PLANET OF GEMSTONES, **SUN JEWEL.**
THERE, YOU WILL FIND THE ONE YOU SEEK.

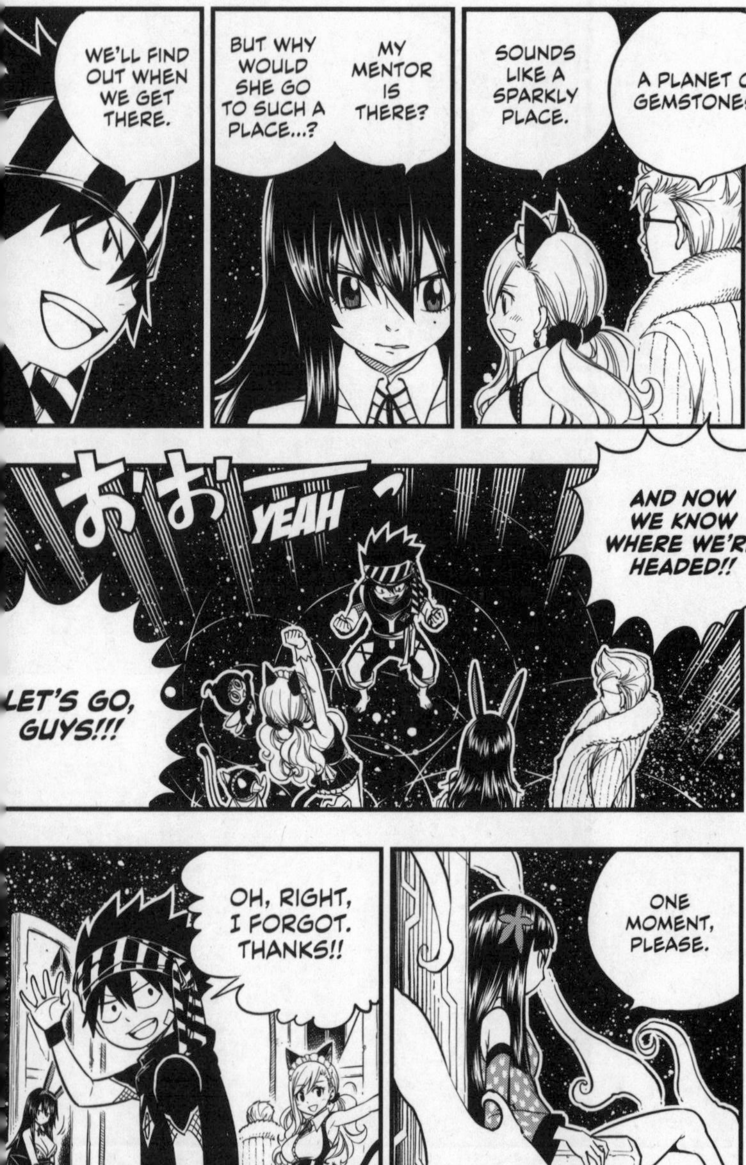
A PLANET OF GEMSTONES?
SOUNDS LIKE A SPARKLY PLACE.
MY MENTOR IS THERE?
BUT WHY WOULD SHE GO TO SUCH A PLACE...?
WE'LL FIND OUT WHEN WE GET THERE.
AND NOW WE KNOW WHERE WE'RE HEADED!!
おおーっ
YEAH
LET'S GO, GUYS!!!
ONE MOMENT, PLEASE.
OH, RIGHT, I FORGOT. THANKS!!

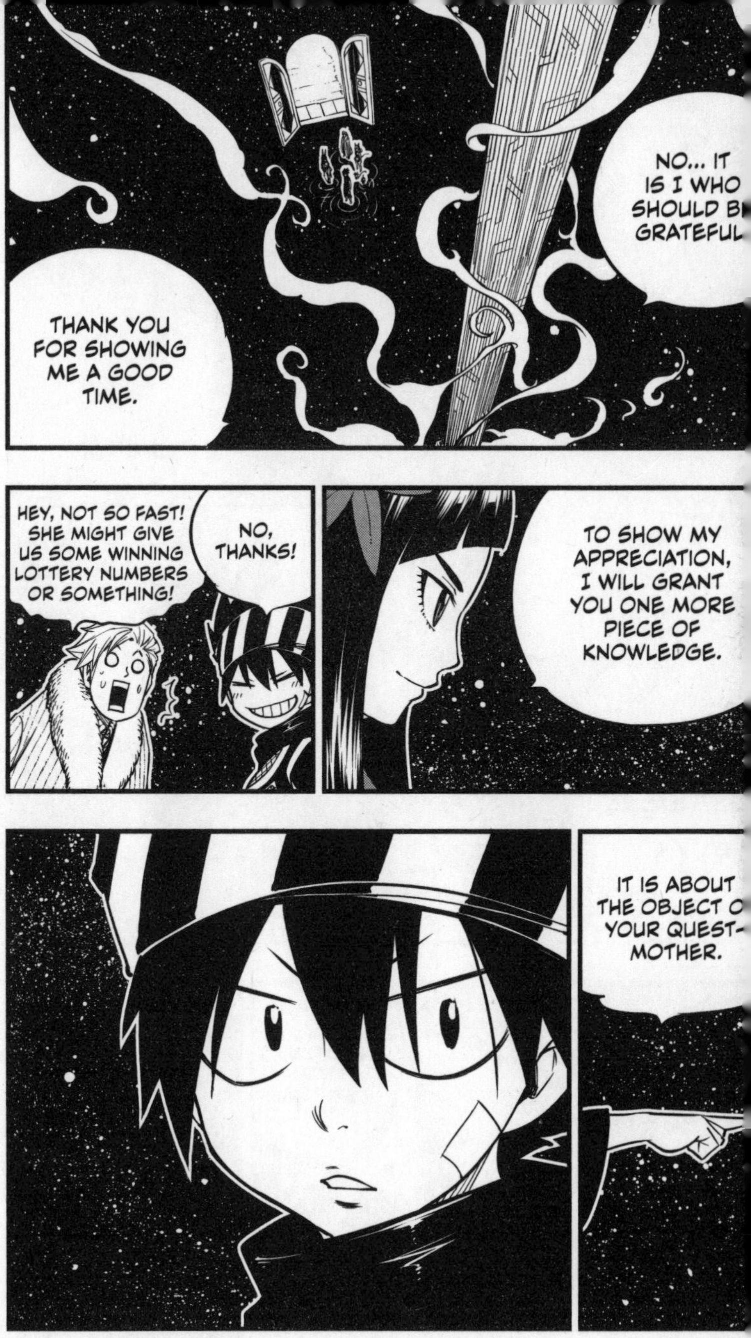
NO... IT IS I WHO SHOULD B GRATEFUL
THANK YOU FOR SHOWING ME A GOOD TIME.
TO SHOW MY APPRECIATION, I WILL GRANT YOU ONE MORE PIECE OF KNOWLEDGE.
NO, THANKS!
HEY, NOT SO FAST! SHE MIGHT GIVE US SOME WINNING LOTTERY NUMBERS OR SOMETHING!
IT IS ABOUT THE OBJECT O YOUR QUEST-MOTHER.

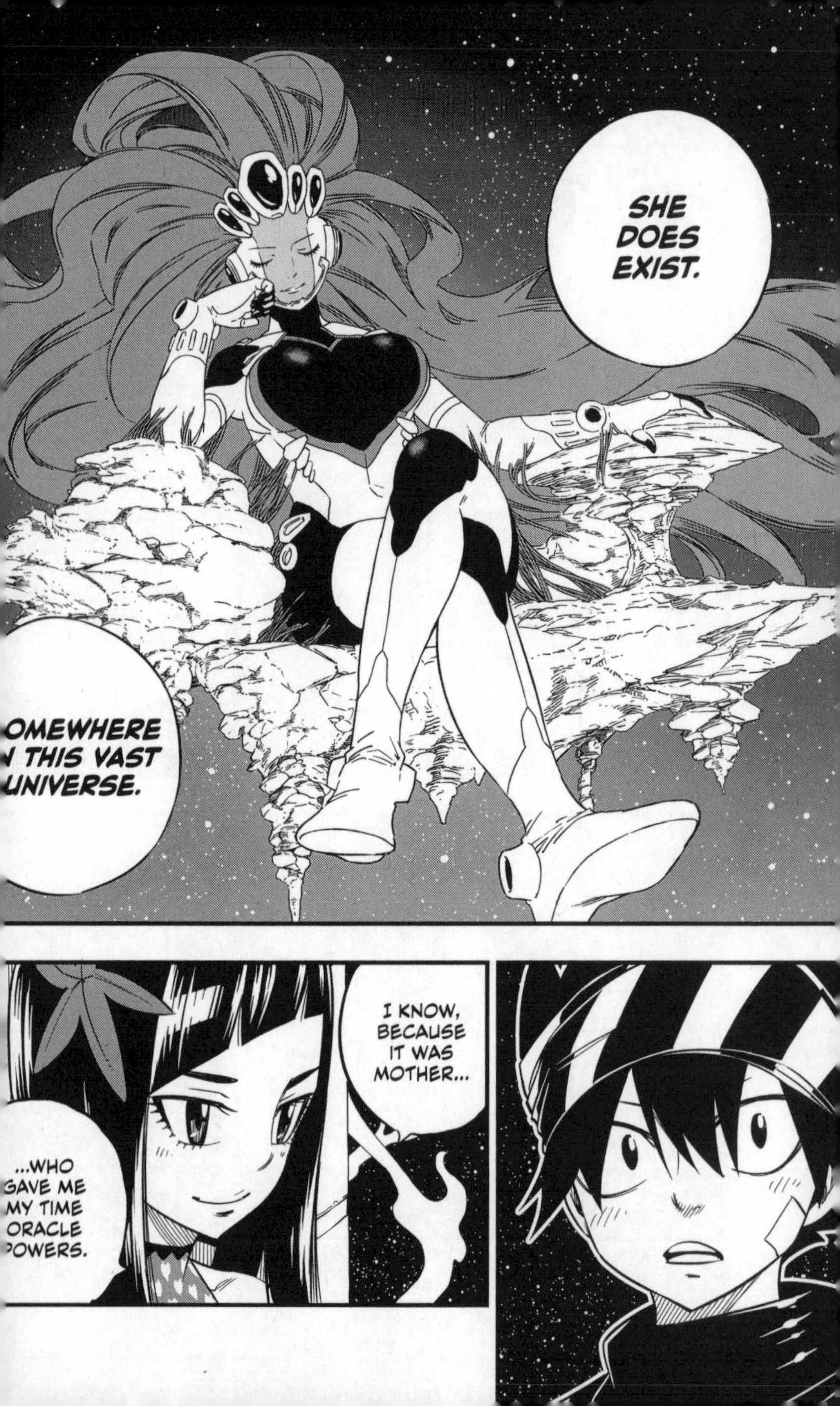

SHE DOES EXIST.
OMEWHERE N THIS VAST UNIVERSE.
I KNOW, BECAUSE IT WAS MOTHER...
...WHO GAVE ME MY TIME ORACLE OWERS.

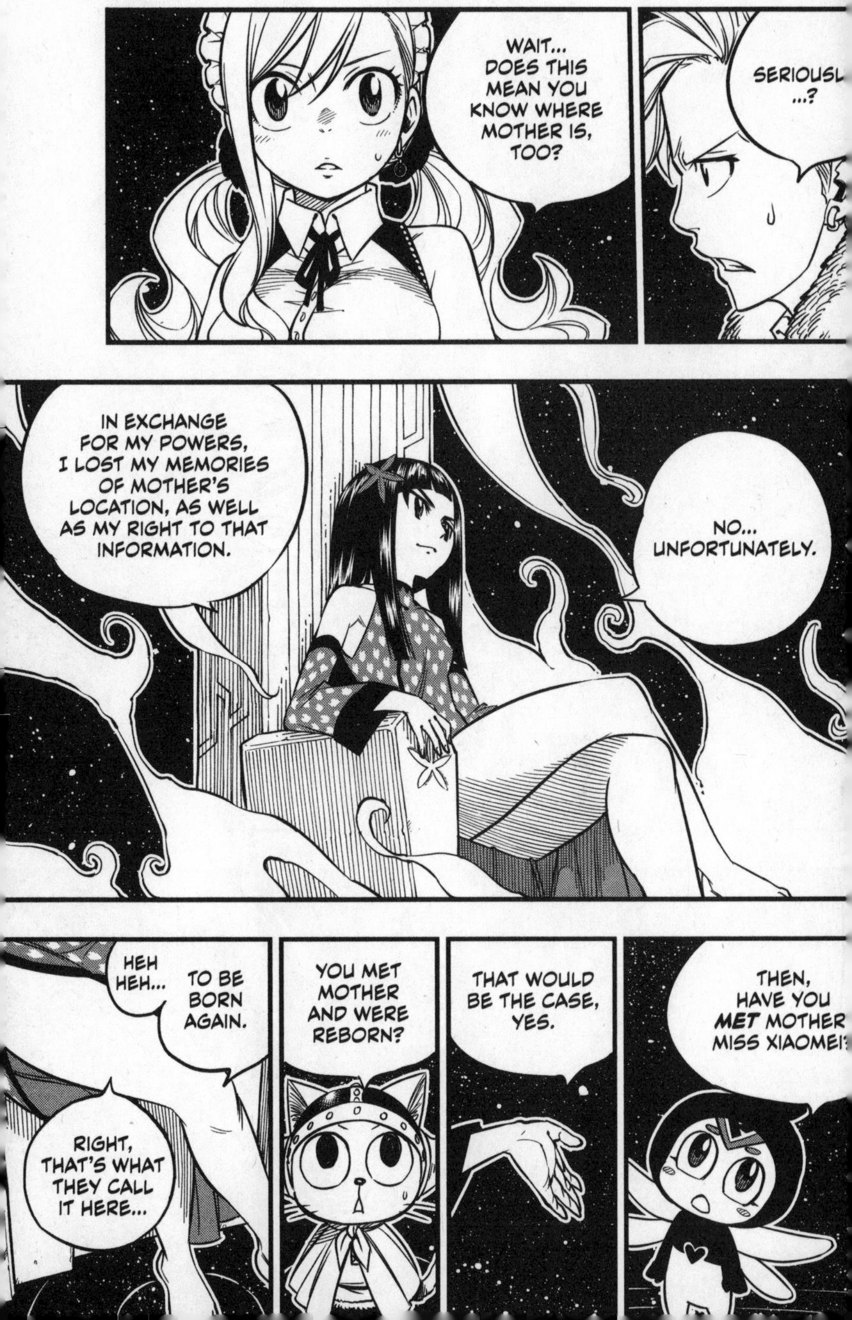
SERIOUSL ...?
WAIT... DOES THIS MEAN YOU KNOW WHERE MOTHER IS, TOO?
NO... UNFORTUNATELY.
IN EXCHANGE FOR MY POWERS, I LOST MY MEMORIES OF MOTHER'S LOCATION, AS WELL AS MY RIGHT TO THAT INFORMATION.
THEN, HAVE YOU *MET* MOTHER MISS XIAOMEI
THAT WOULD BE THE CASE, YES.
YOU MET MOTHER AND WERE REBORN?
TO BE BORN AGAIN.
HEH HEH...
RIGHT, THAT'S WHAT THEY CALL IT HERE...

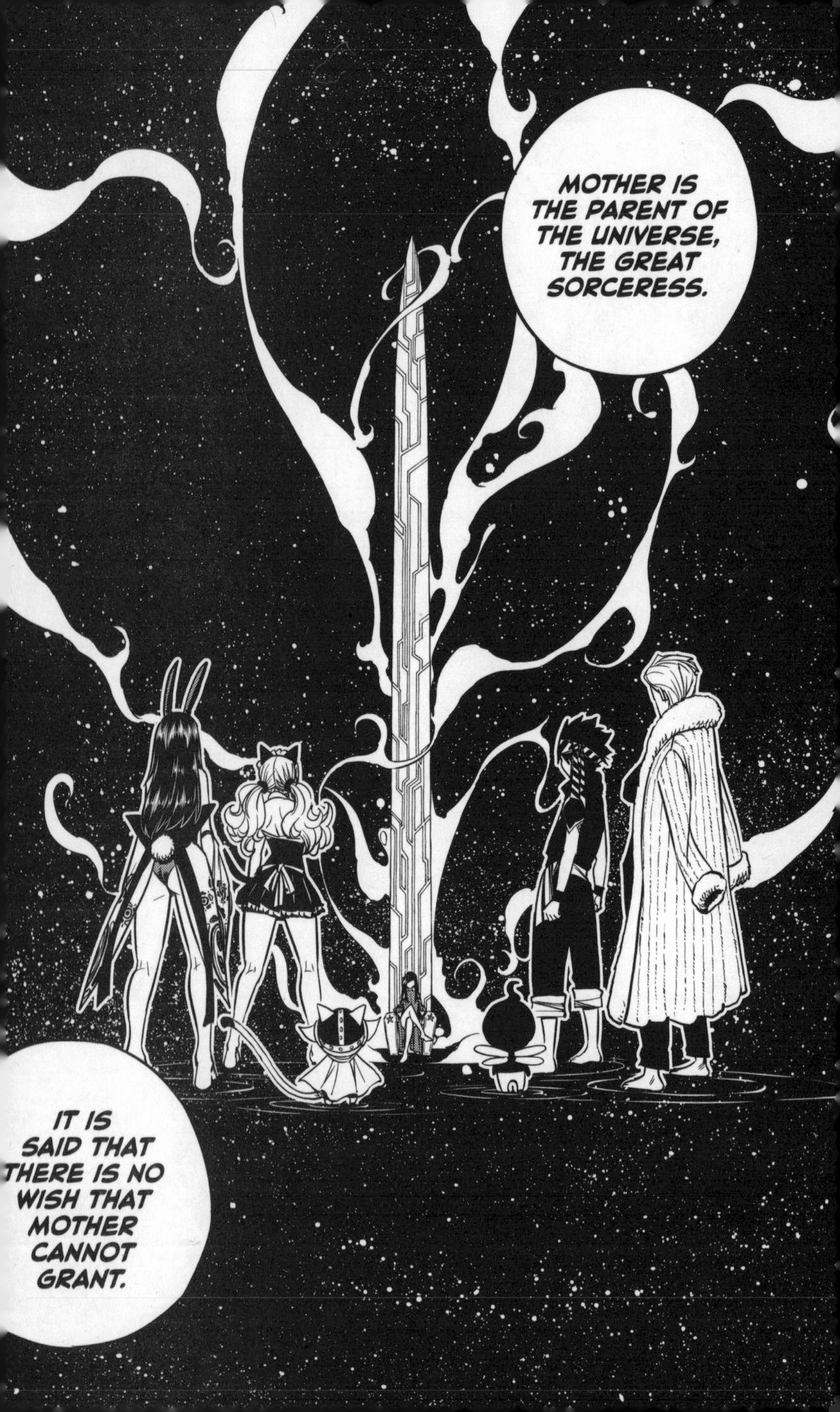
MOTHER IS THE PARENT OF THE UNIVERSE, THE GREAT SORCERESS.
IT IS SAID THAT THERE IS NO WISH THAT MOTHER CANNOT GRANT.

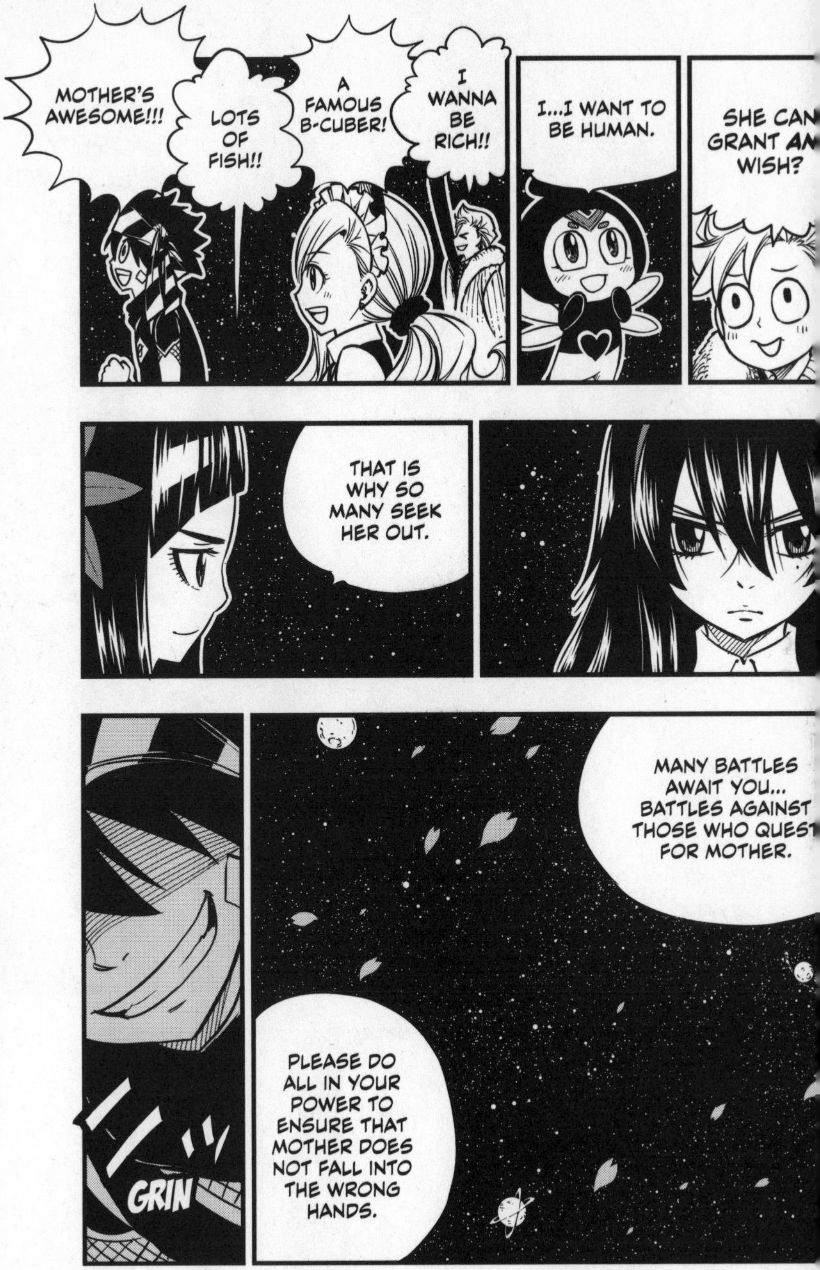
SHE CAN GRANT AN WISH?
I...I WANT TO BE HUMAN.
I WANNA BE RICH!!
A FAMOUS B-CUBER!
LOTS OF FISH!!
MOTHER'S AWESOME!!!
THAT IS WHY SO MANY SEEK HER OUT.
MANY BATTLES AWAIT YOU... BATTLES AGAINST THOSE WHO QUEST FOR MOTHER.
PLEASE DO ALL IN YOUR POWER TO ENSURE THAT MOTHER DOES NOT FALL INTO THE WRONG HANDS.
GRIN

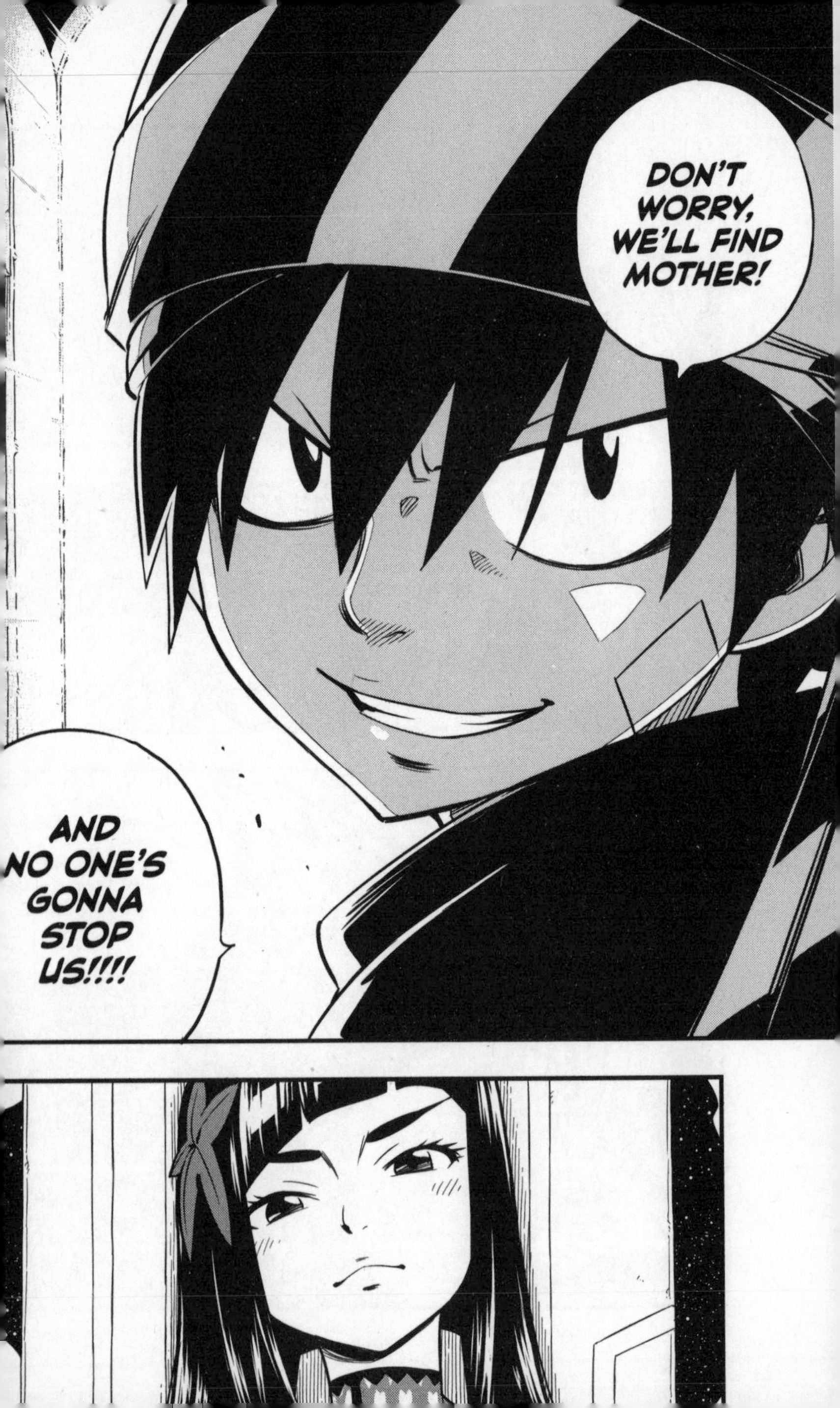
DON'T WORRY, WE'LL FIND MOTHER!
AND NO ONE'S GONNA STOP US!!!!

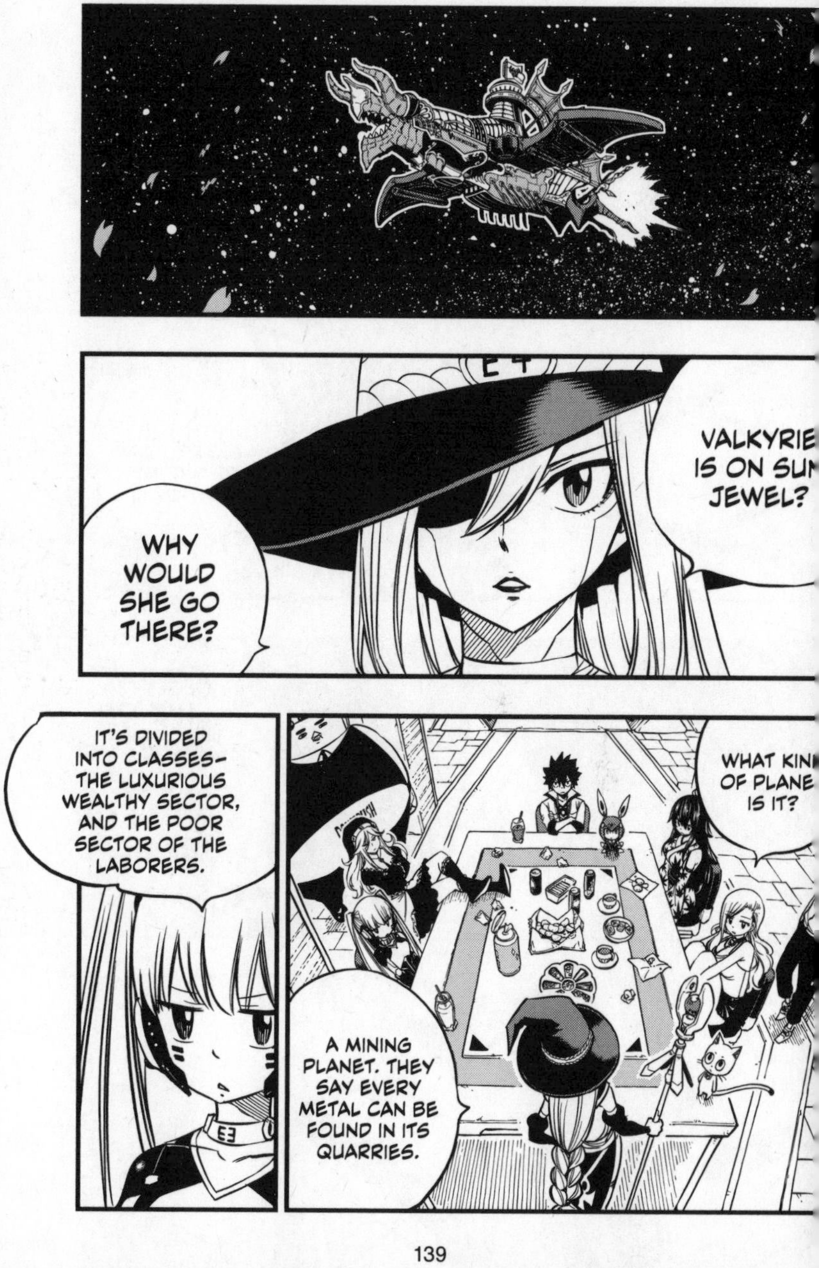
VALKYRIE IS ON SU JEWEL?
WHY WOULD SHE GO THERE?
WHAT KIN OF PLANE IS IT?
A MINING PLANET. THEY SAY EVERY METAL CAN BE FOUND IN ITS QUARRIES.
IT'S DIVIDED INTO CLASSES-THE LUXURIOUS WEALTHY SECTOR, AND THE POOR SECTOR OF THE LABORERS.

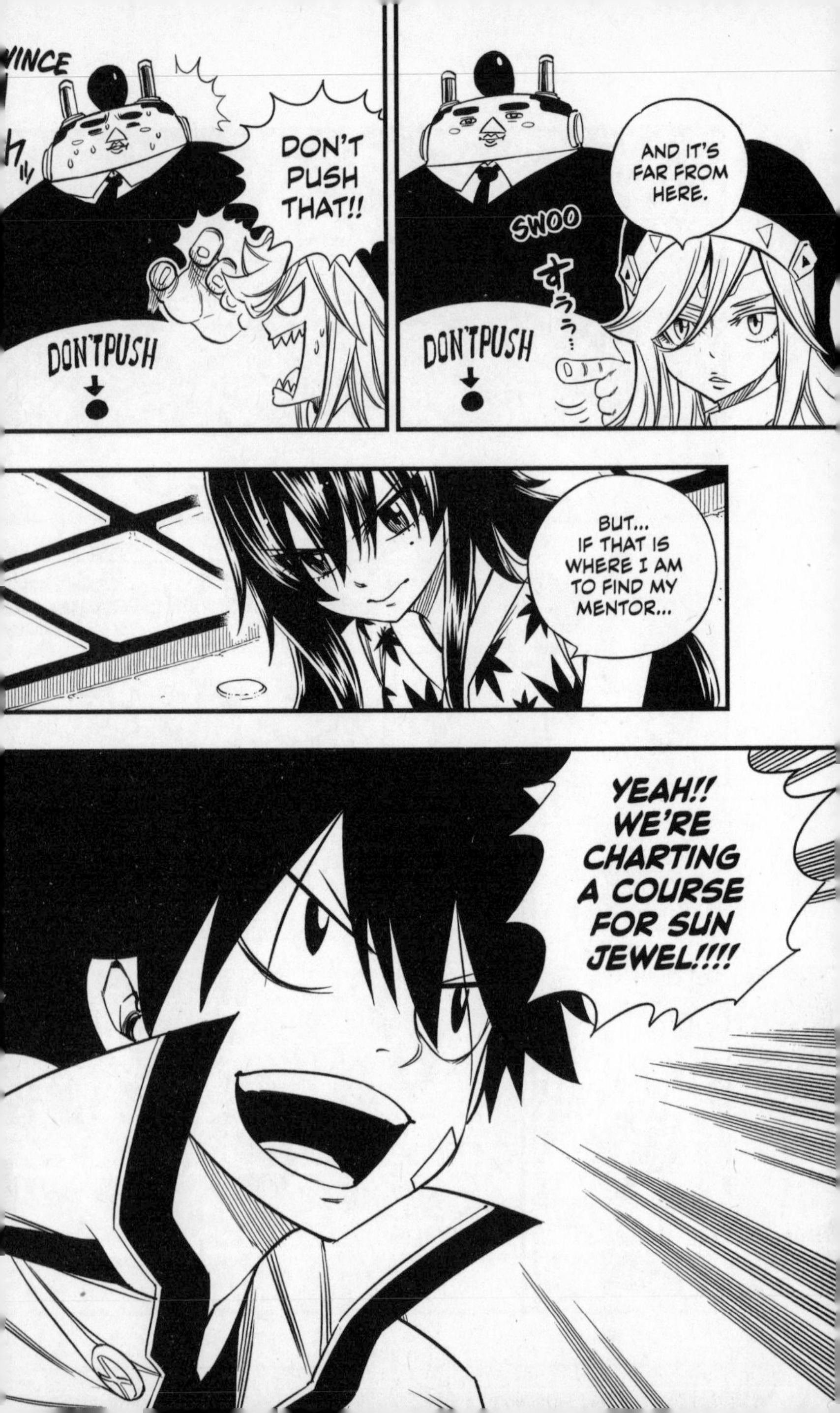
AND IT'S FAR FROM HERE.
SWOO
DON'T PUSH
WINCE
DON'T PUSH THAT!!
DON'T PUSH
BUT... IF THAT IS WHERE I AM TO FIND MY MENTOR...
YEAH!! WE'RE CHARTING A COURSE FOR SUN JEWEL!!!!

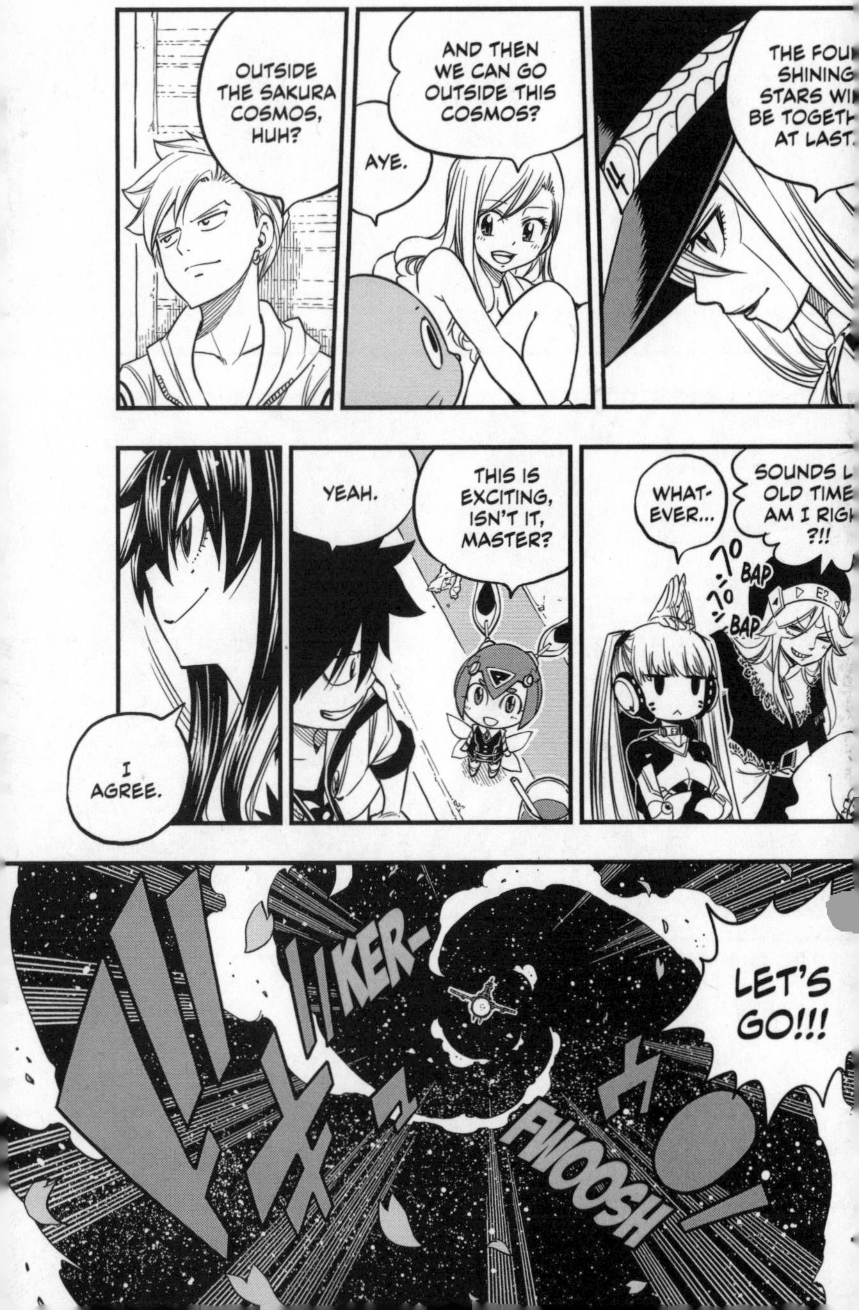

THE FOU SHINING STARS WI BE TOGETH AT LAST.
AND THEN WE CAN GO OUTSIDE THIS COSMOS?
AYE.
OUTSIDE THE SAKURA COSMOS, HUH?
SOUNDS L OLD TIME AM I RIG ?!!
WHAT-EVER...
BAP
BAP
THIS IS EXCITING, ISN'T IT, MASTER?
YEAH.
I AGREE.
LET'S GO!!!
KER-
FWOOSH

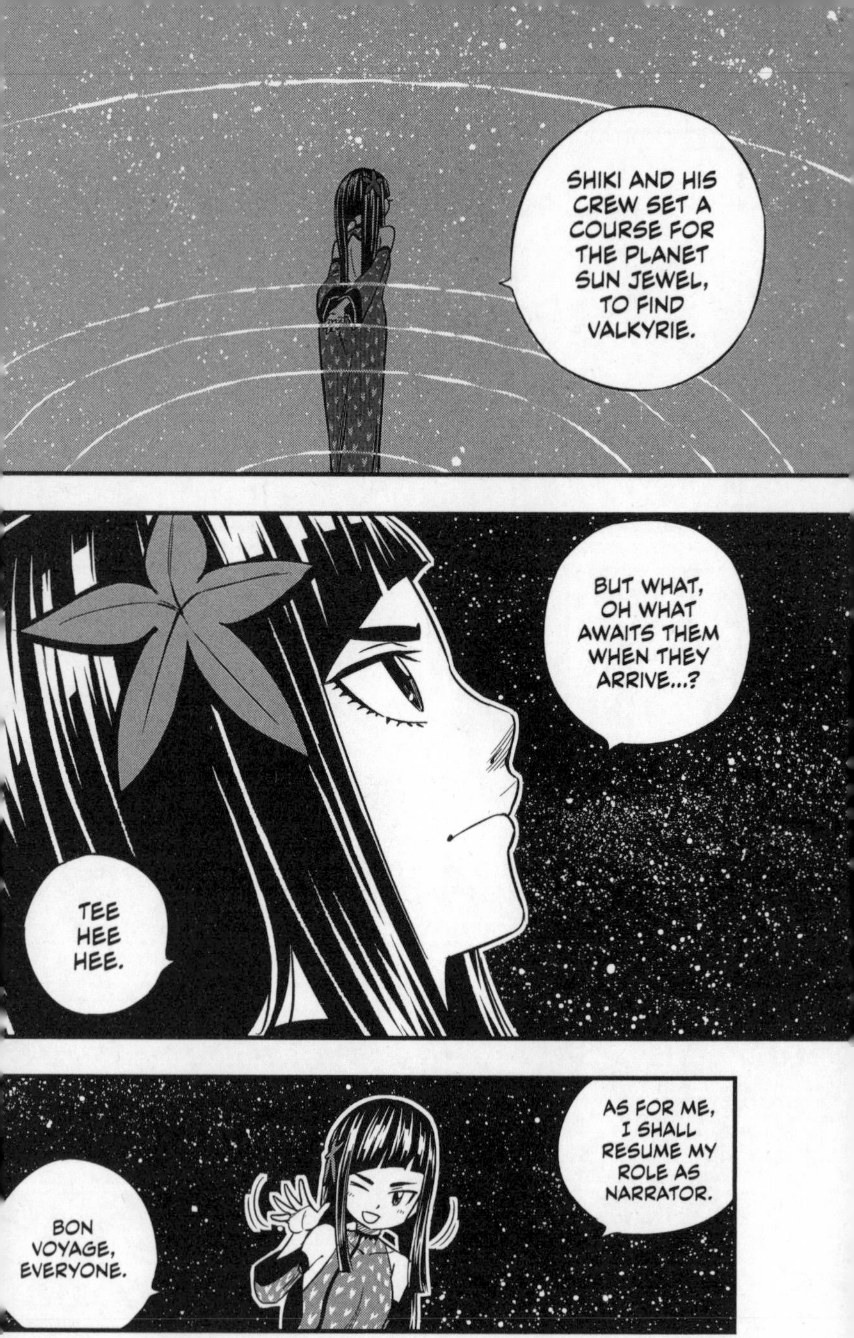
SHIKI AND HIS CREW SET A COURSE FOR THE PLANET SUN JEWEL, TO FIND VALKYRIE.
BUT WHAT, OH WHAT AWAITS THEM WHEN THEY ARRIVE...?
TEE HEE HEE.
AS FOR ME, I SHALL RESUME MY ROLE AS NARRATOR.
BON VOYAGE, EVERYONE.

EDENS ZERO

CHAPTER 49: CAPTAIN CONNOR

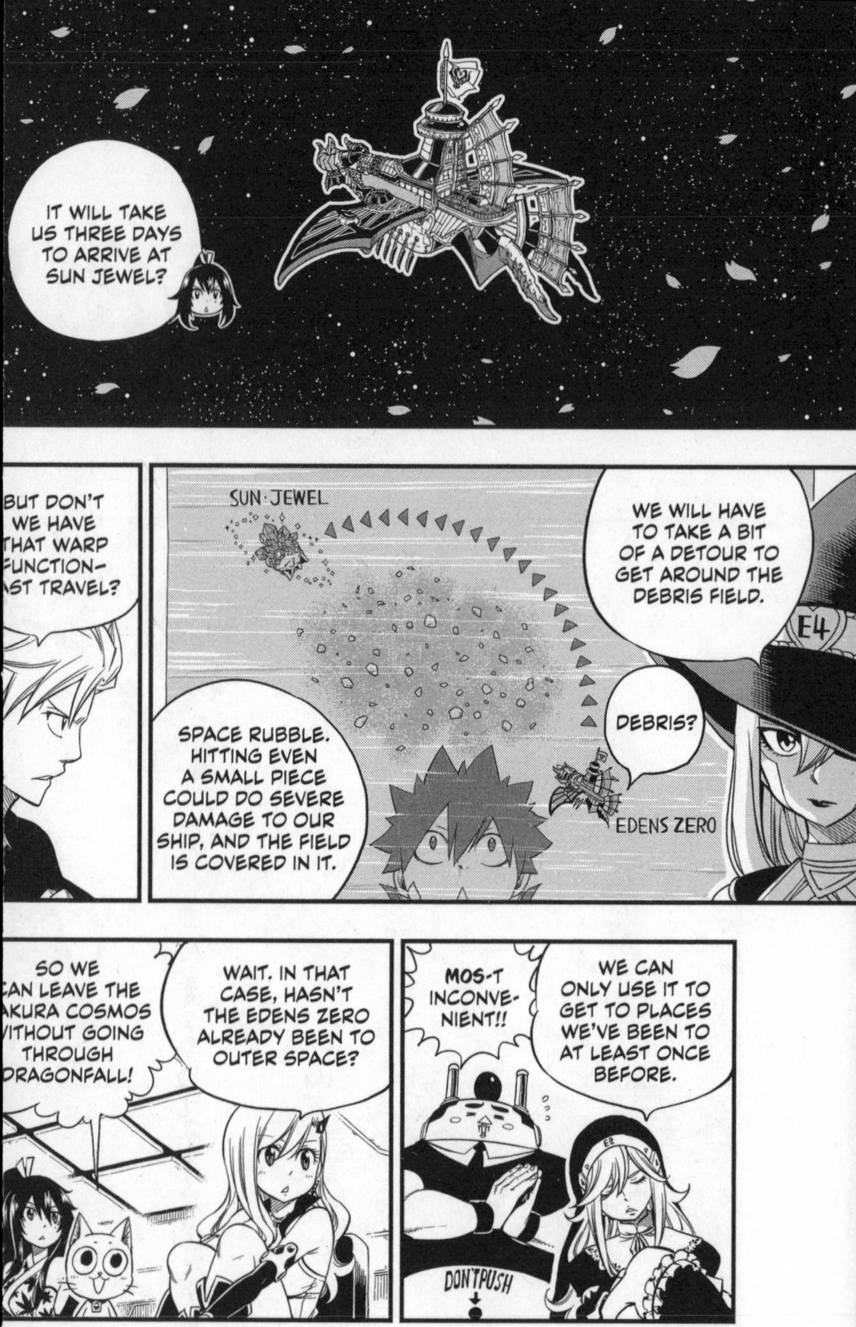
IT WILL TAKE US THREE DAYS TO ARRIVE AT SUN JEWEL?
WE WILL HAVE TO TAKE A BIT OF A DETOUR TO GET AROUND THE DEBRIS FIELD.
SUN·JEWEL
DEBRIS?
EDENS ZERO
SPACE RUBBLE. HITTING EVEN A SMALL PIECE COULD DO SEVERE DAMAGE TO OUR SHIP, AND THE FIELD IS COVERED IN IT.
BUT DON'T WE HAVE THAT WARP FUNCTION– AST TRAVEL?
WE CAN ONLY USE IT TO GET TO PLACES WE'VE BEEN TO AT LEAST ONCE BEFORE.
MOS-T INCONVE-NIENT!!
DON'T PUSH
WAIT. IN THAT CASE, HASN'T THE EDENS ZERO ALREADY BEEN TO OUTER SPACE?
SO WE AN LEAVE THE AKURA COSMOS ITHOUT GOING THROUGH RAGONFALL!

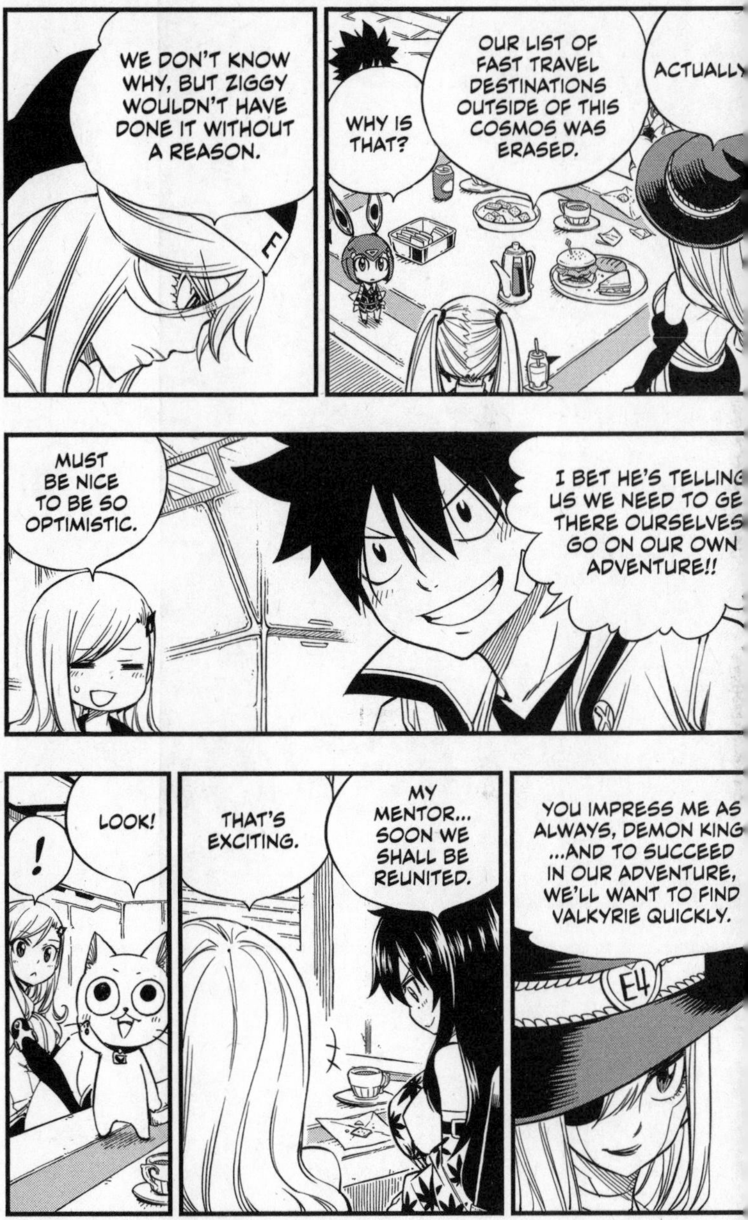
ACTUALLY
OUR LIST OF FAST TRAVEL DESTINATIONS OUTSIDE OF THIS COSMOS WAS ERASED.
WHY IS THAT?
WE DON'T KNOW WHY, BUT ZIGGY WOULDN'T HAVE DONE IT WITHOUT A REASON.
I BET HE'S TELLING US WE NEED TO GE THERE OURSELVES GO ON OUR OWN ADVENTURE!!
MUST BE NICE TO BE SO OPTIMISTIC.
YOU IMPRESS ME AS ALWAYS, DEMON KING ...AND TO SUCCEED IN OUR ADVENTURE, WE'LL WANT TO FIND VALKYRIE QUICKLY.
E4
MY MENTOR... SOON WE SHALL BE REUNITED.
THAT'S EXCITING.
LOOK!
!

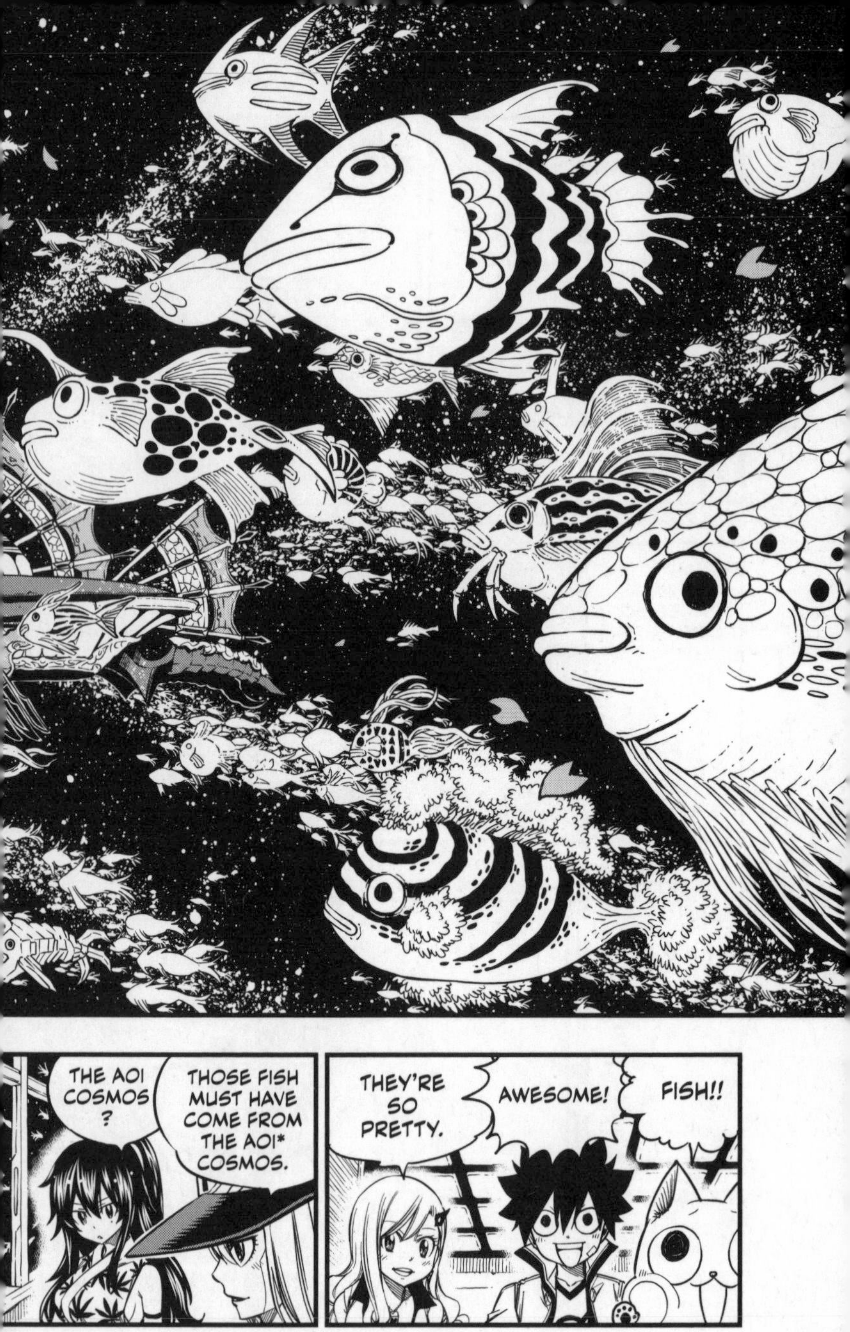
FISH!!
AWESOME!
THEY'RE SO PRETTY.
THOSE FISH MUST HAVE COME FROM THE AOI* COSMOS.
THE AOI COSMOS ?

*"Aoi" is Japanese for Hollyhock.

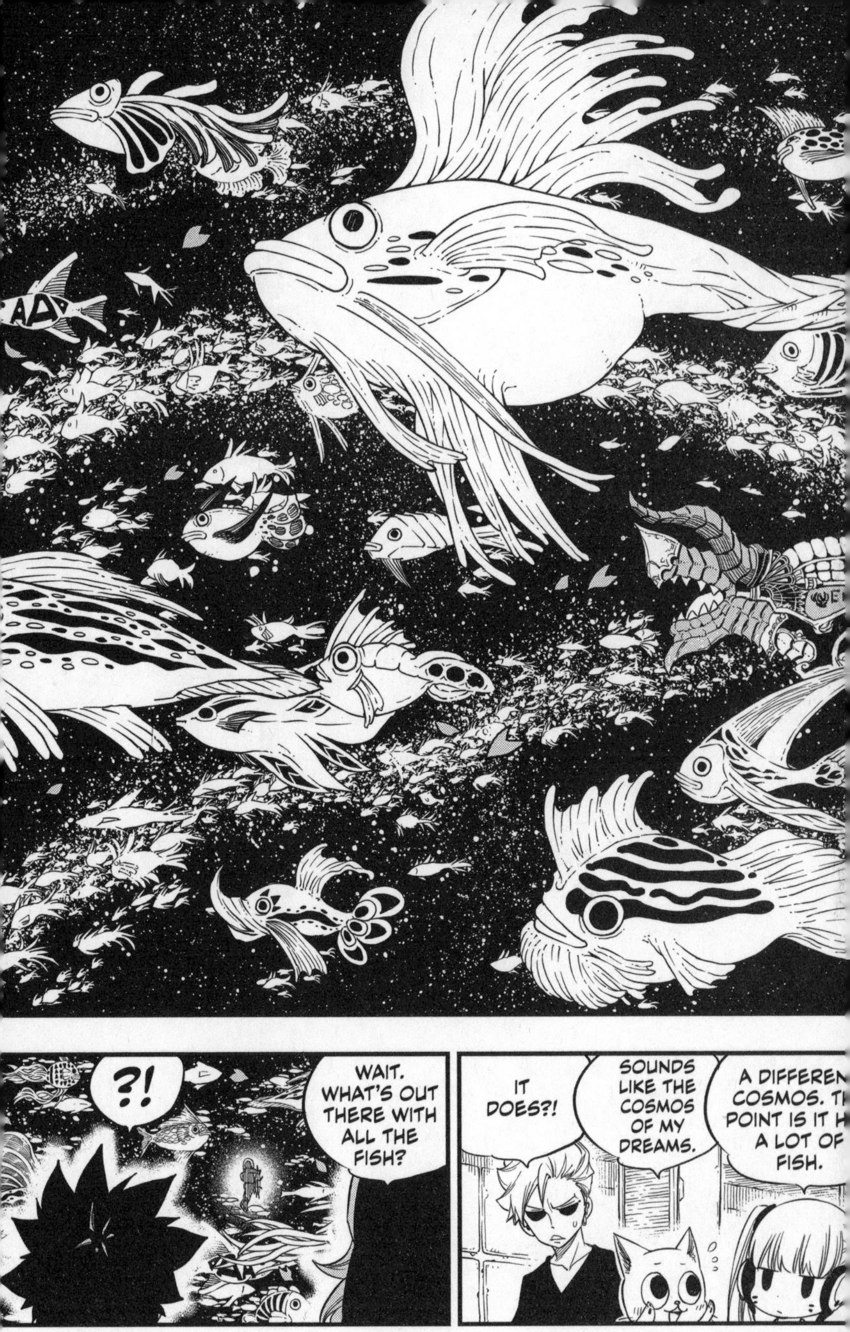
A DIFFEREN COSMOS. T POINT IS IT H A LOT OF FISH.
SOUNDS LIKE THE COSMOS OF MY DREAMS.
IT DOES?!
WAIT. WHAT'S OUT THERE WITH ALL THE FISH?
?!

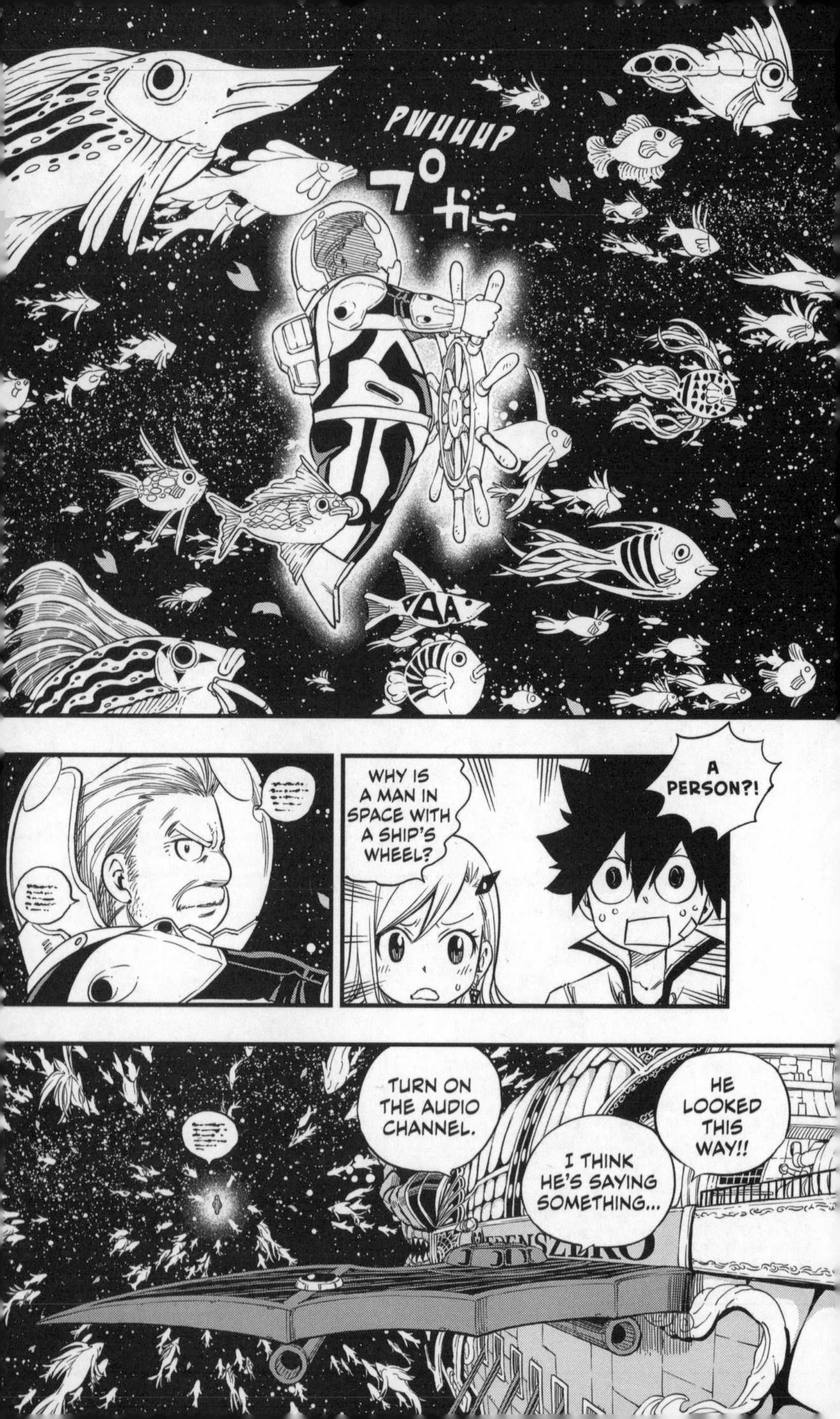

PWUUUP
A PERSON?!
WHY IS A MAN IN SPACE WITH A SHIP'S WHEEL?
HE LOOKED THIS WAY!!
I THINK HE'S SAYING SOMETHING...
TURN ON THE AUDIO CHANNEL.
EDENS ZERO

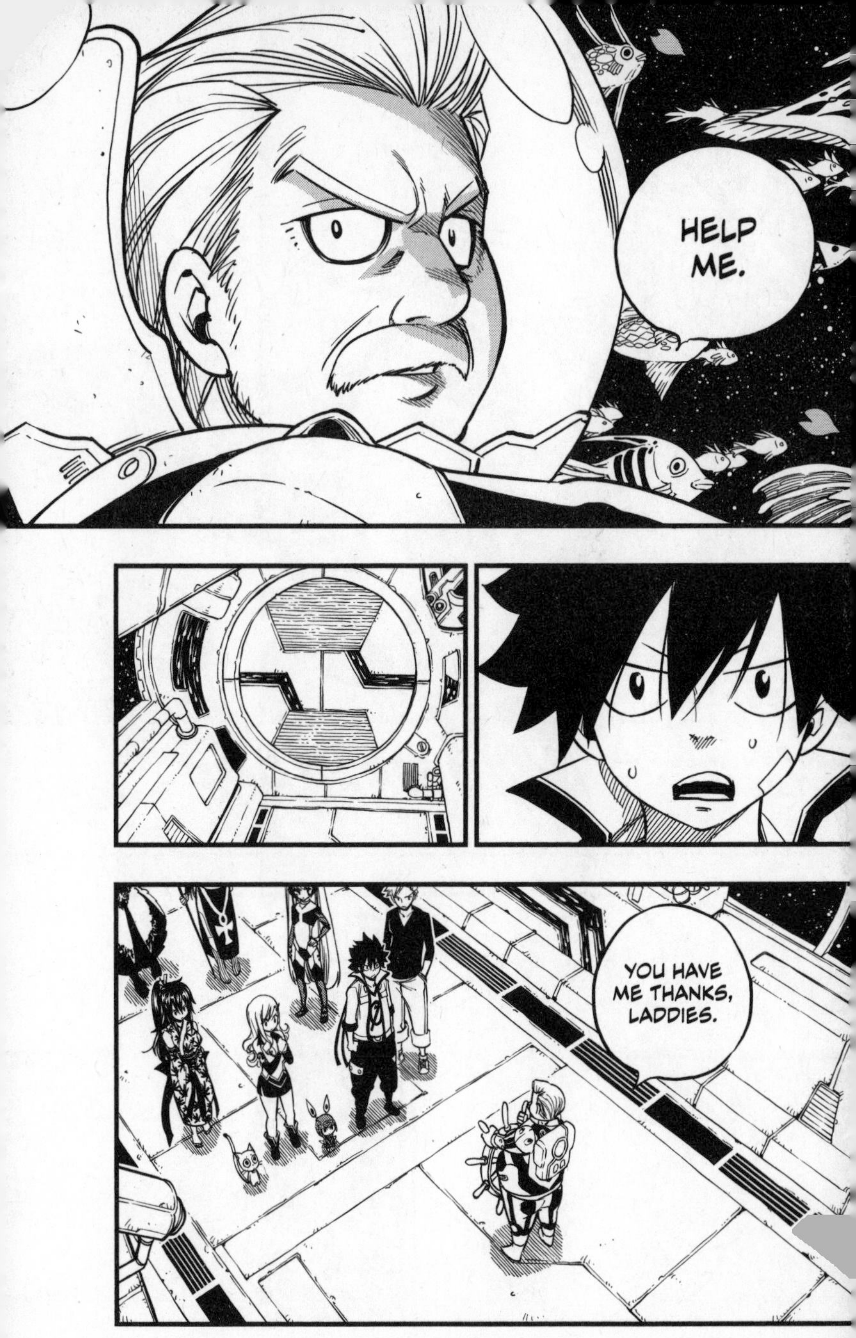
HELP ME.
YOU HAVE ME THANKS, LADDIES.

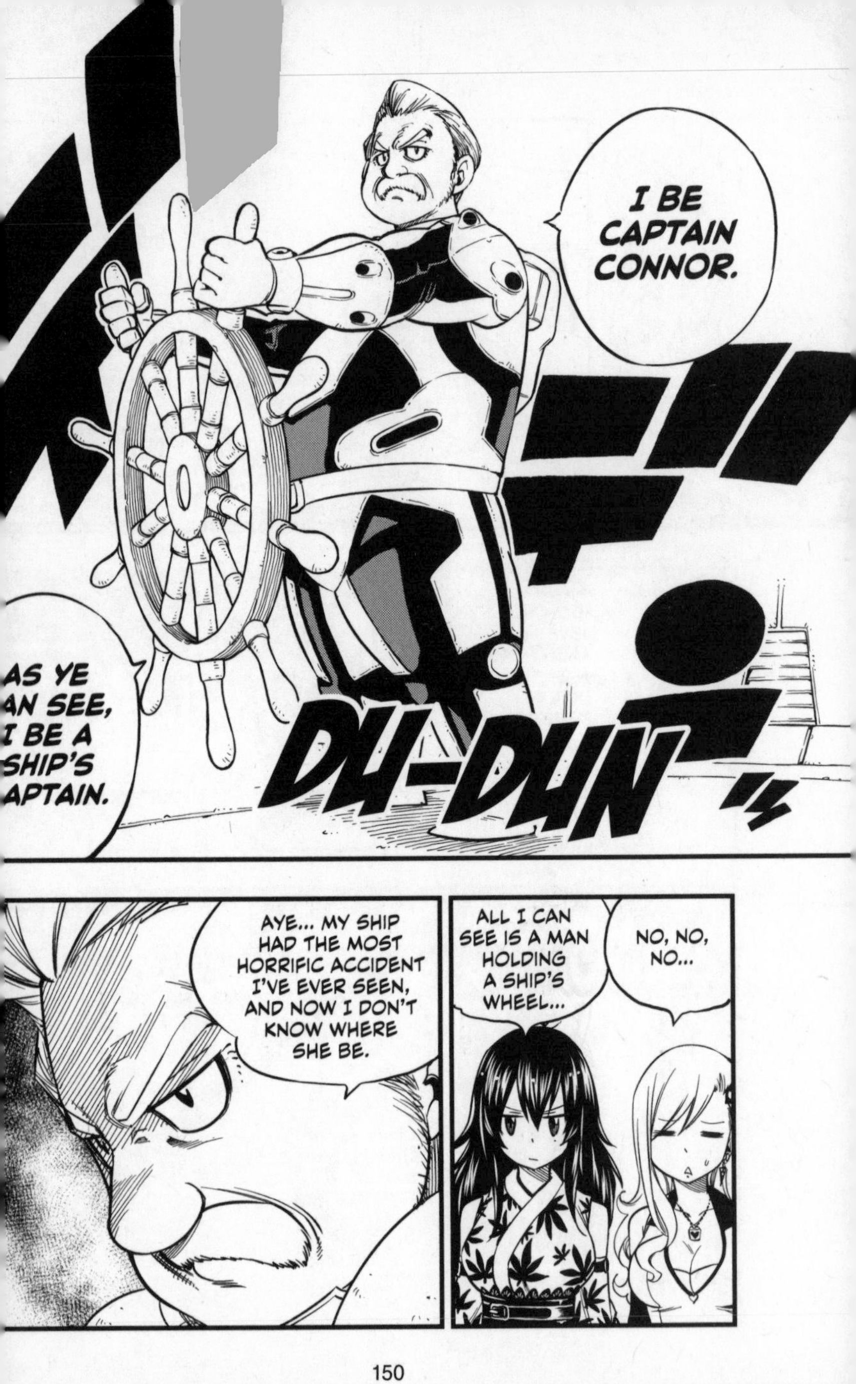

I BE CAPTAIN CONNOR.
DU-DUN
AS YE AN SEE, I BE A SHIP'S APTAIN.
NO, NO, NO...
ALL I CAN SEE IS A MAN HOLDING A SHIP'S WHEEL...
AYE... MY SHIP HAD THE MOST HORRIFIC ACCIDENT I'VE EVER SEEN, AND NOW I DON'T KNOW WHERE SHE BE.

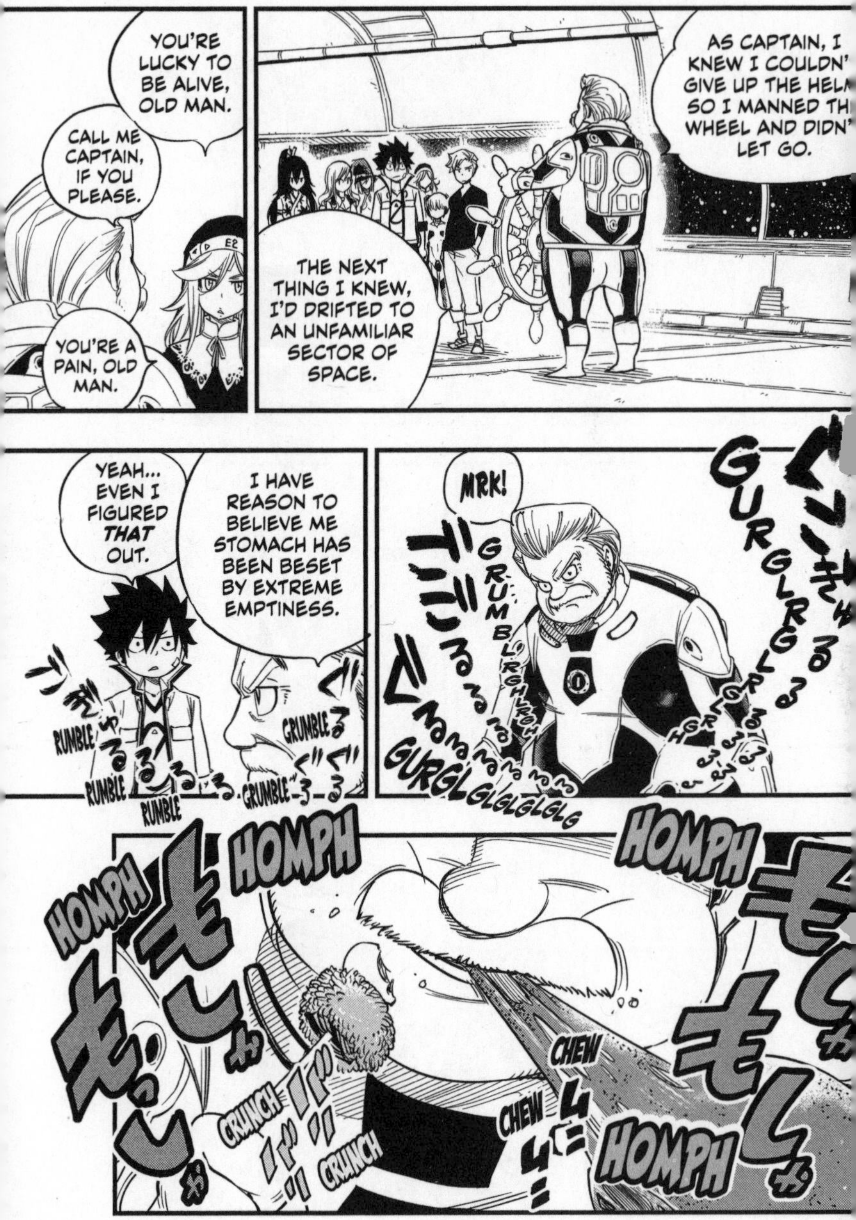
AS CAPTAIN, I KNEW I COULDN' GIVE UP THE HEL SO I MANNED TH WHEEL AND DIDN' LET GO.
THE NEXT THING I KNEW, I'D DRIFTED TO AN UNFAMILIAR SECTOR OF SPACE.
YOU'RE LUCKY TO BE ALIVE, OLD MAN.
CALL ME CAPTAIN, IF YOU PLEASE.
YOU'RE A PAIN, OLD MAN.
MRK!
GURGLRGLRGLRGHGR
GRUMBLRGHLRGH
GURGLGLGLGLGLG
I HAVE REASON TO BELIEVE ME STOMACH HAS BEEN BESET BY EXTREME EMPTINESS.
YEAH... EVEN I FIGURED ***THAT*** OUT.
GRUMBLE
GRUMBLE
RUMBLE
RUMBLE
RUMBLE
HOMPH
HOMPH
HOMPH
HOMPH
CHEW
CHEW
CRUNCH
CRUNCH

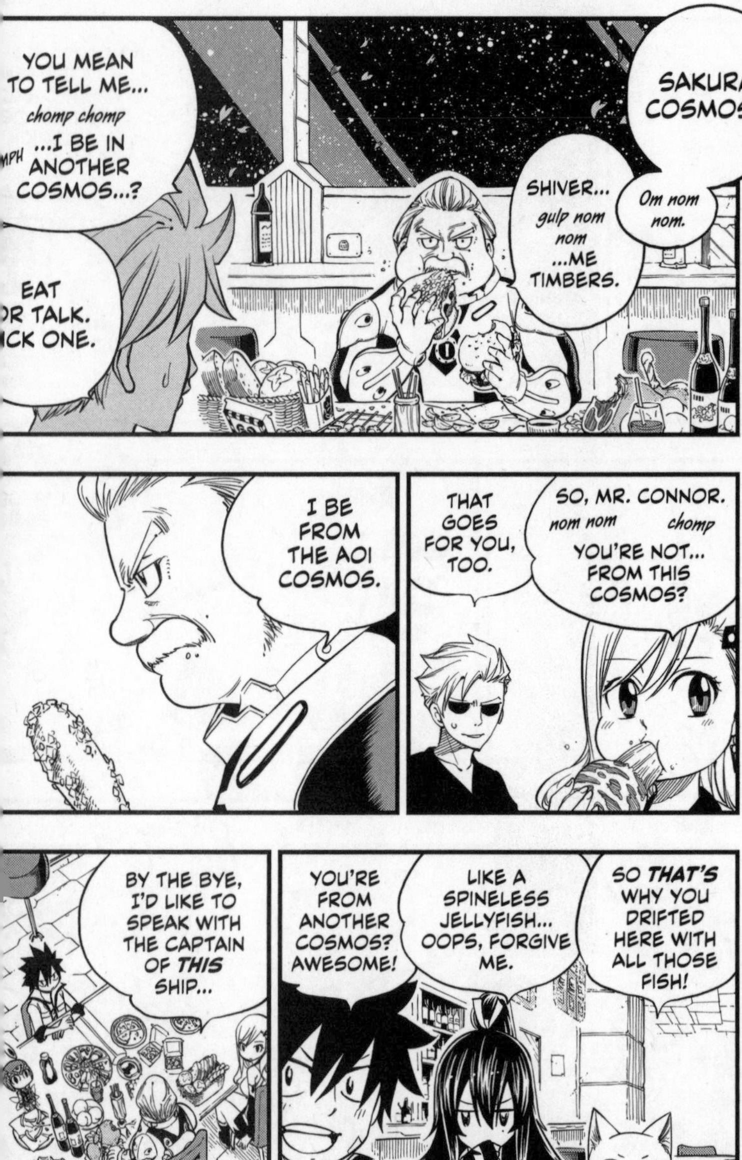
SAKURA COSMOS?
Om nom nom.
SHIVER... gulp nom nom ...ME TIMBERS.
YOU MEAN TO TELL ME... chomp chomp ...I BE IN ANOTHER COSMOS...?
MPH
EAT R TALK. CK ONE.
SO, MR. CONNOR. nom nom chomp YOU'RE NOT... FROM THIS COSMOS?
THAT GOES FOR YOU, TOO.
I BE FROM THE AOI COSMOS.
SO *THAT'S* WHY YOU DRIFTED HERE WITH ALL THOSE FISH!
LIKE A SPINELESS JELLYFISH... OOPS, FORGIVE ME.
YOU'RE FROM ANOTHER COSMOS? AWESOME!
BY THE BYE, I'D LIKE TO SPEAK WITH THE CAPTAIN OF *THIS* SHIP...

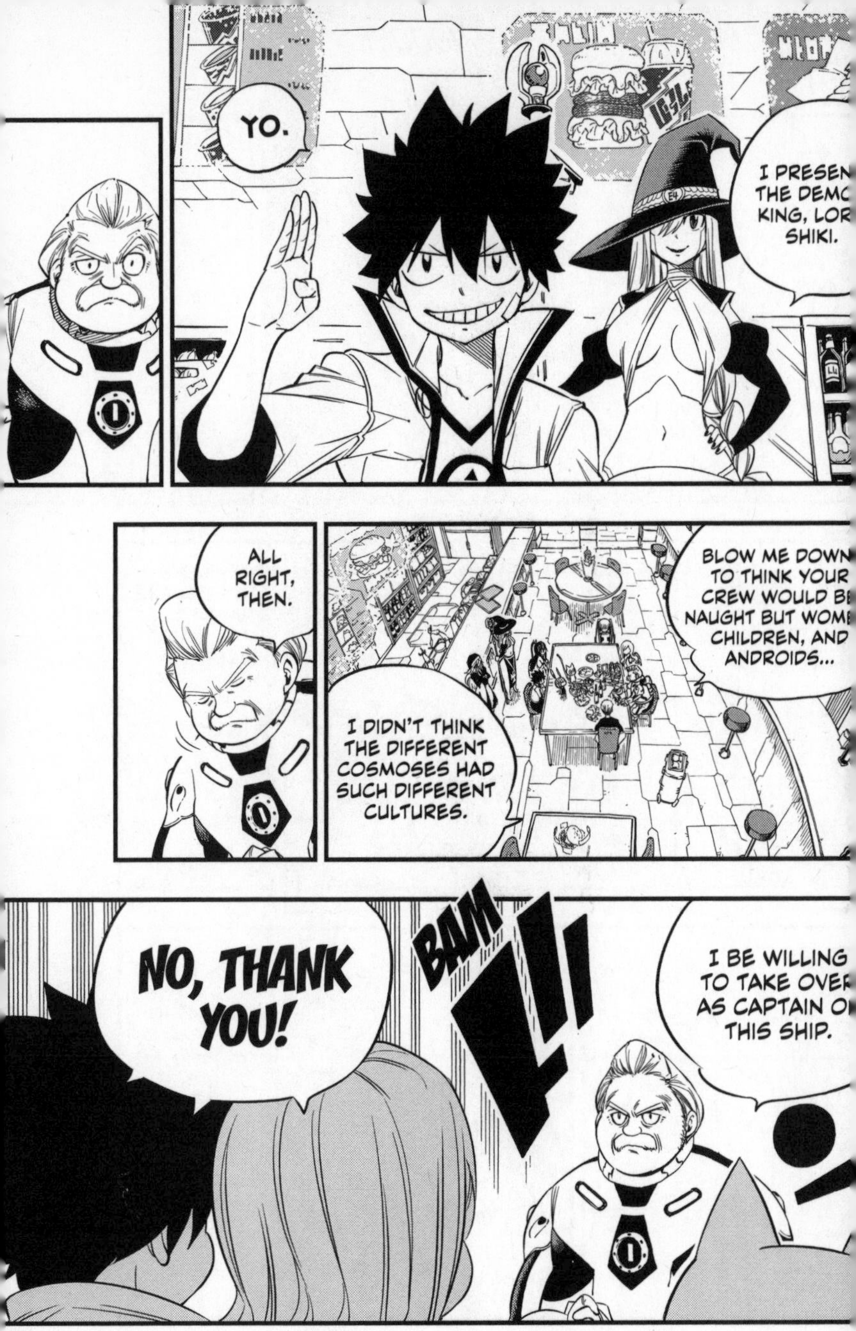
I PRESEN THE DEMO KING, LOR SHIKI.
YO.
BLOW ME DOWN TO THINK YOUR CREW WOULD BE NAUGHT BUT WOME CHILDREN, AND ANDROIDS...
I DIDN'T THINK THE DIFFERENT COSMOSES HAD SUCH DIFFERENT CULTURES.
ALL RIGHT, THEN.
I BE WILLING TO TAKE OVER AS CAPTAIN O THIS SHIP.
BAM
NO, THANK YOU!

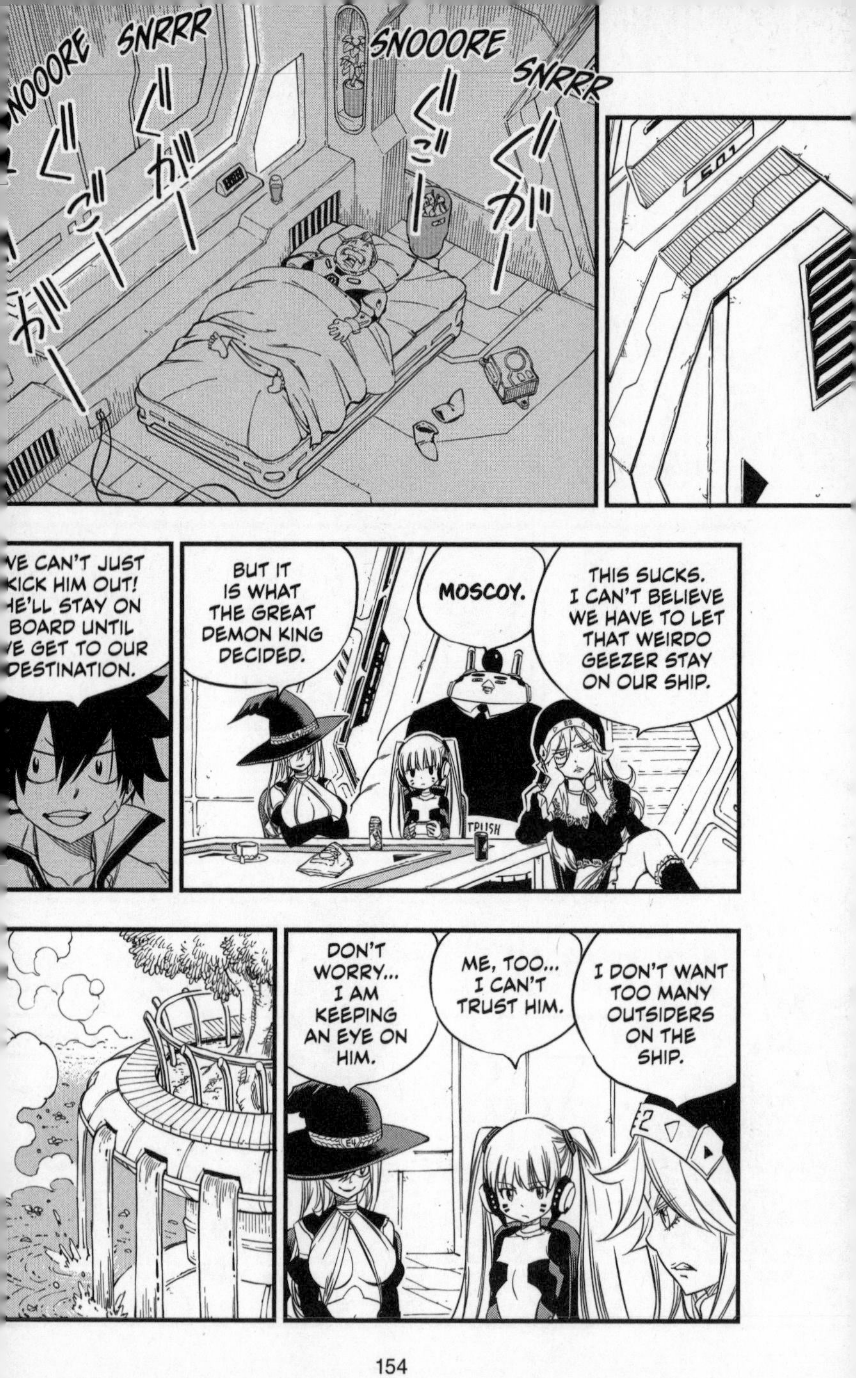
SNRRR
SNOOORE
SNRRR
SNOOORE
THIS SUCKS. I CAN'T BELIEVE WE HAVE TO LET THAT WEIRDO GEEZER STAY ON OUR SHIP.
MOSCOY.
BUT IT IS WHAT THE GREAT DEMON KING DECIDED.
VE CAN'T JUST KICK HIM OUT! HE'LL STAY ON BOARD UNTIL VE GET TO OUR DESTINATION.
I DON'T WANT TOO MANY OUTSIDERS ON THE SHIP.
ME, TOO... I CAN'T TRUST HIM.
DON'T WORRY... I AM KEEPING AN EYE ON HIM.

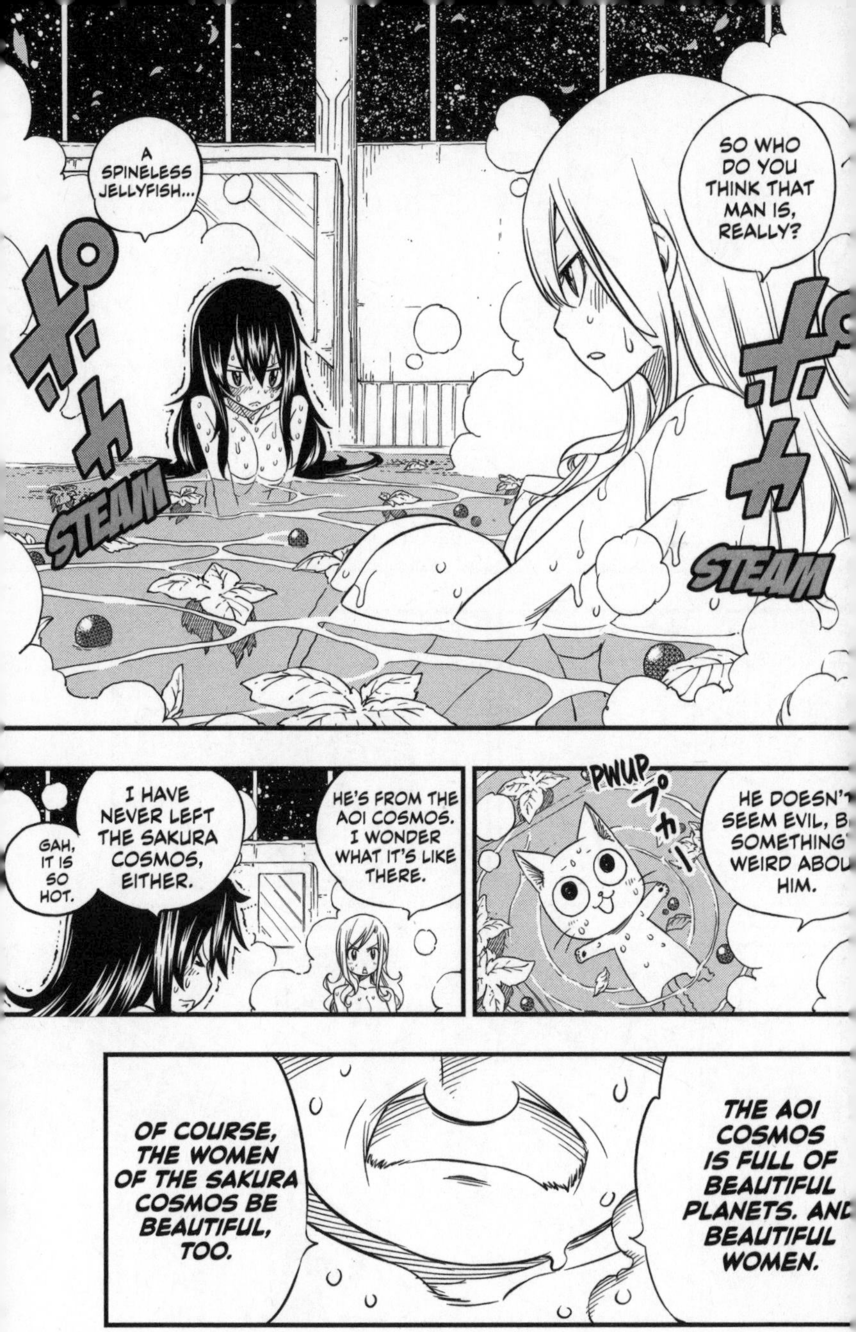
SO WHO DO YOU THINK THAT MAN IS, REALLY?
STEAM
A SPINELESS JELLYFISH...
STEAM
PWUP
HE DOESN'T SEEM EVIL, B SOMETHING' WEIRD ABOU HIM.
HE'S FROM THE AOI COSMOS. I WONDER WHAT IT'S LIKE THERE.
I HAVE NEVER LEFT THE SAKURA COSMOS, EITHER.
GAH, IT IS SO HOT.
THE AOI COSMOS IS FULL OF BEAUTIFUL PLANETS. AN BEAUTIFUL WOMEN.
OF COURSE, THE WOMEN OF THE SAKURA COSMOS BE BEAUTIFUL, TOO.

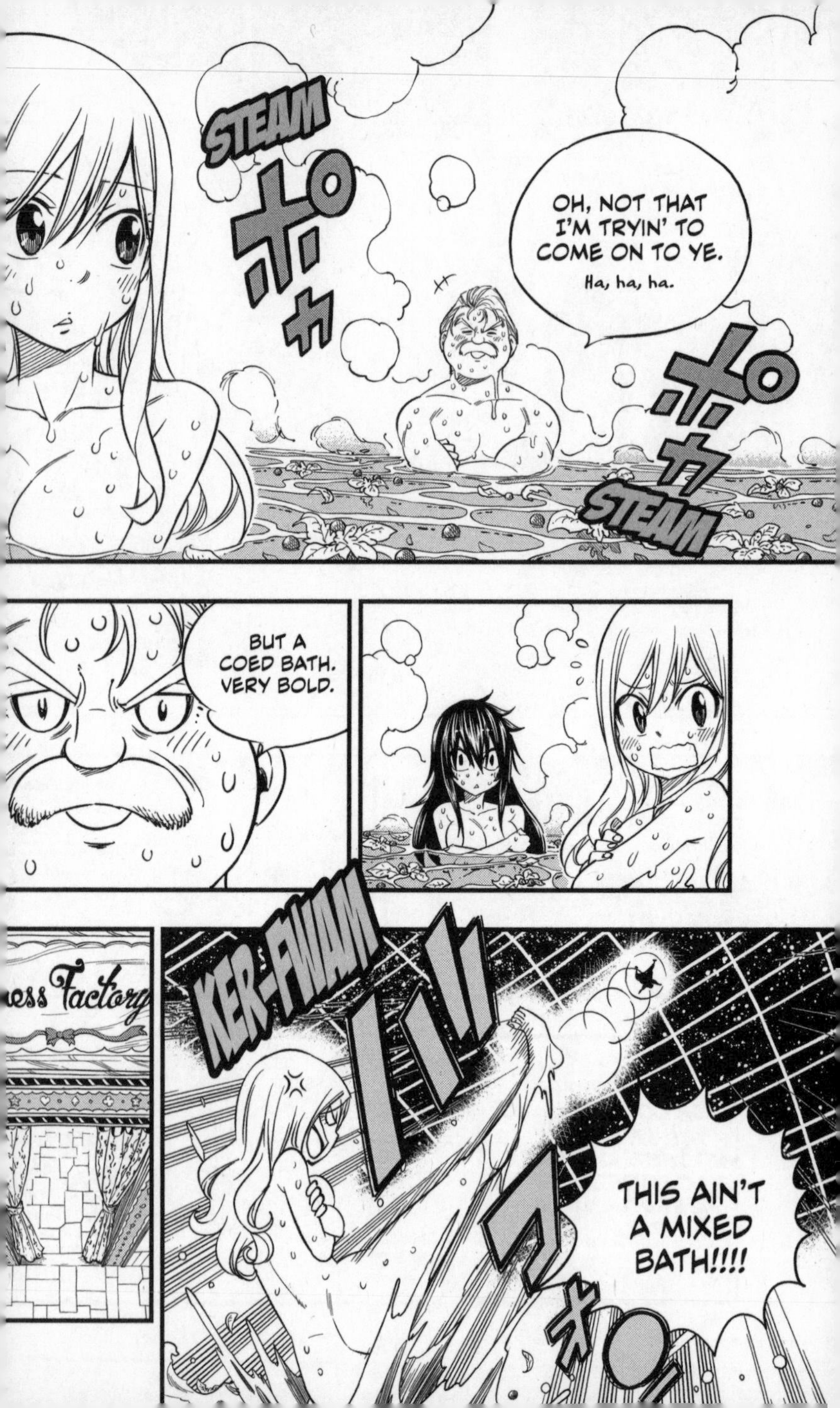
OH, NOT THAT I'M TRYIN' TO COME ON TO YE.
Ha, ha, ha.
ポカ
STEAM
STEAM
ポカ
BUT A COED BATH. VERY BOLD.
KER-FWAM
THIS AIN'T A MIXED BATH!!!!
ess Factory

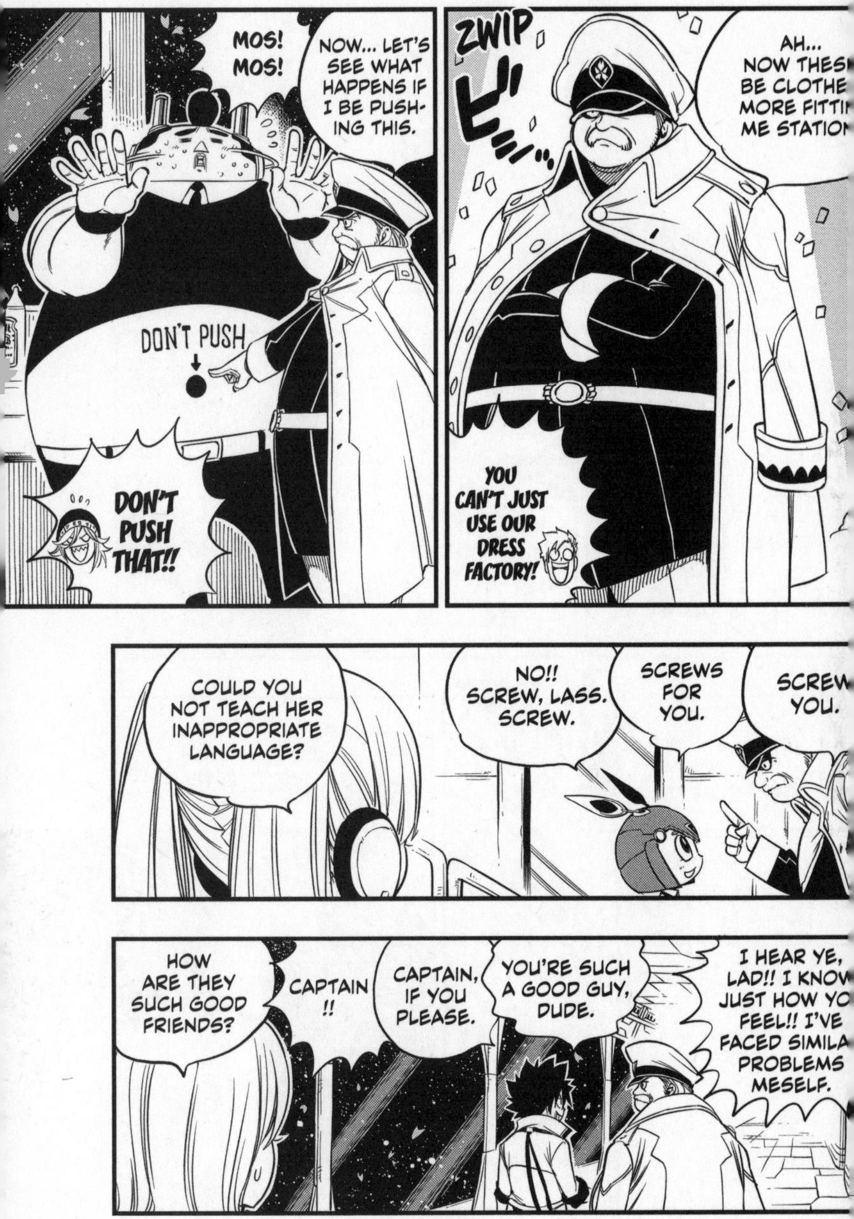

ZWIP
AH... NOW THES BE CLOTHE MORE FITTI ME STATIO
YOU CAN'T JUST USE OUR DRESS FACTORY!
NOW... LET'S SEE WHAT HAPPENS IF I BE PUSHING THIS.
MOS! MOS!
DON'T PUSH
DON'T PUSH THAT!!
SCREW YOU.
SCREWS FOR YOU.
NO!! SCREW, LASS. SCREW.
COULD YOU NOT TEACH HER INAPPROPRIATE LANGUAGE?
I HEAR YE, LAD!! I KNOW JUST HOW YO FEEL!! I'VE FACED SIMILA PROBLEMS MESELF.
YOU'RE SUCH A GOOD GUY, DUDE.
CAPTAIN, IF YOU PLEASE.
CAPTAIN!!
HOW ARE THEY SUCH GOOD FRIENDS?

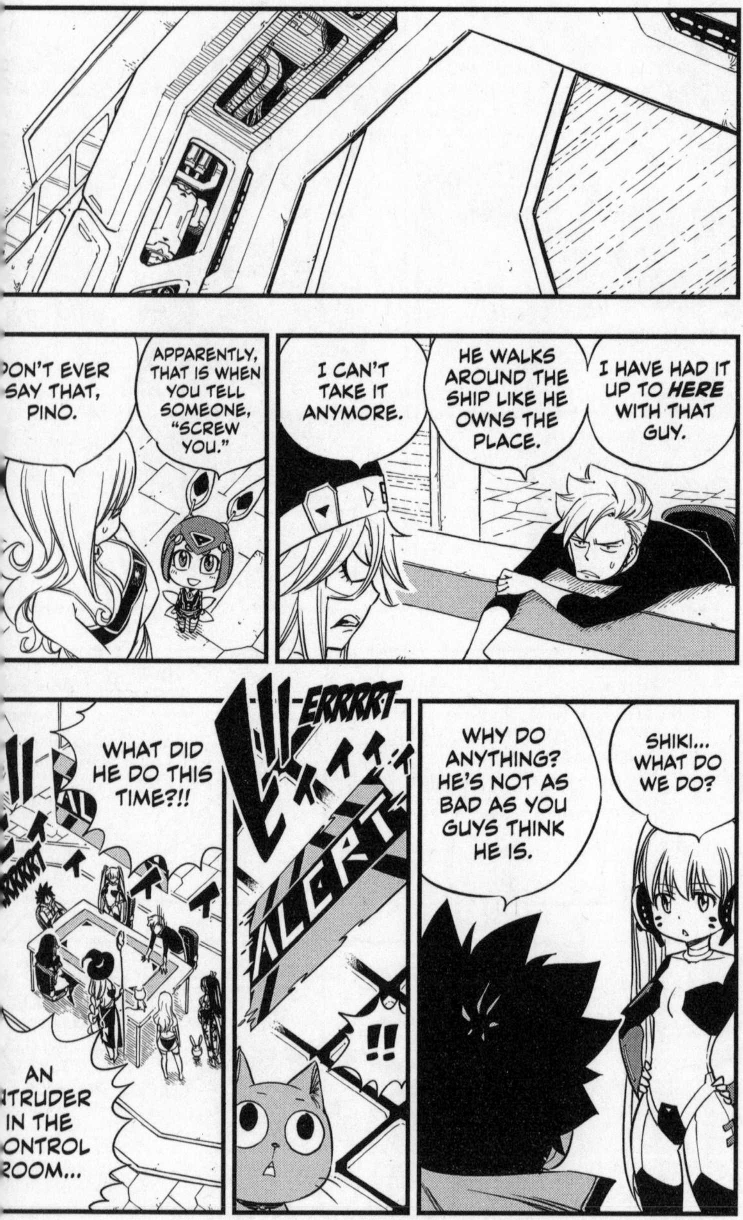
I HAVE HAD IT UP TO *HERE* WITH THAT GUY.
HE WALKS AROUND THE SHIP LIKE HE OWNS THE PLACE.
I CAN'T TAKE IT ANYMORE.
APPARENTLY, THAT IS WHEN YOU TELL SOMEONE, "SCREW YOU."
ON'T EVER SAY THAT, PINO.
SHIKI... WHAT DO WE DO?
WHY DO ANYTHING? HE'S NOT AS BAD AS YOU GUYS THINK HE IS.
ERRRRT
ALERT
!!
WHAT DID HE DO THIS TIME?!!
RRRRT
AN NTRUDER IN THE ONTROL ROOM...

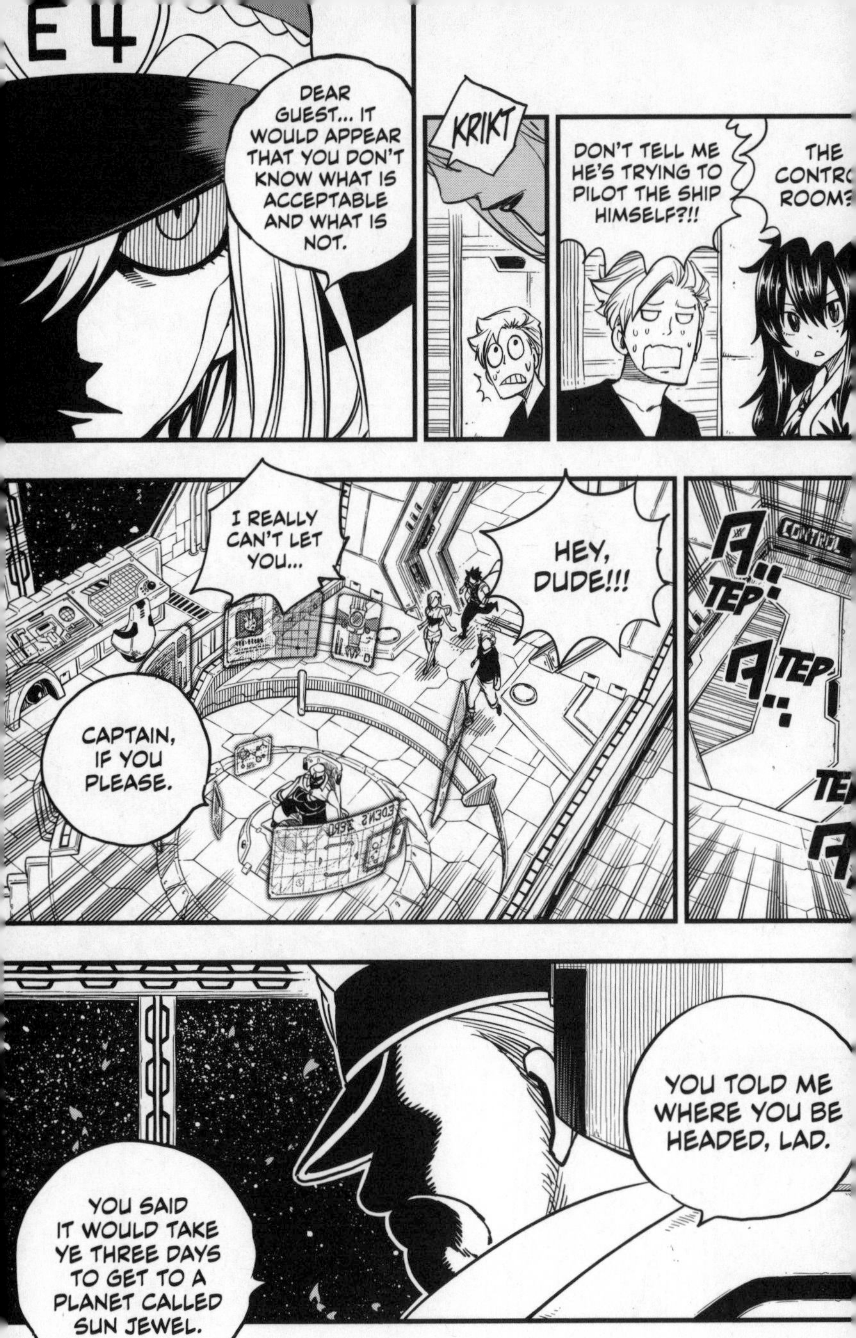
THE CONTRO ROOM?
DON'T TELL ME HE'S TRYING TO PILOT THE SHIP HIMSELF?!!
KRIKT
DEAR GUEST... IT WOULD APPEAR THAT YOU DON'T KNOW WHAT IS ACCEPTABLE AND WHAT IS NOT.
CONTROL
TEP
TEP
HEY, DUDE!!!
I REALLY CAN'T LET YOU...
CAPTAIN, IF YOU PLEASE.
YOU TOLD ME WHERE YOU BE HEADED, LAD.
YOU SAID IT WOULD TAKE YE THREE DAYS TO GET TO A PLANET CALLED SUN JEWEL.

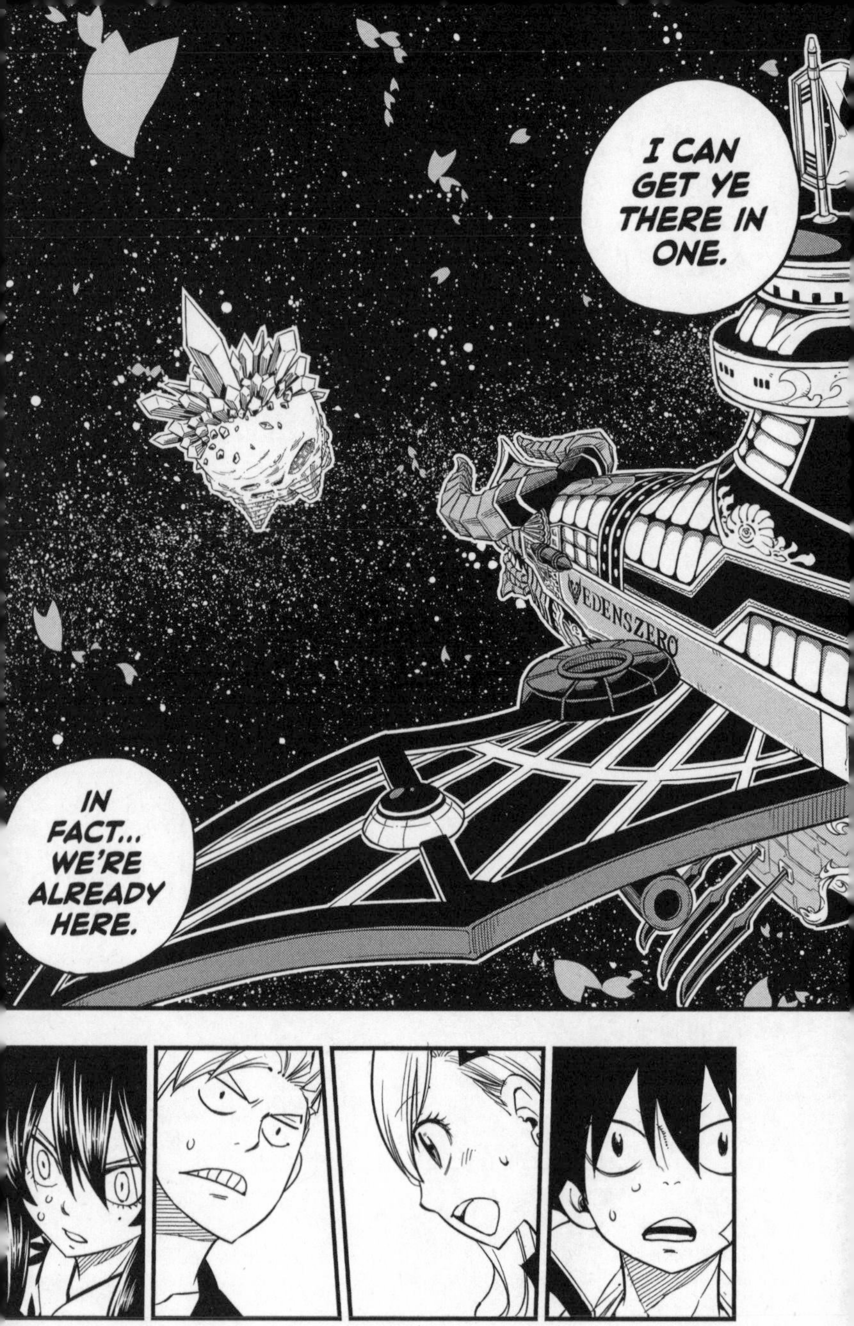
I CAN GET YE THERE IN ONE.
EDENSZERO
IN FACT... WE'RE ALREADY HERE.

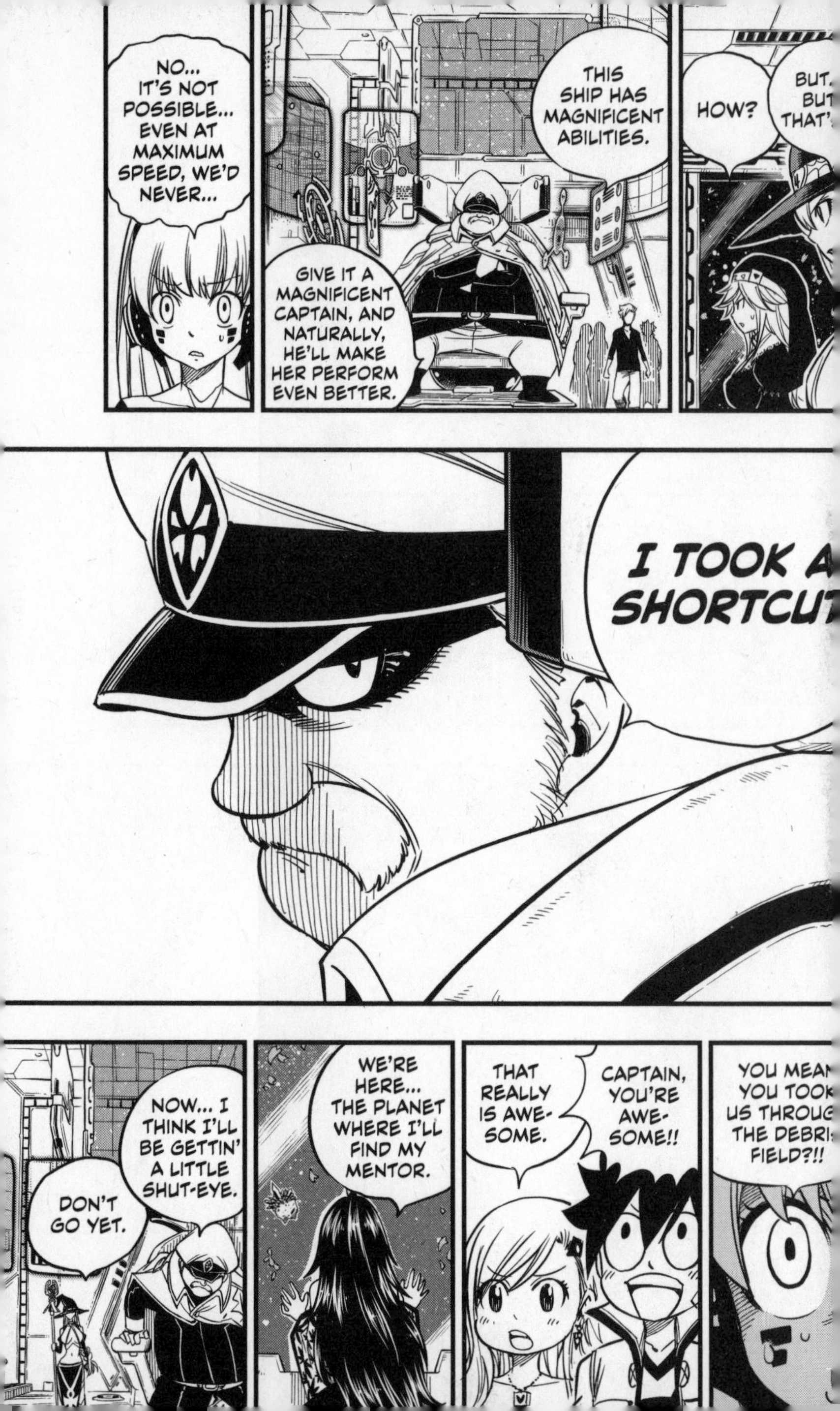
BUT. BUT THAT'
HOW?
THIS SHIP HAS MAGNIFICENT ABILITIES.
GIVE IT A MAGNIFICENT CAPTAIN, AND NATURALLY, HE'LL MAKE HER PERFORM EVEN BETTER.
NO... IT'S NOT POSSIBLE... EVEN AT MAXIMUM SPEED, WE'D NEVER...
I TOOK A SHORTCU
YOU MEAN YOU TOOK US THROUG THE DEBRI FIELD?!!
CAPTAIN, YOU'RE AWE-SOME!!
THAT REALLY IS AWE-SOME.
WE'RE HERE... THE PLANET WHERE I'LL FIND MY MENTOR.
NOW... I THINK I'LL BE GETTIN' A LITTLE SHUT-EYE.
DON'T GO YET.

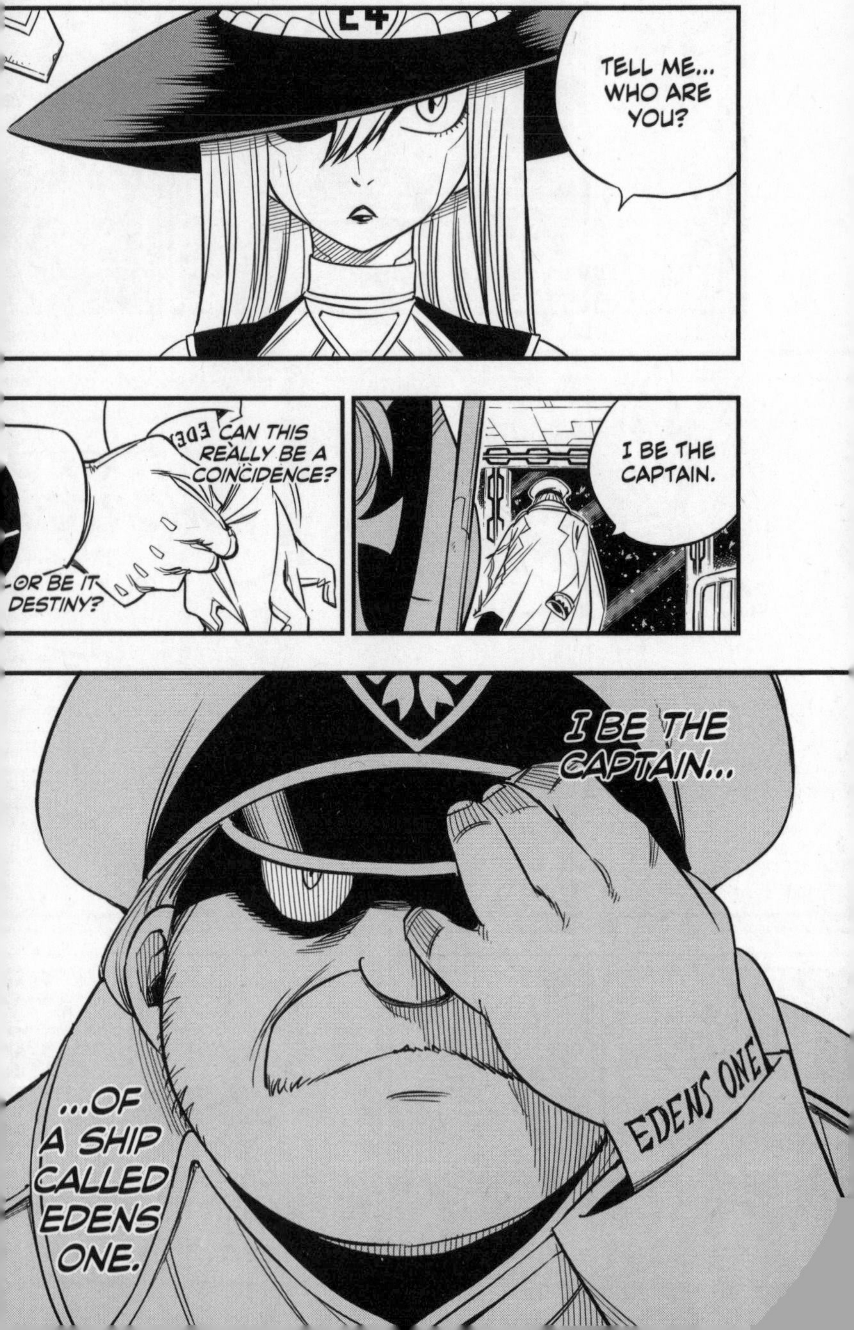

TELL ME... WHO ARE YOU?
I BE THE CAPTAIN.
CAN THIS REALLY BE A COINCIDENCE?
...OR BE IT DESTINY?
I BE THE CAPTAIN...
EDENS ONE
...OF A SHIP CALLED EDENS ONE.

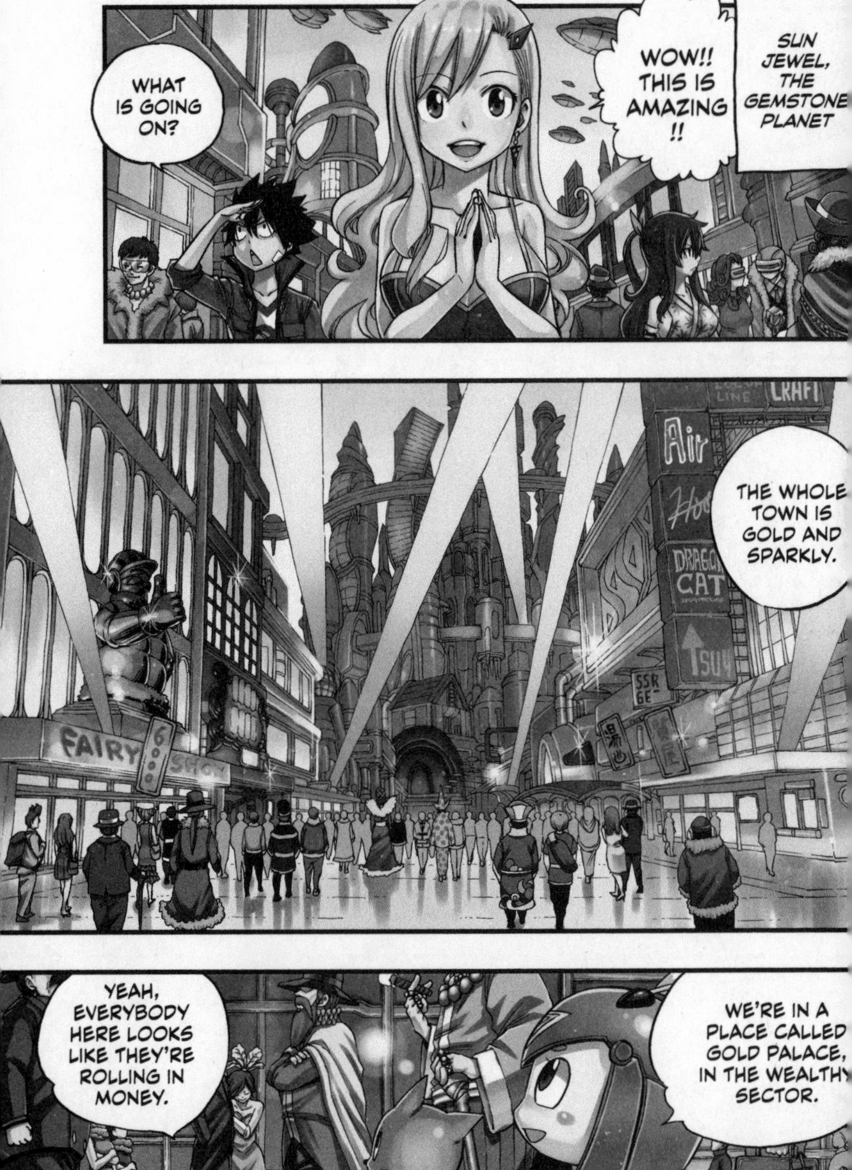
SUN JEWEL, THE GEMSTONE PLANET
WOW!! THIS IS AMAZING!!
WHAT IS GOING ON?
THE WHOLE TOWN IS GOLD AND SPARKLY.
WE'RE IN A PLACE CALLED GOLD PALACE, IN THE WEALTHY SECTOR.
YEAH, EVERYBODY HERE LOOKS LIKE THEY'RE ROLLING IN MONEY.

Chapter 50: Madame Kurenai

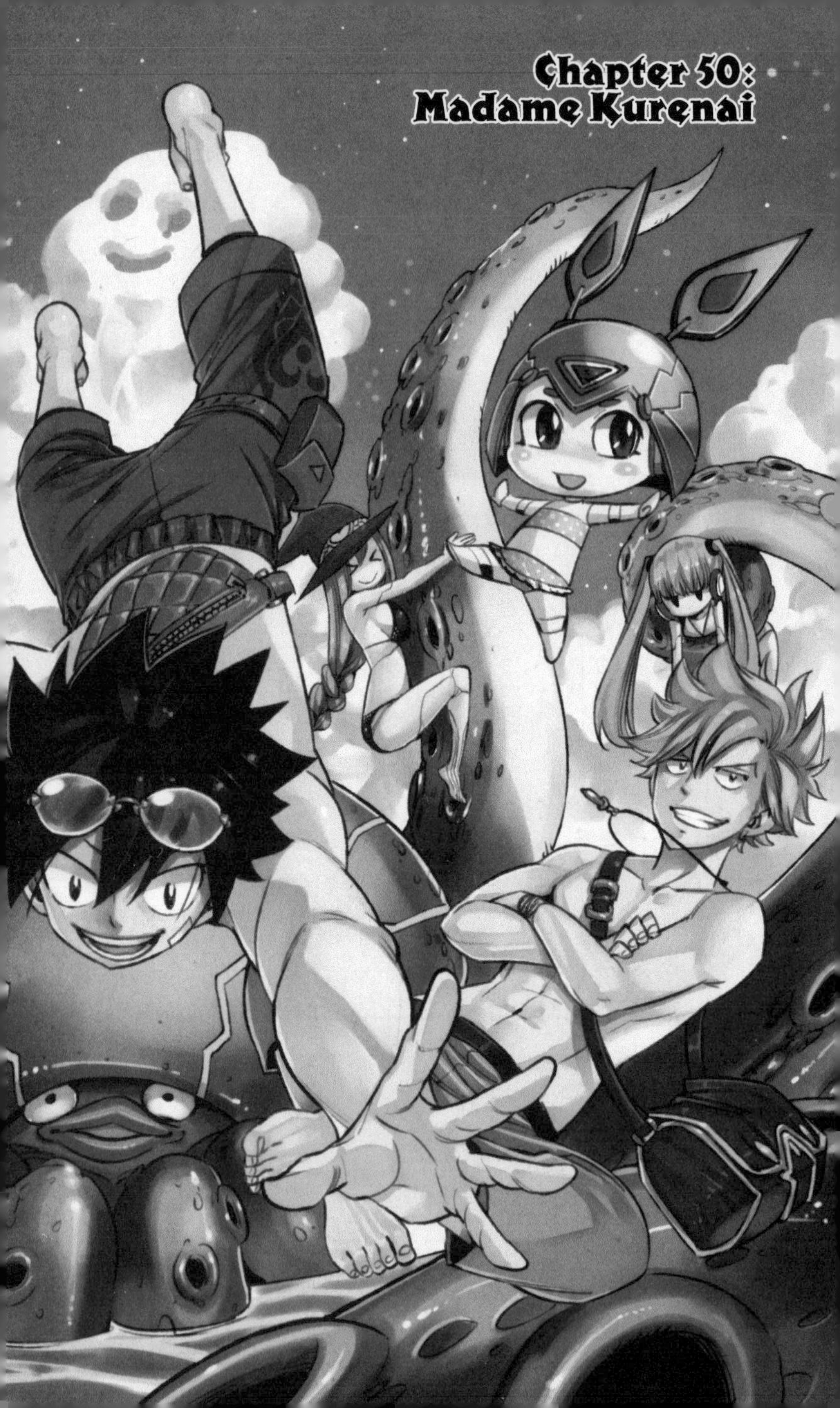

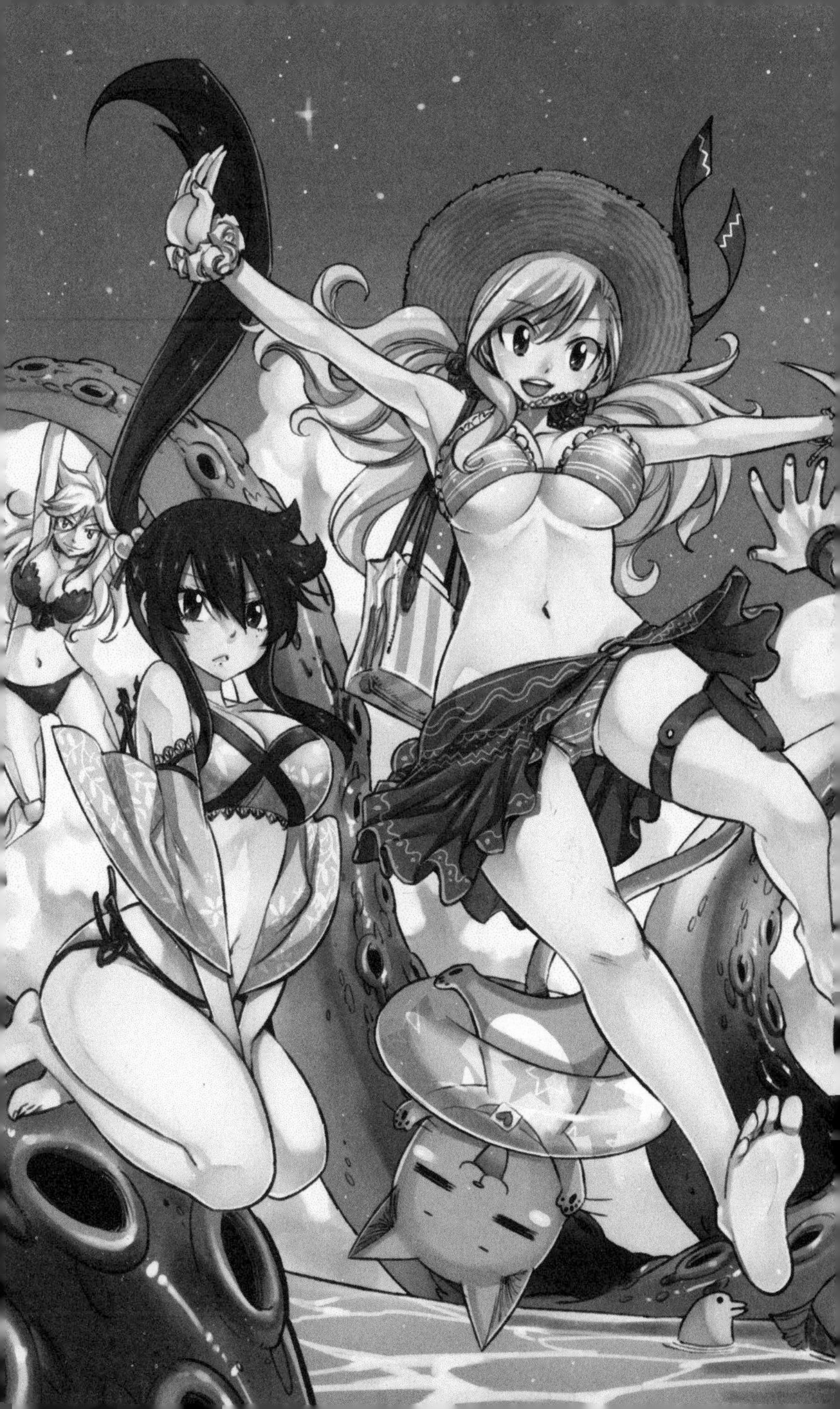

EDENSZERO

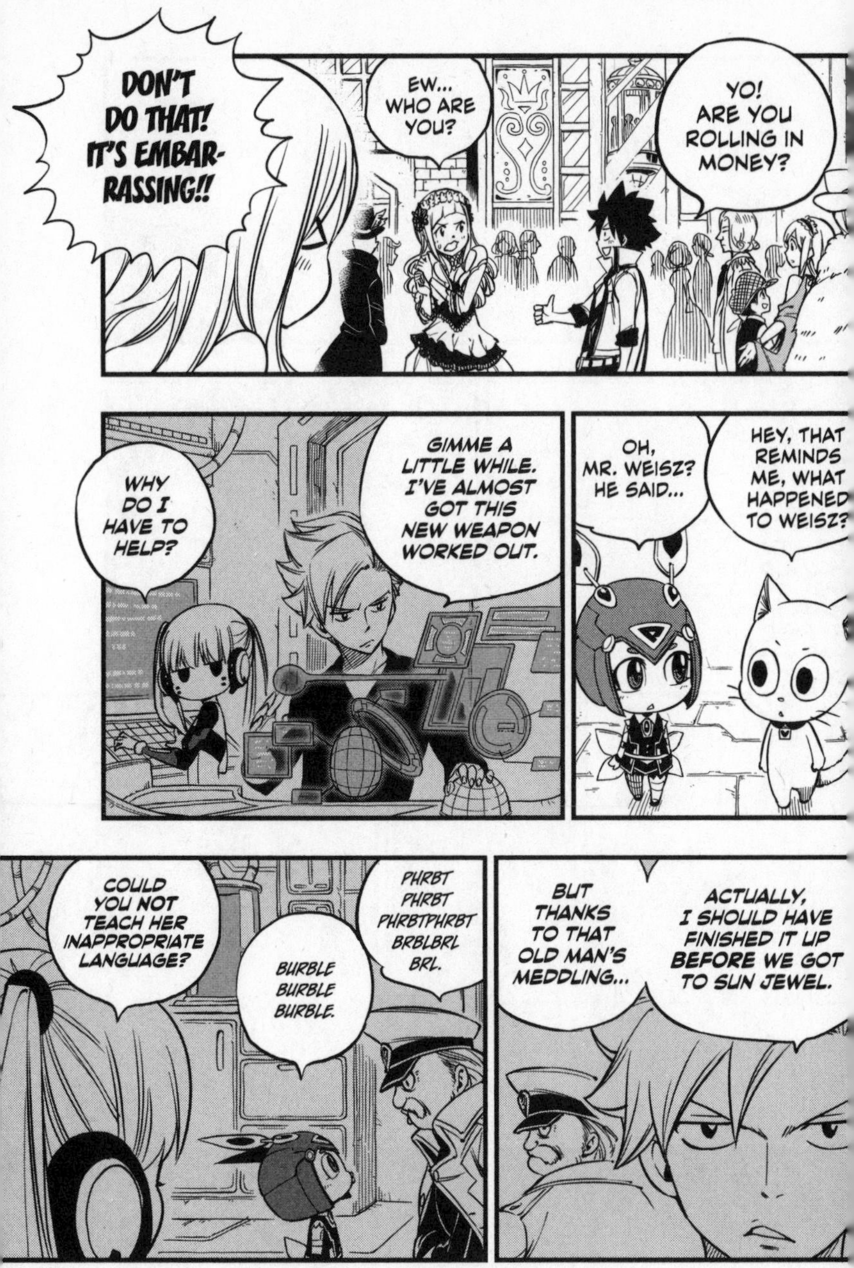
YO! ARE YOU ROLLING IN MONEY?
EW... WHO ARE YOU?
DON'T DO THAT! IT'S EMBARRASSING!!
HEY, THAT REMINDS ME, WHAT HAPPENED TO WEISZ?
OH, MR. WEISZ? HE SAID...
GIMME A LITTLE WHILE. I'VE ALMOST GOT THIS NEW WEAPON WORKED OUT.
WHY DO I HAVE TO HELP?
ACTUALLY, I SHOULD HAVE FINISHED IT UP BEFORE WE GOT TO SUN JEWEL.
BUT THANKS TO THAT OLD MAN'S MEDDLING...
PHRBT PHRBT PHRBTPHRBT BRBLBRL BRL.
BURBLE BURBLE BURBLE.
COULD YOU NOT TEACH HER INAPPROPRIATE LANGUAGE?

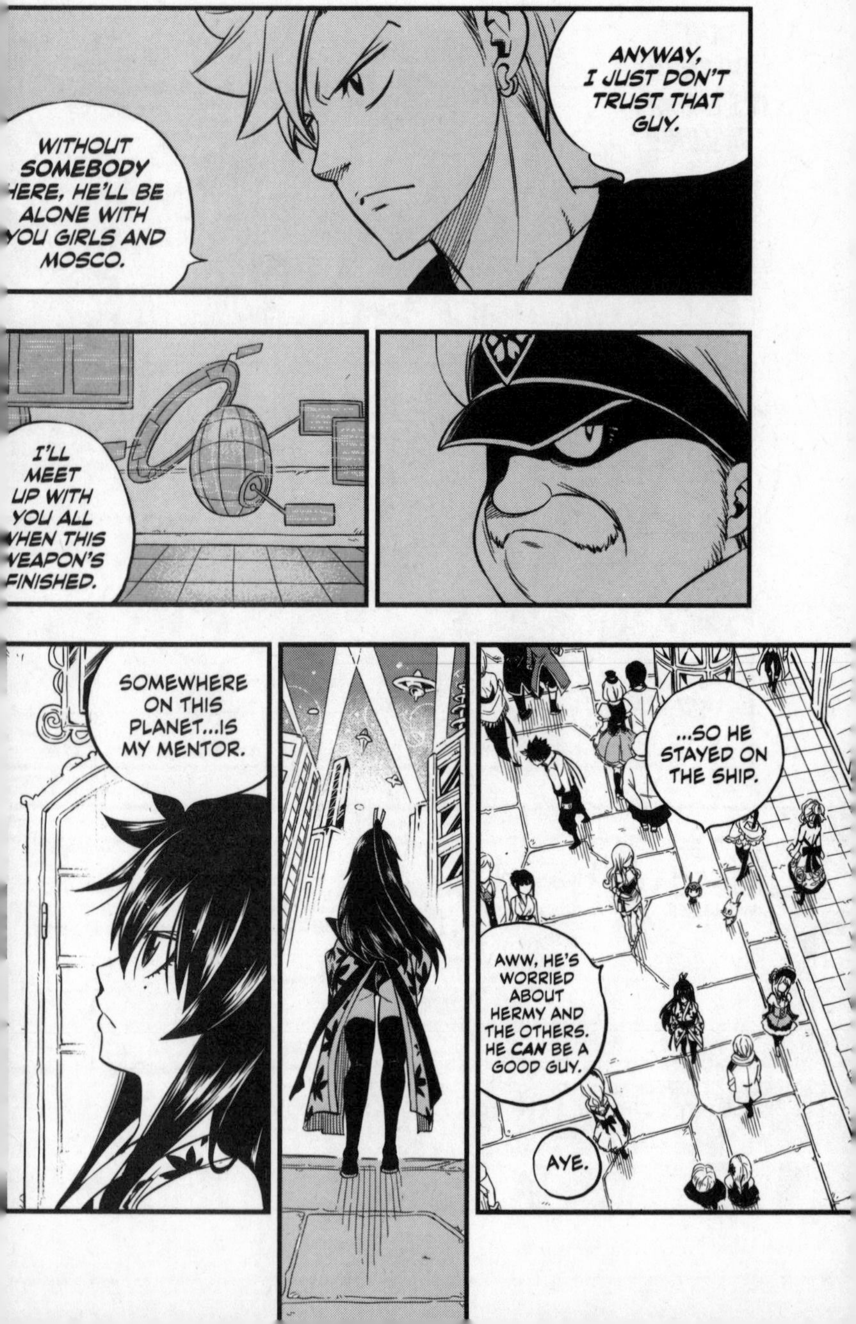
ANYWAY, I JUST DON'T TRUST THAT GUY.
WITHOUT SOMEBODY HERE, HE'LL BE ALONE WITH YOU GIRLS AND MOSCO.
I'LL MEET UP WITH YOU ALL WHEN THIS WEAPON'S FINISHED.
...SO HE STAYED ON THE SHIP.
AWW, HE'S WORRIED ABOUT HERMY AND THE OTHERS. HE **CAN** BE A GOOD GUY.
AYE.
SOMEWHERE ON THIS PLANET...IS MY MENTOR.

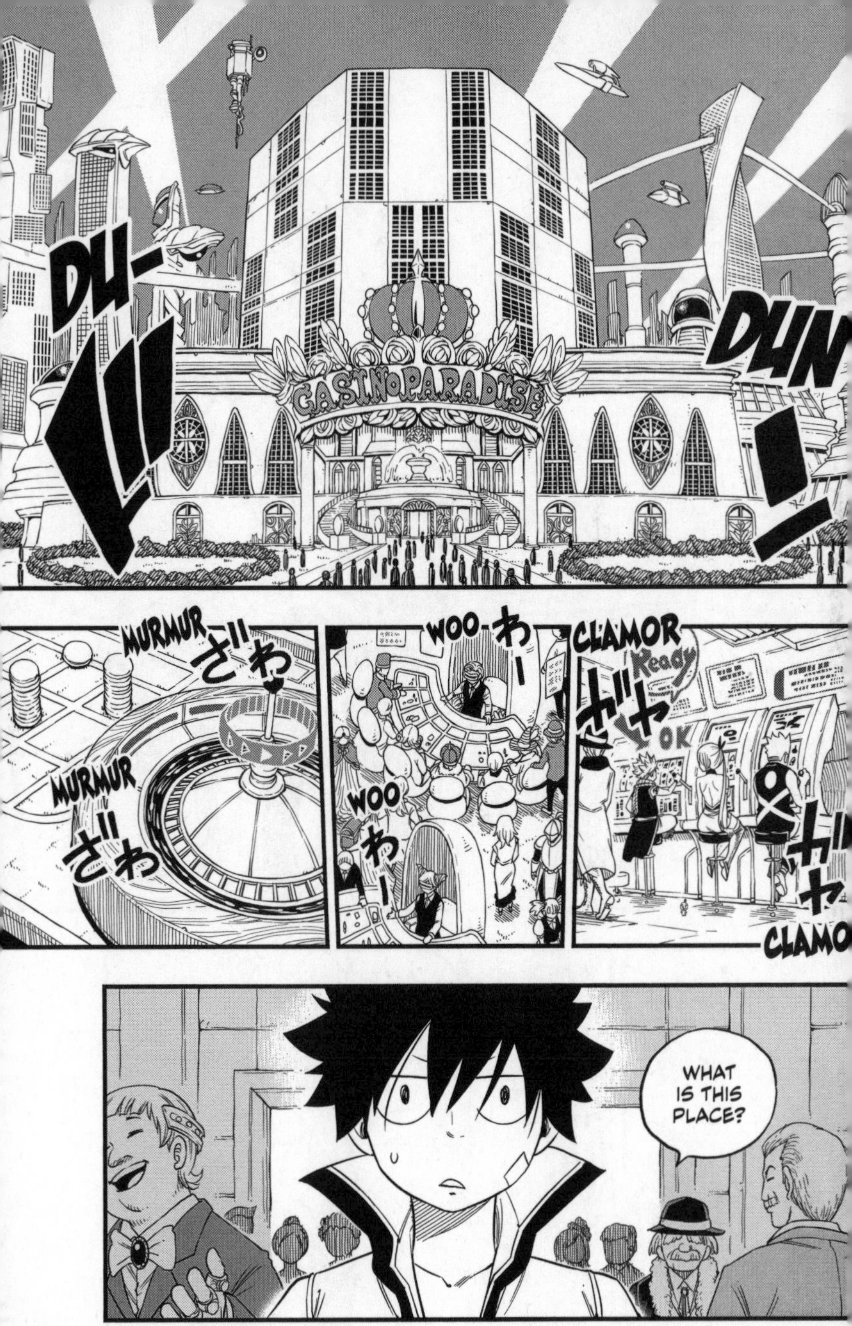
CASINO PARADISE
DU-
DUN
CLAMOR ガヤ
Ready
OK
ガヤ CLAMO
WOO わー
WOO わー
MURMUR ざわ
MURMUR ざわ
WHAT IS THIS PLACE?

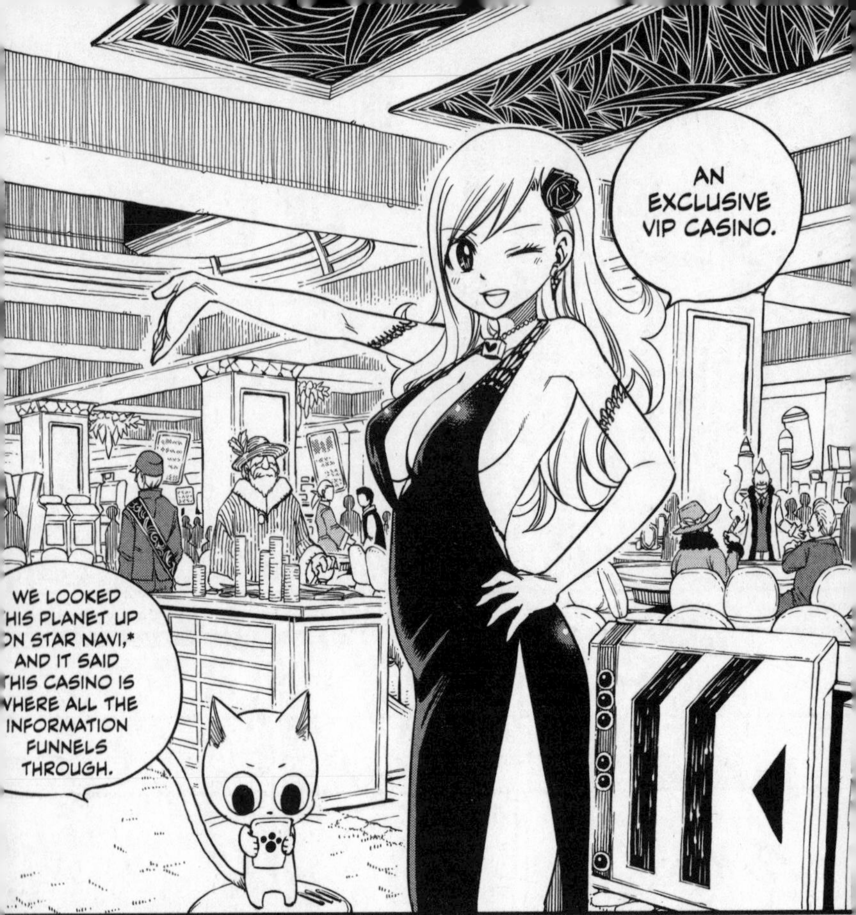
AN EXCLUSIVE VIP CASINO.
WE LOOKED HIS PLANET UP N STAR NAVI,* AND IT SAID THIS CASINO IS HERE ALL THE INFORMATION FUNNELS THROUGH.

vigation.com: A general information site specializing in tourist information for the various planets.

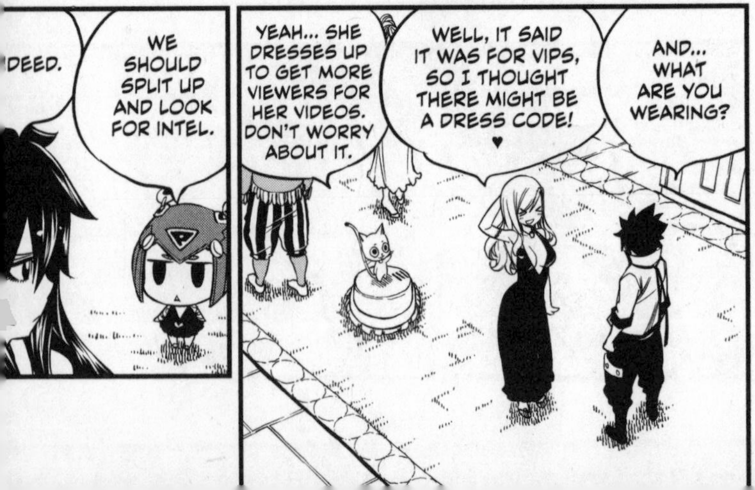
AND... WHAT ARE YOU WEARING?
WELL, IT SAID IT WAS FOR VIPS, SO I THOUGHT THERE MIGHT BE A DRESS CODE! ♥
YEAH... SHE DRESSES UP TO GET MORE VIEWERS FOR HER VIDEOS. DON'T WORRY ABOUT IT.
WE SHOULD SPLIT UP AND LOOK FOR INTEL.
DEED.

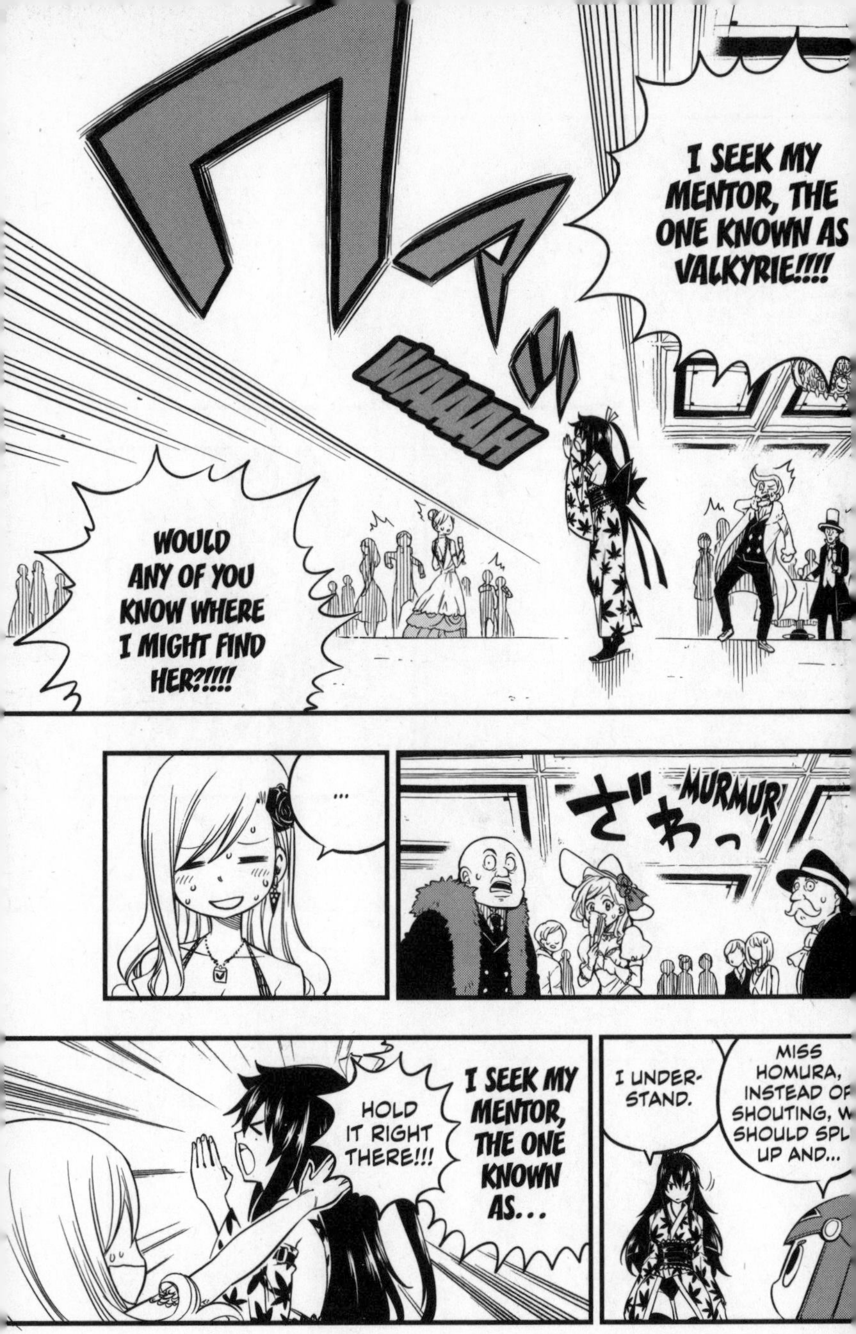
I SEEK MY MENTOR, THE ONE KNOWN AS VALKYRIE!!!!
WAAAH
WOULD ANY OF YOU KNOW WHERE I MIGHT FIND HER?!!!!
ざわっ
MURMUR
...
MISS HOMURA, INSTEAD OF SHOUTING, W SHOULD SPL UP AND...
I UNDER-STAND.
I SEEK MY MENTOR, THE ONE KNOWN AS...
HOLD IT RIGHT THERE!!!

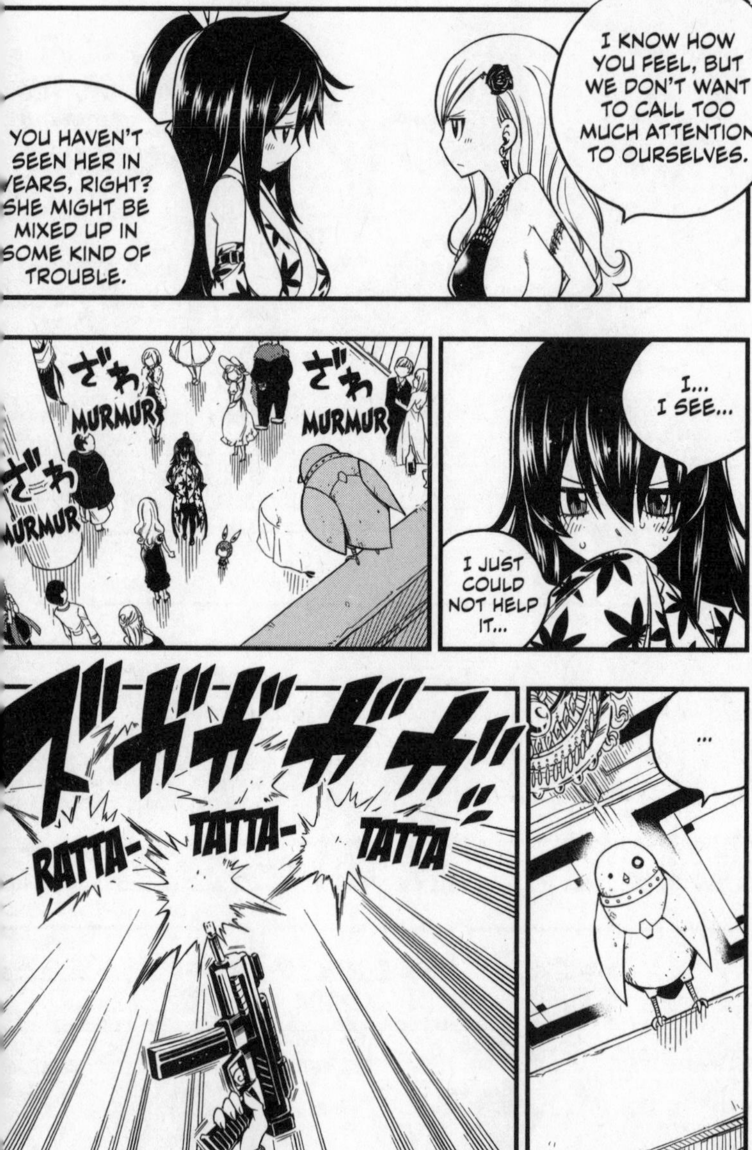
I KNOW HOW YOU FEEL, BUT WE DON'T WANT TO CALL TOO MUCH ATTENTION TO OURSELVES.
YOU HAVEN'T SEEN HER IN YEARS, RIGHT? SHE MIGHT BE MIXED UP IN SOME KIND OF TROUBLE.
I... I SEE...
I JUST COULD NOT HELP IT...
ざわ
MURMUR
ざわ
MURMUR
ざわ
MURMUR
...
ズガガガガ
RATTA-
TATTA-
TATTA

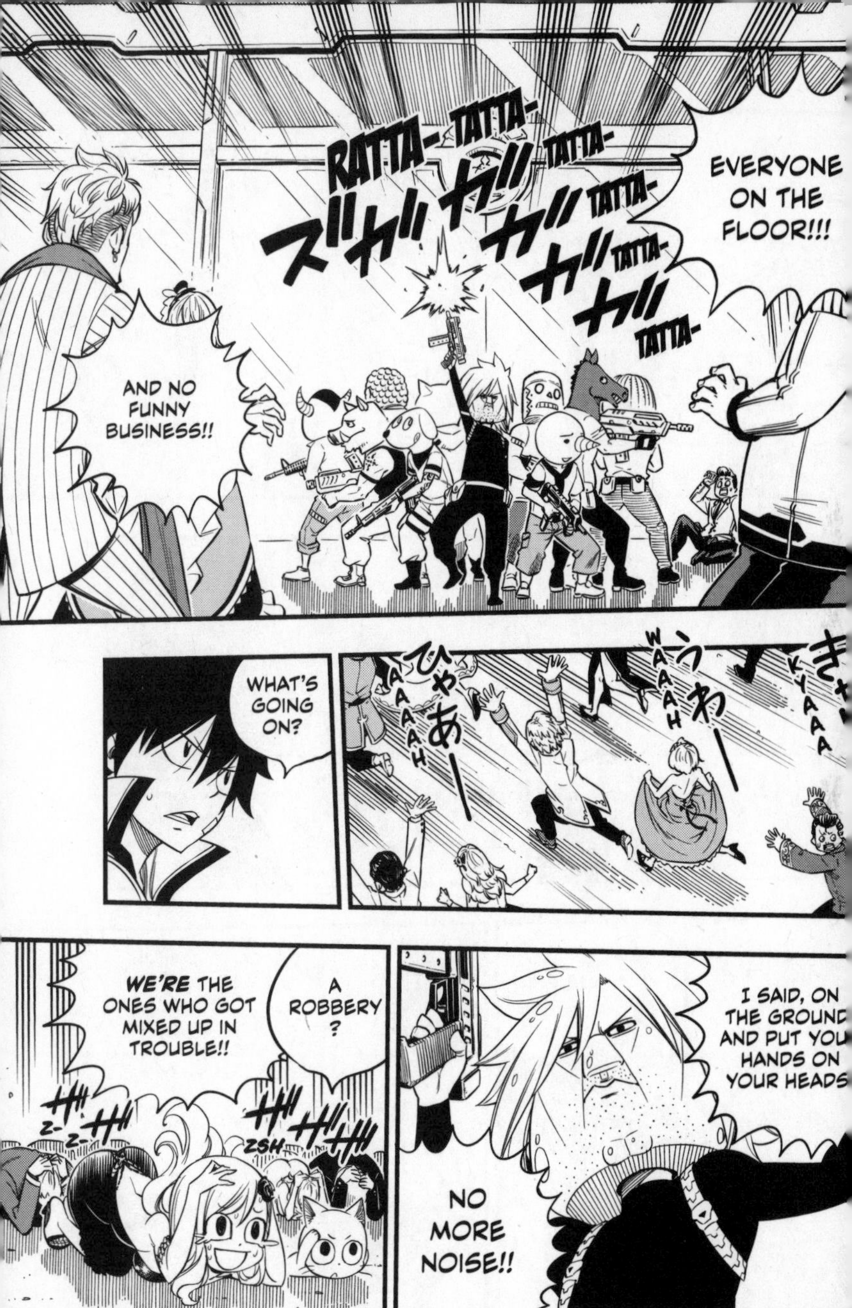
EVERYONE ON THE FLOOR!!!
RATTA- TATTA- TATTA- TATTA- TATTA- TATTA-
ズガガガガガ
AND NO FUNNY BUSINESS!!
きゃ KYAAAA
うわー WAAAAH
ひゃあー AAAAAH
WHAT'S GOING ON?
I SAID, ON THE GROUND AND PUT YOU HANDS ON YOUR HEADS
NO MORE NOISE!!
A ROBBERY?
WE'RE THE ONES WHO GOT MIXED UP IN TROUBLE!!
ZSH
Z- Z-

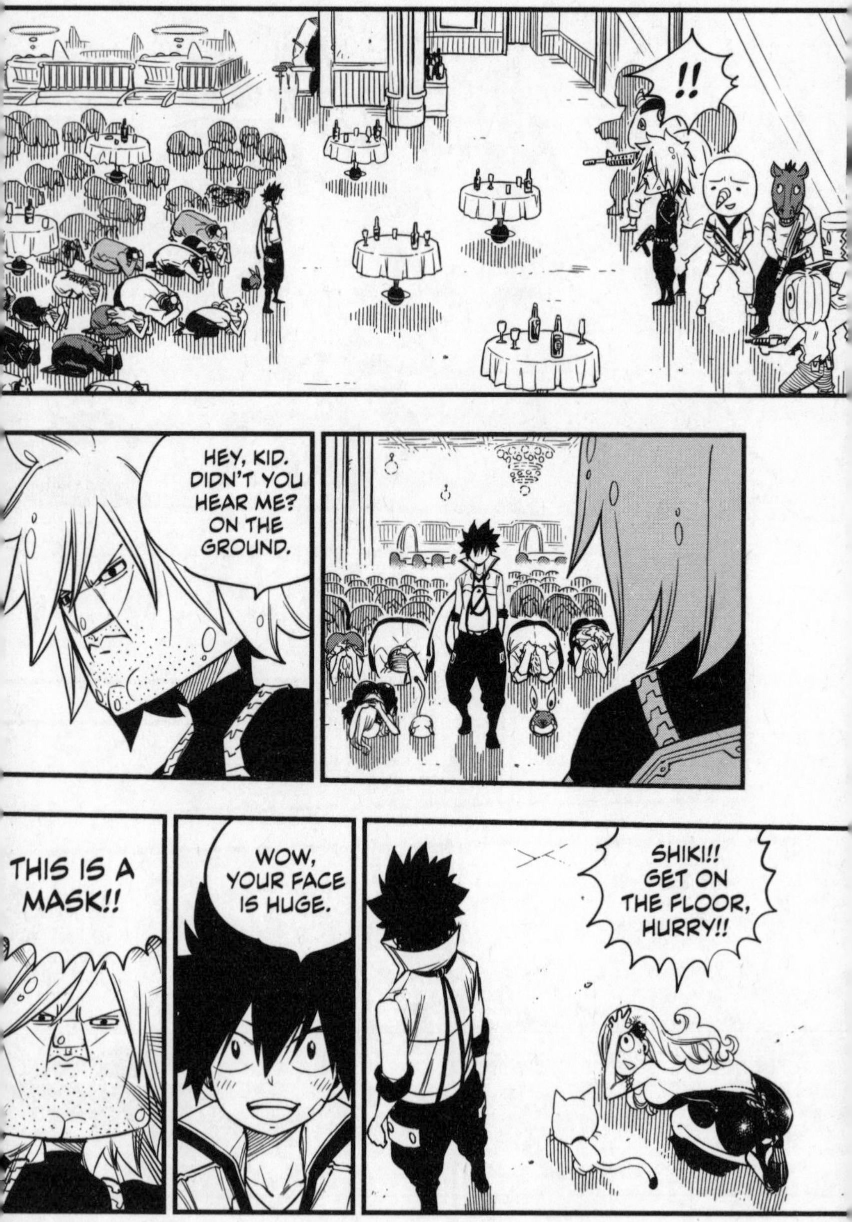
!!
HEY, KID. DIDN'T YOU HEAR ME? ON THE GROUND.
SHIKI!! GET ON THE FLOOR, HURRY!!
WOW, YOUR FACE IS HUGE.
THIS IS A MASK!!

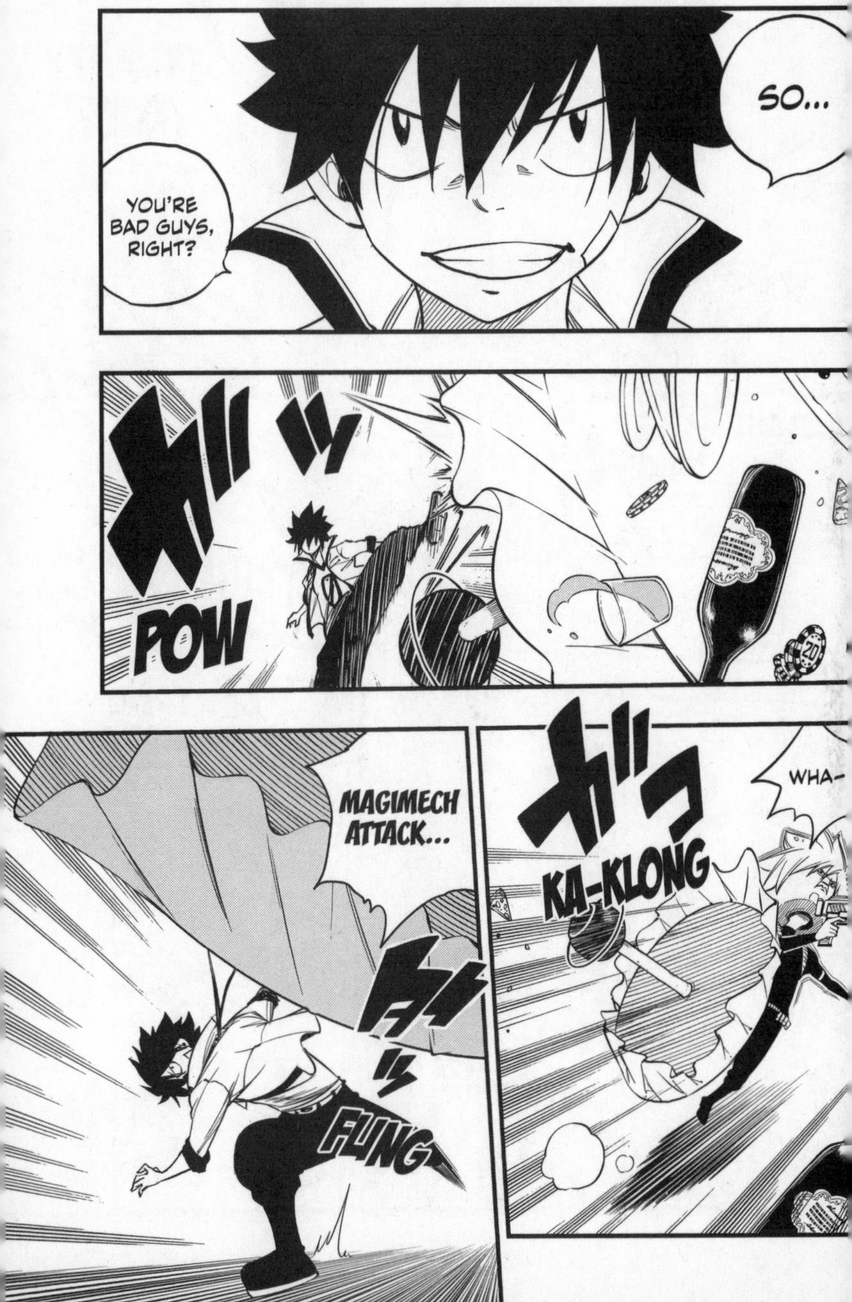
SO...
YOU'RE BAD GUYS, RIGHT?
POW
WHA-
KA-KLONG
MAGIMECH ATTACK...
FLING

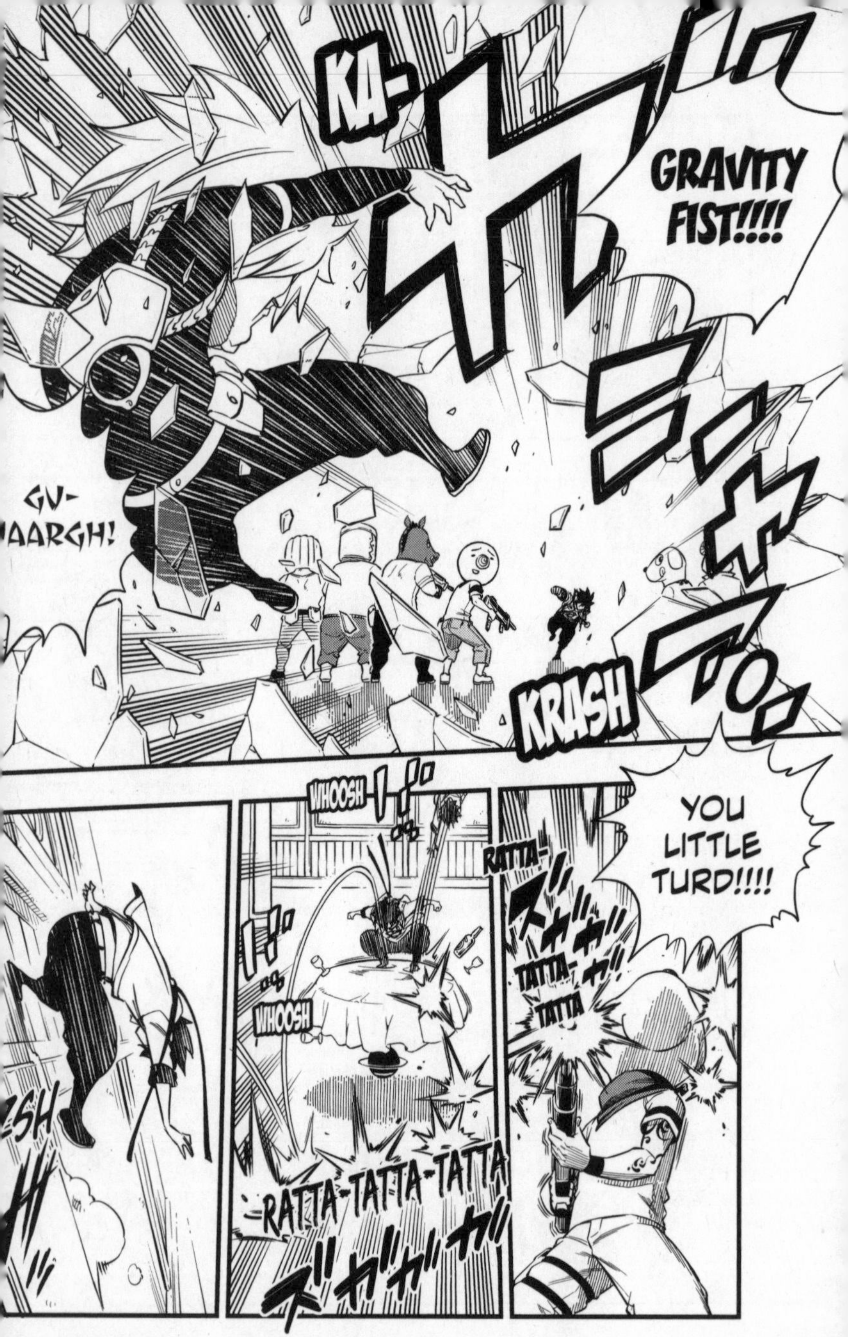
KA-
GRAVITY FIST!!!!
GU-AARGH!
KRASH
YOU LITTLE TURD!!!!
RATTA-
TATTA-
TATTA
WHOOSH
WHOOSH
RATTA-TATTA-TATTA

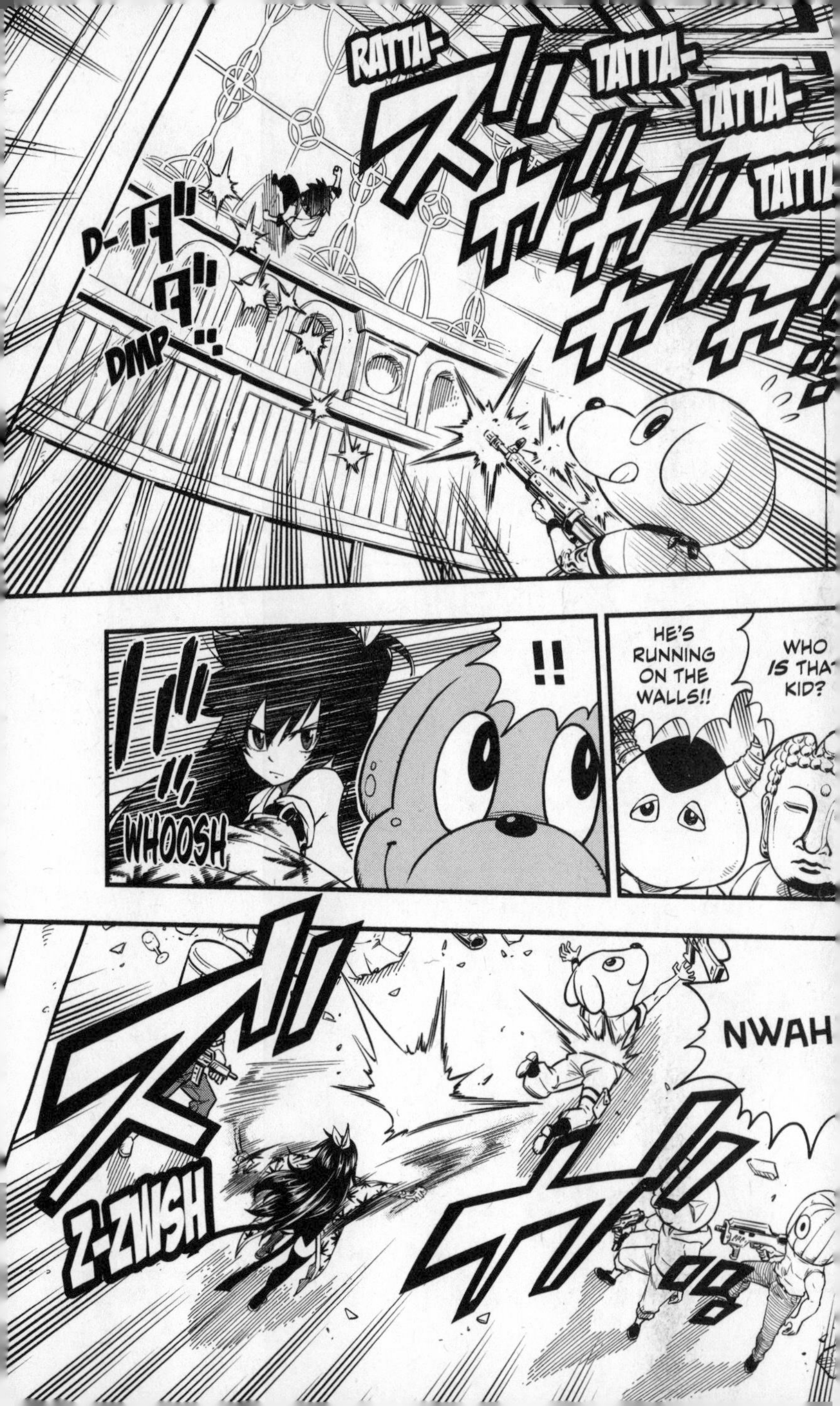

RATTA-
TATTA-
TATTA-
TATTA
D-
DMP
WHO IS THAT KID?
HE'S RUNNING ON THE WALLS!!
!!
WHOOSH
NWAH
Z-ZWISH

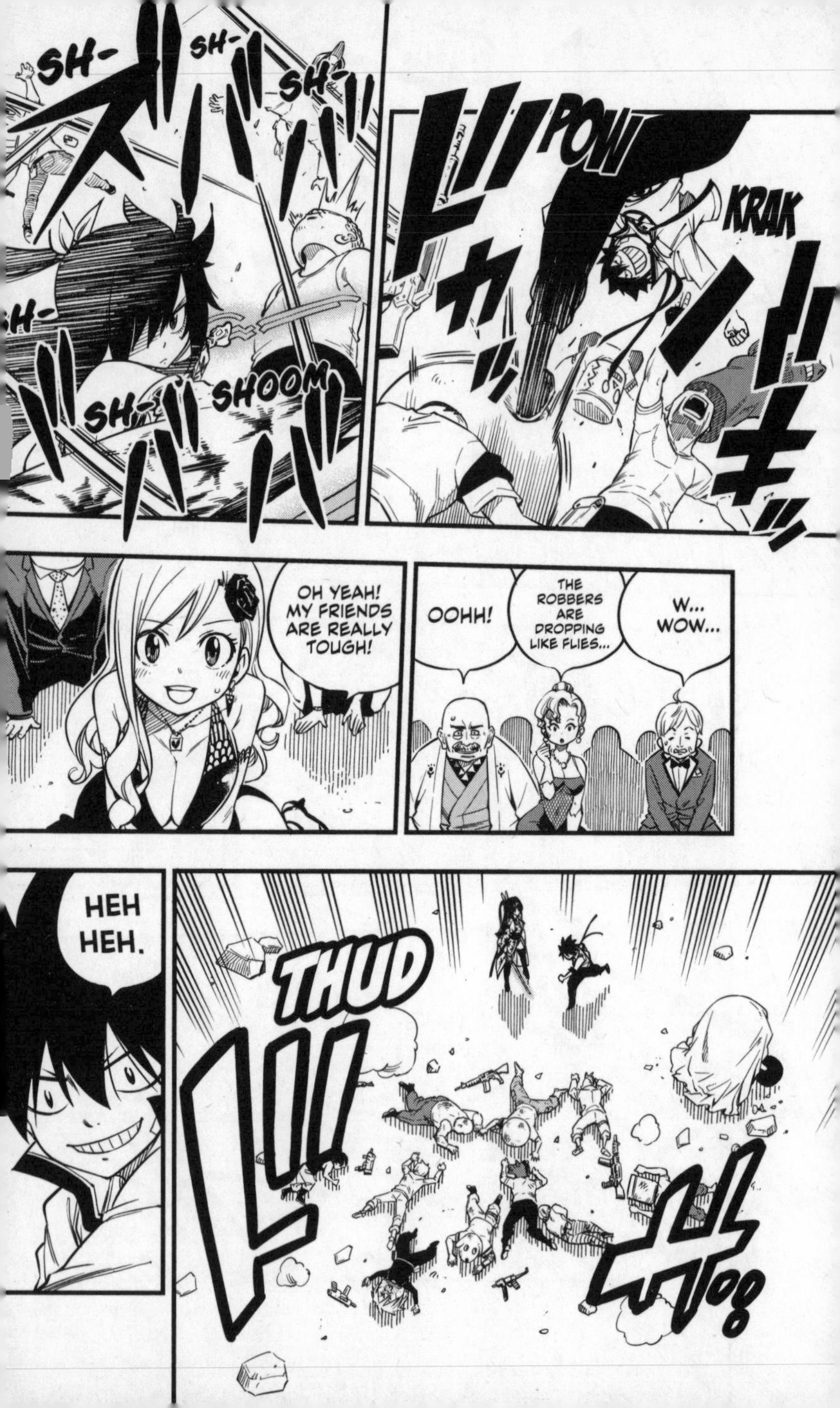
POW
KRAK
SH-
SH-
SH-
H-
SH-
SHOOM
W... WOW...
THE ROBBERS ARE DROPPING LIKE FLIES...
OOHH!
OH YEAH! MY FRIENDS ARE REALLY TOUGH!
THUD
HEH HEH.

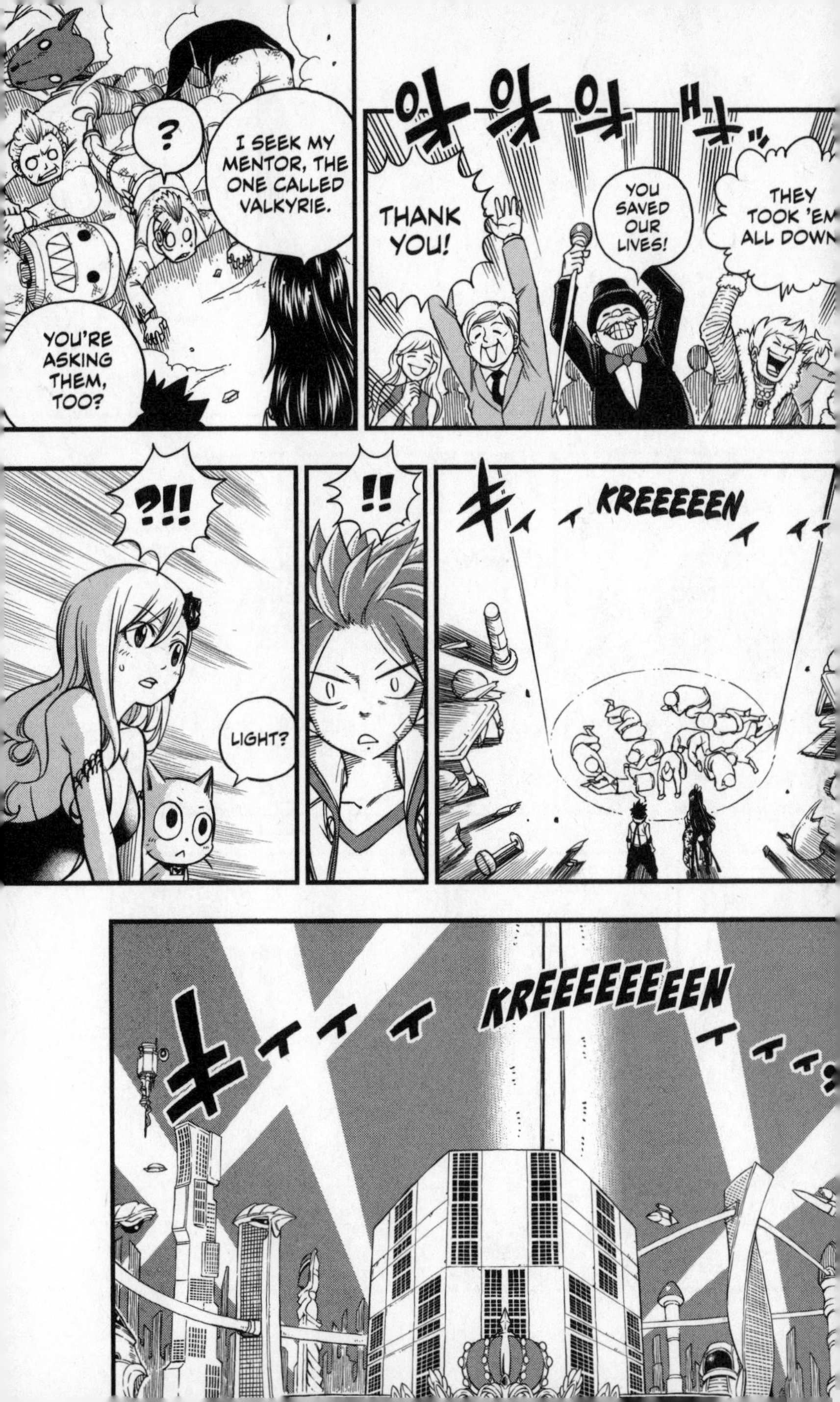
THEY TOOK 'EM ALL DOWN
YOU SAVED OUR LIVES!
THANK YOU!
I SEEK MY MENTOR, THE ONE CALLED VALKYRIE.
?
YOU'RE ASKING THEM, TOO?
KREEEEEN
!!
?!!
LIGHT?
KREEEEEEEEN

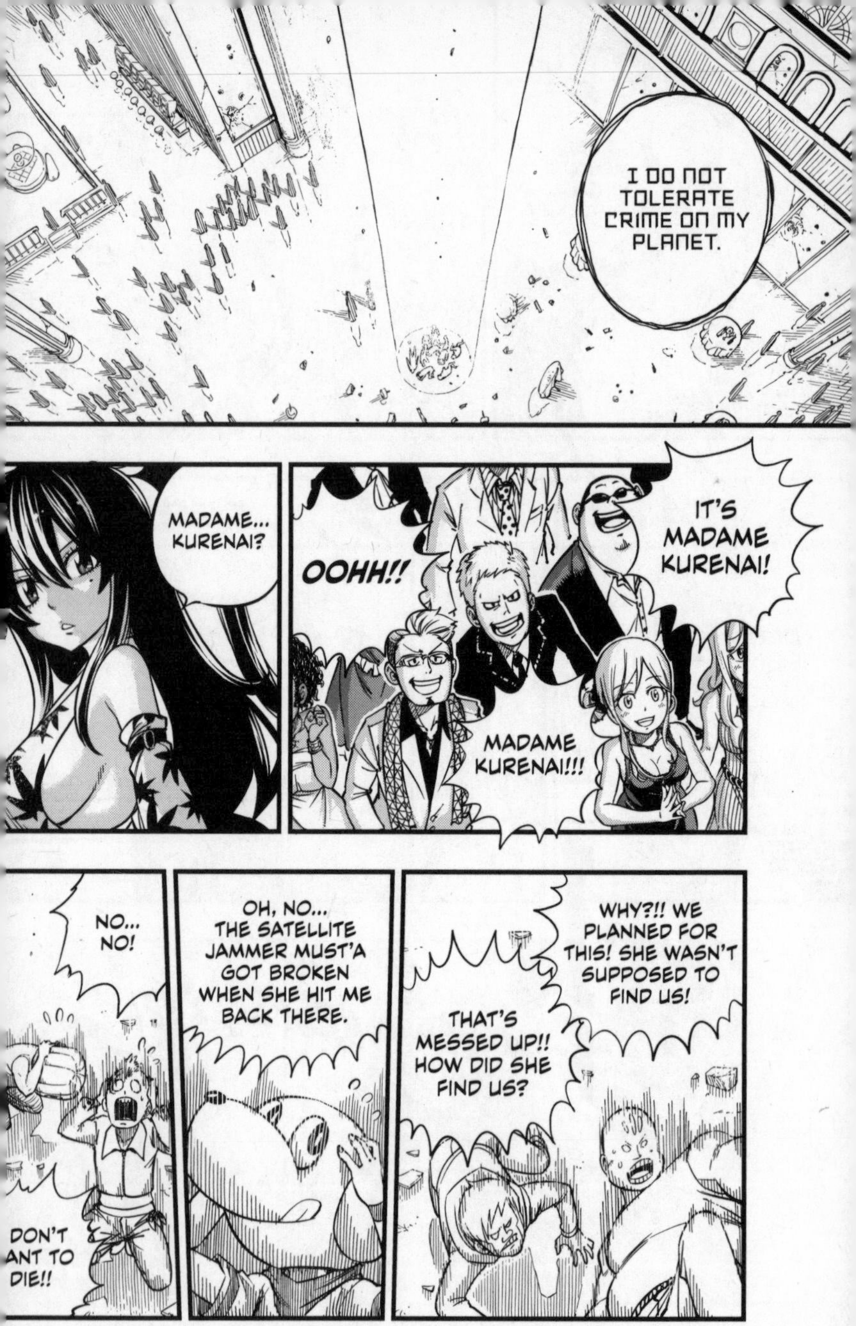
I DO NOT TOLERATE CRIME ON MY PLANET.
IT'S MADAME KURENAI!
OOHH!!
MADAME KURENAI!!!
MADAME... KURENAI?
WHY?!! WE PLANNED FOR THIS! SHE WASN'T SUPPOSED TO FIND US!
THAT'S MESSED UP!! HOW DID SHE FIND US?
OH, NO... THE SATELLITE JAMMER MUST'A GOT BROKEN WHEN SHE HIT ME BACK THERE.
NO... NO!
DON'T ANT TO DIE!!

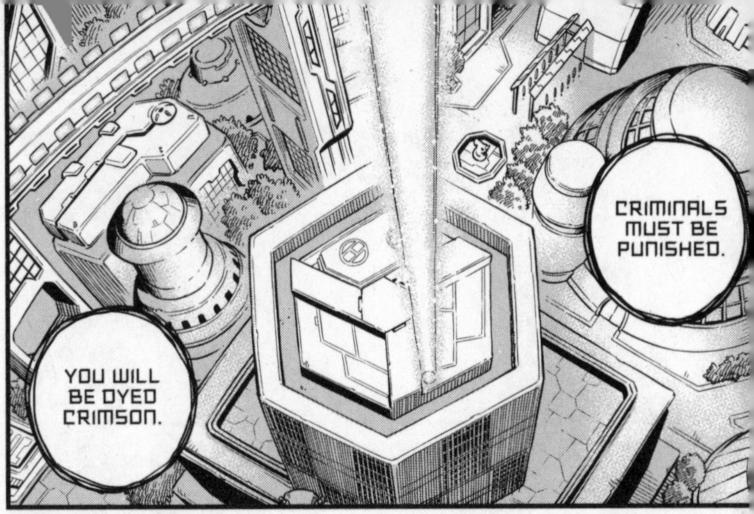
CRIMINALS MUST BE PUNISHED.
YOU WILL BE DYED CRIMSON.

Kurenai means "crimson" in Japanese.

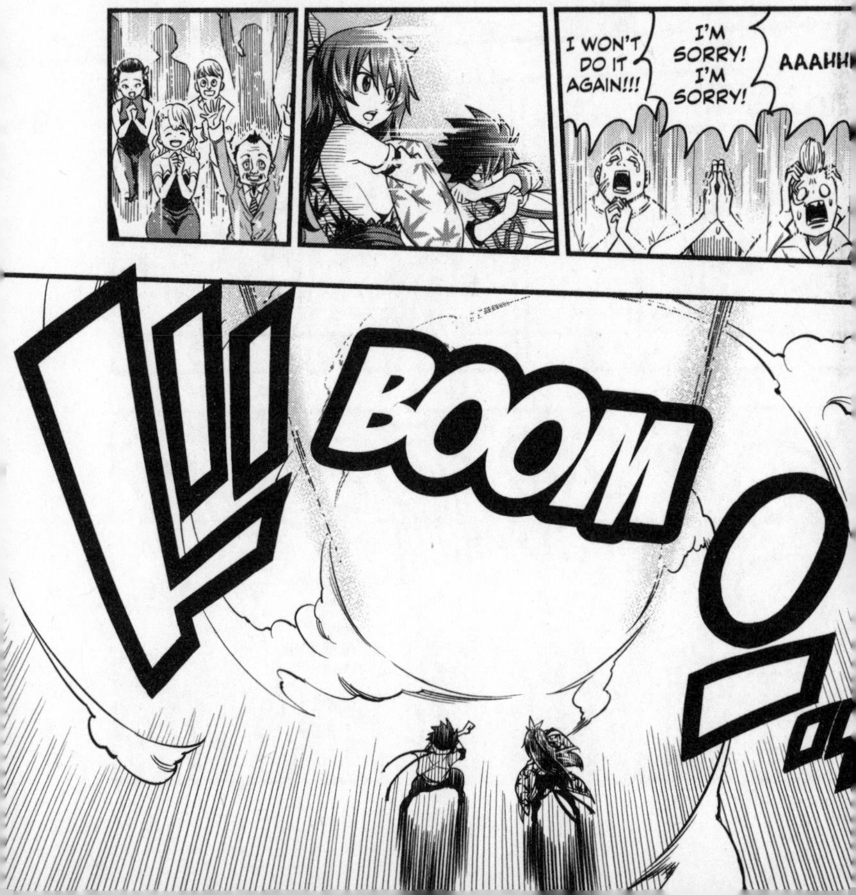
AAAHH
I'M SORRY! I'M SORRY!
I WON'T DO IT AGAIN!!!
BOOM

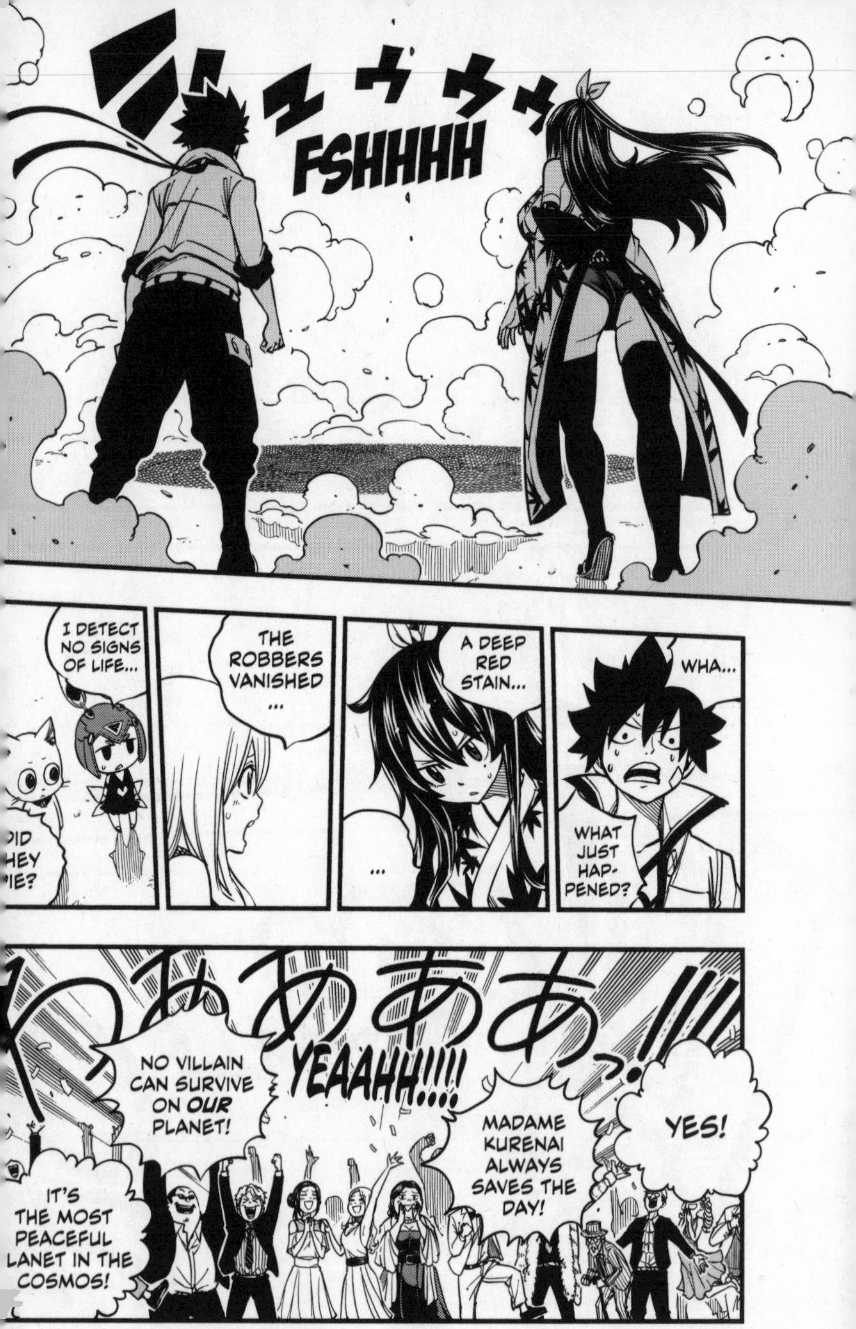
FSHHHH
WHA...
WHAT JUST HAP-PENED?
A DEEP RED STAIN...
...
THE ROBBERS VANISHED ...
I DETECT NO SIGNS OF LIFE...
DID HEY IE?
YES!
MADAME KURENAI ALWAYS SAVES THE DAY!
YEAAHH!!!!!
NO VILLAIN CAN SURVIVE ON *OUR* PLANET!
IT'S THE MOST PEACEFUL LANET IN THE COSMOS!

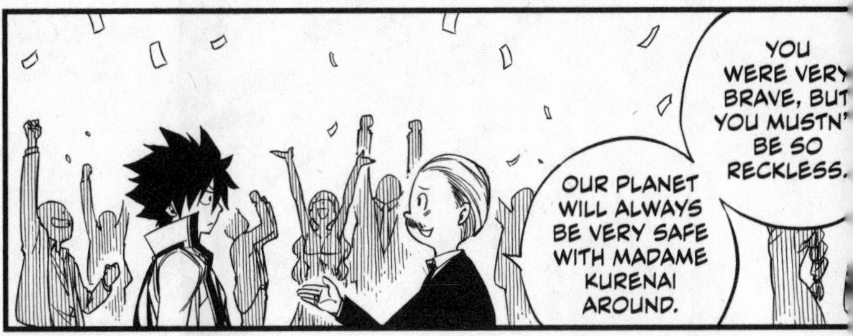
YOU WERE VERY BRAVE, BUT YOU MUSTN'T BE SO RECKLESS.
OUR PLANET WILL ALWAYS BE VERY SAFE WITH MADAME KURENAI AROUND.

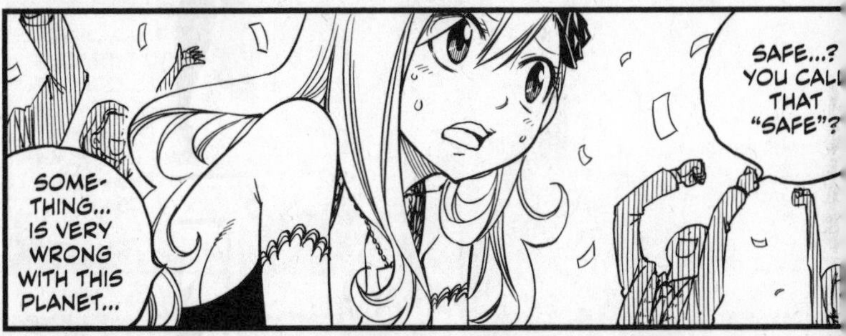
SAFE...? YOU CALL THAT "SAFE"?
SOME-THING... IS VERY WRONG WITH THIS PLANET...

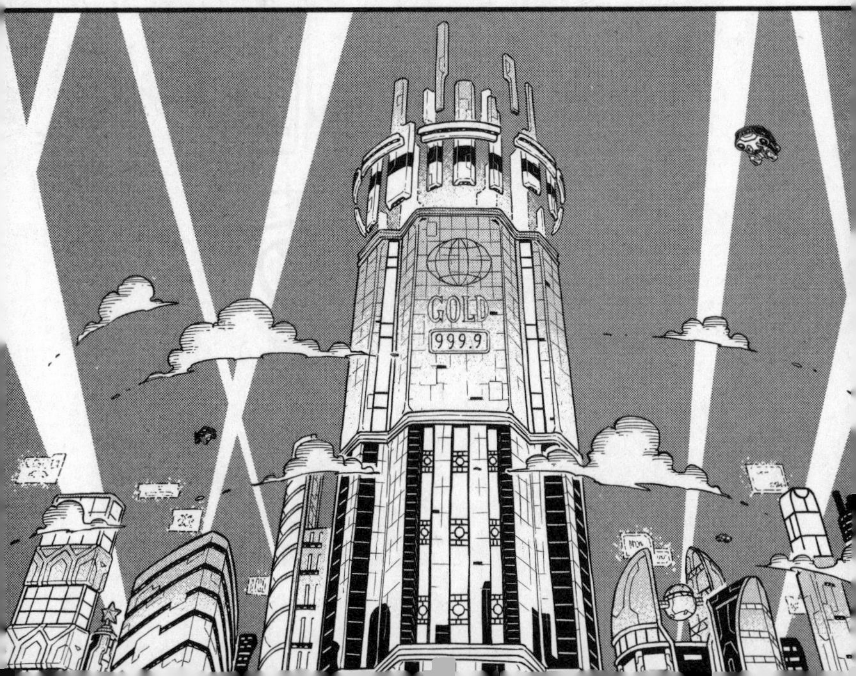
GOLD
999.9

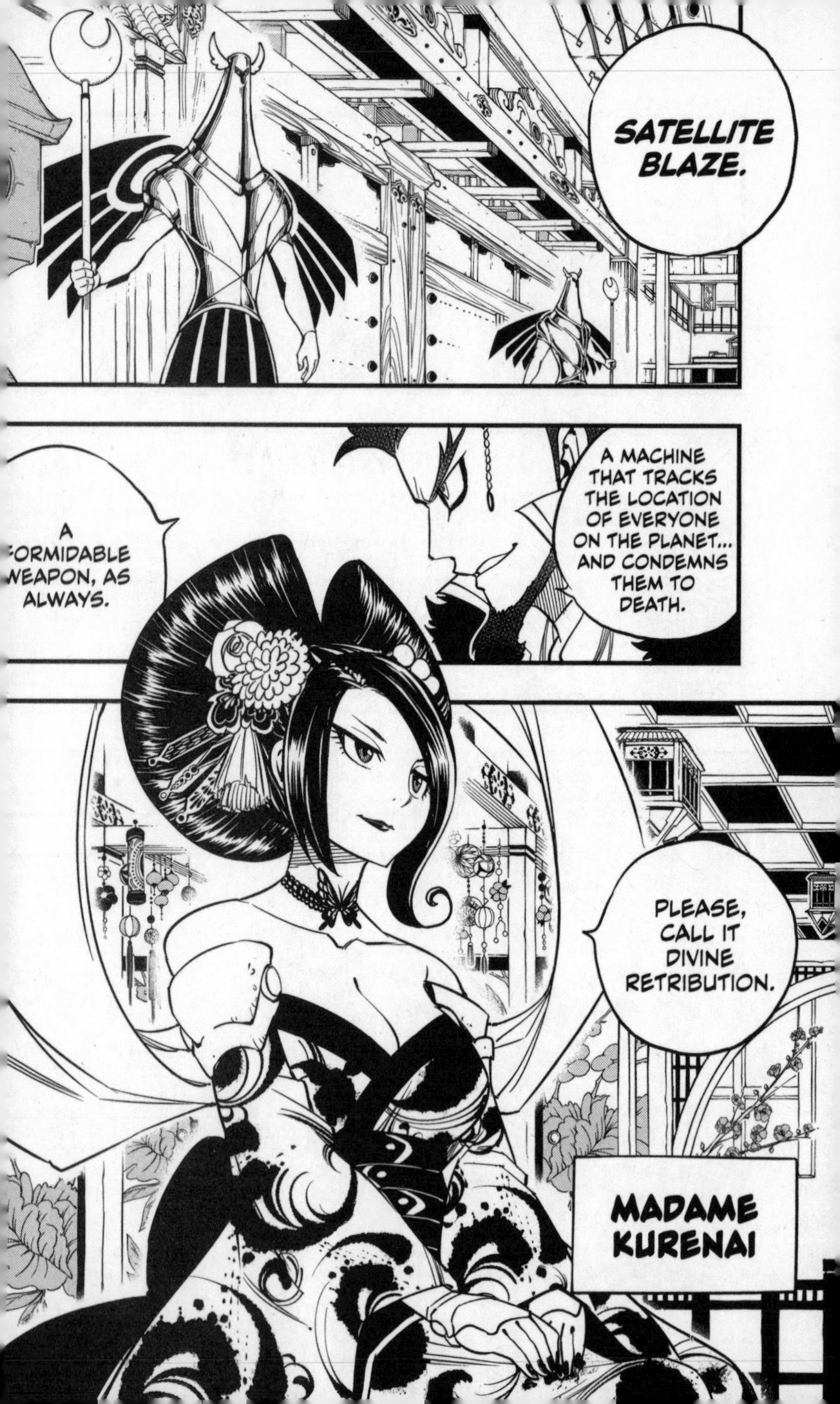
SATELLITE BLAZE.
A MACHINE THAT TRACKS THE LOCATION OF EVERYONE ON THE PLANET... AND CONDEMNS THEM TO DEATH.
A FORMIDABLE WEAPON, AS ALWAYS.
PLEASE, CALL IT DIVINE RETRIBUTION.
MADAME KURENAI

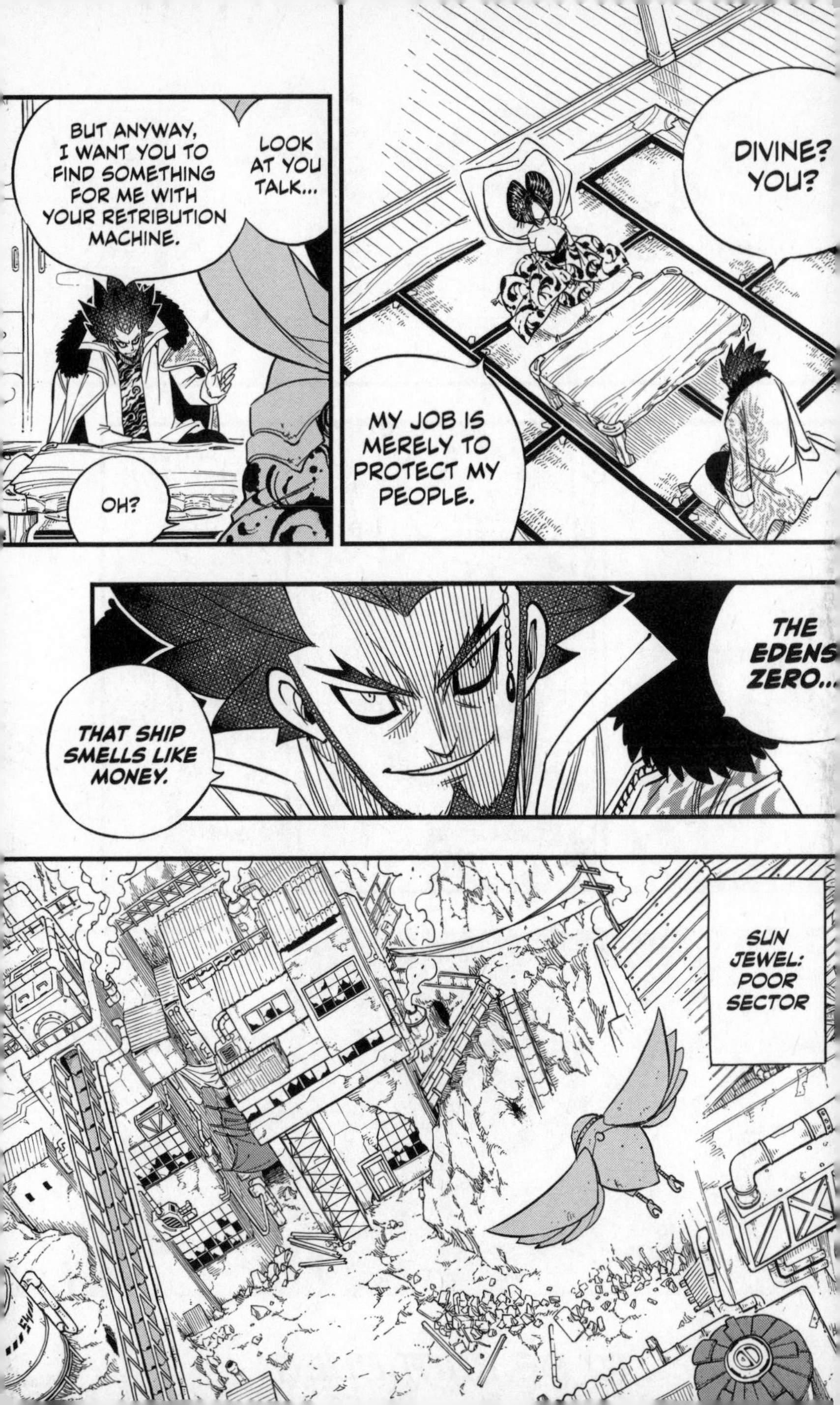
DIVINE? YOU?
MY JOB IS MERELY TO PROTECT MY PEOPLE.
LOOK AT YOU TALK...
BUT ANYWAY, I WANT YOU TO FIND SOMETHING FOR ME WITH YOUR RETRIBUTION MACHINE.
OH?
THE EDENS ZERO...
THAT SHIP SMELLS LIKE MONEY.
SUN JEWEL: POOR SECTOR

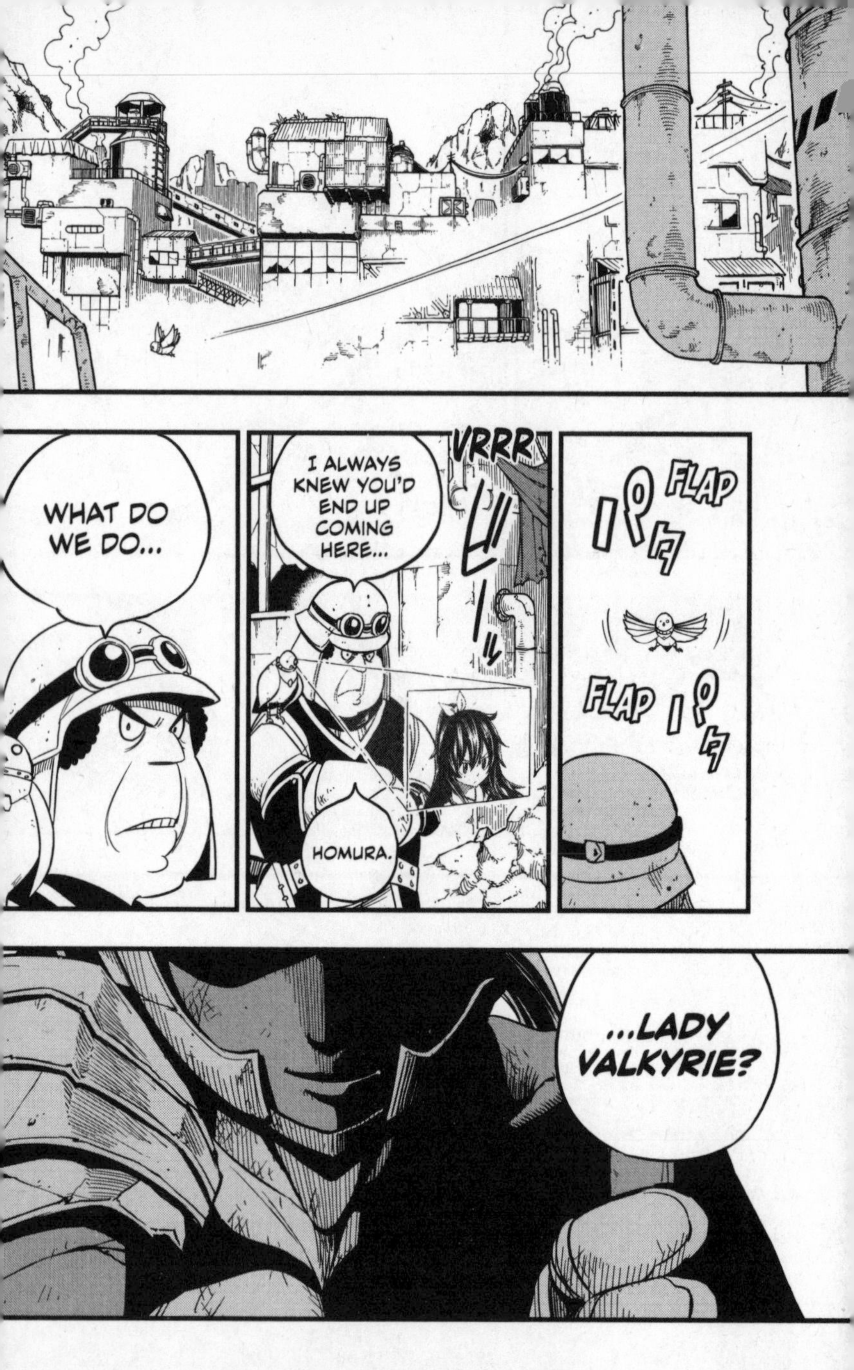
FLAP
FLAP
VRRR
I ALWAYS KNEW YOU'D END UP COMING HERE...
HOMURA.
WHAT DO WE DO...
...LADY VALKYRIE?

TO BE CONTINUED...

AFTERWORD

In this volume, Xiaomei got to be a part of the main story. I created her as a narrator, and she tells the tale from the omniscient narrator's perspective. She can talk about things the characters have no way of knowing, using meta-expressions. That means I have to be very careful about putting her in the main story. But because she "knows everything about the entire world," I actually managed to get her in there without too much trouble.

This character still has tons of backstory and character traits that have yet to be revealed. They may gradually come to light in the future.

And now the other character we all have questions about has made his debut—Captain Connor. His look changed a lot since he was first conceptualized—at first, he was a thinner, more attractive old man, then I gave him a receding hairline, and then I gave him silky smooth hair; I just could not decide on a design for him. I didn't settle on the current design until after I storyboarded his appearance. It was after my editor told me, "It's not very interesting to have an old man doing all that stuff when he's good-looking." The female contingent on my team wasn't too happy about it—there were complaints of, "Why didn't you make him hot?!" But I like this design.

And what in the world is the EDENS ONE he was talking about? Actually, I haven't decided that myself! ...Just kidding. I do have it worked out to a degree, but there are still parts I haven't quite settled on. I've said it a thousand times, but I work out those final details when I do the storyboard, and that's how we get to the final manuscript.

Story elements like these affect the overall narrative, so I get cautious when I work on them.

In the next volume, we'll finally get closer to the mystery of Valkyrie. And we'll finally start acting like a real battle manga!

Hope you're looking forward to it!

WE HAVE ANOTHER 10 DRAWINGS FOR OUR FOURTH INSTALLMENT!

(YURIKA NATSUME-SAN, FUKUOKA)

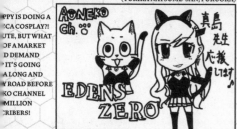

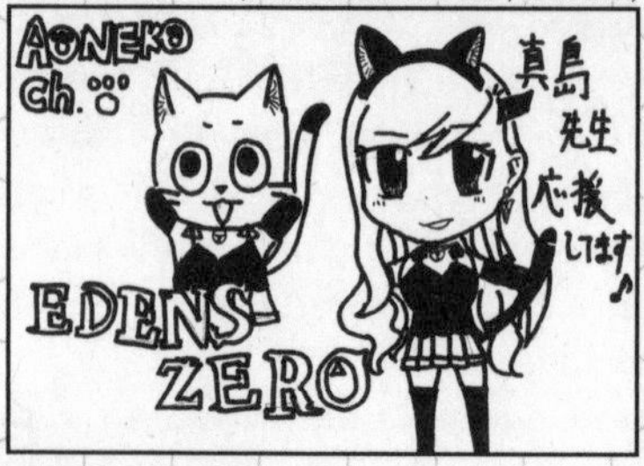
AONEKO Ch.
真島先生応援します♪
EDENS-ZERO

PPY IS DOING A
CA COSPLAY?!
UTE, BUT WHAT
OF A MARKET
D DEMAND
' IT'S GOING
A LONG AND
Y ROAD BEFORE
KO CHANNEL
MILLION
RIBERS!

MASHIMA'S ONE-HIT KO

(DR. U-SAN, HOKKAIDO)

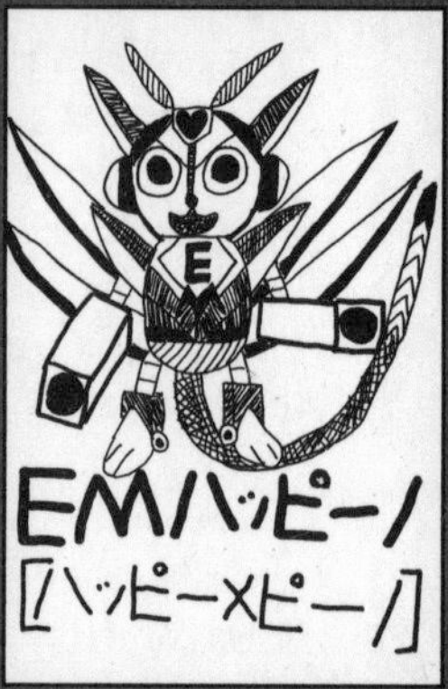
EMハッピーノ
[ハッピーメピーノ]

▲ I DON'T BELIEVE IT—A SUPER MERGE! EVERY GUY REALLY DOES DREAM OF ROBOT SUPER COMBOS. DOES THE LOOOONG TAIL HOLD A SECRET WEAPON...? THIS DRAWING HAS ME GOING, "ARE YOU FOR REAL RIGHT NOW?" BUT IN A MOST EXCELLENT WAY.

(RUBY-SAN, KANAGAWA)

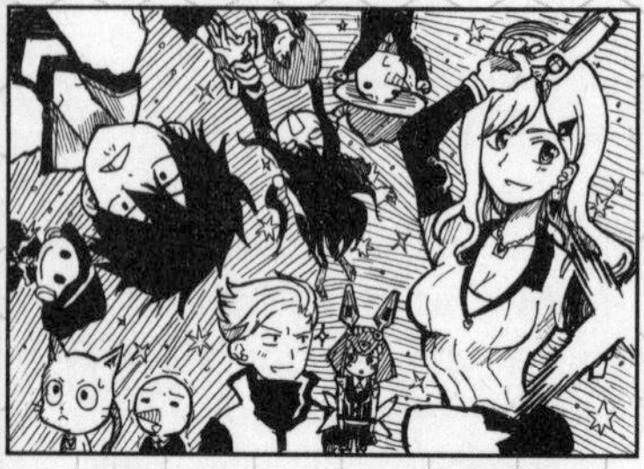

◀ THIS DRAWING KIND OF MAKES YOU FEEL LIKE THEY'RE IN AN ANTI-GRAVITY SPACE. DOES HAPPY LOOK KIND OF NERVOUS BECAUSE HE'S WORRIED ABOUT THE NIKORA (PLUE) BEHIND HIM?!

(YUSUKE HAGA-SAN, NIIGATA)

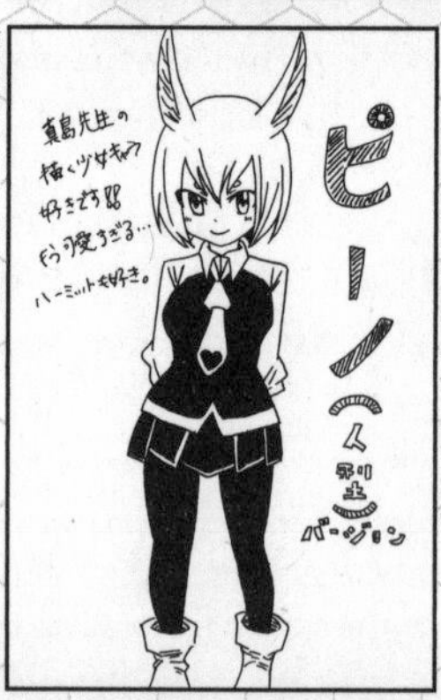
真島先生の
描く少女キャラ
好きです!!
もう可愛すぎる…
ハーミット好き。
ピーノ

◀ PINO IN HUMAN FORM ONCE MORE. I THINK THAT HER HEIGHT INCLUDES THOSE THINGS SPRINGING OUT OF HER HEAD? AND WILL THE DAY EVER COME THAT HER DREAM COMES TRUE?

(YUGO TAKEHARA-SAN, AOMORI)

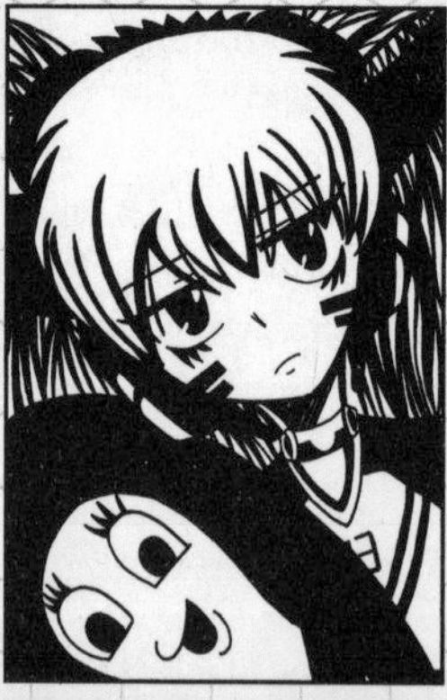

◀ AN UNHAPPY HERMIT AND WHAT IS THAT NEXT TO HER?! WHO IS IT?! WHAT IS IT?! I'M DYING TO KNOW!! AND IT HAS A NICE CONTRAST BETWEEN BLACK AND WHITE—THE WORLD OF THIS DRAWING REALLY PACKS A PUNCH!!

EDITOR'S NOTE: DRAWING SUBMISSIONS LIMITED TO JAPAN

EZ DRAWING

(NINJIN-SAN, OKAYAMA)

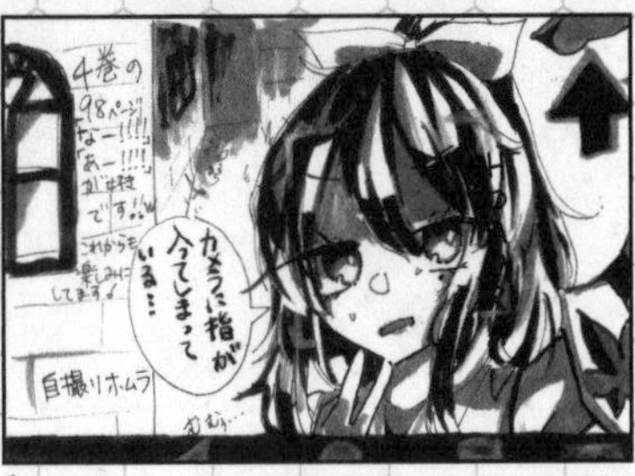
カメラに指が入ってしまっている……
自撮りホムラ

▲ THIS HAPPENS ALL THE TIME WITH SELFIES. HOMURA'S SKILLS WITH A SWORD ARE TOP-NOTCH, BUT SHE'S STILL IN TRAINING WITH A CAMERA?! AND IF SHE IMPROVES, WILL SHE TRY TO BE A B-CUBER?!

(SORA-SAN, KANAGAWA)

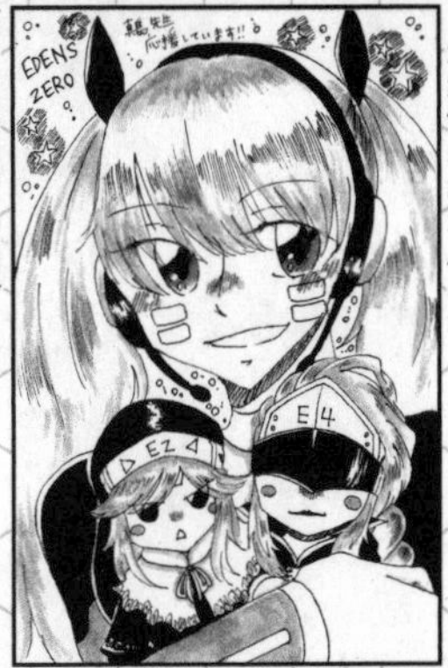
EDENS ZERO
真島先生 応援しています!!
EZ4
E4

◀ A DELIGHTED HERMIT, HOLDING DOLLS OF WITCH AND SISTER. SHE REALLY DOES LOOK BEST WITH A SMILE! IT'S SOOTHING TO LOOK AT.

(NATSUMI-SAN, TOCHIGI)

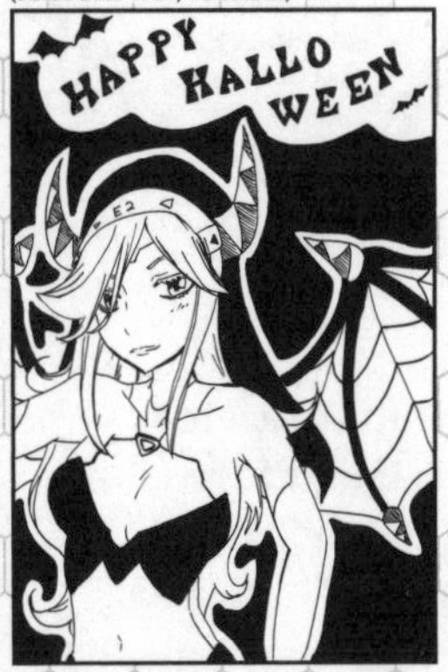
HAPPY HALLO WEEN

▲ SISTER IS JUST AS SEXY DRESSED UP FOR HALLOWEEN. ANYWAY, HER NAME SOUNDS LIKE A MEMBER OF THE CLERGY, SO WHY IS IT THAT SHE LOOKS BETTER AS A DEVIL THAN AN ANGEL? (HA HA)

(RYOKA KAWASHIMA-SAN, HOKKAIDO)

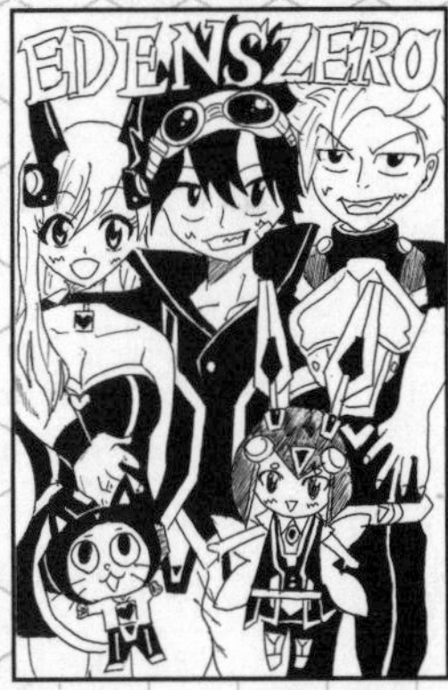
EDENS ZERO

▲ ALL OF THE ORIGINAL FIVE CREW MEMBERS. FOR ALL THEIR TALK, IT LOOKS LIKE WEISZ HAS REALLY STARTED TO BLEND IN. SHIKI'S GONNA JUST KEEP GETTING MORE FRIENDS. THANKS FOR SUPPORTING HIM.

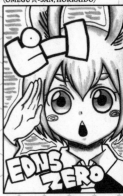

(OMEGU☆-SAN, HOKKAIDO)

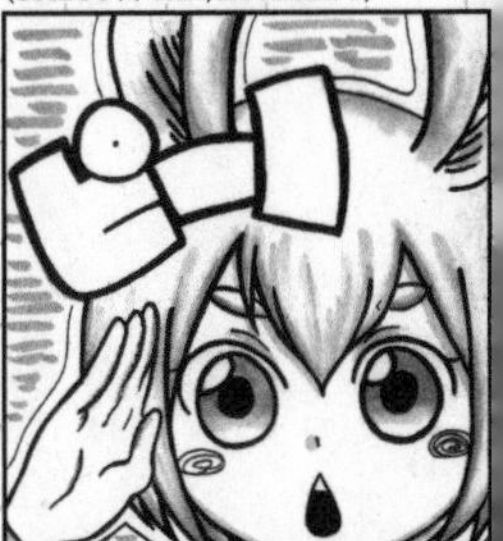
EDNS ZERO

▲ PINO, WHO APPEARED IN HUMAN FORM ON DIGITALIS. HER EXPRESSION IS VERY LIVELY, AND HER POSE IS PERFECT!! YOU CAN SEE THAT SHE REALLY ENJOYS BEING A MEMBER OF THE EDENS ZERO'S CREW.

KAMOME SHIRAHAMA

Witch Hat Atelier

A magical manga adventure for fans of Disney and Studio Ghibli!

Witch Hat Atelier © Kamome Shirahama/Kodansha Ltd.

The magical adventure that took Japan by storm is finally here, from acclaimed DC and Marvel cover artist Kamome Shirahama!

In a world where everyone takes wonders like magic spells and dragons for granted, Coco is a girl with a simple dream: She wants to be a witch. But everybody knows magicians are born, not made, and Coco was not born with a gift for magic. Resigned to her un-magical life, Coco is about to give up on her dream to become a witch...until the day she meets Qifrey, a mysterious, traveling magician. After secretly seeing Qifrey perform magic in a way she's never seen before, Coco soon learns what everybody "knows" might not be the truth, and discovers that her magical dream may not be as far away as it may seem...

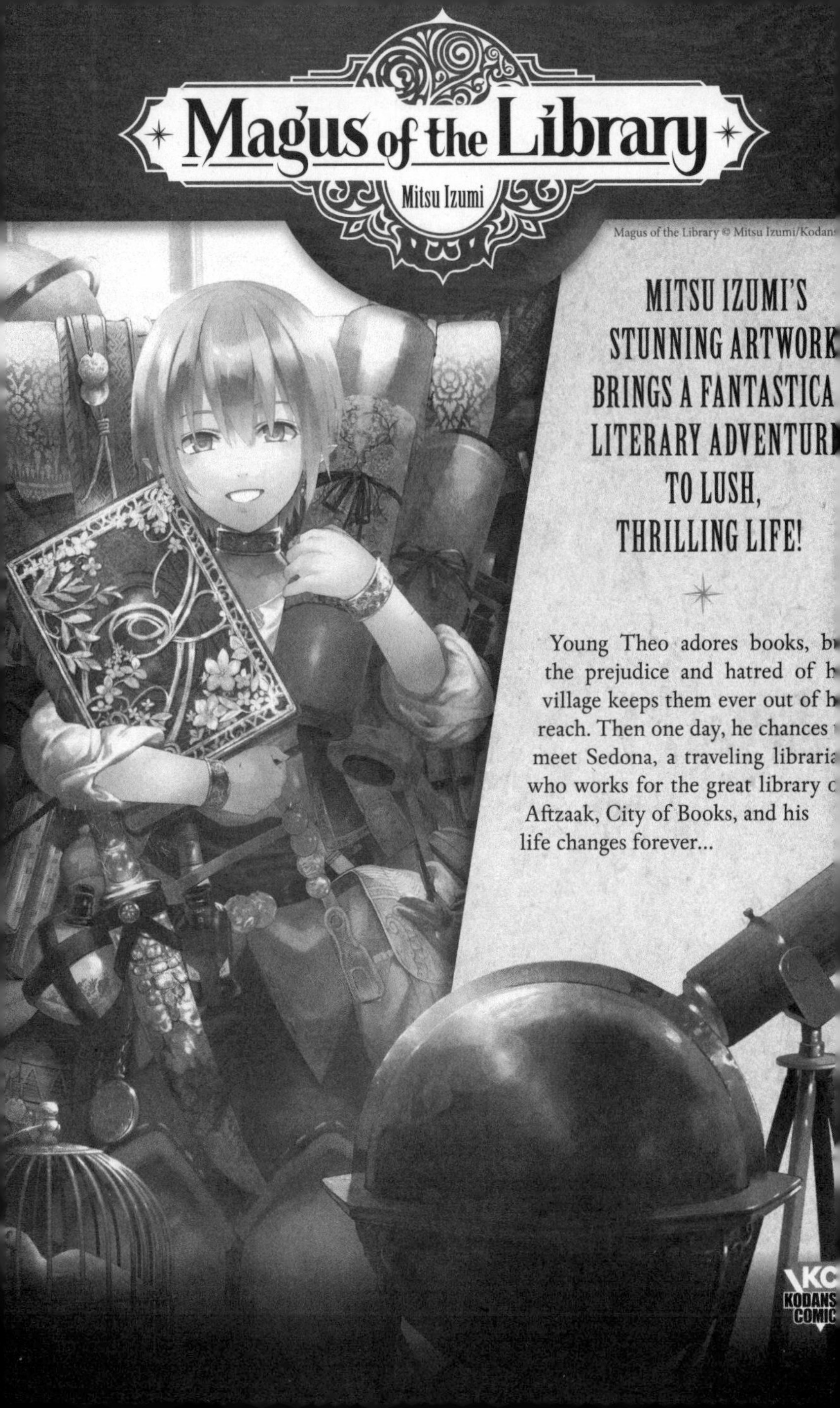
Magus of the Library
Mitsu Izumi
Magus of the Library © Mitsu Izumi/Kodans
MITSU IZUMI'S
STUNNING ARTWORK
BRINGS A FANTASTICA
LITERARY ADVENTUR
TO LUSH,
THRILLING LIFE!
Young Theo adores books, b
the prejudice and hatred of h
village keeps them ever out of h
reach. Then one day, he chances
meet Sedona, a traveling librari
who works for the great library c
Aftzaak, City of Books, and his
life changes forever...
KC
KODANS
COMIC

A Kodansha Comics Trade Paperback Original
EDENS ZERO 6 copyright © 2019 Hiro Mashima
English translation copyright © 2020 Hiro Mashima

All rights reserved.

Published in the United States by Kodansha Comics, an imprint of Kodansha USA Publishing, LLC, New York.

Publication rights for this English edition arranged through Kodansha Ltd., Tokyo.

First published in Japan in 2019 by Kodansha Ltd., Tokyo.

ISBN 978-1-63236-833-1

Original cover design by Narumi Miura (G x complex).

Printed in the United States of America.

www.kodanshacomics.com

9 8 7 6 5 4 3 2 1
Translation: Alethea Nibley & Athena Nibley
Lettering: AndWorld Design
Editing: Haruko Hashimoto
Kodansha Comics edition cover design by Phil Balsman

Publisher: Kiichiro Sugawara
Managing editor: Maya Rosewood
Vice president of marketing & publicity: Naho Yamada

Director of publishing services: Ben Applegate
Associate director of operations: Stephen Pakula
Publishing services managing editor: Noelle Webster
Assistant production manager: Emi Lotto, Angela Zurlow